TIGER'S EYES

ANNE-MARIE PRICE

ISBN: 978-0-9942761-5-5

DEDICATION

To Greg Price
The cuddly big bear brother
We wish you were still here with us.

ACKNOWLEDGMENTS

Many thanks to my beta readers
June Earle and Lynne Doyle

ABOUT THE AUTHOR

Anne-Marie Price is predominately a writer of fiction, to not only give voice to the stories that are given to her through her dreams; but to make it possible to be someone else. Live someone else's life as she tells their story and escape from the world of reality.

For reality is a constant uphill battle. Suffering from not just chronic pain but also manic depression, well mostly depression; it is nice to live in someone else's shoes for a while. To live in another time or place. To be able to share with her characters the emotional highs and lows that they are going through, without having to actually experience the physical pain that she makes them endure. As they struggle to live, love and cheat death… most of the time.

Also By This Author

Hostage Of Diplomacy

The Search For The King James Bible

Stirling Trilogy
Stirling Breed
Stirling Masquerade
Stirling Conspiracy

AFRICA

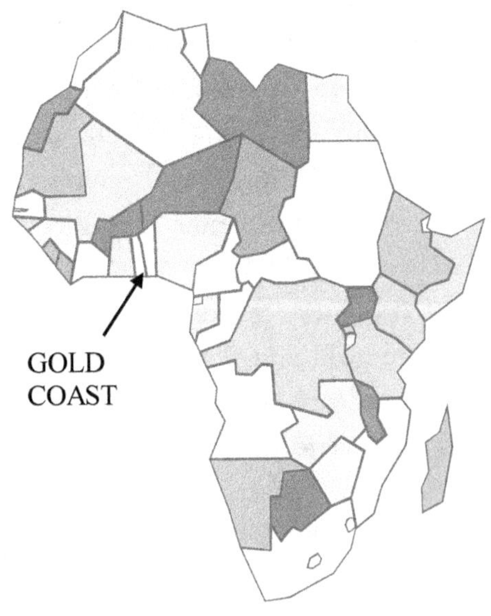

GOLD COAST

A LITTLE BIT OF HISTORY

Before independence was declared in 1957, Ghana, a west African country situated between the Ivory Coast and Toga; was known as the Gold Coast. When the Portuguese arrived in the 15th century, they found so much gold between the rivers Ankobra and the Volta that they initially called the country 'Mina' - meaning mine. Later the European colonizers would adopt the name 'Gold Coast'. In the 16th century, the Dutch joined the Portuguese but there was no idea of peaceful sharing as the trade in gold and slaves was very profitable business. By the mid 18th century other European traders, the English, the Danes and the Swedes wanted a share of the wealth.

The Slavery Trade in Great Britain was abolished in 1807, but it was not until 1833 that it was abolished in every part of the British Empire. The Dutch and the British out lasted the other European traders and when the Dutch finally withdrew completely in 1874, the Gold Coast became a crown colony for Britain. Although the British developed a good relationship with the coastal people, the Fantes, the northern people, the Ashanti, were their enemies. They did not want to be a jewel in someone else's Empire.

The Gold Coast had a vast array of assets to offer the Colony. From ores such as gold, silver, iron, manganese ore and diamonds, to fuels such as forest resources, off shore fishing, petroleum and natural gas. The tropical climate was perfectly suited to crops such as cocoa, coffee, coconuts, bananas, peanuts, tobacco, cotton and rice. The northern two thirds of the country were undulating savannas, the west had heavily forested hills with many streams and rivers, and the coastline was sandy with no natural harbours. In the east, the White Volta and Black Volta Rivers joined to become the Volta River. There was also lush tropical forests, cascading waterfalls and rolling hills.

TUESDAY

A Desperate Race

Margaret Munroe was running through the jungle with all the speed that God had granted her. Dressed in male attire and her long blonde hair flying behind her, Margaret was not at all currently concerned about her appearance as she caught a glimpse of the huge creature that was chasing her.

A flash of light vanished into the trees as the fully-grown white tiger attempted to cut across Margaret's path. Weaving through the jungle, she concentrated upon her breathing, trying to keep it even. Her goal, a clearing, wasn't that far ahead but out of the corner of her deep blue eyes Margaret could see the tiger gaining upon her. In desperation, she attempted to find additional speed but had no more energy to draw upon.

The tiger streaked passed Margaret, reaching the clearing ahead of her and there was a loud splash as the large cat hit the water of the River Volta. Margaret's pace didn't slow as she also burst into the clearing and dove straight in the crystal clear water.

You Cheated!

Surfacing and breathing hard, Margaret splashed water into the face of the tiger as he swam beside her. Margaret's hair was the same colour as the tiger's fur, a pure white.

'Not fair Sebastian! You were supposed to have given me a thirty second head start!' Margaret wrapped her arms around the tiger's neck and playfully wrestled with him. There was no disguising the smug look on the tiger's face.

10 years old, Sebastian was pure white with chocolate coloured stripes and very blue eyes. A similar blue eyes to Margaret. He had achieved his adult body length of nine feet, excluding his tail, and weighed over 700 pounds. If he'd had any intentions of hurting Margaret, she would not have had any chance of escape. Sebastian, though, had been hand raised by Margaret and her parents and would no sooner hurt her than he would hurt his own mother.

Are We In Danger Here?

The sound of running feet coming towards them caused Sebastian to lose his playful nature, as he immediately became protective of Margaret. He relaxed as two young native men he knew burst through the trees and jumped into the water beside them.

Kobbi and Tano were assigned to keep an eye on Margaret and Sebastian when they ventured away from the Munroe farm, situated in the northern jungle running along the Volta River in the Eastern Region of the Gold Coast in Western Africa.

'I'm sorry Miss Margaret, he wouldn't wait until we had counted to 30 before starting out,' apologized Tano.

Margaret splashed water at Sebastian. 'You did cheat!'

The tiger, though, was looking over the treetops at the smoke that was rising in blooms in the cloud-free sky, and sniffed at the air. Margaret followed his gaze before casting a concerned look at the two young guides.

'How close are we to the border of Ashanti?' She asked.

'Not far Miss,' Kobbi gathered his bearing from the surrounding landmarks. 'There haven't been any recent conflicts between the Ashanti people and the British soldiers.'

This did not relieve Margaret's fears. 'Even so, I think we'd better head home.' They waded out of the river and having shaken off any excess water, they didn't hang around in case there was any trouble nearby.

The Munroe Family

For nearly all of her 24 years, Margaret Munroe had lived on a farm in the north of the Eastern region of the Gold Coast in western Africa with her parents, Doctor Edward and Isabella Munroe. When Margaret was a month old they had moved from the capital city of Accra, and Doctor Munroe had built a hospital, a home and a profitable farm, called The Haven.

Doctor Munroe was well respected by both the colonists and the native people, as he was a quiet and patient man. Isabella Munroe was treated with awe as like her husband, she was quiet and patient, but she also appeared to be always cool and calm. Whether it was helping her husband dealing with the very sick, coping with the savage heat or humidity, or running the farm, Isabella always appeared the picture of a proper Victorian lady.

Unlike Margaret, who lived in male clothes, Isabella was always impeccably dressed, often making her own clothes designed from pictures in magazines, so that she kept up with the latest fashions of 1888.

An Air Of Menace

Approaching The Haven, Margaret's alarm increased by the lack of people and activity. *It's late afternoon and there should be the farm workers finishing up for the day. Also the verandah around the hospital is normally full of recovering patients, playing chess, chatting or having a smoke, something Papa won't permit inside the hospital but today it is eerily empty,* she mused.

Kobbi and Tano exchanged a nervous look and kept a hand on the daggers in the waistbands of their trousers. As they approached the homestead, Isabella emerged from the doorway and although she smiled in greeting, the lines of worry upon her face told Margaret that all was not well.

'Mama? What's wrong?' Margaret reached out to take her mother's hand.

'Nothing dear; just news that there has been some trouble in Ashanti. Your father has sent scouts out to determine if there are any local problems. Come, you must be hungry.' Isabella brushed her hand lovingly against her beautiful daughter's cheek before leading them all inside. Sebastian and the two boys went eagerly into the kitchen to the native Housekeeper, Busara, but Margaret drew her mother to one side.

'I'm no longer a child, Mama, if there's any danger then I have a right to know.' Margaret tried to read her mother's feelings, but Isabella was very good at hiding her emotions.

'I'm sorry, but no matter how old you get, you'll always be my baby girl. I suppose that's my fault as I've never been able to give you brothers or sisters.'

Margaret recognized this gambit and was not about to be side tracked. 'Sebastian is enough of a brother. Don't change the subject! You and Papa have been on edge for some time now. Has this got anything to do with the snake that Papa found in one of the boxes of medical supplies?'

'There have been other similar incidents.' Sighing, Isabella placed her arm around Margaret's waist and led them to her daughter's bedroom and sat down beside her on the bed. 'Today a man came to the hospital with talk that the Ashanti are fighting amongst themselves.'

'That's nothing new Mama!' *I can't not see why that would worry my parents.*

Isabella hesitated before finally nodding, 'There is a threat much closer to home from our own people.'

Margaret started in surprise and disbelief, 'Our villagers?'

'No, our own relatives, I'm... I'm not sure that the Haven is completely safe for us any more.'

Stunned for a moment, Margaret did not immediately speak. 'What security measures have you already instigated?'

I'm still hesitant about telling my daughter everything, but Margaret will only worry if she doesn't know all the details. 'Night and day there are armed sentries around the Haven. Someone checks up on them every hour. We have alerted the surrounding villages to the possibility of trouble as well as the nearest white settlers. Any unusual activities and we will be alerted.'

Contingency Plan

'What do you need me to do, Mama?'

This is the question that I've been dreading, as I know Margaret is not going to like the answer. 'Your father and I have discussed several options, and we need you to obey our decision without argument or hesitation.'

'Mama!'

Isabella smiled. 'I know, but we feel this is the best solution. Firstly you'll pack two-canvas carryall, one with food and water, the other with clothes, personal items, your compass and map. Also I want you to pack your pebble people.'

'Surely we're not going to be driven out of our home?'

Her mother shook her head. 'Not we, Margaret, but you. Hear me out please!' She added as Margaret burst into protest.

Not until Margaret was silent did Isabella continue, 'When there is any trouble, you, Sebastian with Tano and Kobbi will make your way to that cave you sometimes use when you spend several days in the jungle. From there you'll head south to Richard's and remain with him until it is safe for you to return.'

'I'm not a child, Mama! I can probably shoot as well as anyone in the village. I'm not a coward. I can't leave you and Papa to fight alone!'

Isabella kissed her daughter's brow. 'You're not a child, or a coward, and you are indeed an excellent shot, but that isn't what this is about. You're our only child and therefore the most precious thing in our lives. If anything happened to you, we'd have no reason to continue living. If we know that you're safe with Richard Evans, then it is one less thing we have to worry about.'

Margaret was far from convinced. 'How useless am I going to feel if anything happens to you and Papa, and I know that I wasn't even here to help you?'

'We need you to continue your father's dream of helping people. Also, though your father doesn't agree with me, I want you to find the man responsible and bring him to justice.'

Tears welled in Margaret's eyes. 'I don't want anything to happen to you and Papa!'

Isabella hugged her tightly, afraid to let Margaret go. 'We don't either, darling, but we need to be prepared in case the worst actually eventuates.'

Resigned to her duty, Margaret wiped her tears away as she glanced around her bedroom. 'So what do you suggest I take?'

Keeping busy means that there is little idle time to dwell upon the future and the dark cloud that hangs over us, mused Margaret. The topic wasn't raised again and the atmosphere at dinner appeared so normal that Margaret couldn't believe that the threat of death could possibly be in their immediate future.

WEDNESDAY
Under Attack!

Reality came thundering home to Margaret as an urgent hand shook her awake at 1 a.m. Isabella's face was deathly pale as they heard shots ringing out all over the Haven. Her mother was already completely dressed.

'You must get away from here immediately.'

Throwing off her bedcovers, Margaret had gone to bed fully clothed apart from her boots, which she now hurriedly pulled on. Isabella picked up the packed canvas bags and ushered her daughter and Sebastian out to the kitchen where Tano and Kobbi were already waiting. The native teens looked as scared as Margaret felt. *This is actually happening! Someone really wants us all dead,* thought Margaret.

'Mama…' Margaret's protest died as she saw that her cool and calm mother was crying.

'We will always be with you!' Isabella embraced her daughter in a hug that could never be long enough but had, by necessity, needed to be kept short.

'I love you Mama.' Margaret choked on a sob as she clung to Isabella. The two guides slung the bags over their shoulders.

'Go now, every minute you delay puts you further in danger.' Isabella pushed them out the back door before picking up a rifle from the table. She positioned herself at the kitchen window so that she could shoot anyone who tried to break into the house.

Fleeing Into The Jungle

Tano led the way, cautiously along the side of the house, towards the edge of the trees. Being the eldest, Tano had a rifle, which he was naturally nervous about using. Kobbi had a hunting knife and Margaret a bow with a quiver full of arrows.

There was a distance of some thirty feet of open ground to cover before they could reach the safety of dense trees. Tano made certain that there was no one about before they made a dash across the open space. They ran hunched over to present less of a target in the moonlight. Halfway across a bullet whizzed through the air quite close to Kobbi's head. Their flight had been seen.

Reaching the edge of the trees and knowing that the gunman would come after them, Tano removed his backpack and passed it to Margaret.

'Kobbi get Miss Margaret to the cave. I'll hold them off,' ordered Tano, already training the rifle back towards the farm.

'Join us if you can brother.' Kobbi led the way as more bullets sought out their position. As they ran through the jungle, they could hear Tano return fire and possibly hit one of the gunmen. *Maybe Tano will be able to join us after all*, prayed Margaret. When they heard Tano cry out as a bullet finally found him, Margaret stopped in her tracks.

'Oh Kobbi!'

The guide grabbed her hand and pulled her onwards. 'We cannot grieve yet Miss, I must get you to safety.'

Although Margaret allowed herself to be dragged further away from The Haven she could not stop the tears that fell.

The Cave

It took nearly two hours to reach the cave, and by the time they dumped their sacks and finally sat down, Margaret felt exhausted. *A long run or hike is nothing new, but I can't stop thinking about poor Tano and what might be happening to my parents and the villagers. No matter what Kobbi says, I can't get rid of the feeling of guilt that I'm not there fighting alongside my parents.* Finally accepting that there was nothing she could do, Margaret was forced to sleep. Sebastian lay down beside her and Kobbi set up an alarm system that would warn them if anyone approached the cave.

Unless someone actually knows that the cave is there it's difficult to see the entrance as a large boulder stands in front of it and appears to be part of the rock face. There is room behind the boulder to slip inside the cave, and it has been my secret place since I was a child. For the moment we're safe and we can sleep the few hours till dawn arrives mused Margaret.

For only one brief moment when Margaret awoke did she think that it had all been a bad dream. That moment didn't last very long as her usual soft mattress turned out to be sand and her pillow, although it was soft, it was Sebastian's stomach. He remained still until Margaret raised herself onto her elbow.

The tiger then got to his feet and stretched every inch of his body before he wandered outside. Kobbi paused at the mouth of the cave to allow Sebastian to pass as the gap wasn't wide enough for both of them. Entering Kobbi handed Margaret a cup of hot black tea.

'How are you feeling this morning Miss?' He squatted down beside her as he went through one of the backpacks for food for their breakfast. Margaret raised the cup to her lips and groaned in delight as the hot sweet liquid hit the back of her throat. Kobbi had been very generous with the sugar.

'I feel like we're living some kind of nightmare. I keep waiting for the jolt that will wake me up and return everything back to normal.'

Kobbi handed her a piece of fruit bread and a banana before tucking into his own rations. 'It's hard to believe it's real, Miss, but we must be strong.'

Looking down at the fruit bread that her mother had baked only the day before, Margaret couldn't bring herself to eat it. *I want to just sit here and cry my heart out, but that isn't about to help anyone.* Slowly Margaret ate her breakfast, but each bite became more difficult to swallow. They removed any rubbish from the cave, made certain that the small fire Kobbi had used to make the tea was completely out, and freshened themselves up.

Margaret had just finished tying her hair back with a ribbon, having brushed it, when Sebastian rejoined them. There was a small trace of blood around his mouth suggesting that he had managed to successfully find his own meal.

Another Destroyed Village

'Where to now?' asked Margaret, pulling on her own backpack. 'Do we still have to head for Professor Evans' farm?'

Kobbi nodded. 'Yes Miss, but not directly. There's a village a little south of here and I thought we might be able to get news there about the Haven.'

A tremor of fear fluttered in Margaret's stomach. *I need desperately to know, and yet I'm afraid of hearing my worst fears confirmed.* 'Let's go then,' she tried to sound positive, but they were both steeling themselves for bad news.

They knew something was wrong before they even reached the village. The smell of smoke hung heavily in the air as they drew nearer. At one point Kobbi wanted to go on alone. *The smoke is a sure sign of danger, but it is my duty to protect Miss Margaret and I can't leave her alone in the jungle.*

Their first glimpse of the village sucked the breath straight out of their lungs. The entire settlement had been burnt to the ground. A crude pyre had been thrown together and all the bodies of the village's entire population seemed to have been thrown on to it. Some of the bodies were barely touched by the flames and the faces were frozen forever with the expressions of surprise and horror.

The smoke was coming from several of the buildings as small flickers of fire continued to devour the abundance of fuel. Margaret turned away from the pile of burnt corpses. *Horror is not a strong enough word for how I feel about this seemingly pointless massacre.*

'I don't understand! Why?' Margaret's voice was croaky with emotion.

Kobbi knelt down beside a body not so badly damaged by the fire. 'I don't know Miss. No guns were used here. This man was speared. This wasn't done by the men attacking our farm.'

The Animals' Secret

Margaret turned her gaze to a group of animals penned together at the other end of the village that had escaped the slaughter and carnage. This puzzled Margaret as she slowly made her way towards them.

'Don't raiders normally take the livestock as prizes?'

'Yes Miss.' Kobbi straightened up to follow her. Sebastian paid little attention to them as he sat on guard duty to prevent any form of surprise attack.

The animals should be spooked by my approach after such a brutal attack upon their village. The livestock had been trapped in their holding, unable to escape as the villagers were murdered and the buildings torched. They gather around me now in the need for reassurance and comfort.

'We can't leave them here, Kobbi, but we can't let them just run free, as they'll be unable to protect themselves from wild animals.'

'And they'll starve if they remain here.' Kobbi glanced around at the destruction about them. 'We must quickly leave this place, Miss Margaret, there is nothing but death here.'

Margaret wasn't listening as she was staring hard at a pile of straw in the corner of the livestock pen.

'Miss Margaret?'

She held up her hand for silence. 'Shh! That straw actually moved,' she whispered. Kobbi looked at her as if she had gone crazy.

'The straw?' He followed her pointed finger and nearly choked as the pile of straw did move. Kobbi stood for a moment stunned then started to laugh.

'It'll only be a wild animal Miss.'

Margaret shook her head. 'No, the livestock would be going crazy if there was a wild animal in their enclosure.' Easily scaling the fence, Margaret cautiously approached the haystack. 'Hello? It's safe to come out now. We won't hurt you.' She spoke softly and encouragingly in the local Ashanti language.

There was another rustle and slowly the face of a ten-year-old native boy emerged from the straw. Seeing Margaret's encouraging smile and the fact that neither Margaret nor Kobbi were armed, the boy came out of his hiding place. He was holding what appeared to be bundle of rags but a gurgle came from inside and a tiny fist emerged. *This frightened young boy is holding a baby!*

Margaret took a step towards the children, but it only caused the boy to tighten his hold on the baby. She decided to try another approach. 'My name is Margaret; my parents run the hospital near here. Perhaps you have heard about them?'

With his eyes constantly flicking between Margaret and Kobbi, the boy nodded.

'This is Kobbi,' continued Margaret. 'And just over there is Sebastian. Don't be alarmed, he's my friend and won't hurt you.' This was added as the boy was startled to see a large animal, which was unfamiliar to him as tigers weren't native to Africa.

Are You Hungry?

'I am Manu, this is Adwoa. When men came in the night, Adwoa's mother gives her to me and tells me to hide. I couldn't see anything, but hear much screaming,' explained the boy, unable to continue as he fought against his tears and the lump in his throat.

'How horrific,' sympathized Margaret, 'I bet you are hungry?' She quickly changed the subject.

Manu nodded his head. 'Yes Miss. I kept baby quiet with milk from the goat.'

'Well done!' *I'm impressed by his resourcefulness.* 'How about we head down to the river and clean you both up a little and then get you something to eat?'

Although he refused to release the baby girl, Manu did accept the hand Margaret held out to him, and led them out of the enclosure.

'Kobbi could you get some milk from the goat please?'

'Must I Miss Margaret?' Kobbi looked across at the goat that was staring blankly at him.

She smiled mischievously. 'Well it is either that or you wash the baby and I'll milk the goat.'

Kobbi glanced from the goat to Adwoa, who although was happily waving her arms around, was quite smelly as she definitely needed a nappy change. He decided that the goat was the lesser of two evils and went in search of a pail.

Sebastian followed Margaret discretely to the river so as not to frighten the children, and while she bathed them, the tiger patrolled the area. *I've met enough children to know that my mistress isn't in danger from them, but I don't like the smell of death that hangs over this village. The sooner we're away from this place the better I will feel,* mused the tiger.

Kobbi was equally worried about Margaret. *It's my duty to see her safely to Professor Evan's farm, but if we take the livestock with us the journey will take us twice as long.* He tried to work out what was the best thing to do as he supplied Manu with some food from their backpack, and Margaret was nursing the baby. Adwoa managed quite well to drink the goat's milk out of Margaret's cup without choking on it too much.

In one of the huts that hadn't been completely destroyed by fire, Kobbi had found some baby clothes and more importantly a sling to help carry Adwoa. Having wiped the little girl clean of any spilt milk; Margaret dressed her and arranged the baby sling around her own neck. She waited until Manu had finished eating before she finally spoke her thoughts to Kobbi.

We Need To Split Up

'I think we should split up, Kobbi. Sebastian and I will take the children to the Professor's, but I want you to muster the animals homeward. I need to know what has happened. I'll wait at Richard's until you come.'

This is exactly what I had been thinking, but even so, I still feel honour bound to protest. 'I mustn't leave you alone Miss Margaret. You'll have no one to protect you.'

Smiling, Margaret shook her head. 'I have Sebastian, and Manu. We'd better take the goat as I don't think Adwoa is old enough for solid food.'

Kobbi almost breathed a sigh of relief. *I don't like goats as they can be terribly stubborn.*

'If anything was to happen to you Miss…' Kobbi trailed off as a look of great sorrow crossed Margaret's face.

'We must all take our chances now. I only pray that when you come for me at Professor Evan's, it will be with good news.' *Neither of us believe that this will actually happen, but it is essential to maintain the pretence if I'm to be able to get myself and the children to Richard's property.*

Kobbi found a piece of rope to loop around the goat's neck and handing the rope to Margaret, he felt a lump in his throat.

'God speed you Miss!' He suddenly embraced her.

'Thank you Kobbi, and may God protect us all.' Margaret returned the hug. Kobbi drew away embarrassed and helped Manu put on the second backpack, while Margaret placed Adwoa into the baby sling around her neck. Adjusting her own backpack, Margaret looked back at Kobbi only once as Sebastian led them away from the smouldering ruins of Manu's village.

The Trek South Begins

We've a long two days walk ahead of us and I'm concerned about how Manu will manage the distance as he drags the goat along. He'd probably barely slept the previous night, and had been frightened out of his wits. When they stopped for lunch, Margaret allowed Manu to sleep for several hours. *It is after all the hottest time of the day, and we can continue walking in the cool of the evening before the light completely disappears. Despite the presence of Sebastian and the children, I feel so alone. I can't help but dwell upon what might have happened at the Haven.* Shaking her head, Margaret tried to concentrate upon the journey ahead of them. *We aren't safe yet, and I need to be constantly vigilant, as there is no predicting where we might meet danger.*

Their progress was seriously hampered during the afternoon, but the only danger was that Margaret would lose her temper. After a good sleep, Manu was quite capable of keeping up, but it was Nan, the goat who was holding them back. She refused to keep up with the pace Margaret set, and Manu was becoming more tired trying to pull Nan along, than the trek itself.

For a couple of hours Margaret tried gentle persuasion but even her patience wore thin. She knelt down and firmly grasping the goat's head, Margaret forced the mutinous animal to look her in the eye.

'You have two choices Nan,' Margaret spoke calmly but firmly. 'You'll either come with us willingly, or you will become dinner, and I'll find another way to feed the baby.' The goat stared back at Margaret with her usual blank expression.

'Don't you believe me?' added Margaret. 'Perhaps a nip from Sebastian will make you realize that I'm deadly serious.'

The goat's gaze travelled to where Sebastian was patiently waiting for a decision and at that moment licked his lips. Nan looked back at Margaret and gave a submissive bleat. When Margaret rose to her feet, Nan didn't have to be urged to keep up as the goat surged forward ahead of them, to show that she had understood exactly the terms of Margaret's ultimatum.

Actually I am relieved, as I can't really think of anything else that we can give Adwoa but milk, sighed Margaret.

Sebastian was a little disappointed that goat wasn't going to be on the menu that evening. *I'm not too worried yet about my next meal. After a really good feed, I can go two to three days before I really need to eat again.*

Travelling south-east, Margaret kept fairly close to the river and every so often she would check her bearings with her compass and map. Although she had no fear of the jungle and its animals, she did have a healthy respect for it. She didn't go looking for trouble and with two children to defend, she occasionally made necessary, though time consuming, detours to avoid danger.

There was a leopard stalking a herd of antelope for her dinner, and Margaret kept her group still and out of sight until the leopard's hunt was successful. Then Margaret led the way around the leopard so that she didn't see them. There was a pack of hyena squabbling over a carcass and Margaret detoured again so as not to provide the scavengers with easy live prey. *Sebastian's size is an incredible deterrent, as most animals will think twice about taking him on. Even so, I want to avoid any unnecessary confrontations.* As it started to grow dark, Margaret was on the lookout for a suitable place to camp for the night.

They heard the rapid approach of many elephants before they actually saw them. The ground shook as a herd of angry and frightened elephants rampaged and trumpeted through the jungle towards them. The noise was deafening and Margaret hurriedly moved her entourage to an area of safety. For such large animals, elephants move pretty quickly and it wasn't long before their calls of distress and the pounding of their feet began to fade.

Manu scanned the direction the elephants had come from, in case the predators followed which could put their group in danger.

'Do you think it was lions, Miss?' Manu checked out the nearest trees to see if they were climbable. Sebastian was suspiciously sniffing the air, and Margaret caught a whiff of what had attracted the tiger's senses.

'No Manu that is gunpowder on the wind. A more dangerous hunter was chasing the elephants; man.'

Jack Phillips

Margaret looked around her and decided they had gone far enough for one day. 'We'll camp here tonight. Have a rest and then we can collect some sticks for a fire.'

Tying Nan to a tree, Manu gratefully flopped down on to the soft green grass in the shade of a tree. Margaret removed Adwoa from the sling and laid her down beside Manu. The baby was awake, but happily amusing herself playing with her toes. Having taken off her backpack, Margaret stretched to ease her aching muscles. The snapping of a twig saw Margaret's bow and arrow immediately in her hands. Sebastian had already risen again ready to defend them.

'Please don't kill me yet,' said an amused male voice. Slowly into view came an Englishman, about 35, handsome and with a slight limp. His hands were held up submissively, but a rifle was slung over his shoulder. *For a brief moment I thought that I recognized him, but now isn't the time to try and remember,* pondered Margaret.

'Place your gun on the ground and keep your hands where I can see them please,' she ordered.

Lowering his weapon, the young man couldn't help grinning. 'You're facing a possibly highly dangerous situation, and yet you still remember your manners. I am impressed!' He continued to approach and made no protest as Manu had risen and patted him down to check for any other weapons. Manu nodded to Margaret, who lowered her bow.

The gentleman's eyes rested mesmerized upon Sebastian, 'I had always thought the native talk about a big white cat was just mumbo jumbo. He is magnificent!'

Margaret's mouth relaxed into a smile of pride. 'Yes he is, but if you are thinking of hunting him, please think again. I will kill anyone who tries to harm Sebastian!'

'I'm not surprised! But where are my manners? I'm Jack Phillips.'

'Margaret Munroe, this is Manu, Adwoa and of course Sebastian. Oh and Nan, the goat.'

Jack acknowledged each of them. 'I'm afraid that the elephant stampede was caused by my father's hunting party. I abhor the sport, but come along to keep Dad out of trouble.'

A frown descended upon Margaret's brow. 'Don't I know you? The name, your face, you're so familiar and yet I cannot place you.'

Jack laughed. 'I'm not surprised! If you are Doctor Munroe's daughter, you would've been only five or six when I was brought to your father's hospital. I was sixteen and while out hunting I tried to save a native guide from being gored to death by a wild boar, I ended up getting my leg ripped open.' Jack tapped the leg he had been limping on. 'Your Dad saved the leg, and I was able to use the experience to let my Dad down lightly about disliking hunting.'

Margaret finally lowered her bow to the ground. 'I remember now.'

Jack grinned. 'You were such an amazing child. You stood beside your father on a chair and handed him surgical equipment as he worked on patching up my leg. Not once did you even flinch at the sight of all that blood and damage.'

Sitting down, Margaret gestured for Jack to join them. He glanced nervously once at Sebastian, but with his mistress' acceptance of this stranger, Sebastian had eased his defensive posture, and laid down again.

'You're a long way from home aren't you?' stated Jack.

Sighing, Margaret nodded and explained what had happened at the farm, and Manu's village. Jack's horror was evident upon his face.

'What is wrong with people?' Glancing around, his expression of horror increased, 'You're all alone! There is no one to protect you!'

This made Margaret smile. 'Sebastian is a very able champion, and I'm very accurate with my bow.'

'Even so…' Jack didn't finish his sentence, as he was already thinking about something else. 'I can't take you to our campsite tonight as Dad and his friends tend to drink a bit, well a lot actually and I can't guarantee that they would behave properly if you were there. Perhaps in the morning I can escort you to Professor Evan's?'

I am touched by his concern for our well-being. 'Thank you, but it really isn't necessary. We only have another day's walk ahead of us.'

'Independent little Miss aren't you?' Jack smirked.

'I'm sorry but it's difficult to know whom to trust.'

'I'll let you carry my rifle,' Jack promised. Margaret couldn't help laughing at his attempt to relieve her concern. 'Please Margaret, at least let me escort you until midday. Then I'll be less concerned as you have only a few more hours before you reach safety.'

Margaret sighed. 'You're not going to take no for an answer are you?'

Grinning, Jack shook his head. 'No, I'm not! I'll be back around dawn. Do you need anything tonight? Firewood, food, blankets?' He rose to his feet. *Rather reluctantly*, he sighed, *as I don't really want to leave.*

'No thank you. We'll be fine.' Margaret also got up and followed Jack to where he had left his rifle. Picking it up, he handed it to Margaret.

'Thank you.'

Her smile makes me want to stay even more. 'I'll see you in the morning.' With a wave of his hand, Jack reluctantly left them.

A Night's Vigil

Sebastian, like all cats, domestic or wild, possesses the useful ability to catnap whenever he likes. This ability to sleep and yet still be aware of what is happening around him means that I don't have to stay awake all night on guard duty. At regular intervals during the night, Sebastian would silently rise, stretch and patrol the area around their campsite. Margaret, though, wasn't prepared to let Sebastian do all the work, and occasionally woke just to make sure everything was still all right.

There's a colony of monkeys in the trees not far from us, and although they're fairly quiet due to being nervous of Sebastian's presence, they will alert us to any approaching danger. They had a quiet night, which was a relief for Margaret, as they still had so much distance to cover before they could truly relax.

THURSDAY

You Are Not Safe

At dawn, Margaret dished up the remainder of their food supplies and milked Nan for Adwoa. *Our next meal will have to come from the jungle around us, but I'm hopeful that we can reach Richard's farm before dinner. Not that I'm worried if we don't keep this schedule. I know what berries and fruits are edible, as well as how to trap an animal or catch fish. My major concern is getting the children to safety as soon as possible.*

While Margaret nursed Adwoa as she drank her milk, her thoughts were focused upon the remainder of their journey and the possible dangers and hazards that might be lying in wait for them. When the monkeys started chattering excitedly and Sebastian rose to his feet with his hackles raised, Margaret laid her hand on Jack's rifle that was on the ground beside her.

Through the bushes and shrubs burst out a highly frightened horse with its rider slumped over the saddle. The rider's hands somehow managed to pull on the horse's reins and bring the horse to a standstill. As if this much effort was too extraneous for the rider, he now fell from his mount and landed heavily upon the ground.

Passing Adwoa to Manu, Margaret immediately went to the aid of the injured man. Kneeling down to turn him onto his back, she was startled to see the extent of the damage Jack Phillips had suffered. He was completely covered with blood; there was a large dent at the side of his forehead, where he had been hit by a blunt object. Opening his jacket Margaret discovered Jack's shirt was absolutely soaked in blood as he had at least three bullet wounds to the chest. She desperately tried to stop the flow of blood. *I know with a sinking heart that I am holding a dying man in my arms.*

Impatiently Jack managed to grab Margaret's hands as she tried to help him. 'There's no time, Margaret,' his words came out as little more than a whisper. 'White men attacked our camp, seeking you. Killed everyone!' Jack suddenly started coughing and the handkerchief she pressed against his mouth came away red with blood.

'I wouldn't tell them where you were… managed to fool them into thinking I was dead. They left but I waited an hour to make sure they didn't follow me here. Take my horse; you'll make better time with the children mounted. You must hurry!'

Margaret stared at him unable to comprehend what Jack was saying. 'They're hunting me? Why? And why kill people who don't even know me?'

Jack coughed again, and this time it was harder to stop the fit. 'All he said was that you had something he wanted. Please Margaret, you must go now!'

She shook her head. 'I cannot leave you like this!'

The hand that reached out to take hers was trembling violently. 'You must! I'm a dead man, I've only kept alive this long so that I could warn you. Whatever it is this monster wants from you, don't give it to him!'

'But I have nothing.'

Jack raised his hand to tenderly touch Margaret's face. 'You have riches beyond the realm of money. Don't let anyone steal that from you.'

'Can I at least ease your suffering?' Tears spilled down Margaret's cheeks.

Shaking his head, Jack struggled to pull himself up onto his elbow. 'I need you to prop me up against a tree. I'll hang on to the rifle and cover your retreat in case I've exposed your location. I may not be able to kill more than one, but at least it'll warn you that they're close.'

Barely knowing what she was doing, Margaret followed Jack's orders and having positioned him seated against a tree, she laid the rifle in his lap. Every breath was now becoming more and more difficult, but Jack managed to curl his finger around the trigger of the rifle.

I cannot just walk away from someone in pain. 'How can I leave you like this?'

Jack sighed. 'If there was any chance of saving me, then I'd agree with you. Please Margaret get to safety. Don't make my death be in vain.'

Very carefully Margaret embraced him. 'I'm so sorry. No one should die because of me!'

'Don't be sorry! Make that monster sorry! Give the innocent justice. Go, now, please!'

Margaret couldn't see through the tears as she stumbled to her feet and away from Jack. She didn't even realize what she was doing as she helped Manu on to the back of Jack's horse and passed Adwoa up to him to carry. Margaret thrust the empty backpack into the other one before flinging it onto her back and took Nan's leash into her hand. Only now as Sebastian headed off to lead the way did Margaret look around once at Jack. His breathing had become faster and shallower, and his eyes appeared glazed.

'I'm sorry,' Margaret said.

'May God guide you safely, Margaret.' Jack's head lolled down onto his chest. Margaret had to control the impulse to go to him. *There's nothing I can do for Jack now.* With Nan's leash in one hand and the horse's reins in the other, Margaret followed Sebastian.

Only when the sound of the horse's hooves had faded did Jack finally raise his head. Already his vision was becoming cloudy and he felt himself sinking into the darkness that was waiting for him. *I must fight against it, though, willing myself to keep living so that Margaret can get a head start on her hunters.*

Jack actually managed to remain awake for another hour. He looked up to find a beautiful young woman with magnificent wings standing in front of him. Suddenly there was no more pain, no more trouble breathing and his vision was clear. Jack took the hand the smiling Angel held out to him, and finally surrendered his fight against death.

Margaret's Anguish

For Margaret, though, there was pain; a great deal of pain. *So many people are dying because of me, and I've no idea what I could possibly have that anyone would kill for. Apart from my parents and Sebastian, the only thing that I value is my pebble people. Although I had always got on well with the children from the local village, it wasn't always easy being the only white child for hundreds of miles. So I had made up a family out of the shiny clear pebbles that I found around the farm. I had given them names and made up stories about their lives, sort of the way a child would with dolls. Mama had encouraged me to collect the pebble people and told me to always keep them close. But what can be the value of the pebbles after all?* Margaret reasoned.

Unable to find an answer that was logical, she tried to concentrate upon keeping them out of danger and collecting food supplies when they presented themselves along their journey. The guilt, though, wouldn't go away, and it started to eat its way through Margaret's soul and kind heart, leaving her feeling very depressed.

Manu's Counsel

Mid-morning they stopped for a rest, water and some of the fruit that they had found along the way. Jack's horse and Nan munched on grass as Adwoa played with Sebastian's tail. *I don't mind this, so long as the baby doesn't put my tail in her mouth. Adwoa may not have teeth yet, but she could still cause pain.* Manu went to sit beside Margaret who was staring intently ahead of her. So deep were her musings that she actually jumped when Manu placed his hand on her arm.

'These feelings of guilt don't do you justice, Miss Margaret.'

She looked at him stunned. 'How did you know I was feeling guilty?'

'I've been watching you all morning as you have wrestled with the questions of why. I understand, Miss, cause I too have been asking myself why. Why was my village destroyed? Could I have done something to prevent it, or save more? Why weren't Adwoa and me found?'

Margaret placed her arm around him and drew Manu closer. 'I'm sorry, Manu. I've been beating myself up with the why questions, and forgot that you and Adwoa are hurting too.'

Manu laid his hand over hers. 'I don't tell you this to shame you, but to show that I understand what you feel. You're not to blame for Mr. Jack's death. Bad men did that, not you. Your soul is not stained with his blood.'

'Those bad men are killing people because of me. I don't know why or how to stop them. I feel helpless and stupid as I don't know what they want from me!'

The boy shook his head. 'You don't have any control over what those bad men are doing. Just like Adwoa and I have no control over the bad men who destroyed our people.'

Margaret kissed the top of Manu's head, 'Then why do I feel so much to blame?'

'You must be strong, Miss Margaret. We can't make this journey without your strength and courage.'

'I'll try not to fail you.' Margaret couldn't believe she was talking to a ten-year-old child, and not an adult.

'I know Miss, but you need to not fail for yourself.'

A Need To Cool Down

The sense of guilt lessened slightly but wouldn't completely go away. They didn't rest too long as the thought that killers could be on their trail meant that they had to keep moving. Even so, by midday, it was so hot and they were tiring, making it essential that they took a longer break. They ate more fruit they had collected and Manu caught a couple of fish.

One was given to Sebastian raw, whilst they cooked the other over a small fire. Margaret was worried that the smoke from the fire would alert others to their position, but Manu insisted that they needed more than fruit and berries to continue, and he would put out the fire as soon as the fish was cooked.

With her belly full of milk, Adwoa was easy enough to get off to sleep, but it was too hot and sticky for Margaret to rest comfortably. She looked longingly at the river that sparkled in the sunlight and glancing across at Manu, she found that he too was still awake.

'What do you say to a quick dip?' suggested Margaret.

Manu jumped to his feet. 'Will Adwoa be all right?'

Rising, she nodded. 'Sebastian will watch out for trouble. Come on.' Her last words were unnecessary as Manu was already ahead of her and plunging into the cool water beside their camp. Margaret didn't immediately follow, as she needed to strip out of her clothes and remove her boots. Once she was completely naked, she plunged into the refreshing, sparkling river.

The water was wonderful and cool, but they couldn't have any fun, splashing or playing games as it might attract attention to their location. Manu was soon out of the water again and lay down besides Adwoa and Sebastian. Margaret, though, remained in the river, enjoying the feel of the therapeutic rhythm of the water lapping against her body. *It's so nice to be able to relax for a minute and forget the horrors that we've been through the past couple of days. It can't last though, as the men hunting me are still out in the jungle somewhere, and we're still several hours away from the safety of Richard Evan's farm.*

Discovered!

It was difficult to say what first alerted Margaret to a sudden change in the atmosphere. *It could've been the abrupt silence of the birds in the trees around us. The foreboding chill that ran down my back, the way Jack's horse pawed at the ground, or the fact that Sebastian had risen to his feet and placed himself protectively in front of Adwoa and Manu.*

Also sensing the change in the air, Manu dragged Margaret's bow and arrows closer to him before locating the hunting knife in the backpack, and throwing it across to Margaret. She nimbly caught the blade and held it under the water ready to use it if necessary. She remained perfectly still; as to emerge from the river was to offer a target. *I finally understand the saying about tension being thick enough you could cut it with a knife.* The suspense may have only been several minutes but it felt like hours.

Through the trees approached a man on foot. He appeared to be unarmed and his wide brimmed hat was pushed forward to shield his face which was adorned by steel rimmed glasses. He was of average height, he was considerably handsome, in repose his expression was often a serious one, but when he smiled, as he did now, it literally transformed him.

'Doctor Livingstone, I presume?' He said in a dry humorous drawl. These had been the first words uttered by

Henry Stanley, a journalist, when in 1871, he found the explorer David Livingstone in the Congo.

Margaret burst out laughing, and Sebastian launched himself at the newcomer, knocking him onto his back and stood on his chest. Manu gasped in surprise but instead of lowering his massive jaws to sink into the man's throat, Sebastian enthusiastically rub his face against the newcomer's.

'Yes, Sebastian, I'm pleased to see you too, now get off! You weigh a ton!' Professor Richard Evans managed to push the tiger off and sit up.

Margaret sighed deeply at seeing an old friend and not an enemy. 'We didn't expect to see you until we arrived at the farm tonight.'

Richard polished the cat saliva off his glasses before putting them on again. 'I must apologize for not meeting up with you sooner Margaret. When the message via the drums came about the hospital being attacked, I was in the middle of an experiment that had taken six month to get to this stage. I knew you'd have Sebastian to protect you, so I completed my research before setting out to help you. I'm sorry.'

Margaret shook her head. 'Don't be, I didn't expect you to come looking for us at all. If you'll just turn around I'll get out of the water.'

Richard looked at her blankly and then down at her pile of clothing that lay on the grass beside him. He turned bright red as he quickly turned around, 'Really Margaret! Have you no modesty?'

Manu, who had lowered the bow and arrow when Margaret had greeted the newcomer, now, looked from one to the other bemused as he wore only a loincloth. Margaret emerged from the river and pulled on her clothes again.

'You English are so prude,' stated Manu. Richard looked at him in surprise but Margaret only laughed.

'Very true Manu,' agreed Margaret, 'but it should be either 'so prudish' or 'such prudes'. Either way I concur.'

Richard was frowning. 'Where are Tano and Kobbi? I thought they were never supposed to leave you? Who are these two youngsters?'

The laughter left Margaret's face. 'I'll explain on the way. It isn't safe for us to stop here long.' Her sudden seriousness communicated itself to Richard, and he immediately rose to his feet.

'I left the wagon just beyond these trees. Can I take anything for you?'

Margaret, having decided not to put her boots on again, had untethered the horse and Nan while Manu had made certain the fire was completely out, prior to pulling on a backpack. 'Can you pick up Adwoa please?' asked Margaret. Richard looked down at the baby who was happily waving her arms around, and he stepped forward to take the animal's reins out of Margaret's hands.

'You'd better pick up the baby; I'd be terrified that I would drop her or something.' Although she shook her head at him in disbelief, Margaret scooped Adwoa up.

In a clearing not too far away from their campsite stood Sophie, the horse attached to Richard's wagon. Sophie was quietly eating grass until she saw the Professor approach leading another horse, and she raised her head to glare at him.

'Calm down Sophie, he's not your replacement.' Richard gently rubbed Sophie's nose, but she didn't stop glaring until the other horse had been hitched to the back of the wagon. A thick layer of straw covered the floor of the vehicle and in each corner stood upright poles, which supported a canvas sheet overhead for shade.

Sebastian jumped up easily into the wagon and buried himself under the straw. *With Richard present to protect us, I'm going to catch up on some sleep.* Manu assisted Richard to lift Nan, the goat into the wagon before the boy tossed in the backpacks and jumped in also. Margaret handed Adwoa to Manu and would have also got in, but Richard stopped her.

Mama Know Best!

Out of the straw, Richard withdrew a cardboard box and handed it to Margaret. 'In my defence, I'm following orders,' He said. Puzzled Margaret opened the box to reveal a dress of pale blue. Her eyes were blazing as she looked back up at Richard.

'Whose orders?'

'Your Mother's,' replied Richard calmly. 'She said that you would hate the idea but that it might save your life.'

Margaret opened her mouth to retort but then closed it again. *It is a well-known fact throughout our locality that I always dress as a boy. That is what the hunters will be looking for.* Margaret took the dress out of the box and shook out the creases. She silently handed the empty box back to Richard and headed behind a tree to change.

I hadn't thought I would actually win that round so easily. When Margaret reappeared, Richard felt his chest tighten and all his breath sucked out of his lungs. *With her white hair trailing wet and loose down her back and the dress accentuating her curves, whereas the male attire hid them, I'm surprised at how much she has grown up since we had first met.* The dress skirt wasn't as full as it should be as there was no bustle, pads or numerous petticoats as was the fashion in Victorian London.

Throwing her male clothes into the wagon, Margaret was closely watching Richard as if she expected some sarcastic comment. When he didn't say anything at all, Margaret became even more wary. She turned around and pulled her hair out of the way.

'You'll have to do me up Professor, but don't tighten it too much. I can barely breathe now.'

Coming out of his trance like state, Richard adjusted the lacing at the back of the dress before securing it. 'That is probably because you're not as small as you had been when this dress was originally made.'

Margaret turned around so suddenly that she took Richard by surprise. 'Are you saying that I'm fat?' She demanded, her eyes alight with the scent of battle.

'No, of course not!' *I'm treading on dangerous ground.*

'What then?'

Swallowing hard, Richard said cautiously, 'Just that you have developed more curves.'

'You're still saying I am fat!'

He sighed exasperated. 'I'm not saying that at all! There's probably not an ounce of fat on you! When this dress was made you weren't as well developed as you are now.' Realizing that his cheeks were burning, Richard quickly changed the subject. 'Can we go now, or is there something else you want to argue about?'

'Not right now.' Margaret smiled sweetly at him.

'Minx!' laughed Richard and led her to the front of the wagon but stopped before he handed her up onto the box seat. 'One last thing,' he reached behind her cascade of long blonde, wet hair and undid the necklace that Margaret always wore. Attached to the necklace was a ring; her grandmother's wedding ring. 'Put this on, just in case.' Margaret looked up into the serious face of the Professor and did not even think to argue as he slid the ring on to her left ring finger.

Hired Killers

Sophie raised her head and neighed, causing Richard to turn as he had also heard the approach of a group of horses. *What surprises me isn't the look of steel that has entered*

Richard's placid and kind eyes, but the fact that he has produced a pistol seemingly out of nowhere.

'Sebastian, stay hidden,' Richard ordered quietly. 'Margaret keep calm, let me do the talking.'

Margaret could only nod her head as a knot of fear was tightening in her stomach. *If these six horsemen are my hunters, then they're cold- blooded killers.*

'Sorry to startle you Sir,' called out the leader of the horsemen as they drew closer. 'We were wondering if you could possibly help us.'

Although Richard lowered the gun, he didn't put it away. 'How can we help you gentlemen?'

Margaret blushed as the men scanned her from head to toe and she moved closer to Richard. *I'd feel more comfortable if I could reach my bow and arrows, but I have to put my faith in the Professor.*

'We're looking for a dangerous criminal that has escaped. A young woman, dressed in male clothing and travelling with a tiger.'

Richard's eyebrows rose and he said in a supercilious manner, 'A tiger? My good man tigers are not indigenous to this continent! Someone has been having you on.'

The leader only smiled. 'It does sound strange, but I assure you it's true. You and your good lady haven't seen anyone fitting that description?

Richard shook his head. 'No, sorry, you're the first people we've seen all day.'

'Are you sure?' pressed the leader, his eyes glued to Margaret's face. 'She's probably with two teenage niggers.'

Richard groaned, but there was nothing he could do to prevent the volcano beside him from erupting.

'Don't you dare use that word in my hearing!' exploded Margaret, her hands clenched into tight fists by her side.

'I call them as I see them, ma'am! They're no better than animals!'

'What right have you got to degrade another race just because they're different?'

Richard quickly placed his arm around Margaret's waist to stop her from charging at the group of men.

The leader grinned at Richard. 'My God, that is a passionate woman you have there! We're pretty sick of black women; I don't suppose you'd be willing to share your good fortune?'

Richard tightened his grip upon a furious Margaret. 'Sorry to disappoint you, but I should warn you, that unless you like the thought of a blade between your ribs, I wouldn't try if I was you. My wife is very good with a knife.'

The leader threw his head back and laughed heartily. 'I wish you joy then! What a temper she must have! Good-day, Sir, Ma'am.'

Richard raised his free hand to the rim of his hat, but did not release Margaret until the horsemen had moved out of sight. She suddenly went limp in his embrace.

'That was them, wasn't it? They attacked the Haven and Jack's hunting party. They want to kill me!' Margaret's words were little more than a whisper.

Richard helped her up on the box seat before getting up beside her. 'You know I don't believe in theorizing without sufficient data. Why don't you tell me what's been happening?' Sighing, Margaret nodded and began to explain the nightmare of the past few days as Sophie headed for home.

Once Margaret had told Richard everything, he suggested that she might want to join the children in the back of the wagon. *It isn't that I don't want to talk to Margaret, but she's emotionally drained and could do with some sleep. Also I want time to process what she has told me, and consider what we need do to in the future.* Sophie required very little guiding which was just as well as he had a great deal to think about.

Richard's Story

Over ten years ago Professor Richard Evans, had arrived in the Gold Coast in western Africa, wanting to study the traditional African roots and herbs in the hope that some of them could be used for diseases that Western medicine had yet to discover a cure or a treatment. When his experiments and research permitted, Richard would spend a couple of days with the Munroes at the Haven. Edward Munroe, on occasional trips down to Accra, the capital city, or Oda, the major city in the Eastern Region; would stop for the night with Richard.

Margaret had always thought, *Richard's life must be a lonely one, for apart from his native workers and despite the fact that he is married, he doesn't have any family or his wife living with him. We never asked, and Richard never volunteered any information about his life before coming out to Africa.* She had also wondered, *Is there some deep, dark secret that makes Richard so serious. I love to tease him, but he is well able to retaliate with a well-chosen barb of sarcasm. There's no animosity, though, and despite thinking Richard a little stuffy, I do like him a lot.*

Uneventful Trip

The remainder of their journey was thankfully uneventful, which caused Richard to heave a sigh of relief as he drove through the boundary of his property. *I hadn't thought we would succeed in fooling Margaret's hunters so easily. Then again, I'd never thought Margaret would submit without a fight to wearing a dress. It had been fortuitous that she had changed before the hunters had come along or we'd probably all be dead now.*

Not wanting to dwell upon that thought, Richard firmly tried to think only of the future. Pulling Sophie up outside the stables, Richard was relieved to see that everything at home was normal. Father and son, Danso and Fynn, who was in his early twenties, came running out to take control of Sophie as Richard descended from the box seat. Danso was the Property Manager and so trustworthy that Richard could safely leave everything on the farm in Danso's hands so that he could concentrate upon his research and experiments.

Fynn led the two horses into the stable to feed, water and rub down. Danso assisted Richard to get Nan out of the wagon.

'Kobbi and Tano are not with Miss Margaret?' Danso looked worried as he and the boys' mother were cousins.

'No, I'm sorry. Kobbi will be here with news soon we hope, of the Haven and the Munroes.'

Sebastian emerged from under the straw, jumped down and stretched. The tiger had been to Richard's farm before, so Danso wasn't frightened of the huge cat, only wary.

'I'll see that the goat and Sebastian have some food and drink, Sir.'

Richard bent down to stroke Sebastian's head. 'Thank you. I need someone to ride over and tell Father Gerard that I have Margaret safe. Also I need his help.'

'Of course Sir, Fynn will go once he has attended to the horses.' Danso led Sebastian away; who went willingly as he knew that Margaret was safe with Richard.

The remaining occupants of the wagon were still asleep, and Richard was loath to wake them. *I have to get them out, though, as I've another use for the vehicle today, before the sun goes down.* From the house, Richard's Housekeeper, Dalila, came running across the yard.

'I was fearful you wouldn't find them Sir.' Dalila looked into the wagon and seeing the two young children, her heart melted, 'Oh the poor darlings! We must get them inside.'

When Richard reached over to pick up Adwoa to hand to Dalila, Manu woke up.

'Sir?' He looked around bewildered.

Richard smiled kindly. 'It's all right. We've reached my home. Dalila will look after you and Adwoa.'

As he scampered out of the wagon, Manu cast a concerned glance at Margaret, who was still asleep. Richard could guess what he was thinking.

'I'll bring Margaret inside. You won't be separated from her.'

Manu smiled and looked considerably relieved. 'Thank you Sir.' He followed the Housekeeper into the house, grateful that they'd finally arrived at their safe refuge.

Watching Margaret as she slept, Richard thought, *she looks so much younger. The stress and worry reflected earlier on her face is momentarily gone. They'll be back as soon as Margaret wakes, and I want to delay that moment for as long as possible.* Meanwhile Fynn saddled up a fresh horse and rode off to the local village.

Carefully, Richard reached into the wagon and scooped Margaret up into his arms to gently lift her out. Despite the care he took, Margaret stirred and sleepily opened her eyes. Casting a brief look at her own body, Margaret groaned as she laid her head against Richard's shoulder.

'I'm dead, aren't I?'

Richard was surprised by the question as he carried her into the house. 'Why do you say that?'

Margaret sighed, 'How else did you get me to agree to actually wear a dress?'

'Impossible child!' Richard chuckled, making his way through the house to his bedroom where he laid Margaret down on his bed.

'Father Gerard should be here soon,' Richard added, 'Don't think that you need to be doing one hundred and one things, everything will be taken care of.'

Margaret opened her mouth to retort, but quickly closed it again. *Even if I wanted to move, I can't. My limbs feel like lead and I feel absolutely drained and exhausted.* Bewildered, Margaret looked up at Richard for answers. 'What's wrong with me?'

Sitting down on the edge of the bed, Richard took her wrist to check her pulse. 'You've spent the past two days living on fear and adrenaline. It is what has kept you going. Now that you can feel some measure of security, the adrenaline drops drastically and can leave you feeling drained.'

'It isn't permanent is it?'

Richard shook his head. 'No, in a few days you'll be getting into mischief like you always do!'

Finding a sudden surge of energy from somewhere, Margaret hit him with a pillow. 'Beast!' Rising to his feet, Richard only laughed as he made sure the mosquito curtain completely surrounded the bed.

'Try and sleep. Tomorrow you'll feel much better.' Leaving the room, Richard only hoped, *that the morrow will also bring welcoming news from the Munroes. The continuing silence is a warning sign, but I will not share that concern with Margaret as she's already worrying enough about her parents.*

Manu's Worries

The house was a lot more elaborate than Richard would have designed for himself. Isabella Munroe decided that Richard needed more than a room to work in and a bit of floor to sleep on. The house was a perfect square with a verandah surrounding all sides. Each room had either windows or doors that opened right up to allow cool breezes to sweep through. There were originally four bedrooms, one for Richard, one for dry storage, and one for experiments and attached to Richard's study, and one spare room that presently contained a lot of junk.

With the arrival of Margaret and not knowing how long she would be staying, Dalila finally had permission to clean out the spare room. The Housekeeper lived in a cottage with her family on Richard's property. She had found the erratic hours Richard worked were too exhausting to keep up with. Besides which, she had a family of her own to raise.

Sitting on a couch holding Adwoa and looking rather forlorn, Manu managed a half smile as Richard looked at him closely.

'Everything all right?'

'Yes Sir!'

'Hmm! You may want to loosen your hold on the baby. Has Dalila gone to get some milk?'

'Yes Sir! Sorry Sir.' Manu released Adwoa so quickly that she nearly slid off his lap.

'Relax Manu.' Richard laid his hand on the boy's shoulder. 'You don't have to keeping calling me sir. Don't apologize either; you've done a magnificent job keeping the baby alive. You're amongst friends now and you can allow some of the responsibility of keeping you and Adwoa safe to us.'

'Yes Sir, thank you.' Manu paused as he thought carefully about how he wished to word his next question. 'What happens now? I mean our biggest goal was to get here alive.'

'A very good question,' Richard leant back and for a moment his eyes focused on the roof.

'You've several options but there is no need to rush into a decision now, as you need to recover a little from the horrors you've endured. You could, if you wanted to, stay here and become one of our families on the farm. You might want to live with a family in our nearest village. There is a possibility that others from your village may have escaped into the jungle, if they can be located you might wish to join them. You might want to stay with Miss Margaret and return to the Haven when she does. Have I overwhelmed you with options?'

Manu shook his head. 'What about Miss Margaret? Do you really believe that her parents are still alive?'

Richard cast a quick glance at his bedroom curtain door to make sure that Margaret wasn't within hearing. 'I don't know! I prayed that some miracle has saved them. The news of the slaughter of the Phillips hunting party doesn't allow for much hope that Edward or Isabella are still alive. Until we hear from Kobbi, we can only speculate.'

Dalila bustled in with milk for Adwoa. The Housekeeper had found a baby's bottle and handed it to Manu. Adwoa proved to be quite hungry.

'The good Padre has just arrived, Sir,' said Dalila.

Richard nodded curtly. 'I'll go and greet him.'

Father Gerard Gothe

He strolled outside, certain the Manu did not need to re-live the story as Richard told it to Father Gerard Gothe. Gerard was a German Missionary, in his late 50's, and had been in the Gold Coast for nearly 30 years. He worked fairly closely with Edward Munroe, gaining basic medical knowledge so that he could treat minor conditions rather having to send them to Edward's hospital.

Once a month, the Priest would ride to the Haven to perform a Sunday service. Gerard's relationship with the reclusive Richard was quite a close one. There was shared dinners, chess games, theological debates as well as discussions about the progress of Richard's research.

It wasn't surprising then; that Father Gerard knew something was wrong the moment he saw Richard's face. He allowed Danso to take his horse as he reached out to grasp Richard's arm.

'What is it, my son? Is Margaret all right?'

Richard sighed. 'Margaret's fine. Come away from the house.' He led the religious man away from where they might be overheard, as he told Margaret's story. They paused under a group of shady trees where a hammock was stretched between two of the trees.

'Verdammt!' swore the Priest when the story came to an end, 'Do you intend to ride to the Munroe's to see for yourself?'

Richard shook his head. 'Kobbi is attending to that mission. What I need to do is to return the bodies of the Phillip's hunting party to their farm. We can't leave them like that to have their carcasses picked over by scavengers and Mrs. Phillips deserves to be told what happened.'

Nodding Gerard said, 'Ja, Ja, but you need to protect Margaret, so I will go.'

'I cannot ask you to do that!'

'No one said you did my son! I volunteered!'

Richard sighed in defeat. 'I'll organize the wagon, a couple of strong men, food and spades for you. Finding their camp shouldn't be too hard as Margaret kept fairly close to the river.'

'I'll just grab a few things I need from home and then I'll be ready to leave. I suggest you write a report to officials in Accra to let them know what has happened.'

Richard nodded. 'That was my next task.' They walked back to the stables together in silence, both deep in their own thoughts.

Richard's Childhood

Entering the house alone, Richard was surprised to find Margaret sitting alone on the couch as she tried to brush her hair.

'Where are the children?' He asked urgently.

Margaret nodded towards Richard's bedroom. 'Dalila borrowed a cradle from her daughter and has settled Adwoa down for a nap. Manu is outside, he needs some time alone.'

'Is he all right?'

Margaret sighed. 'I suppose the magnitude of losing everyone in his family has finally sunk in.'

Richard took the brush out of Margaret's hands and sat her in a dining chair. Standing behind her, he began to brush out the knots for her.

'I was Manu's age when both my parents died. I would've been better off, though, if I'd no other relatives. It was a devastating feeling that none of them wanted me.'

Margaret turned in her seat to take his hands between hers as her eyes reflected her horror. 'That is cruel! I can't see you as being a naughty child. Were you that difficult to look after?'

'Far from it!' Richard returned the pressure of her hands before turning Margaret round again to continue brushing her hair. 'So long as I had my books and ink and paper, they hardly knew I was there. Even so, they couldn't send me off to boarding school quick enough.'

'Monsters!'

Richard chuckled. 'It suited me fine. Except for the summer holidays, I could spend all other holidays on campus. I basically had the library to myself which was fantastic.'

'How lonely!' *I can't imagine spending such long periods of time away from my parents.*

Reminiscently, Richard smiled. 'Not really. I made some really good friends at school. Surprisingly, for a bookworm, I was very good at cricket. It is the one thing I miss out here.'

'You'll have to teach me how to play.' Margaret uttered a little 'ouch' as Richard tried to untangle a stubborn knot.

'Sorry. You should have brushed your hair as soon as you came out of the water.'

She cast him a speaking glance. 'Strangely enough I had more important matters to think about.'

'That reminds me I have to send off a report to officials. I had better talk to Danso about additional security.'

'If they supposedly know so much about me, wouldn't they know that I would come to you for protection?' Margaret fidgeted restlessly in her seat.

'I don't know, but if they do come, they won't leave here alive!'

Margaret turned around to stare at Richard in surprise. 'You don't believe in violence!'

He shrugged his shoulders. 'Edward said to me that if anything happened to him and Isabella, I was to look after you. Your father said that I was to protect you no matter what, even if that meant dying trying.'

'Why?'

A tender smile appeared. 'You're the most precious thing in their life. They want to protect you at all costs.'

'But why does someone want me dead?'

'I don't know.' Richard's smile vanished.

The Killers Reappear

Moving silently on such large paws, Sebastian ambled into the house. He affectionately brushed against Richard's legs before sitting down at Margaret's feet and laid his head upon her knee.

'Hello beautiful boy!' Margaret scratched the tiger behind the ears, who closed his eyes and began to purr. The tranquillity of the moment was shattered by a scream from outside.

Without pausing to consider the danger, all three charged out to see what the problem was. Dalila stood on the verandah; one hand covered her mouth in horror as she pointed to where a group of six horsemen were riding towards the house.

The source of her horror was the sight of Kobbi, bound by the hands, looking half-dead as one of the horsemen dragged him stumbling along behind him. From all over the farm, men came running in answer to Dalila's scream. The sight of Kobbi, who wasn't yet a man, caused the workers to pull up short in shock.

Margaret, though, was beyond shock, she was bloody angry. Ignoring the danger to herself, she ran to meet the horsemen and surprising the one leading Kobbi, she grabbed the knife from his belt and cut through the rope tied around Kobbi's wrists. The young man fell into Margaret's arms.

'I'm sorry Miss Margaret. They'd killed your parents. They made me tell them where you were.' Kobbi passed out, his head lolling back against Margaret's shoulder. Danso and Richard rushed forward to relieve Margaret of the youth.

'Take him inside Danso. Dalila, there are extra medical supplies in my bag if you need them.' ordered Margaret. Danso carried the boy away and the Housekeeper quickly followed to tend to his injuries. Seething with fury, Margaret turned to stare at the leader of the horsemen as he casually dismounted.

'Very clever Professor,' complimented the leader, 'Getting Miss Munroe into a dress before we found her.

Just too bad that we came across the little nigger riding one of Munroe's horses. He probably thought it was the quickest way to get to you with the news of the body count we had left behind.'

'You needn't sound so pleased with yourself!' Margaret's eyes were now ablaze at his casual attitude. 'I didn't think anyone could be stupid enough to be fooled by a simple change of clothes, but we fooled you!'

'Margaret, be careful what you are saying,' warned Richard quietly.

'Why? He's only going to kill me any way! Why shouldn't I have the opportunity to say what I feel?'

The leader was amused as he came down out of his saddle. 'Go ahead little one. Let us make your death more interesting.' He cupped her chin in his hand and Sebastian, taking exception to this familiarity, moved to defend Margaret, but she held out her hand for him to stay back.

'Sebastian, no, not yet!' Margaret ordered. Reluctantly Sebastian sat down beside Richard, but the tiger refused to look anywhere but at the leader.

Pushing his hand away, Margaret looked the leader in the eye and quietly asked, 'Why?'

'Ah, the eternal question!' He appeared even more amused. 'Why what, little one?'

'Why did you kill my parents? Why are you hunting me?'

The leader smiled. 'Money!'

'What grudge could you have against us?'

'My beautiful child, we're paid to eliminate people. It's nothing personal, just a business arrangement.'

Margaret shook her head. 'You kill not for food, self-defence or protection of a loved one, but because someone pays you? I feel sorry for you.' Her last words caused everyone gathered to look at her stunned.

One of the horsemen started to laugh, 'People about to die, usually feel sorry for themselves!'

Calmly Margaret shook her head. 'I've no reason to feel sorry for myself. When you kill me, I'll be joining my parents in heaven. On the other hand, with the atrocities you've committed, you have condemned your immortal soul to Hell. With every additional innocent life you take, you increase the severity of your punishment, and the amount of time you must spend in purgatory.'

The horseman, who had laughed, wasn't laughing now as he glanced at their leader in concern. 'Andy, you never said anything about an eternity in Hell!'

'Shut up you fool!' The leader snapped.

'But you should be worried,' Margaret added. 'You might escape justice in this life, but when you die, you must face God, the Ultimate Judge and Redeemer of mankind. He knows every single detail about your life. You cannot lie to Him; you cannot hide, nor can you escape His punishment. Eternity is a very, very long time.'

There was a rumbling of concern amongst the horsemen, but the leader was smiling again. 'Are you trying to convince us to let you go free?' He asked Margaret.

'No,' her answer shocked them again. 'You took on a contract, you have to honour it. I do ask, though, that you don't kill all these people as well. Although, I know that Richard will look after Sebastian, I'm afraid that since we've hardly been apart since he was a new born cub that he might pine for me. I don't know what is best to do in his case.'

Facing A Harsh Reality

Richard strode forward and grabbing Margaret by the shoulders turned her around to face him. 'The best thing to do is not to leave him at all! Really Margaret I've never known you to give up the fight for justice!'

Margaret's composure shattered as tears began to fall down her cheeks. 'You don't understand, Richard. They're dead! My parents are gone, and I have nothing left! I don't know if I have the strength to go on without them. Whatever this man wants, he can have it, because apart from Sebastian, nothing was more precious to me than Mama and Papa. I don't know if I can stay at the Haven with all those memories of them, and not go completely insane. I don't know what to do Richard! I don't think I can cope in a world without them!' By now she was sobbing uncontrollably and the men looked away embarrassed as Richard drew Margaret into his arms to comfort her.

'Don't give up Margaret. I know it hurts now, but it does get easier. You must be strong. I'll get you through this.' Ignoring everyone else, Richard soothingly ran his hand down Margaret's hair as she sobbed into his shoulder.

'It hurts so much I can barely breathe!' She gasped out. 'It's like I've already died and I'm just waiting for my body to catch up. There is so much pain. I just want it to go away.'

The leader cleared his throat. 'Sorry to interrupt this touching scene, but we'd like to get our job completed so we can be on our way. I promise you, Miss Munroe that we won't kill anyone else so long as they don't try to stop us.' At his signal, the other horsemen removed their firearms and pointed them at Margaret.

Richard refused to release Margaret as she tried to push him away to a safe distance. Sebastian rose to his feet and moved to stand beside his mistress, ready to protect her.

The horsemen seemed to be waiting for someone else to begin shooting first. They appeared loath to be the one to actually kill Margaret. The leader looked around at his men and in exasperation pulled out his own weapon.

No sooner had he raised his gun level with Margaret's head, than a shot rang out. It came not from the leader's gun but the nearby trees, and wasn't aiming for Margaret, but the horsemen. The second bullet took the leader cleanly between the shoulder blades and he was dead before he even hit the ground.

The sniper was hidden by foliage, but it didn't stop the other horsemen from firing blindly at the trees. The sniper's bullets were much more accurate, taking out each of the horsemen. The horses were spooked by the gunfire but although they ran they didn't go far, and were easily caught by Richard's men.

Drawing away from Richard, Margaret went from one horseman to the next until she found one not quite dead yet.

'Who hired you?' She demanded.

The man shook his head. 'Don't know! A white man! Said… We wouldn't… have any problems.' His head lolled back as his heart finally stopped beating.

Guiding Margaret away from the scene of carnage, Richard kept glancing around to see if the sniper wanted to add them to the corpses. *I think I know who our guardian angel is, but it does still surprise me.* Danso was standing in the doorway of the house; he had come running outside when the first shot had been fired.

'What… what would you have me do with them Professor?' *Nothing like this has ever happened before on the farm.*

'Make sure that they're dead and not just injured. Remove any personal items of identification from them so I can inform the authorities of their deaths. Then I suppose we had better bury the bodies. For the time being, settle the horses in the stables.' Richard continued into the house with Margaret who now appeared numb. Sebastian trailed closely at their heels. Dalila looked up from where she had been tending to Kobbi, who lay on a couch.

'Miss Margaret? Is she all right Sir?' The Housekeeper cast a worried look from one to the other.

'Alive, but not all right just yet,' Richard steered Margaret into his bedroom and forced her to lie down. Her eyes were blank as she looked up at him. *Shock*, Richard supposed.

'Sleep Margaret, I'll take care of everything.' Obediently she closed her eyes, but Richard doubted that sleep would be so easily obtained. Kobbi was sitting up when Richard came back out of the bedroom; he checked the boy over and was relieved that it was mainly bruising.

'A quiet place, a comfortable bed, some food, Dalila and plenty of water. Let me know if you need additional balm for Kobbi's feet.'

Dalila nodded. 'I'll take him home now Sir, if that is all right?'

The Sniper

Richard agreed and looked around as Father Gerard Gothe entered the house. His expression was rather grim, and over one shoulder was slung a powerful rifle. Dalila hesitated but Richard urged her to take Kobbi home. He waited until he was alone with the Priest before he spoke, 'So who does a Priest go to for absolution?'

Gerard threw the rifle onto the couch and bent down to pat Sebastian. 'Out here, I go to God! Have you got anything strong my son?'

Although Richard's eyebrows rose in surprise, he didn't say anything as he went to a cupboard in the kitchen and unlocked it. He pulled out a bottle of Scotch and poured a shot into a glass. Taking the glass, Gerard tossed it down and silently Richard refilled his glass. Only when this had gone down the same way as the first, did the tension finally leave the Priest's stance.

'I'll face whatever punishment God gives me for killing those men, but I could not allow them to just slaughter that innocent child.'

Richard nodded. 'I know. I should never have allowed Margaret to leave the house. I didn't think that they would get here so soon.'

Gerard laid his hand on Richard's shoulder. 'You're not to blame. They forfeited the right to a long life the moment they started taking away innocent lives for money.'

Putting the bottle of Scotch back into the cupboard and locking it again, Richard sighed. 'I suppose now that Margaret is not being hunted I should go and collect the bodies of the Phillips party.'

Placing his empty glass into the sink, Gerard was frowning. 'Margaret needs you more than ever now. She has lost the only family that she had ever known, and you need to be here for her. If her behaviour outside is any indication, then you're going to have your hands full. In a week or two, that absolute despair will ease, but until then you cannot let her out of your sight.'

Moving Gerard's rifle, Richard sat down on the couch and distractedly ran his hands through his chestnut coloured hair. 'Surely your spiritual guidance would be better for her?'

Shaking his head, Gerard sat down beside him. 'You know what she is going through. I might be able to sympathize, but you can empathize. Besides night time may be when she needs you most.'

'What do you mean?'

'Dreams, my son, nightmares; the need to have someone to cling to and feel the reassurance in touch.'

Richard's cheeks turned bright red and he took off his glasses to clean them to cover his confusion, 'Have you forgotten that I am still married?'

Gerard looked at him amused. 'Nein! Nein! I haven't forgotten. I didn't mean sexual contact. It would be more like comforting a frightened child. If you cannot keep your libido under control in that situation, then you're not the man I thought you to be!'

Richard had the grace to meekly apologize for jumping to conclusions.

'Come, my son, I want to be on my way. Unpleasant tasks cannot be put off.'

Following the Priest to where Gerard's horse and a fresh horse was ready with the wagon, Richard still felt guilty about not undertaking this unpleasant task himself. Gerard only chuckled and said that after a day or two of tears, anger, nightmares and degradation, Richard wouldn't feel that his task was the easier. Although Richard laughed, he privately agreed that the immediate future was not going to be smooth sailing.

Babysitting Duties

Having watched Gerard ride off with three of the men from the farm in the wagon, Richard left Danso and several of his men to the burial of the assassins. He took their personal effects back to the house to attempt to identify the dead murderers so that the authorities could alert their families, if they had any. Before sitting down to write his report, Richard checked up on Kobbi, who was enjoying a hearty meal, Manu, who had cried himself to sleep in the hammock, and Margaret and the baby. Margaret appeared to be asleep, but Adwoa was awake and she gurgled happily at him and waved a fist in the air.

Not wanting the baby to disturb Margaret, Richard gingerly picked the little girl up and carried her through to his study. Seated at his desk, which was covered with papers and books,

Richard nursed Adwoa on one knee as he carefully wrote an account of the past few days.

Adwoa was really a very good baby. She didn't mind being handled by a stranger, and happily amused herself playing with a necklace of amber beads that Richard had found lying around.

The assassins weren't hard to identify from their belongings, and having added their details to his report, Richard wrapped up their personal effects in brown paper. These he would send down to Accra with his report. *I still don't know what to do with the horses.* There was no need to make a hasty decision, as the horses would be well looked after by Danso.

Still holding on to Adwoa, Richard took the report and parcel outside to find his Property Manager. *I need a rider to head to Accra at once, but I'm uncertain whom Danso can spare.*

The Property Manager looked surprised to see the Boss carrying a baby, but made no mention of this strange phenomenon. Danso promised to have someone ride off immediately, but couldn't help casting a searching look from Richard to Adwoa, who was happily waving her hands to Danso. Richard caught the look and laughed. *I'd forgotten I had Adwoa, as she was so well behaved and quiet.* Danso, a father of five children, and a grandchild on the way privately wondered, *Is there hope for the Boss after all?*

Coming from her own cottage, Dalila was also pleasantly surprised by Richard's change in behaviour. She was reluctant to remove Adwoa, but the baby needed changing and another feed. *Besides which,* she mused, *there is only so much change you can expect in a person in one day.* Richard wasn't sorry to relinquish the baby as Manu had woken up and he wished to have a quiet talk with the boy. They sat down on the verandah and Manu gulped down two large glasses of lemon squash from the jug Dalila had provided.

Richard's Advice

'I know this is a hard time for you, Manu,' started Richard gently. 'You must be feeling pain, anger, hurt and guilt. All these are natural, but I want you to remember that you weren't the cause of the attack upon your village. You and Adwoa were very lucky but don't begin thinking that you could have saved others, or stopped the attackers. If you had tried, neither you nor Adwoa might be alive now.' Richard paused to take a sip of his own drink.

'Don't try to bottle up your grief and pretend it didn't happen. Something momentous and life changing did occur. You will never forget that. If you need time alone, just make sure someone knows where you are. But if you need to talk, I can understand what you are going through. I lost my parents in an accident when I was your age. Dalila is a mother and will also help you through any doubts or worries.' He paused to consider how to word his next thought carefully.

'I know Margaret has been a pillar of strength for you and Adwoa since finding you, but she has just learnt that her own parents are now dead. I'm not saying that she won't want to talk to you or spend time with you, but like you she'll need time alone, and time to grieve. If you have any problems can you come to Dalila or me?'

Manu nodded, 'Of course Sir! I wouldn't wish to burden Miss Margaret.'

Richard shook his head. 'I didn't mean it quite like that. There may be times when it feels like Margaret doesn't want your company or anyone else's. It isn't a reflection on you, but her need for time alone. Like you, her emotions will be in a great deal of turmoil.'

Manu smiled. 'I understand Sir. I don't want to talk about it at the moment, but when I do, I'll seek out you or Dalila.' He held out his glass for more squash, and they sat there quietly, not needing any more words as they understood the need for time to think and reflect.

I Didn't Know You Had A Sister

Richard had just filled his pipe when Sebastian came out onto the verandah and laid one of large paws on Richard's knee. Placing his pipe on the table, Richard frowned as he looked down into Sebastian's face.

'What is it Seb? Is Margaret all right?' Richard rose to his feet as Sebastian headed back inside and led Richard to his bedroom. Margaret was sitting on the edge of the bed, brushing her hair in such a savage way that it was coming out in handfuls. Richard took the hairbrush from her and gently caressed her hair.

'I need scissors, Richard! Hair is vanity! I must rid myself of all sins!' Margaret gathered all her hair up in one hand and tried to pull it out. Richard pulled her hands away and kept hold of them as he sat down on the bed beside her.

'Don't be silly Margaret! You're not vain, and you haven't sinned. God isn't angry with you, but I will be very angry with you if you cut off your hair.'

Margaret gasped for a steading breath. *Anyone more placid than Richard would be difficult to be found.* 'Why do I feel so guilty, like this is all my fault?'

Releasing her hands, Richard placed his arm around Margaret's shoulders and laid her head against his shoulder. 'There are so many 'what ifs' that you end up believing that you are guilty. Come on, turn around, and I will finish your hair.'

Richard gently brushed and then began to plait her hair. She was rather surprised at how well he did it.

'Where did you learn to braid hair?'

Richard sighed reminiscently. 'My mother used to sometimes let my sister and I brush her hair before bed, and plait it.'

Margaret looked around to stare at him is surprise. 'In all the time I've known you, you never once mentioned you had a sister!'

Richard turned her back so that he could finish doing her hair. 'Eloise didn't have a very happy life after our parents drowned. She's two years younger than I am, but the relatives actually fought over whom would be her guardians. They parted us and they even refused to allow us to communicate. Eloise's Governess devised a way for us to send and receive letters in secret.' Richard broke off as he cleared his throat. With a ribbon, he tied off the end of her plait.

'Why did they want to keep you apart?' Turning around to study his face, Margaret felt a sinking sensation in her stomach.

Richard shrugged his shoulders. 'Probably so that I wouldn't learn what they were doing to Eloise.'

'Oh no!' Margaret gasped in horror, 'They didn't beat your sister or starve her?'

Again Richard cleared his throat. *This is a difficult topic for me, but I had started it.* 'No, perhaps if they had been, the outward signs would have been more noticeable to others. My uncle was sexually abusing Eloise, and she was sworn to secrecy or bad things would happen to her.'

Margaret laid a supporting hand on his arm. For the moment, as she listened to his painful past, she wasn't so weighed down by her own grief. 'How did you discover the truth if Eloise couldn't tell you?'

'In her letters, she told me how unhappy she was and frightened. Eloise mentioned that uncle's love was not at all like that of our parents. I couldn't get any details out of her, so I wrote to her Governess and she agreed to spy on uncle when he was alone with Eloise. She was only ten at the time.' Again Richard cleared his throat.

'I went to my Grandfather, but he refused to do anything that would cause a family scandal. I went to my Headmaster and he agreed that we should contact my grandfather's lawyer and the police. The Governess managed to secretly take Eloise to a Doctor to be examined. When the police came to arrest uncle, they actually caught him in the act of assaulting Eloise. My aunt tried to blame my sister, saying she led uncle on. That defence was dismissed immediately, especially when uncle's own daughters came forward and admitted that he had abused them for years.'

'The family was furious with me, but I had got Eloise away from them all! She was placed with a foster family, who were good people with a strong religious faith. We could then write openly, and I was allowed to visit, although it wasn't possible for me to spend all the summer holidays with them.'

'It was through the Church that Eloise met her husband, Randall North. He is a lawyer and a very nice chap. My family, of course, did not approve. Threatened to cut off Eloise's inheritance, but I discovered that they could do no such thing. So when I was 21, I became Eloise's legal guardian and gave them permission to marry.'

Richard sighed. 'They have four children now, and are exceptionally happy. At least one of us found happiness in marriage.' This last sentence was barely audible, but Margaret had heard and she was surprised by the bitterness in his voice.

'You weren't happy in your marriage? Is that why your wife didn't come out to Africa with you?'

Richard looked at her startled. *I hadn't realized that I'd spoken aloud my lament.* Embarrassed, he pulled at the collar of his shirt as if it was suddenly choking him. 'I… that is… well…'

Dalila entered the room. 'Dinner is ready Sir.' She took in the strained atmosphere in the bedroom and wondered, *what powder keg of emotions have I walked in on?*

The Crash Of Reality

They followed Dalila to the dining table where she had managed to carefully move enough of Richard's research and books so that she could set two places. They ate mostly in silence. Margaret wondered, *how can I rectify my faux pas as I consider the man sitting beside me? At times Richard seems quite cold and clinical, but this mention of his wife has touched something raw and painful. It's a topic we've never talked about before and I feel that Richard is still not ready to share this with me. I know that I've no right to ask awkward questions, but when Richard had been telling me about his sister, I had seen a little beyond the facade of scientist to the man underneath. It's only natural that I want to know more.* It wasn't long before Margaret's thoughts returned to her own tragic loss and the emptiness she felt inside.

After dinner, she sat on the couch with her knees pulled up under her chin as she stared blankly at the wall opposite. Sebastian lay protectively at her feet and Manu, recognizing the signs didn't disturb her.

He helped Dalila in the kitchen as she put Adwoa to bed. The cradle and a blanket on the floor were set up for the children in Richard's room. For the next couple of nights they would stay close to Margaret until they were used to their new surroundings. Until the second bedroom was cleaned out and made ready, Richard would sleep on a couch. *I want to stay close by just in case either Margaret or the children need me during the night.*

Looking up from the books he was working on, Richard saw the forlorn look on Margaret's face as tears fell noiselessly down her cheeks. He went briefly to his experiment room and returned to the living room a few minutes later with a glass of clear liquid. Sitting down beside Margaret, he gently shook her shoulder before putting the glass in her hand. She glanced at him in enquiry, and he smiled reassuringly.

'It'll help you to sleep.'

Obediently Margaret drank the mixture and pulling a face at the taste, she handed the empty glass back to Richard. He carried a candle as he led Margaret into the bedroom. Sebastian followed them and jumped up onto the bed as Richard undid the laces of Margaret's dress. He helped her to undress and into one of his nightshirts. She slipped into bed under the mosquito netting and drew the sheet over herself. Richard sat down on the edge of the bed for a moment.

'You're not alone, Margaret. I'm here for you. Together we will conquer your pain.' He rose again, but Margaret reached out to grab his hand.

'Will it always hurt?'

Richard didn't hesitate. 'Yes. Hopefully time will make it hurt less. They say "What doesn't kill you makes you stronger". This is what experiences are all about, making us stronger; tougher. I'm not saying it is going to be easy, but that is why they call them challenges. If they were easy, it wouldn't be a test of our faith, strength, courage and resourcefulness.'

'What if I fail the test?' Sighing, Margaret released his hand.

Richard shook his head. 'You won't! You love your parents too much to want their dream of helping others, to die too. They'll be kept alive through you. Try not to worry about more than a day at a time.' Leaving the candle behind, Richard headed outside to sit on the verandah and smoke a pipe. *I've doubts about my capability to competently deal with the current situation, and hope that Father Gerard won't be gone for too many days.*

FRIDAY

A Violent Awakening

In the early hours of the morning, Richard woke up on the couch drenched in sweat and his heart racing. *I'd been dreaming that I was locked in a house with no door or windows, and outside people were screaming for help.* It took him a moment to realize that the screaming wasn't just in his dream, but real. Lighting a lantern Richard hurried into his bedroom. He pulled up short at the sight that met him.

Even though she was screaming, Margaret's eyes were closed, as she was still asleep despite Manu's attempts to wake her. Adwoa, woken by the screaming also was bawling. Sebastian sat beside the cradle, looking worriedly at the baby, and wondered, *what can I do to stop that noise?*

Snapping out of his stupor, Richard picked up Adwoa and placed her into Manu's arms. 'Take her outside, walk her around a bit, some milk and a clean nappy would help. If you have troubles then go to Dalila for assistance. I'll quieten Margaret down.'

Manu nodded, but looked concerned at Margaret, he added to Richard, 'I didn't touch her Sir! Honest!'

'I know, Manu. It's just a nightmare.'

Richard waited until Manu had left the room before he slipped under the mosquito net and grabbing Margaret by both shoulders shook her.

'Wake up Margaret! It's only a dream.'

Her eyes flew open and she was panting as if she had been running. Her hands reached out blindly to cling to the front of Richard's nightshirt, and her eyes reflected the horror she was remembering. For a moment she was robbed of the power of speech. Richard was glad she had stopped screaming, and he could finally think about what he could say to sooth her fears.

'It was only a dream Margaret. You're safe with me. A dream can't hurt you.'

Tears fell uncontrollably as her mouth opened and closed as she tried to say something, but it was a few minutes before she could get anything audible out.

'Why?'

Richard groaned. *I know what she's referring to.* 'I know of no logical reason why anyone would want you and your parents dead. I mean to discover the answer and bring that person to justice. As much as I want to Margaret, I cannot bring back your parents.'

'It… hurts… so much!'

Richard could feel her pain, and taking a deep breath, he did something he knew he would regret later. He lay down beside Margaret and pulled her into his protective embrace.

'I know! The pain feels unbearable now, but you must be strong. It is what your parents want.' He caressed his hand down Margaret's back as she clung to him, her face pressed against his shoulder as she cried.

'I'm not strong!'

'Yes you are!' Richard looked around and seeing Sebastian lying on the floor beside the bed called to him, 'Come on Seb up here.' Sebastian jumped up and lay on the other side of Margaret.

'You have to be strong, Margaret. What would happen to Sebastian without you? What about the villagers who rely upon your farm for work to feed their families? What about me? How do you think I'll feel if you would rather be dead than in my company?'

Richard rolled Margaret over so that her arms wrapped around Sebastian's neck, and her supple, sensual body was pressed against the tiger's and not his. *I won't leave the bed, but I'm grateful for my sanity's sake, to put a few inches between our bodies.*

'I don't want to be responsible for anyone else!'

Richard sighed. 'Tough! That's life! We have to take the hand that is dealt to us and make the best of it. It's not easy, at times it feels damned impossible, but that is what challenges are about. We have to extend ourselves out of our comfort zones. They're not pitfalls, but opportunities to learn and grow.'

Margaret sniffed in an unladylike manner, and Richard handed her a handkerchief to wipe her eyes and blow her nose.

'Do you honestly believe all that?' She finally asked, rolling onto her back so that she could look at him.

Richard grinned ruefully. 'Not when I was feeling like you do now.' He ran a caressing finger down her cheek. 'Focus on how your death would affect others. What you would really miss if you were dead. Besides which, Margaret, if our mystery man is desperate to have you dead, why hand it to him on a platter? Why not irritate the hell out of him by being very much alive and prepared to fight?'

'That won't be easy Richard.' Reaching for his hand, Margaret sighed.

He uttered a harsh laugh, which surprised her. 'Not easy? You want to try lying in a bed with an utterly desirable young woman and keep your hormones under control!'

She stared at him in surprise. 'Oh Richard, I'm so sorry! This grief has made me so caught up in myself that I don't see how it is affecting others around me.'

'That is only natural.'

'And your hormones aren't?'

'Margaret!'

'Well?'

'That's not the issue here.'

'I thought it was an issue, or is it your way of distracting me from my own worries?'

I am acutely embarrassed by this conversation, which hadn't been my intention when I had blurted out my thoughts. 'Perhaps you should try to go back to sleep,' He suggested, trying to keep his tone of voice calm. Margaret nodded but retained a hold on his hand.

'Will you stay with me please?'

Richard grimaced. 'Why? So that you're not the only one facing a challenge?'

She punched him on the arm. 'No! Because I feel safe when you're near.'

Sighing, Richard relented, 'All right. No more talking though.' To his relief, when Margaret rolled over onto her side it was towards Sebastian. The tiger began to purr as Margaret wrapped her arms around him, and Richard sighed, *I hope that there will not be too many nights like this one.*

Sanity Restored

Light was filtering through the windows when Richard next woke. Richard took a deep breath and let it out slowly. Almost instinctively, without looking, he knew that Margaret was already up. *It's a relief, as I had said more during the night than I'd meant to say. I've never spoken about my feelings for her, as there had seemed little point whilst I remained married.* The thought of his marriage caused a muscle in Richard's cheek to spasm. *Not only do I not want to talk about it; I don't even want to think about it.*

Shaking his head, as if to throw off the memories, Richard got out of bed. *I have to focus all my attention upon getting Margaret and Manu through the emotional roller coaster that will be their lives for a while. There's no time for self-pity or regrets, but it isn't always possible to control the direction of one's thoughts.*

Breakfast was waiting on the table for Richard. Dalila was in the kitchen and Kobbi and Manu were playing checkers on the verandah. Sebastian had found a cool spot to lie down under the trees. Margaret, having had a long relaxing bath, had washed her hair and was now standing out in the sunshine as she brushed it. Finishing his breakfast, Richard also bathed, shaved and dressed.

Stepping out of the house to check up on Margaret, Richard was disappointed that she was once more attired in clean male clothing. *She looks great in both, but there is something so feminine and sexy about a dress.* Tactfully Richard did not mention this. Margaret looked up and gave him a tired smile as she paused in combing out her wet hair. She expected some comment about her clothes, but when it didn't come, her smile softened into fondness for him.

'You always know when not to say something.'

Richard chuckled. 'Why ask a question if you already know the answer? How are you feeling?'

Sighing Margaret continued to brush her hair. 'Better. Not good, but definitely better. I still feel so empty, but you're right, I'm not going to let some mystery man get away with killing my parents.'

Richard's brows descended into a frown. 'Don't even start to think about revenge. Don't go looking for him!'

Margaret shook her head. 'How could I, Richard? I don't even have a clue as to who he is or why he wants us dead. Besides which if he's desperate to get rid of me, once he knows his assassins are dead, he will come after me again.' *Somehow this doesn't seem to comfort me in the least,* mused Richard.

An After Shock

Without warning, the ground suddenly shook beneath their feet, and Margaret reached out to Richard to steady herself. It was over in a matter of seconds, but although Margaret was surprised, Richard was not.

'An earthquake?' She asked, releasing him.

Richard shook his head, 'No, only an aftershock. The main tremor was late last night. This is about the third or fourth after shock. Are you all right?'

Margaret nodded, 'Just surprised that I didn't notice an earthquake.'

Richard smiled grimly. 'The potion I gave you to sleep was quite a powerful one. That is why it took so long for Manu and I to wake you when you were having a nightmare,' he explained.

'Oh,' Margaret looked away at the sound of pounding hooves as they approached the farm.

'Go inside,' Richard ordered, determined this time to protect Margaret more efficiently.

'Our mystery man can't know his killers are dead yet. It could be several days before he could possibly descend upon us,' argued Margaret.

'What if they have come for the children?' He demanded. It had the result Richard wanted as Margaret flew inside to protect Manu and Adwoa. Richard relaxed, as it became obvious that the rider wasn't only native, but also a woman.

'Danso, we've got company,' called out Richard.

The woman who came off the horse was barely a teenager.

'Abena, isn't it?' Richard reached out to support the girl as she started to collapse.

'Yes Sir! Oh Professor, you must help us! Our village, 'tis covered in earth. The earthquake brought down half the hill on top of us. We've been digging the alive and dead out since first light.'

'Danso! Margaret!'

Margaret appeared in the doorway, and immediately came out to help Abena inside as Danso came running around the corner of the house.

'The child is exhausted Margaret, see that she gets something to eat and drink. Danso, gather together every able bodied person. We'll need tools to help with the digging. I'll have Dalila arrange food rations for us to take,' ordered Richard.

Margaret glanced over her shoulder. 'Don't forget fresh water supplies. We need to prevent an outbreak of cholera and dysentery.'

Danso nodded. 'Yes Miss.'

As Margaret assisted Abena inside the house, Dalila rushed forward to help the girl to the couch. Richard filled the Housekeeper in on the situation as Margaret urged Abena to drink some water.

'I'll get the food ready Sir.' Dalila paused as she glanced across at Margaret tending to Abena. 'Will you be going too Professor?'

Richard was frowning, 'Of course! Why shouldn't I help?' Following the Housekeeper's gaze, he swore. 'Damn! I can't leave Margaret alone.'

Margaret looked at him in surprise. 'But I'll be coming with you! I'm the closest you have to a fully trained Doctor!'

Frustrated, Richard ran his hands through his hair. 'True, but I can't let you go. You're not strong enough after what you've been through. I can't risk you collapsing in exhaustion.'

Margaret wanted to argue, but knew deep down that he was right. 'I'll be all right. It will be days before anyone can do anything about the killers being dead. You must go Richard. It is the right thing to do.'

Richard groaned. 'Damn you Margaret! Why does life get so complicated when you're around?' He strode out of the room without waiting for a reply; which was just as well as neither woman knew what to say.

Within twenty minutes, two cartloads of men were heading for Abena's village, which was a couple of miles south of their own settlement. Fynn was sent to the local village to gather food, blankets and anyone else able to help in the rescue. Richard hesitated getting on his own horse to grasp Margaret by her shoulders.

'For goodness sake, be careful! Stick close to the house. If we desperately need your help, I'll send someone for you.'

Margaret wrapped her arms around his neck and hugged him. 'I'll be careful if you will do the same,' she promised.

Embarrassed, Richard pulled himself out of her embrace, but placed a kiss on her forehead. 'I'll try!' He threw himself up on to his horse and followed the carts southward.

He Will Come Back

Margaret waited until they were out of sight before she went back inside. Her deep dejected sigh caused Dalila to look up worried from refilling Abena's glass.

'Miss Margaret?'

Margaret jumped, startled at being addressed, 'Hmm? Sorry, I was miles away,' she apologized.

'Yes I know.' The Housekeeper came around the couch to place her arm around Margaret's shoulders. 'He will come back, you know. The Professor understands that you can't handle another loss. He won't desert you.'

'I know.' Margaret managed a weak smile. 'I just feel so useless. I'm the closest thing this region has to a Doctor now and I feel like I am some weak insignificant female.'

'The Professor never said...' Dalila was shocked.

Margaret shook her head. 'Richard would never say that, but it's exactly the truth. As much as I want to help that village, I couldn't actually do it. Richard was right; I would be exhausted in a matter of a few hours. Then instead of helping I'd be in the way, a nuisance.'

Dalila didn't agree. 'You've been through an ordeal of your own Miss Margaret. You're going to need time to recover, to get back to peak condition.'

Sighing again, Margaret nodded. 'I know and understand that, Dalila, but it doesn't stop the feelings of guilt and uselessness.' She wandered out the back, and flopped listlessly into the hammock.

Abena glanced up at Dalila in concern. 'Will Miss Margaret be all right?'

Watching Margaret through the kitchen window, a sudden chill ran down Dalila's spine. 'I certainly hope so, my dear, for her sake and the Professor's.'

That morning, Dalila had no time to think about cleaning out the spare bedroom, as she was kept extremely busy. Margaret slept for most of the morning out in the hammock, and it was a great comfort to the Housekeeper when Sebastian went to keep an eye on his mistress.

Abena insisted on going home after lunch to help the rescue effort. With her she took two large saddlebags full of supplies. There were the homemade bandages, more food, blankets, water and additional medical supplies that Professor Evans might need.

I Need Something To Do

After managing to eat something at midday, Margaret's listlessness became restlessness and frustration. *I need to be doing something, anything, just so long as I can keep my mind from thinking about what Richard might be going through, or thinking about my parents.* Pacing discontentedly up and down the living room, Margaret realized that she was just using up important energy. She turned to Dalila for help.

'I need to keep busy. I feel like my head is bursting with millions of thoughts and feelings.'

Dalila put down the cloth she was using to dry the dishes. 'You can help me clean out the spare bedroom. I've been putting it off as I've been hesitant to throw anything out.'

'Spring cleaning! Oh, can we start now?' Margaret brightened up immediately.

Dalila laughed as Margaret hugged her. 'Of course, Miss.'

When they had fed Adwoa and put her down for a nap, Dalila finally opened the curtains of the spare bedroom. *Taking a look inside, I can see why Dalila hadn't known where to start. Everything that has ever needed mending has been placed in the spare bedroom.*

'Oh my goodness!' exclaimed Margaret, as they couldn't enter the room properly.

'Well the Professor is an extremely busy man. He is exceptionally intelligent, but not very good with the handyman jobs.' Dalila made her way through the piles of junk to open up the two large exterior doors to let in more light.

Margaret nodded. 'Papa is… was the same. He could design anything, but actually building it was the challenge.'

Dalila looked around her doubtfully. 'Should we sort as we go, or what do you suggest?'

Margaret joined her by the window and made a decision. 'We'll remove absolutely everything from the room. Start afresh. Clean the room from top to bottom and then only return the furniture that we want in it.'

Dalila cast her a look of uncertainty, 'But what about all the rest?'

'We can sort it into two piles, what can be fixed, and what is beyond repair. The rubbish can be either turned into firewood or salvaged to repair the other pieces,' startled, Margaret glanced horrified at the Housekeeper as she started to cry.

'What is it, Dalila? Did I say something wrong?' Margaret placed her arm around the older woman's shoulders.

'No Miss, it's just a shame that it was impossible for the Professor to ask you to marry him when you turned 18. You're exactly what he needs!'

Margaret's arm slid down to her side as she stared at Dalila stunned. 'Richard has never shown any hint of romantic inclinations. He has always treated me like a sister.'

Sniffing, Dalila wiped away her tears. 'How could he do anything else? Tied to a disastrous marriage, that he cannot escape, the Professor is too much of a gentleman to offer less than all of himself.'

'I never knew! I mean Richard didn't like to talk about his marriage, and I didn't want to pry. Oh, it is pointless talking about it. I'll get the boys to help us haul everything out.' Margaret marched away to find Kobbi and Manu, but she couldn't stop thinking about what Dalila had revealed.

Transforming The Spare Room

The boys really got into the chore of cleaning out the spare room. Once all the furniture was out, as Margaret and Dalila washed over the ceiling, walls and floor, Manu and Kobbi leant the mattress against a tree and took turns hitting it with Richard's cricket bat. This wasn't mindless vandalism, but beating out the dust, mites and musty smell. With that completed, they joined the women in sorting out what furniture was worth saving.

Actually, they all had a good time, laughing themselves to tears as the boys rummaged through old clothes and paraded around in them looking ridiculous. They moved the best of the furniture back into the room when the floor was dry. With sheets and pillows on the bed, a mosquito curtain up and a vase of flowers that the boys had collected for Margaret, they had to admit that the room looked immensely improved.

Margaret put aside clothes that she could mend during the evening and the rest were consigned to rags. The boys took great enjoyment in breaking up the unsalvageable furniture, but were very careful in transporting what Margaret intended to mend, to the workshop beside the stables.

Why Stop There?

The transformation of the room was more than they had hoped for, but it did make the rest of the house look a little worn. Dalila was a very house-proud woman, but she battled against Richard's eccentricity.

He didn't confine his work or research just to the study or experiment room, therefore books and notebooks could be found in every room. Richard refused to allow a single book to be moved, which made cleaning a challenge. Margaret was thinking about that as she sat down to a well-earned dinner.

'I think we should spring clean the whole house.' Her suggestion caused Dalila to drop the spoon with which she had been serving.

'Oh Miss Margaret, we couldn't possibly do that! The Professor is very particular about any of his papers being moved.'

Margaret looked up at her from under her long eyelashes, her blue eyes sparkling with mischief. 'But he's not here, and by the time he finds out, it'll be too late.'

'Oh Miss, he would rightly kill me!'

Margaret chuckled. 'No, I'll take the blame, don't you worry about that. He has that huge study; it just seems ridiculous that he has work spread all over the house.'

'Oh Miss, do we dare?' Dalila caught some of her daringness.

Again Margaret laughed. 'We'll start first thing in the morning. I'll look after Richard's papers and books that way I'll take complete blame for his anger.'

'Oh how I'm going to enjoy you staying here, Miss Margaret.'

They both laughed and while Margaret set about mending clothing, she and Dalila discussed their schedule for cleaning.

A Quiet Night

That night, Margaret slept more peacefully. She had moved into the spare bedroom and Sebastian had taken the move in his usual placid manner. He had kept out of the way whilst the room had been cleaned. *I have a vast experience of Margaret's cleaning frenzies, and it leading to a bath for me, is a possibility I like to avoid. To take a swim in the river is one thing, but all those bubbles are too much for a man to bear.*

The boys slept on the couches; they had bonded despite the age difference. They both wanted to be close to Margaret in case she needed them during the night. Although Margaret did cry herself to sleep, she didn't experience the horrifying nightmares of the previous night. *Even if I keep busy during the day, there is no escaping my grief once alone at night.*

It is then, when I really want Richard to be here to hold me, but I know that I have to sort out my own feelings for him before he returns. It is one thing to use his shoulder to cry on, but to go beyond that will bring misery to us both. Is it just the need to have someone to love and protect me with the death of my parents? Or had there always been some underlying attraction between us? And if there is, what the hell are we supposed to do about it?

SATURDAY

Cleaning Zeal Continued

The arrival of morning did not bring any answers to Margaret's questions, but by throwing herself back into cleaning; she could momentarily forget these other problems. The boys helped move furniture again before disappearing out of the way. Sebastian had escaped as soon as breakfast was finished and wouldn't be seen again until it was all over.

Adwoa was being babysat by Dalila's daughter, Nbulungi, who along with her husband, Fynn were expecting their first child in another three months. Thus Dalila and Margaret could focus their full attention upon cleaning. Margaret had begun on the living area, while Dalila concentrated on Richard's bedroom.

Margaret's work was more time consuming as she carefully sorted Richard's books and research into categories before she moved it into his study. Piles of laundry were building up, but that just made the women happier as it meant that they were being thorough.

The storeroom, bathroom and kitchen were the easiest rooms to clean, as there was none of Richard's work in any of them. Also, they were mainly Dalila's domain, and thus kept clean to her own standard.

By the time they stopped for lunch, they had gone throughout the house with the exception of Richard's study and experiment room. These rooms Dalila was not prepared to even look at let alone touch, but Margaret was determined to rearrange the study so that Richard had no excuse for working anywhere else.

The furniture was returned to the rest of the house, and in the case of the living area, rearranged to make better use of the space available. Completely drenched in sweat, Margaret went outside to tip a bucket of water over herself to cool down.

Deciding to change before attacking the study, she went through Richard's old clothes for something that might be cool to work in. A pair of torn trousers were soon cut up to make shorts, which needed a belt to keep them up, and a singlet, completed Margaret's new outfit. Dalila's mouth dropped open in surprise, and shock, when Margaret appeared in her daring, revealing clothes. She had also pulled her hair up into a bun.

'Oh Miss, I don't think that is suitable!'

Margaret looked at herself and laughed. She was showing an awful lot of skin and the singlet strained against her supple breasts. 'No one will see me, Dalila. It's only while I'm working.' Margaret promised before disappearing into the study.

Richard's Study

Throwing open the windows, Margaret paused to look around her and took a deep breath. *I've come this far; it's essential that I complete the job. It seems an overwhelming task as there are books and papers everywhere.* Margaret, though, had a plan of action, and it just needed patience to bring it to fruition. As she dusted the shelves Margaret grouped the books together in similar categories.

Any fiction books Margaret moved to shelves in the living area, organizing them alphabetically by author. Margaret put Richard's notebooks on the shelves next to Richard's writing desk, in chronological order.

Hidden under a pile of papers, Margaret discovered a Remington typewriter. Margaret set up the typewriter on its own table and arranged around it the papers Richard had already typed, and on the other side the papers ready for typing.

The experimental room, Margaret didn't touch except to remove a pile of books no longer being used. These were shelved into the relevant categories. By the time Margaret had finished, she felt justified in disobeying Richard. *With everything so organized and easy to find, he should be able to work more efficiently, and keep his work out of the rest of the house.*

There is no guaranteeing his response, after all, Richard is very passionate about his work, and men can be very touchy about their things being moved. Margaret decided that facing his anger would be worth it as she was extremely proud of the work she and Dalila had achieved.

Danso's Report

When they heard the sound of horse's hooves in the late afternoon, both Dalila and Margaret ran outside to see who had arrived. Margaret had picked up a shirt and slipped it on over the singlet, but didn't do the shirt up.

A tired and dusty Danso, driving one of the carts was alone, which was perhaps just as well considering his response to Margaret's attire.

'My goodness, Miss, I'm glad I sent the men straight home! It would not be seemly for them to see you so attired!'

Margaret waved his protest away as he came down from the cart, 'Never mind that! What's happened? Is Richard all right? I didn't expect anyone back so soon.'

Danso sighed. 'The Professor is fine, I'll just stable the horse and come and report.' He wasn't prepared to say any more at that moment, so the women went back inside to prepare food and drink for Danso.

They sat on the verandah as they listened to Danso, between mouthfuls, describe the last two days.

'When we arrived, the villagers who were digging were nearly exhausted, so as we took over the search for bodies, the Professor organized everything. You would've been proud of him, Miss.'

'Those who could be attended to by anyone, Professor Evans instructed a few helpers what to do, before he attended the more serious injuries himself. Mostly it was cuts and broken bones, some people only suffered from shock, but there were several more serious cases. By nightfall, we had accounted for everyone one way or another.' Danso took a long drink before he continued.

Margaret could tell that they were getting a much cleaned up version of the story. *Danso is trying to spare us from the horror of so many dead bodies, so much suffering, the chaos and tragedy that natural disasters can wreck upon a community.*

'This morning, while some tried to salvage what they could from the destroyed houses, others were either on nurse duty, food duty, digging graves or helping to build new homes. Some of our people will remain another day or so to help the villagers finish rebuilding, but everyone else was sent home today. I expect the Professor to return tomorrow morning.'

Slowly Margaret nodded her head. 'How many dead and wounded?' She asked.

Although Danso had heard her perfectly, he pretended that he hadn't. 'I'm sorry Miss. I didn't quite catch your question,' he apologized. *I'm trying to remember what the Boss had said I can reveal to the women.*

'Danso, I want the truth. Never mind what Richard said to tell us.' Margaret sat watching him and waiting, and Danso knew she would wait all night until she got an answer.

He sighed in resignation. 'About half, miss. Roughly a quarter dead and a quarter injured. The Professor said we shouldn't burden you with the details.' He tried to salvage some of his promise to his boss.

'I know, I appreciate the concern,' Margaret admitted.'

The Professor's Return

While Dalila prepared dinner, Danso went home to clean up, and Margaret ran a bath for herself. The boys were spending the night with Nbulungi and Adwoa, so there was plenty of room in the living area for Sebastian to sprawl out on the floor when he knew it was safe to come back. Preparing to step into the bath, Margaret had thrown off her shirt and boots and socks when she once again heard the approach of horse's hooves.

Instinctively knowing that it was Richard and not pausing to think about how she was dressed, Margaret ran outside to greet him. The man who came out of the saddle was not the same one that had left her two days before. Richard was absolutely exhausted, covered with dirt, sweat, blood, and appeared to have injured his left arm.

His horse was taken away to the stables by Fynn and Richard stumbled slightly as he headed for the house. Margaret reached out to steady him, and was surprised that Richard was frowning as he looked at her.

'What on earth are you wearing? Have you lost your mind? That outfit will not be worn when my men return to work!'

I know he's tired and therefore irritable, but I hadn't thought to receive this sort of greeting. 'Of course I won't wear it when they get back, but I've been cleaning and this was comfortable.'

'Cleaning?' Richard stopped walking and firmly placed one hand on Margaret's shoulder. 'Cleaning what? Not the house?' There was a touch of hardness in his voice that Margaret wasn't used to, and it brought a lump to her throat.

'Please don't be angry until I can explain what I've done. You'll see it makes sense, but not tonight, you're too tired.' She tried to keep her voice light and even, but she could feel tears welling up in her eyes.

All the tension left Richard as he exhaled slowly and released Margaret's shoulder. 'Yes, I am tired. We'll discuss it tomorrow.' They continued into the house, and although Richard glanced around, he really didn't take much in.

'I've just run a bath, why don't you hop in first and then head off to bed?' Margaret suggested.

'You mean I still have a bed to go to?' Richard teased and as Margaret blushed, he relented and carelessly flicked a finger down her cheek. 'Don't go moving the house while I'm in the bath, all right?'

'All right.' Margaret managed to laugh, even though it felt like her throat was closing up on her. *This is turning out to be a lot harder than I had envisaged.*

A Hot Bath

A couple of minutes after Richard had entered the bathroom, Margaret realized that although the towels had been washed and folded they had not been returned to the bathroom. Carrying a couple of towels, Margaret called out to Richard, but when she received no answer, she cautiously poked her head around the curtain that hung instead of a solid door. Richard was still fully dressed, seated upon a chair, his head lying against his chest. Margaret put the towels down before gently shaking his shoulder.

'Come on, why don't you go straight to bed?' She suggested.

Stirring slightly, Richard managed to open his eyes. 'No. I want to get rid of the smell of blood and sweat.'

Even so, he didn't appear capable of moving. Margaret knelt down in front of him, and removed his boots and socks before beginning to undo his shirt. It wasn't until

Margaret unbuckled Richard's belt that he managed to rouse himself. He took her hands between his own and drew her to her feet.

'I'll take it from here, thank you.' He rose unsteadily and saw Margaret out before completely stripping and stepping into the warm bath.

I Must Be Dreaming

Emerging from the bathroom twenty minutes later, with a towel wrapped around his waist, Richard felt decidedly more human. On his freshly made bed, he found a nightshirt laid out for him. *I would debate about arguing that it is too early to go to bed, but I've decided that my body is not up to supporting such an argument.*

No comment was made by Dalila as Richard sat down at the dining table, but she watched him cautiously. The table was completely bare of books and papers, but Richard didn't appear to notice as he gulped down a glass of water.

The Professor was halfway through his dinner when Margaret appeared fresh from her own bath. Her hair hung down loose and to everyone's surprise, she was wearing a dress.

'Is this more to your taste, Professor?' Margaret asked as she sat beside him at the dining table.

'You look very beautiful.' Richard's eyes twinkled slightly behind his glasses.

Margaret was put out. *That wasn't the answer I had been expecting.* 'I wasn't asking how I looked, but if I met with your approval!' she retorted.

He smiled rather ruefully. 'I never said I disapproved of your earlier outfit, only when and where you chose to wear it.'

'I don't understand.' Margaret looked at him puzzled.

'I only ask that you're careful what you wear outside the house where others may see you.' Margaret remained in stunned silence and chuckling, Richard leant closer to her. 'Do you know what I wanted to do when I saw you in that outfit when you came running out to welcome me home?' Unable to speak, Margaret could only shake her head.

'Only this.' Rising to his feet, Richard drew Margaret into his arms and kissed her. This was not the usual peck on the cheek or forehead, but a proper kiss on the lips.

Margaret stood frozen, not knowing what to do or how to react. *This is not the man that I know! I've never seen this side of him before, and I'm a little frightened!*

'Professor Evans! You mustn't do that!' Dalila protested in horror.

Although Richard lifted his head away from Margaret's to look at Dalila, he didn't remove his arm from around Margaret's waist. His eyes were distinctly glazed and his speech was a little slurred but it had nothing to do with alcohol, as he didn't really drink.

'Please stay out of this Dalila. It's my dream and for once I will have what I actually want!' His gaze returned to Margaret, who stood very still, not sure that if she tried to pull away, Richard might react violently. *If he truly feels he is really dreaming, then Richard isn't completely to blame for his actions.* He raised his free hand to cup Margaret's face and gently caressed his thumb along her jaw.

'Do you know what I want to do when I see you in a dress?' Again Margaret could only shake her head.

Sebastian had risen to his feet when Dalila had cried out in protest, and the tiger approached the entwined couple cautiously. His eyes never left them, *I dislike Richard's hand upon Margaret's throat, but I've never had reason to distrust the Professor, and Margaret isn't trying to fight.* Sebastian watched and waited; *I won't allow anyone, even Richard, to hurt my mistress.*

Oblivious to the danger, Richard had eyes only for Margaret as he slowly caressed his hand down her throat, along her bare shoulder and across to the swell of her breasts. Margaret's breathing quickened as his fingers caressed her supple bosom, and he lowered his head to trail kisses following a similar path.

Margaret had never been kissed like this before and she began to tremble in Richard's embrace. Not in fear, but in a pleasure that was alien to her. When Richard claimed her mouth once more with his, Margaret couldn't contain the sigh of desire as she found herself responding to his lovemaking.

I know I have to put a stop to this immediately, but all I can think about is how firmly Richard holds me against him, how pleasurable is his hand caressing my breasts, and how intoxicating are his kisses. I know that it's wrong, but I can't make myself draw away from him. It wasn't until she felt him start to undo the fastening of her dress that she was brought back to reality with a thud. For the first time Margaret resisted and Dalila grabbed Richard by the shoulders and pulled them apart.

'No sir! You must not! You're tired, you must go to bed!' Dalila urged.

Sighing, Richard's shoulders slumped. 'I don't even get what I want in my dreams!'

Margaret reached out to brush her trembling hand against his cheek. 'Perhaps you will when you're not also dreaming about being tired.'

'Will you still be waiting for me?' He took her hand into his and pressed her palm against his lips.

'I'll wait forever if need be.' Margaret smiled.

Nodding Richard stumbled slightly as he headed for the bathroom. It was only instinct that got him through cleaning his teeth and preparing for bed. When he reappeared, his eyes were actually closed and Margaret had to place her arm around his waist to guide him towards his bedroom.

She threw back the sheet and eased Richard down onto the bed. Margaret made no protest as he pulled her down beside him. Dalila, who had followed them into the bedroom, did protest.

'Miss Margaret, this isn't right!'

Margaret shook her head. 'Richard doesn't have the strength to do anything. I'll stay until he falls asleep.' She permitted Richard to wrap his arms around her and laid his head upon her shoulder. Carefully Margaret removed his glasses and placed them on the bedside table. Dalila was not prepared to leave them alone, so she sat down on a chair to act as chaperone. *I want to be able to say categorically that nothing untoward happened.*

Margaret brushed her hand against Richard's hair. *I'm confused by how right it feels to be lying in his arms, and yet how wrong it is because Richard is a married man.* As his breathing slowed and deepened to indicate that he finally slept, she reluctantly slid out of his bed. Dalila placed her hand beneath Margaret's elbow to ensure that she left the room.

He Might Not Even Remember

Sebastian stood by the dining room table waiting for them and rubbed reassuring against Margaret's legs as she reappeared. Falling into a chair, she bent down to wrap her arms around Sebastian's neck and bury her face in his fur. *I don't know how I should be feeling about what has just happened.* Dalila sat down beside Margaret and sympathetically placed her hand over Margaret's.

'Do you feel up to eating some dinner?'

Dumbly Margaret shook her head. 'Sorry,' was all she could manage to say.

'Then perhaps you too should go to bed. Don't worry my dear, I'm sure the Professor won't remember any of this in the morning.' *Dalila meant it to be a comfort, so why does it leave me feeling cold and forlorn?*

Feeding their uneaten dinner to Sebastian, Dalila waited until Margaret had changed and settled in her own bed before she even thought about going home. *Even though the Professor is exhausted and now in a deep sleep, I doubt that I should leave him and Margaret alone.*

If he thinks that he's still dreaming, then there's no saying how far he will go. The Professor wouldn't behave in this manner when he is in his rightful mind, and I feel it is my duty to prevent him doing anything that he would later regret. As it is, the events of this evening will have to be kept secret for the sake of Margaret's reputation. If any hint of misconduct ever got out, there will be no way to maintain that Margaret has remained as innocent as a child, while in Richard's protection.

As she cleaned up the dishes, Dalila decided that the only thing she could do was spend the night on one of the couches. She would duck home for a minute to make sure that everything was all right before returning. *Just in case anything is to happen before I can get back, I'll make Sebastian lie down in the doorway of Miss Margaret's bedroom. That way the Master will have to fall over Sebastian to reach her, and the tiger would not like that.*

Curled up in bed with tears streaming down her face, Margaret couldn't stop thinking about what had just occurred with Richard. *I know that I'll never be able to forget this night, and I am almost afraid that Richard will never remember. That he might never know the turmoil of emotions that he has awoken in my breast is more heartbreaking than the thought of Richard remembering his actions and actually regretting them.*

I'm reliant upon Richard until I know what is to happen to my parents' property. If I've fallen in love with him, is staying with Richard only going to make it more painful when I need to leave? This evening has made it more obvious how he feels about me. Where can we go from here though? Even if Richard is unhappy in his marriage, he is still married. More than ever, I wish my parents were here to guide and advise me. I have never felt so alone. By the time she eventually fell asleep, her pillow was soaked with tears.

SUNDAY
Margaret's Despair

Dalila wasn't in any hurry to wake either Richard or Margaret. She kept Manu and Kobbi busy with simple tasks away from the house and urged Sebastian to head out to do a little hunting. When Margaret emerged, she was dressed once more in shirt and trousers, her face showed how badly she had slept, and was disinclined to want to talk.

Dalila's concern increased as Margaret refused anything to eat and went to sit on the verandah, staring blankly into the distance. *I want so much to reach out to the child, but in all honesty, I don't know what to say to ease Margaret's grief. Having already lost so much, and having just realized she is in love, is Margaret to lose that as well?* Shaking her head as she watched Margaret, Dalila thought, *that is too unfair and cruel.*

Richard's Injury

It was mid-morning before Richard finally appeared out of his room. Sleep had done a lot to restore his energy, but he still held his left arm rather stiffly. He accepted breakfast and although he ate well, he appeared distracted and solemn.

I'm desperate to know if he remembers the previous evening, but I don't have the courage to ask the Professor. When he asked so casually about Margaret's whereabouts, I can only presume that he remembers nothing. The difficulty Richard had using his left arm caused Dalila to finally speak.

'Can I get you something for your arm, Sir?'

Grimacing, Richard rubbed his upper arm. 'I'll have to make up a liniment. Hopefully it's only muscle damage.'

'How did it happen, Sir?' Dalila placed a cup of tea on the table before him.

The Professor sighed. 'There was a child trapped in a hole under some rubble. We couldn't lift the debris off; as the area was unstable under foot, so I reached down to pull the child out. The rubble collapsed into the hole, trapping the child and my arm. My men worked frantically to clear the rubbish so that we could pull the girl up. It was a miracle that she had only cuts and bruising.'

The Housekeeper stared at him in disbelief. 'You held on to her even though it could have cost you your own life?'

Richard took a sip of his tea as he looked at Dalila over his the top of his glasses. 'Margaret would never have forgiven me if I hadn't done everything possible to help those villagers.'

Dalila fell silent at the mention of Margaret's name. Richard didn't seem to notice her distraction as he was deep in thought.

'I want to do something for the men, to say thank you for their rescue efforts, but I don't want to insult them. I know that they would consider money to degrade what they did, but I want to show them how proud of them I am.'

Dalila nodded, her brow puckered in thought. 'Hmm! Let me think it over.'

A smile swept away Richard's worried expression. 'Thank you. Now where is Margaret? I think she should show me my new organized life.' His words were lightly spoken, and Dalila prayed that they would stay that way.

It Wasn't A Dream

Outside, Margaret sat on the verandah with her knees folded up under her chin. She looked up, a little frightened, as Richard came out to sit beside her. He smiled kindly at her as he placed his cup of tea on the table in front of him.

'What's up kitten? You look as bad as I'm feeling.' His teasing tone did much to relieve some of Margaret's fears.

'Oh Richard, please don't be angry with me. Once you've seen how I've organized your work, you'll realise how much easier it will be to keep track of everything.' The anxiety in her voice made Richard reach over to take her hand into his own. Her hand trembled, but she didn't pull it away.

'Was I very angry with you last night? I'm sorry Margaret, but I don't really remember anything, only that you and Dalila had been cleaning. Everything else is a blank. Was I an utter beast?' He brushed his free hand against her hair.

Margaret tried to choke back a sob as tears streamed uncontrollably down her face. Disturbed that he had caused Margaret further pain, Richard drew her into his arms and let her cry into his shoulder as he stroked her hair.

'It's all right Margaret. If I behaved badly please forgive me. Sleep deprivation doesn't have a good effect upon me.'

'You remember nothing?'

'Not really.' Richard frowned as he thought about it. 'I had some really wild dreams though.'

Margaret took the handkerchief that Richard held out to her and wiped her eyes before blowing her nose. 'Anything interesting?' *I know I'm pushing my luck, but I have to know.*

'Well, yes, but I don't really want to talk about it.' Colour rushed up Richard's tanned face.

'Why?'

Richard cleared his throat. 'I don't want to upset you further, and besides which it could only ever happen in a dream.'

Margaret dragged in a deep shuddering breath. 'What if it was really to happen?'

'Then I would be a cad!' He sighed.

Margaret tried again, 'What if it was possible to happen without you being a cad?'

He groaned, 'If only that was true!'

'Is it impossible?'

For a moment Richard was silent as he considered the problem, 'Difficult, but not impossible. You speak as if you actually know what I was dreaming.'

Looking him straight in the eyes, Margaret took hold of both his hands. 'Richard, I...' Dalila calling out her name from the kitchen interrupted her.

'You can tell me later, Kitten.' Richard raised her hand to press against his lips. At that moment he realized the truth. As Margaret ran inside to help Dalila, Richard knew that his dream had been real. Groaning in disbelief, Richard buried his head into his hands.

What have I done? How much of my secret desires have I revealed? How is this going to affect my relationship with Margaret? The only way we can be together is for me to divorce my wife, but can I do that to her? She has suffered so much all ready? How can I adhere to a promise made in the past when all I want to do is make a future with Margaret?

Job Well Done

Just before the midday meal Dalila sent Richard to address the workers with several large baskets of freshly baked bread and just picked vegetables. Richard gave the basket to Danso before he thanked the men for their efforts in helping their neighbouring village. When Richard left them to have their lunch, then Danso brought out the basket to be shared around. This was well received by the workers, who were very grateful to have such a considerate boss.

Lunch up at the house was a very quiet affair, as neither Richard nor Margaret knew how to overcome the awkwardness of their situation. *When Richard had kissed my hand, I'd seen the dawning of realization in his face. I know that he has remembered the previous evening and that it hadn't been a dream.* They both knew that they needed to discuss what happened, but neither wanted to be the first to bring the subject up.

Kobbi and Manu joined them for the meal, but sensing the tension, they talked quietly together and escaped outside as soon as they had finished.

We Need To Talk

Battling one fear, after lunch, Margaret led Richard into his study. He listened attentively as she explained how she had arranged everything into categories and made the room tidy enough to work in. *In all honesty, I am rather pleased with the transformation.* An awkward silence fell between them as they had exhausted the topic of the organized room. Richard sighed. *I know that the only way we can move forward is to discuss exactly how we feel. We also need to come to a decision as to what we can do about these feelings. We can't leave our relationship hanging in limbo as it creates more stress than we need at the moment.*

'Margaret, we…'

'Richard, I…' They both started speaking at the same time and broke off laughing.

'Come and sit down, we need to talk.' Richard suggested, showing Margaret out of the study and on to the verandah, so they could enjoy the cool breeze. Richard sat staring at the ground before he cleared his throat and decided to get it over with.

'Me kissing you last night wasn't a dream was it? It really occurred?'

Margaret nodded her head and clasping her hands tightly together she thought, *I hope Richard is not about to say he regretted it.*

'I'm sorry if I upset or offended you, but I'm not sorry I did it. Obviously I've more gumption when I think I'm dreaming to do what I really want to do, than when awake.'

Margaret gave a small sigh. 'I was dreading that you would say that you regretted it,' she admitted.

Richard unclasped her hands and held one between his own. 'Never that! Only that I'm unsure that I can give you all that you deserve. I need to explain something about my marriage and it might take some time.'

'I'm not going anywhere at the moment.' Margaret gently squeezed the hand holding hers.

Richard Opens Up

Richard took a deep breath and slowly let it go before he began his story. 'I need to go back to when I was at school. There was a boy in my year who needed a little help with studying for tests. When he was sent to me to tutor, Peter Dickson and I thought we had very little in common. I was a bookworm, and he was an athlete. It was through Peter that I first became interested in cricket. I showed Peter easy ways to remember what he needed to pass his exams. A friendship grew from there.'

Margaret interrupted to clarify something. 'Didn't he come out here to visit you about five years ago?'

Richard nodded. 'Yes, he stayed for about six months with me.'

'I spent all but my summer holidays on campus and Peter didn't think this was right. He asked his parents if I could come home with him the next holidays. They said yes, and it was the best holiday I'd ever had since my parents' death.'

'When they invited me to come the next holidays, I wrote to Mrs. Dickson to tell her that I'd really enjoyed myself last time, but they didn't have to feel obliged to have me again. Mrs. Dickson's response was that she and her husband had come to think of me as a second son, and that I was welcome to call their place home.'

'I discussed it with Peter, as I didn't want to put a strain on our friendship by intruding on his holidays. Peter said not to be stupid, as he got to do a lot more with me there and got him away from his younger sister Alice.'

Richard cleared his throat. 'During my last year at University, Alice was engaged to a man called Austin Stanley. He ran off with a married woman a couple of months before he was due to marry Alice.'

'What a scoundrel!'

Richard sighed. 'It was worse than that! Austin had convinced Alice that as they were to be married anyway, it wouldn't matter if they had sexual relations before the wedding. The day Austin ran off, Alice had just told him that she was pregnant. When Alice discovered later that day that Austin had deserted her, she became hysterical and was forced to tell her parents everything.'

'Poor girl! That must have been devastating,' sympathized Margaret.

'The scandal would have destroyed her parents. It was decided that a notice should be placed in the newspaper saying that Alice broke off her engagement, before the news of Austin's running off became known. That just left the problem of Alice being pregnant. Either Alice would have to have the baby in secret, or another husband had to be found quickly.'

Richard sighed as he twisted the gold ring on his left hand. 'I believed at the time that I was doing the right thing as I wanted to spare Kurt and Erica Dickson as much pain and shame as possible. So I married Alice.'

Margaret nodded. 'That way you kept the scandal contained within the family.'

'Yes,' Richard agreed, 'but that was when my nightmare truly began. For some time Alice's volatility had been growing worse, even before Austin disappeared. She was more moody, easily sick and irritable.'

'That is understandable if she was pregnant,' interjected Margaret, trying to be fair.

'True, but there were other characteristics not common to being pregnant according to Mrs. Dickson. She wanted her daughter to see a Doctor, but Alice absolutely refused. A rash covered most of Alice's body, her hair was actually falling out by the hand full, she had ulcers all the time, and she complained about muscular pain.'

'I'm afraid I wasn't able to help Mrs. Dickson much as any time Alice saw me, she would start screaming blue murder, and throwing things. She would accuse me of things I'd never done, and constantly threatened to kill me. So I was sent back to Cambridge to finish my education.'

Frowning, Margaret rose to her feet and paced up and down the verandah. 'That's a bit harsh, considering all that you had done for her.'

Richard shrugged. 'When the baby was born, the poor boy was malformed and puny, his limbs not fully formed and several organs had not developed properly. He died within minutes of being born. Alice took one look at the baby and her mind just snapped. She was beyond reason or logic.'

'Mrs. Dickson finally brought a specialist Doctor in to examine Alice. They never told me what the problem was or the medicine that the Doctor prescribed. Mrs. Dickson said it was best if I didn't know. Funny, there was one question that she insisted that I answer completely truthfully.' Richard hesitated. *I'm not quite sure that I should reveal this much.* Margaret, though, was certain that she already knew what the question was.

'She wanted to know if you had consummated your marriage with Alice.'

'How did you know?' Richard looked at her stunned as she sat down again beside him.

Margaret sighed. 'I have a good idea what was Alice's problem. I'll explain in a minute. Go on with your story.'

'The Doctor arranged for her to go into a private clinic, where they had fully trained staff to deal with people with her problems. The Dicksons decided that there was nothing I could do for Alice now, and that I should come out to Africa as I had originally planned after I had graduated. I had no interest except my work so I didn't foresee how being married could hinder my research. I'm afraid of causing further pain to the Dicksons if I divorce Alice, but I can see no other way of being able to be with you. I can't ask you to live in sin. Besides which, you mightn't even want to marry me.'

'In a heartbeat,' whispered Margaret, her eyes bright with unshed tears. 'I must know, though, your answer to Mrs. Dickson's question.'

Puzzled, it took a moment to realize what Margaret was referring to, 'Oh about consummation? Of course not! Alice was like a sister,' Richard admitted.

'Thank Goodness!' Margaret let out a sigh of relief. 'What I believe Alice had and more than likely given to her by Austin, was syphilis. I'm not surprised she worsened on medication, as current treatment I believe is mercury and arsenic. The baby's malformed limbs are also a classic sign of syphilis. If you had been intimate with Alice, immediate treatment for you could lead to a cure. Alice had left it too long before seeking treatment. It would already be eating away at her brain and her muscles.'

'So you're saying that bastard had infected her and she had gone insane?' Richard was obviously horrified.

Margaret nodded. 'If she isn't already dead, then by now Alice wouldn't even remember who you are.'

'I keep in contact with the Dicksons. They would've informed me if Alice had died,' replied Richard as he rose shakily to his feet, and this time he paced up and down the verandah. 'I must write to them. I want this matter cleared up. To think of the years we could've been together!'

Margaret surprised him by shaking her head. 'I don't know that I could've been parted from my parents even for you.'

Richard's features lightened as he laughed. 'I would've packed this all in and built a home on your parents' property so that you were closer to them.'

'But your farm, the villagers, your work! Everything you've built over ten years is here!'

'They mean nothing compared to you!' Richard pulled Margaret up into his arms, but at that moment they were interrupted.

Father Gothe Returns

'Wunderbar! It's about time you told Margaret everything,' stated Father Gerard Gothe as he stepped up on to the verandah. Richard released Margaret, but wasn't embarrassed.

'Hello Gerard. We weren't expecting you back so soon.'

The Priest groaned as he lowered himself into a chair, 'Encountered no problems. Put the kettle on Richard, I could do with a cup of tea.'

Margaret sat down beside Gerard as Richard strode inside. 'Have you heard about the village south of us?' asked Margaret.

Gerard nodded, 'Heard on the jungle vine, also about Richard's wonderful work. I stopped there this morning on my way homeward. The people there couldn't stop singing Richard's praises. I'll return in a couple of days to make sure they are treating the injured correctly.' Gerard yawned and scratched his full white beard.

'Did you notice any other damage due to the earthquake on your trip?' Richard asked from the doorway as he returned to join them.

'Nein, not really.' Shaking his head, the Priest yawned again, 'Some minor cracks in the ground, but nothing like that avalanche our neighbours suffered.'

There was one vitally important question that Margaret had wanted to ask the moment she had seen the Priest, but she was worried about what the answer was going to be. 'Father, how did your mission go?' She chose her words carefully, not wanting to picture the carnage that Gerard would have come upon. He took her hand between his and gently squeezed it.

'Successfully, my dear, we returned the bodies and helped Mrs. Philips to bury her family. She told me to tell you that she doesn't want you to blame yourself for their deaths. She was also relieved that the killers weren't allowed to escape justice.'

Richard's eyebrows rose sardonically. 'Did you mention to her how the killers met their justice?'

Gerard nodded. 'Oh ja. Actually she thought it a fitting end to their evil ways.'

Dalila brought out a pot of tea and three cups and placed them on the coffee table. When the tea was sufficiently brewed, Dalila poured out before retiring again.

'So,' asked Margaret, 'where do we go from here?' No one immediately answered as they considered the question and sipped their tea.

A Gift From The Dead

Frowning, Father Gerard stroked his beard. 'I believe it is time that Margaret received the box Isabella left for her.'

'What is this?' demanded Margaret as Richard rose and disappeared into the house.

'When I visited you, a couple of weeks ago,' explained Gerard, 'your mother gave a box for me to leave with Richard for safe keeping.'

'Why didn't you tell me about this earlier?'

Gerard sighed as he shook his head. 'To be truthful, dear child, I didn't feel you were ready to deal with what the box may contain. Isabella warned me that the contents might upset you.'

'Do you know what is in there?'

Again Gerard shook his head. Richard returned with a beautifully carved wooden box about the same size as the tea tray. There was a hushed silence as he placed the container onto Margaret's lap.

She sat staring at the box, of two minds about opening it. *On the one hand I don't want to know what dark secrets it'll reveal. On the other, I know that I have to know, or forever wonder what it really is.*

Her two companions sat in silence as her fingers trembled slightly as they ran lightly over the carvings. Neither of the men knew what the box contained and were eager to find out, but wouldn't force Margaret to open the chest until she was ready.

Taking a deep breath, Margaret finally lifted the lid of the box and peered fearfully inside. Nothing jumped out to attack her, which was a relief. There appeared to be an assortment of papers. On top was a letter addressed to Margaret in Isabella's hand writing. Her hands were shaking so much that Margaret dropped the letter twice back into the box as she tried to open it up. Finally it was opened out flat and Margaret began to read it out aloud,

'My dearest darling daughter,

If you're reading this letter then we're no longer with you. I can't give you all the answers that you seek, but I'll endeavour to tell you all that I know. Firstly and most importantly you must know that your Papa and I love you with every fibre of our being. From the day you were born, you were our most important and valuable treasure.

It'll come as a shock to you, that we're not your biological parents. We didn't love you any the less because of this, or the fact that we couldn't have any children of our own. You were our golden child.

Your mother was my sister, Felicia, who along with my other sister, Hester, never had a serious thought in their pretty heads. I was considered an outsider in the family because I did charity work, and volunteered at the hospital in Accra, where I met Edward.

Two of the richest and most eligible bachelors in Accra were the Barnsby brothers. My sisters ignored all the warnings against the Barnsby's wild and volatile ways, and they were married. Hester s a lot more timid than Felicia was and she just took the abuse her husband dished out. Felicia had a passionate temperament herself and she fought back. Their fights were colossal and violent but when Felicia fell pregnant, her husband, George, calmed down a fraction.

That was until when Felicia was nearly full term and had returned home from a visit to your Grandmama earlier than expected and found George in their bed with a mistress. Felicia could not believe that George would flaunt his affairs in front of their servants.

A rage possessed Felicia as she attacked her husband. George hit back, and continued to beat her until Felicia lay bleeding on the ground. Fearing for the life of her unborn child, Felicia reached for the nearest thing to defend herself, which happened to be the fire poker. When George went to strike her again, Felicia swung with all her energy and smashed the poker into his head.

The servants took them both to the hospital where Edward was on duty. George died from a massive brain haemorrhage. Felicia lived only long enough to see you born.

The family came rushing to the hospital, hoping to salvage something from the scandal of a double murder by the birth of an heir. One look at your sweet angelic face and both your grandfathers walked away in disgust. You were only a girl, what use were you to them? My mother, Elizabeth, was not about to let them treat you like an old newspaper.

She went to the family lawyers, and firstly made certain you were safe by allowing Edward and I to adopt you. In Hester's household, you would've been abused or treated like a servant. Secondly, my Mama ensured that George's fortune was held in trust for you until you were 25 or married. The Barnsby family fought tooth and nail against this, but the law was on Mama's side.

Thirdly, Mama arranged for us to receive a piece of land my father owned, that was according to him was worthless. We were given enough money to start the farm and the hospital, but Father made a clause that the farm could only be passed on to our natural children. We were young, and could not foresee that we would never have our own babies.

So, my darling daughter, the home you have known for nearly 25 years must pass back to your grandfather. I have no knowledge as to what extent your inheritance amounts to. I believed that you would be happier not knowing our family's dark past. I hope that you can find it in your heart to forgive us. We will always love you.

Isabella Munroe.'

Margaret was crying as she laid the letter down on the coffee table. Richard drew her into his arms to comfort her. Margaret accepted his offered handkerchief.

'Do you forgive them?' Gerard asked gently.

'No,' Margaret shook her head, stunning the Priest, 'but that's because there is nothing to forgive. Mama was right. I was happier not knowing. I had to learn the truth eventually, but I am glad that it was only when it became necessary.'

'How do you feel?' Richard brushed her hair away from her face.

Margaret sighed. 'Confused, a little. They will always be my real parents despite not being biologically so.'

Gerard was satisfied with this answer. 'What else is in the box?'

Returning her attention to the box on her lap, Margaret began pulling out each piece of paper, opened it up and laid them on the coffee table.

'Papa's will, leaving all his possessions to Mama, unless she predeceases him, then to me,' Margaret read each document out loud, 'Mama's will, same provisions as Papa's, my Birth certificate, their wedding certificate, the death certificates of George and Felicia. A list of items I may remove from the farm, and my adoption papers. Oh!' Margaret broke off with a tremor in her voice as she lifted out of the box two simple gold rings. A lump formed in her throat making it impossible to speak for a moment.

'Mama's and Papa's wedding rings,' Margaret finally managed to say, looking up from the rings glinting in the sun, to Richard's serious face. 'Why were they murdered? Was it for the Haven? Why does someone want me dead? Is it the same reason or is it this inheritance? Why wait this long to get their hands on it?'

'I don't know,' sadly Richard shook his head. 'I promise that I will get to the bottom of this.'

Margaret was trying valiantly not to cry. 'I would've given them the money in a heartbeat, if it meant that Mama and Papa could be with us now!'

The rings fell back into the box as Margaret jumped to her feet and ran to her bedroom to throw herself onto the bed. Richard began to rise from his chair to follow, but Gerard waved him back down again.

'Give her time to grieve, Richard. This has been a great shock.'

Richard nodded. 'Yes, but what surprise will spring upon us next?' Neither knew the answer.

Duty Rings

Carefully Richard folded each document before placing it back into the wooden box. The two men sat in silence, reflecting on their own private thoughts, as Gerard lit up a cigar. Neither had previously had any inkling about the bombshell that Isabella's revelations had just landed upon them. *There are still so many questions that are unanswered, and from Isabella's words, she couldn't have shed light on these questions either.*

A strange ringing sound broke through Gerard's musings and as he looked around for the source of this noise, he noticed that it hadn't penetrated Richard's consciousness.

'Either I'm going senile, my son, or there is a bell ringing.'

Blankly Richard's eyes turned towards the Priest as he brought his thoughts back to the present. When the noise finally registered, Richard jumped to his feet.

'Hell and damnation! That's my experiment!' He was about to dash off inside but paused to glance appealing to Gerard. The Priest only smiled; he was used to Richard's absorption in his experiments.

'Go, I want to talk to Margaret alone anyway.'

With a word of thanks, Richard raced into his experiment room, leaving Gerard alone to enjoy his cigar in peaceful solitude.

Father Gerard's Comfort

When Gerard entered Margaret's bedroom, his heart was touched by the sight of her lying on her bed curled up in a foetal position. She was staring, dry-eyed; up at the ceiling but she didn't look at the Priest as Gerard sat upon the edge of her bed.

'Why are people so cruel, Father?'

Gerard sighed, wearily. 'Since the time Adam and Eve were thrown out of the Garden of Eden, humans have lusted after what is not theirs. The eternal battle between knowing the difference between right and wrong, and this greed and lust for property is like a set of scales. For most people, they're able to subdue the demon of lust. Others, though, lack self-control and just want more and more and more. There is no logic behind the demon of greed and lust, it cannot be rationalized.'

Finally Margaret lowered her gaze to the Priest. 'Is it pardonable to take another's life?'

Hesitating before answering, Gerard stroked his beard, 'If it is in the pursuit of greed, most definitely not! There are a few exceptions though, if you are defending yourself or someone else, if it is an accident, or if the person is beyond medical aid and suffering terrible pain.'

'What if I came face to face with the man who negotiated my parents' murder?'

Gerard took one of her hands into his. 'That is a dark and dangerous path, and there is no guarantee that you'll be able to return to the path of the righteous. You're grieving right now and it's natural that you want to lash out at the one whom has brought you this pain, but you must forget all thoughts of revenge. It won't bring your loved ones back to you, and will leave you only feeling emptier than before.'

'What if he is beyond our laws?' Margaret's eyes returned to the ceiling.

Kindly Gerard smiled. 'My child, you said yourself to the assassins that no one is beyond God's laws. This man will face his punishment. Remember, eternity is a very long time.'

Slowly Margaret pulled herself up into a sitting position on her bed. 'I need to go back to the Haven. I don't want to be there when some stranger takes over. I want to say goodbye to my parents in private and I should explain to the villagers about the changes ahead.'

Gerard considered this and finally nodded. 'Depending on this current experiment of Richard's if he cannot escort you, then I'll go with you.'

Thanking him, Margaret added, 'What happens then?'

'Well I suppose you'll stay with Richard until this inheritance business is sorted out and you turn 25.'

'And then?'

'My dear, one day at a time for now.' *I can understand how the future can possibly frighten her.* Margaret didn't answer, but just sat looking at him.

Gerard hastened into speech again, 'I'm honest enough to say that it would please me if you and Richard could marry. I'm not saying it'll be easy, but it isn't your only option. You are limited by what you can do with Sebastian. I can hardly see you living in London with a fully grown tiger!'

'The Gold Coast is our home. I don't see us ever leaving it.' Margaret agreed. 'Father, if Richard cannot divorce Alice; would it be a sin for us to still be together?'

I so do not want to answer that question. 'It would be an injustice if you can't be together, but it would be wrong not only in the eyes of the law, but also the eyes of God. Have faith Margaret, miracles have been known to happen.' Gerard squeezed Margaret's shoulder. 'The tide must turn soon. I'll head off home now, but any time you need a sympathetic ear, you know where to find me. Auf Wiedersehen.'

'Thank you.' Margaret watched Gerard head for the stables, and she wondered, *how much more will we have to contend with?*

Kobbi's Options

When Kobbi and Manu along with Sebastian returned to the house, Margaret had gone back out to the verandah and gestured for them to join her. The boys were making a fuss of Sebastian and she couldn't help but smile as the tiger rolled onto his back so that Kobbi could scratch his belly. Sebastian was certainly lapping up all the attention.

'There is something I need to discuss with you Kobbi,' Margaret said, serious again.

Manu began to rise to his feet. 'Would you like me to leave Miss?'

Margaret shook her head. 'In a way it affects you as well.' Taking a deep breath, she continued, 'Due to some legal mumbo-jumbo, when my parents died their property reverts back to my grandfather.'

'That's terrible!' Kobbi was shocked. 'What are you supposed to do Miss Margaret? The Haven is your home!'

Trying to not cry, Margaret shrugged her shoulders. 'Apparently I'll inherit some money when I'm 25, if I'm allowed to live that long! In the meantime, Richard has offered me a home here.'

Solemnly Kobbi nodded. 'The Professor is a good man.' Margaret could only agree with that.

'In a couple of days,' She continued, ' I'll go back to the Haven to collect what items I am allowed to keep before leaving there forever. Now I know how close your family is Kobbi, and I assume that you'll wish to return to your village. I ask only that you wait here until my grandfather or his representative arrives so that you can escort them to the Haven.'

'Of course Miss Margaret,' Kobbi swallowed hard, 'are you dissatisfied with my service to you?'

'No, of course not!' Margaret's eyes were beginning to mist over.

'Then why do you wish to send me away?'

She reached out to take his hand. 'Oh Kobbi, I don't want that at all! What I also don't want is to keep you from your family. Having lost two of the most important people in my life, I don't want to deprive you of your family.'

'What if I was to divide my time between the two? Remain in your service, but visit home regularly?' Kobbi sniffed, trying manfully not to cry.

Deep in thought, Margaret nodded. 'Is that what you want to do?'

'I don't know, Miss,' the native guide scratched his head. 'I just know that I can't just leave you alone. I know the Professor will protect you, but I still feel that is my job.'

Margaret wasn't surprised by this answer. 'Even if you make a decision and want to change your mind later, there'll be no problems.'

'Thank you Miss Margaret.' Kobbi's face lit up as he smiled.

Major Raoul Marconi

At the sound of several horses approaching, Kobbi jumped to his feet, his hand on the dagger in his belt as he placed himself protectively in front of Margaret. Calmly she shook her head. 'Don't panic, it's too soon for anyone to know the first assassins are dead. Kobbi go and tell Richard we have visitors. Manu go and warn Danso.'

The boys stared at her for a second, but didn't consider questioning her orders. As they disappeared, Sebastian sat up, pressed close to Margaret's side. She might be sang froid about the nearing riders, but he was still wary. Margaret placed her arm around the tiger's neck and gave his a reassuring kiss on the nose.

'It'll be all right Seb, I don't feel that today is the day either of us is going to die!'

'I am glad to hear that!' Came a dry voice from the doorway. Margaret looked up to find Richard standing, looking rather grim as he held a rifle in his hand. *Obviously he isn't as certain as I am that the riders mean no trouble.* Danso came running up to join them on the verandah, and ordered the boys into the house for safety.

The steady clip-clop of the horses' hooves came closer and closer and the tension continued to build until one thing became clear. That was the colour red; red jackets, to be precise. These horsemen were British soldiers. With a sigh of relief Richard lowered the rifle and headed down the steps to meet the riders.

One of the men who slid from the saddle was so dark in features and colouring, that he appeared more Mediterranean than English. Major Raoul Marconi approached Richard with his hand extended and his eyebrows raised.

'We heard rumours that there was trouble in this area, and came to discover the truth. The fact that you greet us with a rifle tells its own story.'

Richard shook his hand and grimaced. 'We've had our fair share of trouble. You'll forgive me for passing you over to Danso, but I'm in the middle of an important experiment.'

'Of course Professor,' the Major bowed, 'I quite understand. Do we have your permission to camp on your land overnight?'

Richard abruptly nodded. 'Of course you're always welcome. Excuse me.' He strode back into the house leaving Margaret wondering, *is there something more between Major Marconi and Richard to make him want to escape so blatantly? Richard's experiments are extremely important but I feel that is more of an excuse than a real urgency.*

As Danso showed the other soldiers where to set up their camp, the Major's gaze had fallen upon Margaret and Sebastian sitting on the verandah. He took in not a single word Danso said, as he stared mesmerized by the sight of beauty before him. One of his men led the Major's horse away to be watered and fed as Marconi placed one booted foot on the verandah in a rather macho stance.

'Miss Munroe I presume?' The Major laughed lightly. 'A silly question, for who else travels in this part of the world with a white tiger? It's strange, I've been to your parents' farm many times, but never actually met you.'

Margaret remained seated on the ground, her arm lightly around Sebastian's neck. 'That is a puzzle isn't it?' Her tone was polite, but not very inviting.

The Major laughed again. 'More than likely your mother wanted to keep you away from such disrespectful men as British soldiers.'

The mention of her mother caused Margaret to bite down on her bottom lip to stop it trembling. 'I'm sorry, but I'm not able to talk to a stranger about my parents just at the moment. Please excuse me.' She hastily rose to her feet and with Sebastian on her heels she hurried inside. Major Marconi rounded on Danso.

'What the blazes has been going on here?' he demanded.

Danso explained everything that had happened over the past couple of days as he led the Major to where the other soldiers were setting up camp, and away from the house. The story once completed left the Major shocked.

'Bloody Hell, no wonder she gave me the cold shoulder! What an ordeal!' He hunted for a moment through a saddlebag, and emerged with a pencil and pad of paper. After careful consideration, the Major wrote a message, folded it and handed it to Danso. 'Can you deliver this apology to Miss Munroe? I hadn't meant to belittle the memory of her parents.'

'Of course Major.' Danso bowed, 'If there is anything else you need, please let me know.'

Lieutenant Elliott Gibbs

Danso had barely walked away before Major Marconi turned to his second in command, Lieutenant Elliott Gibbs, and slapped him on the shoulder.

'My God, what a woman! I doubt I've ever seen anyone more beautiful! I'd lay you odds that she's as wild as that tiger in bed. Definitely worth getting scratched to find out.'

Elliott Gibbs, far from approved of the Major's womanizing ways, had always kept his opinions to himself. Now, though, he felt compelled to speak.

'Sir, the young lady has just lost her parents! I hardly feel it is appropriate to try and seduce her in such circumstances.' Elliott kept his voice low so that the other soldiers couldn't hear.

The Major's eyebrows rose, mockingly. 'Even more reason to have a manly shoulder to cry upon. Never fear Elliott, I've never failed to win a woman over yet!' He strode off to supervise the setting up of the camp. Lieutenant Gibbs glanced thoughtfully up at the house. *I didn't think Margaret looked like an easy conquest. Perhaps the Major is about to meet his first failure?*

Hospitality

Entering the house, Danso was surprised to see Richard in the kitchen instead of his experiment room. *It makes me wonder if the Boss' experiment was as urgent as he had made out.* The Property Manager waited, not wishing to intrude on the conversation Richard was having with Dalila.

'I'm sorry it is such short notice Dalila, but do you think it's possible to offer the soldiers a meal?'

Frowning in thought, Dalila stared at the dining table. 'Did you want to have them all join you at the table?'

'Hell no! I suppose I should invite the Major and his Lieutenant to dine with us. What do you think, Danso?' Richard turned to include Danso in the conversation.

The Property Manager chose his words carefully, 'Protocol expects you to offer. I suggest you keep an eye on

Miss Margaret, as the Major has already upset her, and I fear that he showed an interest in her that was far from honourable.'

'Damnation! They've barely arrived! What happened?'

As Danso explained, Richard's expression grew darker. Danso handed him the Major's letter, which Richard glanced at and grunted.

'At least he apologizes! I'll take this to Margaret. Can you let the Major know that he and his Lieutenant are welcome to join us at the table, and that Dalila will supply dinner for the rest of the men?'

Danso nodded, 'Of course Sir.' He strode out of the house.

Rather worried, Dalila closely watched Richard's face. 'Is Miss Margaret in any real danger?'

Slowly Richard shook his head. 'If her response, so far to his charms is anything to go be, he won't get anywhere.'

Dalila still looked worried. 'Some men do not take rejection well.'

Richard smiled grimly. 'Perhaps not, but he has to go through me and Sebastian. I don't like his chances!'

Am I Supposed To Be Honoured?

Under the trees, swinging in the hammock, Sebastian lay stretched out, looking rather relaxed to the uninitiated. Richard, though, as he crossed the yard, noticed that the tiger's eyes were only partially shut. He was keeping an eye on Margaret and the two boys as they sat in the shade on the ground beside the hammock.

Kobbi was dealing out a pack of cards. Sebastian lifted his head for a moment as he heard Richard approach, but lowered it again when he was satisfied that Margaret wasn't in danger. Kobbi was carefully explaining the rules of the game that he had been teaching Manu, but broke off as Richard squatted down beside them.

'What have we got here, my little gamblers? Gin, Rummy or Poker?'

'Neither,' looking up into his eyes, Margaret laughed. 'Snap or Go Fish are our limits. How is your experiment going?'

Richard looked rather rueful. 'This afternoon's work is actually finished. I just didn't want to deal with Marconi.'

Laughing, Margaret caressed her hand against Richard's cheek, 'I'm afraid he's absolutely no match for you intellectually. My diagnosis of him is an excess of ego and testosterone.'

Remembering the Major's note, Richard handed it to Margaret. She read it through before crumbling it up and tossing it across to Sebastian who caught it nimbly in his mouth. Realizing that it was not remotely edible, Sebastian spat it out again.

'Am I supposed to be honoured by his condescension?'

Richard shook his head. 'He certainly wants to make a good impression on you and from what Danso said, Marconi only succeeded in upsetting you.'

An impish grin appeared. 'Mama always said I'd make a good actress.' At Richard's surprised expression, Margaret added, 'I certainly did not desire to discuss my parents with him, but it was either let him down gently or laugh at his macho posing. I decided to be prudent, as someone with his ego can be very dangerous if angered.'

'I see Sebastian isn't the only one to possess claws!' Although he shook his head, Richard couldn't help laughing. 'I've had to invite him to dinner. Can you stand that?'

Unconcerned, Margaret nodded, 'So long as you don't disappear into your experiment room.' A thought suddenly struck her. 'Is Dalila cooking a meal for all those men?'

'Yes, why?'

'I'll go and help.' Margaret jumped to her feet. 'Sorry boys, I'll play cards with you later.'

'But we will help also.' Kobbi began to collect up the cards. 'Dalila has done much for us.' Manu nodded in agreement and even Sebastian got up to follow them to the kitchen. *I'm never one to pass up the opportunity for food.*

Richard Reflects

Although Richard retired to his study, it was just as well he wasn't in serious research mode, as a great deal of noise and laughter floated through the house from the kitchen. Richard had feared that the boys would be more of a hindrance than a help, actually surprised him. They proved to be very adept in the kitchen, and quick to learn.

Leaning back in his chair, Richard allowed their youthful laughter and enjoyment to flow over him. He began to imagine what it would be like if he and Margaret were married, and the children laughing were theirs. As soon as the image was fully formed, Richard felt a stabbing pain in his chest as he looked down at the wedding ring on his left hand.

The indulgent smile was wiped clean off his face, and reminded him that he had several letters to write. *If I want a future with Margaret, I'll have to swallow my pride and ask Alice for a divorce. I hate to hurt her after all Alice has been through, but don't I have the right to seek my own happiness?*

A Very Uncomfortable Meal

For the second time in five minutes, Major Marconi checked his fob watch as he, Lieutenant Gibbs and Richard silently drank their soup. The Major wondered, *is the absence of Miss Munroe from the dinner table a statement against my failed attempt at humour earlier?* There was a strained atmosphere that the

Lieutenant tried valiantly to rectify, but although Richard would answer him, he would not willingly interact with the Major.

As Dalila cleared away the soup bowls, Sebastian padded in silently and sat down beside Richard. Sebastian rubbed his head against Richard's arm, causing him to look down and smile as he stroked the big cat's head. Marconi, following his host's movement, knocked his chair over as he jumped to his feet at the sight of Sebastian sitting so close.

'Jesus Fucking Christ! Where the fuck did it come from?' The Major backed to the far end of the dining table as Sebastian looked at him in curiosity. Richard gazed at his startled guest over the top of his glasses, his hand lying soothingly upon Sebastian's head.

'Firstly, Sebastian is a he and not an it. Secondly, sudden and abrupt movements are not advisable around any animal. Thirdly, cats big or small have to either be able to move swiftly or silently to be able to catch their prey.' Richard didn't even attempt to conceal the condescension in his tone of voice.

'Fourthly,' came a voice from behind them. 'It's not appropriate to take The Lord's name in vain, even if you are scared!' Margaret moved forward to join them, making the men momentarily speechless as she was attired in a dress. Her hair was pulled up into a bun or chignon, and secured with decorative pins. Dalila had assisted with her hair.

Rising to his feet, Richard pulled out a chair for Margaret beside the Lieutenant. Once she was seated, Sebastian came round to sit beside her, and she wrapped her arms around his neck.

'I'm all right, darling, why don't you go and get some dinner.' She suggested, kissing the top of the tiger's head.

He padded silently out of the house. Only when the tiger had departed did the Major pick up his chair and be seated.

'My apologies for being late Richard, but the Sergeant wished to show his appreciation by singing such a touching Welsh air,' Margaret explained as she shook out her napkin before laying it upon her lap.

Frowning, Marconi snapped. 'So these are the morals your parents have left you with, by letting you run wild? You don't waste your time bedding a man, but I hardly think you needed to change into fine clothing to act the part of a whore!' Margaret's cheeks weren't the only ones to go crimson, as Elliott Gibbs looked horrified at his superior officer.

'Major, how dare you speak to Miss Munroe this way! You don't know enough about her to make such wild accusations.' The Lieutenant spoke calmly but he was deeply mortified.

Marconi's face was going red in anger. 'Well then, what was she doing so that one of my men would want to show his appreciation?' He demanded smugly.

Dalila was in the process of serving the main course and looked worriedly from the Major to her boss. 'Forgive me, Sir, but to assist me, Miss Margaret and the two boys carried dinner down to the soldiers. My daughter usually helps me, but she is currently looking after the baby. I hope I've not done anything wrong, Professor.'

Richard smiled reassuringly. 'Of course not, Dalila, I'm afraid the Major merely jumped to erroneous conclusions.' His tone was light and soothing.

Quite suddenly, Major Marconi started laughing. 'My God, you're the most bewitching and frustrating woman I have ever met!'

With her head tilted slightly on one side, Margaret studied him. 'If that is an apology Major, I do not think much of it!' She turned her gaze to Richard. 'Perhaps I should eat elsewhere since my presence appears to disturb the Major so much?'

'No fear!' Richard shook his head. 'Sebastian would have a fit if I let you out of my sight whilst he has left you in my care.'

Using this to quickly change the subject, Elliott asked, 'Is your livestock safe? I mean Sebastian is a wild animal after all.'

Nodding, Richard replied, 'He has been trained to know what is off limits on the farm. If something is given to him it is acceptable; otherwise hunting is beyond our perimeters.'

Elliott laid his cutlery down as a thought struck him. 'Don't you worry about him becoming prey to hunters?'

A shiver of fear ran down Margaret's spine. 'I'm always worried about Sebastian getting hurt. The white farmers in this district know that Sebastian won't harm their livestock, and leave him alone. The villagers are more in awe of him because he doesn't belong to this continent; Sebastian takes on a mythical like status.'

The Lieutenant tried to laugh, but felt Dalila's excellent meal sticking in his throat. *Neither Marconi nor the Professor are doing anything to ease the tension between them, and I am afraid that one wrong word would ignite a battle that no one needs.*

Swallowing some water, Elliott tried to ignore the hostile atmosphere as he addressed Margaret, 'I know it must be painful for you to discuss, Miss Munroe, but I would like just to say how sorry I am to hear about your parents' deaths. They were very good people, and will be greatly missed.'

Although Margaret's eyes shone with unshed tears, she managed to smile. 'Thank you Lieutenant. Your kind words illustrate how wide their influence has spread, and gives me comfort at this sad time.'

The Major reached across the table to lay his hand over Margaret's but she quickly drew hers away. 'I would've expressed my sympathies before now, but I felt the topic of your parents was too painful for you,' Marconi glared at Elliott, whose colour heightened under his tanned skin.

'Thank you, but it was your frivolous comments about my parents that I found unacceptable.'

Margaret refused to glance in Richard's direction, as she knew that if she did she would start laughing. *Richard is obviously enjoying seeing Marconi so eloquently put in his place. This is one maiden who is not going to be won over by the Major's good looks and smooth moves.*

To cover the moment of embarrassment, Elliott rushed into speech, 'What do you intent to do now Miss Munroe? Do you plan to run the farm yourself?'

Sighing heavily, Margaret shook her head. 'No, Lieutenant, I'm afraid that due to the way my parents inherited the property, it reverts back to my grandfather. I'll return home just once to collect what I've been allowed to have. Richard stands as guardian until I come into an inheritance. After that is settled, I have no idea what I will do.'

Richard placed his hand over Margaret's and she laced her finger through his. 'You'll always be welcome here, Margaret. You never have to be without a home.'

'Thank you.' Margaret managed a half smile.

Scowling, Marconi did not like the intimate nature of the Professor's touch, or Margaret's ready acceptance of it. Seeing the rising signs of danger in his Commander, the Lieutenant spoke quickly, 'When do you mean to head home?'

Sighing, Margaret shrugged her shoulders. 'I don't know. It depends upon when Richard can leave his experiment for a few days, otherwise Father Gerard has promised to take me.'

'Permit us to escort you.' Major Marconi's offer stunned everyone at the table. His eyebrows rose in surprise. 'We're heading that way anyway, and how much safer would you be with a troop of soldiers to protect you?'

Not quite sure how to say 'no', Margaret chose her next words carefully. 'That is most generous of you Major, but I wouldn't like to hold you up or be a hindrance to your duty.'

'Nonsense!' Marconi waved away her protest. 'It would be a pleasure to serve such a beautiful lady.'

Margaret could feel bile rising to her throat. 'Thank you, I'll have to think about it.'

Leaning back in his chair, the Major's eyes gleamed. 'Don't think too long, as we intend to move out tomorrow afternoon.'

Surprise was written all over Lieutenant's Gibbs face. *That is news to me!* He wondered, *what game is my Commander playing at now, and how does it involve Margaret?*

I Don't Know What To Do!

The noise of a baby crying broke the awkward silence that surrounded the dinner table. As Nbulungi entered the house, highly agitated, she held a screaming Adwoa, and Margaret was already on her feet to meet her.

'Oh Miss Margaret, Professor, I'm sorry to disturb you but I was looking for my mother,' Nbulungi explained over the top of Adwoa's cries.

'She isn't here at the present, what is worrying Adwoa?' Margaret willingly took the baby who held her arms out to her, although she stopped howling, Adwoa was still peevish.

'I don't know, Miss, that is why I brought her to see Mother.'

Margaret brushed her hand against the baby's soft hair. 'You would have checked the obvious, nappy, hungry, wounds!'

'Oh yes Miss! Adwoa is also drooling a lot as well as being irritable.'

This news changed Margaret's frown of concern to a smile. 'Ah!' She gently ran her finger along the inside of the baby's mouth.

'Teething?' Richard enquired as he rose to join them.

Margaret nodded, 'Swollen and painful gums and hard lumps beneath the surface where the teeth are trying to break through.'

'I thought it might be sickness as she has been such a good baby. I didn't know what to do!' Nbulungi sighed in relief.

Richard shook his head. 'Incorrect, Nbulungi, you did the best thing you could do, when in doubt seek help. I have something that will relieve some of Adwoa's pain.' He headed off to his experiment room.

Adwoa had calmed down considerably with Margaret and led Nbulungi to wonder, *if I'm really ready for motherhood?* Smiling, Margaret shook her head.

'You'll be fine. Adwoa is using my finger to chew on, that is why she is quiet. A hard food to rub against her gums will help her teeth to break through.'

'There is so much to learn,' groaned Nbulungi.

'True but there is always someone willing to help you. There won't be too much you'll face that your elders haven't already confronted before and overcome.'

Richard returned with a small jar, which he handed to Nbulungi. 'Place a small amount on your finger and rub it against her gums. It's a natural product so it won't harm her if swallowed. Don't over use it though, only when Adwoa's gums are inflamed.'

Nbulungi took Adwoa back from Margaret as the baby decided to chew upon her own thumb. 'Thank you so much! I won't keep you from your dinner any longer.' A much-relieved Nbulungi left and Richard and Margaret sat down once again.

Margaret's Magnificent Exit

The Professor was about to apologize for the interruption when a look of disgust on Marconi's face arrested him.

'Are you feeling unwell Major?' Richard asked, causing Margaret to lay down the knife and fork she had just picked up.

'How could you touch one of them?' blurted out Marconi.

Elliott Gibbs groaned in disbelief. *My superior officer is about to make an ass of himself.*

Richard's eyebrows rose. 'What? A baby? She is hardly contagious!'

'No, no! One of them!'

Margaret stiffened and Elliott groaned, *I wish the ground beneath my feet would open up and swallow me whole.*

'Are you referring to the fact that the baby was African?' Margaret's tone was very cold.

'Of course!'

Richard sighed. *The Major is obviously a bigger idiot than I had previously presumed. If I'm expecting Margaret to explode, I'm to be disappointed.* Although her eyes flashed in anger, she remained calm as she rose majestically to her feet.

'I'm sorry Richard, but I will not eat with a racist, chauvinistic bigot!' With a swish of her dress, she headed for the back door. 'I'm going to check up on the boys. And for your information Major Marconi, they too are African. Strangely enough, we seem to be surrounded by them in this country!' On this magnificent shot, Margaret sailed out of the house.

'Well,' Richard stated calmly, 'If it was your intention to make an impression upon Margaret, then I would say that you have succeeded!'

Grinding his teeth as his hands clenched into angry fists, Major Marconi fought against the desire to land Richard a facer. Elliott's alarm grew as he watched the two men. *I can see significant repercussions if all-out war is declared between the Major and the Professor.*

'I think you'll excuse us if we say goodnight Professor,' Elliott rose to his feet and bowed slightly. 'We won't trespass upon your hospitality any longer.'

Richard also rose as the Major felt compelled by the Lieutenant's actions to leave.

'You're always more than welcome, Lieutenant,' answered Richard, the meaning behind his words more than clear and brought an angry flush to the Major's cheeks. Richard saw them out, and waited in the doorway until the soldiers returned to their makeshift camp.

That Man Could Be Dangerous

The Professor felt rather than heard or saw Sebastian join him on the verandah. The tiger brushed affectionately against Richard's legs and began to purr as a hand scratched his head.

'That man is going to be trouble Seb! I think the Major is extremely dangerous.'

'I agree Sir, but what can we do about him?'

Startled, Richard jumped and for a brief second glanced down incredulous at Sebastian, before turning to face Dalila as she approached him from inside the house. He uttered a nervous laugh.

'For a moment I thought Sebastian was actually talking.'

This brought a slight smile to the Housekeeper's lips. 'Sorry Sir, but he most likely agrees.'

Richard rubbed a weary hand over his face. 'The Major has offered to escort Margaret home. I don't know if that would be safe for him.'

Frowning, Dalila looked puzzled. 'Forgive me Professor; I don't quite understand you. Do you mean from him? Safe from him?'

'No, I mean not safe for him.' A twisted lopsided smile appeared. 'If he keeps talking the way he has been Margaret will kill him and if he tries to lay a hand on her, Sebastian will tear his throat out. I don't really want either of them turned into murderers because of that fool!'

'Miss Margaret doesn't have to go with them does she?' Dalila set about cleaning up the dining table. Sebastian followed her into the house, hopeful of scraps. Richard also came back inside.

'No, she doesn't. Even so, apart from Major Marconi, it would be the safest escort Margaret could have.'

Dalila paused in collecting plates, her brow puckered as she thought carefully about that. 'I doubt their generosity would extend beyond escorting Miss Margaret there. She still has to make the journey back here again. Miss will be more vulnerable then.'

Richard sighed. 'Well that answers that then. We'll wait until the soldiers head out and then I'll take Margaret home.'

Smiling, Dalila continued her work. 'Miss Margaret is safest with you Professor. Why don't you head to bed Sir? Fynn will bring Miss back to the house.'

'I worry about her!' Another sigh was dragged from Richard.

An understanding smile touched Dalila's eyes. 'Of course, Sir that is what happens when we truly love someone!'

May I Stay With You?

Just dropping off to sleep, Richard was suddenly jerked awake by the sensation of someone slipping under the sheet beside him. 'Margaret?' He rubbed his eyes, trying to jump-start his brain, as his companion wrapped her arms around his waist.

'I certainly hope you weren't expecting anyone else?' Margaret teased as she rested her head against his shoulder. She was dressed in a nightshirt.

Richard propped himself up on one elbow as he fumbled to light a candle on the bedside table. 'I wasn't expecting anyone, least of all you!' He retorted. 'This isn't right Margaret.'

'I know.' Although Margaret sighed, she didn't argue. 'I didn't intend on staying, but I wanted to talk to you before going to sleep.'

I know that she isn't about to leave until she has said her piece, I'll just have to work hard to not think about the supple body that is pressed against mine. 'Go on then.'

It seemed impossible, but Margaret actually moved closer to him. 'I'm sorry for deserting you but that man was making me think un-lady-like thoughts.'

Placing his arms around her waist, Richard chuckled. 'That's all right. I was having un-gentlemanly thoughts of knocking his teeth down his throat!' He admitted.

Margaret gave a gurgle of laughter. 'I'm just so grateful that you're nothing like that man!'

Richard laughed; he could feel his resistance to Margaret's soft curves beginning to wear thin. 'Keep Sebastian by your side until the soldiers leave. I don't want you or Seb getting hurt.' Tenderly he kissed her on the forehead. *I don't dare touch her lips, as I can't be certain that I could stop at one kiss.* A shiver ran down Margaret's spine.

'I'm frightened Richard! Oh not of Marconi! Someone wants me dead, and have already killed my parents.'

Richard also felt a chill. 'I'm not going to let anyone hurt you! We will discover who is behind all of this, and they will be made accountable for their sins!' He promised, feeling

Margaret's tears soaking into his nightshirt, and didn't want to let her out of his sight or his arms for that matter.

'Please Richard; can I stay with you tonight? Is it too much for you to bear?'

Richard couldn't help smiling ruefully as he tried very hard not to think about his erection now pressed against Margaret's thigh.

'Of course you can stay.' Richard caught sight of Sebastian sitting in the doorway so he patted the bed beside him.

'Come on Seb, you may as well join us and play chaperone,' he added. When the tiger had settled down on the bed, Richard reached over to put the candle out, but suddenly decided against it. *I hope that the reassuring flicker of the light as it dances around the dark room will help to sooth Margaret's fears, and some of my own.*

MONDAY
Elliott Makes A Good Impression

The next morning, Lieutenant Elliott Gibbs sat on the front verandah, eating breakfast as he talked to Margaret. Their meeting had initially been strained, but Elliott made her laugh by reassuring her that he wasn't a bigot, racist or a chauvinist. Margaret was pleased to discover that he was easy to talk to and quite knowledgeable about a vast range of subjects.

When Sebastian rose to his feet and began growling, instinctively Elliott placed his hand on his sidearm as they looked up to watch a horse being ridden full speed towards them.

Relaxing, Margaret laid her hand upon Elliott's arm. 'It's Father Gerard. He doesn't, though, normally ride his horse hard and fast.' She placed her arm around Sebastian's neck and whispered against his ear. 'Go and find Richard. He's cultivating plants in the garden.'

Sebastian brushed his head against Margaret's before he trotted along the verandah and out into the trees. Elliott eyebrows rose. *I'm surprised that Margaret actually expects the tiger to not only find Richard, but convince him to come back to the house.*

The Earthquake Victims

The Lieutenant kept his misgivings to himself as Father Gerard drew his horse up in a spray of dust. The Priest came unsteadily off his mount and Elliott jumped to his feet to offer the older man a supportive hand. Margaret drew up a chair on the verandah and assisted Elliott to place the Priest into the seat.

'What is it Father? What has happened?' Margaret knelt down beside Gerard and took his wrist to check his pulse.

'Our south neighbours… the avalanche victims… they were raided last night. The bandits stole what water and food supplies the village had… killed anyone who got in their way and kidnapped several dozen girls.'

The noise of Gerard's arrival had brought Dalila to the door, but she now returned quickly, a glass of water in her hand, which the Priest gratefully accepted.

'Shall I fetch the Professor, Miss Margaret?' asked Dalila.

Margaret shook her head. 'Sebastian has gone to find him. We do need Danso though, as we'll need two teams of men. One team to help Richard with the injured, and the other team to go after the abducted girls.'

Nodding Dalila ran off towards the stables in search of the Property Manager. Gerard turned his hand so that Margaret's now lay inside his.

'Nein! Nein! My dear child, Richard cannot leave you again! There is no telling when the assassins may come after you.'

Again Margaret shook her head. 'That doesn't matter Father. Richard is the only one who can help these people. I'll be safe enough here until he returns.'

'It'll mean another couple of days away from you and I thought you wanted to return to the Haven before your Grandfather repossessed it?'

'It doesn't matter.' She shrugged her shoulders. 'This is about saving people's lives! You'll need to go with the team to retrieve the girls so that they know and understand that they are being rescued and not just a different set of kidnappers. My journey can wait. These people don't have the luxury of time.'

You Have To Go

Danso arrived, puffing and out of breath, just as Sebastian managed to drag Richard to the house by tugging on his sleeve. As Gerard repeated his story, Dalila went to the storeroom to see how much more they could spare for the stricken village.

Richard agreed that two groups of men were needed, and Danso ran off to pull men from their regular duties and to ready the horses. Frowning, Richard stared for a moment down at Sebastian, who was now comfortably sprawled on a mat on the verandah.

Margaret could guess what he was thinking, and laid a hand on his arm. 'You have to go, Richard, don't worry about me. I'll wait until you return. This is more important!'

Raising his eyes to meet hers, Richard surprised her by the fire in his eyes. 'You are more important than anything upon this planet, but neither of us will be happy until this is sorted out.'

I Offer My Personal Protection

Up to this moment, Elliott hadn't said a word since the Priest's arrival. He spoke now, 'The Major's offer still stands open. We can see Miss Munroe safely home and then when you're free; you can bring her back.' A stunned silence followed as the others stared at each other.

'It is one option, Richard,' Father Gerard said quietly. *I'm uncertain if it is a good option; by the way Richard is frowning again.*

'It's just…' Richard broke off, as he looked hard at the Lieutenant. 'It's just that I'm not happy about being indebted to Major Marconi, or having Margaret further exposed to his presence.' He flushed at having to speak so frankly about his doubts about the Major's morality.

'I understand, believe me!' Elliott smiled in response, 'I promise to protect Miss Munroe to the best of my ability. I can't promise to make the Major behave; I think that is beyond the capabilities of a mere mortal!'

Although he didn't laugh, Richard's frown did lighten. 'I'll leave that decision to Margaret. If she can stomach Marconi, then an armed guard of a dozen men will mean that she is well protected. Thank you.'

Margaret pulled a face as she considered the situation. 'Can I kill him if he becomes too obnoxious?' Elliott raised his hand quickly to hide a smile, but Gerard openly laughed.

'My dear child, you must learn to deal with people of all types, even the obnoxious ones.'

Richard's eyes twinkled. 'Even if killing him would bring a great deal of satisfaction to many people, you'd better control the impulse. I must pack some medical supplies, Margaret, and Dalila may need your help in the storeroom.' He gently brushed his hand against Margaret's cheek before striding inside to prepare for another medical emergency.

Margaret waited until he was gone before turning to Elliott. 'Thank you for the offer. I'll just help to get Richard on his way before I give you an answer.'

Elliott nodded. 'I understand.'

Smiling gratefully at him, Margaret went inside to find out what Dalila needed her to do.

A Moment Of Doubt

In less than half an hour, the team of riders, to be led by Father Gerard, had already left to rescue the abducted girls. Two cartloads of workers were just preparing to depart. Margaret felt a stab of pain as she watched Richard mount his horse to leave her again for another medical mission.

I'm equally worried about leaving Margaret but what else can I do? debated Richard. *As Margaret had said, she'll be safe enough here until I return, and these other people are in urgent need of my assistance. It doesn't make it any easier to leave, but I have to put my faith in the protective possessiveness of Sebastian.*

Elliott was a silent watchful onlooker to these proceedings, and was beginning to have doubts about allowing the British soldiers to escort Margaret home. *She's extremely vulnerable; despite how well she appears to be dealing with her parents' deaths. There's a full day's journey to reach the Haven, and I'm experiencing doubts as to whether I can actually deal with the Major if he tries to do something reprehensible, or if Margaret became hysterical and unmanageable. By re-enforcing the Major's offer of an escort, I wonder if I've bitten off more than I can chew?*

The Lieutenant regretted his moment of cowardice as he watched the tender scene as Richard caressed his hand fondly against Margaret's cheek. She refused to cry, but couldn't control the forlorn look that was reflected upon her face as Richard led his men off to assist their southerly neighbours. Not until the horses were out of sight did Margaret finally turn around to lift tear filled eyes to Elliott's face.

'Does the Major still really wish to escort me or did I burn my bridges last night?'

Elliott laughed. 'He's more determined to make up for last night's disagreement. How long the noble feeling will last though, I cannot say.'

Slowly Margaret nodded. 'It's only a day's ride, how much trouble can we get into in that short time?'

Boyishly Elliott grinned. 'Not to burst your bubble of optimism, but it was only yesterday that you met Major Marconi, and it was only a matter of minutes before you had the desire to scratch his eyes out.'

'I just want to get this journey home over and done with as soon as possible.' She sighed.

'I know.' He placed his hand on Margaret's shoulder. 'Just to be on the safe side, I think we should have a contingency plan if something goes wrong.'

'Your optimism about the future is over-whelming,' Margaret murmured dryly.

'I prefer to be over cautious!'

Elliott's Contingency Plan

'Depending upon whether the Professor's home, or the Haven is closest, the Major will assume you'll head for the nearest for safety,' Elliott stated.

'That would be logical,' agreed Margaret, stretching out her hand to caress down Sebastian's back.

'If he's determined to go after you, then the logical thing to do is not head for either. Go east instead. Mention the name of Richard Evans or your father and any village in this district will offer you sanctuary. It should also give you time to get a message to the Professor.'

'What if we arrive at the Haven without mishap?'

Elliott was not about to be as flippant as Margaret appeared to be treating this. 'Then I'll breathe a huge sigh of relief and offer a prayer of thanks to God!'

Please Don't Do This!

Without saying another word, after lunch Dalila assisted in packing a canvas carry-all for Margaret; some food, her compass and map, a change of clothes and a hunting knife. Everything else Margaret had brought with her to Richards, like the pebble people, she would leave with Dalila for safe keeping.

Aware that the Housekeeper was bursting to say something, Margaret gave Dalila plenty of opportunity to speak, but it wasn't until Fynn was preparing Sophie and the cart, that Dalila finally spoke.

'Please Miss Margaret; don't go with these men. The Major is not a good man!' She grasped hold of Margaret's hand to detain her as Fynn lifted her canvas bag into the cart.

'Lieutenant Gibbs has promised to protect me.'

Sighing, Dalila shook her head. 'You're not going to listen to reason are you, my dear?' Sebastian jumped up into the cart and made himself comfortable. Margaret raised her hand to scratch his ears.

'I should be back within a week.'

'A week!' Dalila's voice rose an octave.

Margaret looked at the Housekeeper in surprise. 'A day to get to the Haven, a day to get back here, a couple of days to organize my parents belongings and convince the villagers that they'll be kept on the farm if it remains in the family.'

'Oh Miss Margaret, please, please be careful!'

'Of course, I plan on coming back alive, Dalila. Take care of the children.' Margaret hoisted herself up onto the box seat and took Sophie's reins firmly into her hands. Dalila followed the cart as Margaret joined the packed up military enclave. Not until the horses were out of sight did Dalila finally return to the house.

A Tense Beginning

The greeting between Major Marconi and Margaret had been cordial, polite, but a little cool. Elliott breathed a sigh of relief that there was no open display of hostility. *They aren't going to have much opportunity to talk during the journey, but we will stop overnight to rest before continuing at first light. I had tried to convince my superior to continue riding through the night, but the Major is not prepared to alter his plans.*

The Lieutenant stuck fairly close to the cart, but Marconi didn't even attempt to speak to Margaret as he stayed at the head of the entourage. Sebastian alternated between lying in the cart and sitting on the driver's box beside Margaret.

It isn't that I'm restless, I could happily sleep the afternoon away, but I do not like Major Marconi and I'm determined to keep Margaret safe. As night began to fall, Sebastian was beginning to get edgy. *I'm hungry for a hunt, and a kill, but can Elliott defend Margaret? My Mistress would ensure that my stomach is taken care of, but the tension with Marconi means that I'm too ready to snap his head off.*

A Not So Quiet Night!

Margaret finally solved this problem when they stopped for the evening and ordered Sebastian to go hunting. The big cat hesitated, glancing across to where the soldiers were dismounting and setting up camp. Bending down, Margaret wrapped her arms around Sebastian's neck.

'It's all right Seb! Go and run off your frustrations. I need you relaxed if you're going to be on guard tonight.' She kissed him on the nose, before letting him go. Sebastian glanced across at Elliott who also felt his concern. When the Lieutenant nodded his head in acknowledgement that he was in charge, Sebastian silently disappeared into the jungle that surrounded them.

A fire was lit, the horses rubbed down, watered and left to chomp upon the grass. Dalila had supplied enough food for all of them and the meal had a surreal, artificial feeling about it.

The soldiers kept glancing from Margaret to Major Marconi as if they expected either of them to suddenly spontaneously combust. Elliott Gibbs was equally nervous, as he knew that Sebastian would kill him if anything happened to Margaret. *The unsettled atmosphere is like the calm before the storm, and there is nothing in that to offer any comfort.*

There was almost an audible sigh of relief all round when Sebastian returned and retired to the cart with Margaret for the night. The stress and strain of waiting for confrontation was actually more exhausting than real hard physical labour. So it wasn't long before the military men were also turning in for the night.

Elliott checked up on Margaret and Sebastian before he reluctantly settled down to try and sleep. *There is no escaping though, the nagging doubt that this apparent calm is masking something very dark and sinister.* It's not surprising then that no one slept very well that night.

TUESDAY

Elliott's Comfort

It was still dark when Elliott woke up in a cold sweat. *Something is desperately wrong, but I can't immediately tell if it's something I'd been dreaming or if reality had actually disturbed my sleep.* Rising, Elliott was surprised that the fire was still burning brightly and hadn't died down like it usually did. This was immediately answered as Sebastian rose from where he sat beside Margaret, who was huddled in front of the fire, and came towards Elliott to check him out.

The tiger allowed the soldier a brief pat before returning to Margaret's side. Casting a quick and anxious glance around, Elliott was relieved to see that the other soldiers appeared to still be asleep. With this concern gone, he sat down on the ground beside Margaret and wondered, *what can I say to comfort her?*

There was enough light from the fire for Elliott to see the tears that fell down Margaret's cheeks. For a brief moment the Lieutenant thought the worst had occurred as Margaret rocked backwards and forward.

'Marconi! Did he…' Elliott was about to jump to his feet to execute retribution, but Margaret reached out to grab his arm.

'No, no, not that! I'm just being silly!' Embarrassed, Margaret wiped away her tears.

Elliott looked at her, stunned. *The last thing I have ever thought of Margaret as being silly.*

'I don't understand.' He handed her his handkerchief and waited for Margaret to explain while his anger subsided.

'This journey home, while I can still call it home, is essential. Until I see it for myself, none of this is real. The problem is that once I know that this nightmare is real, then I must accept that my parents are indeed dead. I'll never see them again. I'm now alone because someone so desperately wants my family out of the way. Will attempt to kill me when he knows that his assassins are dead. Why? My parents only ever wanted to help people. They only ever wanted a simple life. What was so important that they had to die for it?'

Swallowing hard, Elliott didn't say a word as he allowed Margaret to cry upon his shoulder. He could not have spoken, even if he had trusted that his throat would allow any sound to come out. *My heart is touched by Margaret's sorrow but I realize that any words of mine could be of little comfort or balm to ease her loss.*

Sebastian had been watching them closely, and now rose to his feet as he tried to lick away Margaret's tears. Wrapping her arms around the tiger's neck, Margaret buried her face into his fur. For a moment she remained like this, but when she finally released Sebastian, she had managed to stop crying. Using Elliott's hanky to wipe away her tears, Margaret apologized to him.

'Sorry, I'm not dealing with reality well at all. I suppose I should have waited until Richard or Father Gerard were able to come with me for support. I just couldn't face the prospect of watching a stranger, all be he my grandfather, take away my home.'

Sympathetically, Elliott laid his hand over hers. 'You've nothing to apologize for. Actually I would've been surprised if this trip hadn't upset you. It just shows how deeply you love and miss your parents. Don't ever be ashamed of that.'

Margaret managed a weak smile. 'Thank you anyway for being so kind about it. Most men don't like women crying all over them.'

He gave her hand a gentle squeeze before removing his. 'I don't think that you make a habit of it, so I'll easily forgive you.'

A hint of a smile appeared. 'You're so generous! I like a man who is gracious with his condescension!'

Laughing, the Lieutenant rose to his feet and held out his hand to assist Margaret up. 'I didn't mean to condescend. Will you try and get some sleep before daylight?'

Slowly Margaret nodded. 'I'll just go and visit a bush.' Elliott laughed, but Sebastian was determined to go with her. Margaret laid her hand upon the tiger's head.

'It's all right Seb, I'll only be a minute.'

Man and tiger waited by the fire as she disappeared into the darkness. Glancing down at Sebastian, Elliott shrugged his shoulders.

'I suppose there are times when you really do need to be alone.' Sebastian yawned as he sat down beside the fire and kept his eyes glued on the place Margaret had last been seen.

Marconi's Moves

Taking a deep breath, Margaret soaked in the night sounds of the jungle. *Reality about my parents' deaths is hitting hard. Harder than I'd thought it would. Running for my life, caring for Adwoa and Manu, learning about my real parents and myself, facing hired killers, innocent people being killed because of me, the loss of my home, an earthquake, and a declaration of love is proving to be too overwhelming.*

I hadn't expected to fall apart before I'd seen my parents' graves, but the stress of the journey has been more trying than I had been prepared for. The cooling night breeze was soothing against Margaret's heated cheeks. After several minutes of solitude, she felt composed enough to return to the camp.

A twig snapping in the darkness caused Margaret to jump, momentarily startled. Her mind snapped back to her present location, and she reached for a small hunting knife that was attached to her belt.

'Sebastian?' She called out cautiously, *it might just be the protective tiger come to see what was taking me so long.*

'No, sorry if I startled you.'

Margaret tried to contain a groan as the soldier who approached was not Elliott Gibbs but Major Marconi. She returned the knife to her belt.

'I'm sorry if I disturbed your slumber Major, I'm afraid this journey is more painful than I thought it would be.' Without wishing to appear too obvious, Margaret tried to quicken her steps back towards the camp.

'Is that what you call letting Elliott fondle you?' Raoul Marconi adroitly stepped in front of her to block her escape.

'Finding me struggling to deal with the overwhelming reality of returning home, your Lieutenant was attempting to comfort me! There was nothing sexual in his manner towards me!'

Unable to fathom what the Major's problem was, Margaret attempted to move around him. Unwilling to let her leave, he grabbed hold of both her arms in a hold that was painful and impossible to break.

'Major, I'm tired and emotionally unstable. We have a full morning's ride ahead tomorrow and I want to get a few hours of sleep before light.' *I'm trying to keep calm but this obstinate man is starting to annoy the hell out of me.*

One arm of steel locked around her waist and pulled her hard against him. His face was only inches away from Margaret's but she couldn't bear to look at him.

'I know a better way to spend the next couple of hours.' The Major lowered his head to kiss her but because Margaret had turned her head, he only managed to kiss her cheek.

'You're insufferable! What part of "no" do you not understand?' Unable to free her arms, Margaret used the heel of her boot to step down hard upon Marconi's foot. This wasn't enough to get him to release her, but as he swore, the Major's hold weakened allowing Margaret to draw slightly away from him.

As Marconi moved to regain his crippling hold, Margaret thrust her knee into his groin. The colourful profanities flew and Margaret was released as a furious Major clutched his privates.

'You little bitch! You'll pay for that!' He spat out venomously.

'I don't think so,' Margaret was momentarily out of reach and had drawn the blade again. 'I'd rather die than allow you to touch me!'

The knife glittered in the moonlight, but not even the sight of it could put the Major off. He was furious and wanted his revenge. He did not care how he got it.

Spoiling For A Fight

Lunging forward to grab the knife from her, Major Marconi was hit from behind by something heavy and extremely solid, and ended up face down in the dirt. Hungry for a fight, Sebastian nimbly jumped off the Major's back and stood protectively in front of Margaret. He growled menacingly as Marconi picked himself up and rose a little unsteadily to his feet.

'My God, I'll make a coat out of that beast!' As his hand descended to his sidearm, Margaret called out to stop him.

'Don't even think of it Major! Attempt to pull out your gun and I will let Sebastian kill you! Believe me; he's much faster than you.'

The Major snarled in disgust and ignoring the warning continued to withdraw his pistol. Springing like lightening, Sebastian latched his massive jaws upon Marconi's gun arm and held on until the screaming soldier dropped the weapon to the ground. Only then did the tiger release him and return to his protective position in front of Margaret.

'I'll kill you both!' Major Marconi swore as he clutched his bleeding arm to his chest.

'You're a fool! It was silly of me to think that you could be anything but a chauvinistic pig! Are you so conceited that you cannot conceive that any woman may not be attracted to you?'

The Major's scream and Margaret's raised voice had brought Elliott double quick and one hasty glance told him what had happened. He groaned in disbelief. *I'll have to act quickly to avoid a blood bath.* Despite the danger, the Lieutenant placed himself between his Commanding Officer and Sebastian.

'Miss Munroe, perhaps you should return to your cart,' suggested Elliott. He acted as a shield but should have first picked up the Major's gun. Marconi swooped down to retrieve his pistol and using his uninjured arm aimed the weapon at Margaret.

'I'll kill you all!'

'You're insane!' As his own hand descended to the gun at his hip, Elliott honestly thought that his Commanding Officer had gone completely mad. *There is no other reason why the Major is acting this way. Who gets upset about being rejected by a woman?*

'Miss Munroe, go back to the camp.' Elliott spoke calmly, keeping his eyes upon Marconi whilst he used his own body to shield Margaret from the Major's gun.

'Damn you Elliott! Stay out of this or I'll shoot you too!'

The Lieutenant ignored this threat and stepped forward as if to take the weapon away from Marconi. The movement startled the Major, and in his highly-strung state, he pulled the trigger. Elliott was knocked backwards off his feet, his hand reaching up to his shoulder where blood began to pour forth.

Enough!

Never in a million years had I thought that Major Marconi would in fact shoot his Lieutenant. Margaret let out the breath she had sharply drawn in as Elliott fell, and knelt down to check his wound. Pressing a clean handkerchief to stem the flow of blood, she was relieved that the wound wasn't life threatening. Margaret picked up a chunky branch that lay nearby.

'I've had enough of this nonsense,' she declared, and before Marconi could train his gun on her, Margaret swung the branch and smacked him over the head with it. Unconscious but not dead, the Major dropped silently to the ground. Margaret threw away the branch and turned back to Elliott who was in a great deal of pain.

At the sound of a gunshot, the other soldiers had awoken and now arrived at the scene, to find Margaret ripping off the Lieutenant's shirt to use strips of it as a pressure bandage. One soldier ran back to the camp for the medical kit, while another checked to see if the Major was still alive. Elliott grabbed hold of Margaret's hand covering it with his blood.

'Go!' He said quietly.

Margaret looked shocked. 'I can't leave you like this!'

Shaking his head, Elliott said, 'The boys will look after me. Leave the cart and ride like hell. Marconi cannot be allowed to be anywhere near you. Get back to the Professor.'

The young Private, Matthew Fraser, who had gone for the medical kit, now dropped to his knees beside them. 'Lieutenant Gibbs is right, Miss. Go now before the Major wakes up. We'll stall him as long as possible, but it's no longer safe here for you.'

Margaret wavered. 'This is ridiculous! I'm not going to run away and leave you to deal with this situation.'

Private Fraser sighed, 'Miss, if you don't leave, he won't stop until he has killed you. We would be forced to mutiny and kill our superior officer. Justifiable it may be, but we would all hang for the crime.'

Glancing round at the worried faces of the soldiers, Margaret finally looked back at Elliott. 'This is wrong!'

The Lieutenant winced as his shoulder was tightly packed and bound. 'Please Margaret, just go! There is no telling when the Major will come round. We only want you to be safe.'

When Margaret finally nodded, Elliott gave a sigh of relief. He issued the order for the others to see Margaret onto Sophie without the wagon, and thundering away eastward. Not until the sound of hooves died away, did Elliott finally give into his pain and the darkness that washed over him as he fainted.

On The Run

Racing eastwards, Sebastian ran happily alongside Margaret astride Sophie. *Although I'm puzzled, when after an hour of hard riding, we're turning south, but so long as it isn't back towards the soldiers' camp, I'm not about to protest. I am extremely angry that Marconi had proven himself to be untrustworthy, and heartily wish that I had bitten the Major more than once,* contemplated the tiger. Their pace slackened to a walk and Sebastian looked up startled as Margaret swore. *She is still on Sophie and hasn't hurt herself,* which left the tiger to presume, *that my mistress is cursing herself for allowing her to misjudge the Major's intentions.* Smiling wryly, Margaret glanced down at Sebastian.

'Dalila will be justified in saying "I told you so!" Damn it! I wish I'd listened to my gut instinct about that man! Oh Sebastian! What a pickle! I was so stupid to believe that monster could actually be human!'

Sebastian could only look sympathetically, as he could not offer the words of comfort that Margaret needed.

'I think we should push on whilst we have the advantage of a lead and darkness. It won't be too many hours before day breaks and we need to seek shelter.'

Margaret hitched up her backpack so that it sat more comfortably on her back. The rhythmic motion of Sophie added to the lack of sleep caused Margaret's eyelids to slowly close. It wasn't possible to tell when she actually fell asleep, or even how she remained on the horse. Sophie and Sebastian just kept silently moving in a southerly direction. *We have to get Margaret to safety before the arrival of dawn makes us easier to hunt,* was what both animals thought.

Sanctuary

It wasn't possible for Margaret to accurately state, what finally woke her. *It could have been the sound of human voices, the bright sunlight streaming down on my face, that Sophie was now standing motionless, although she tossed her head in nervousness, or the fact that Sebastian was uttering a low growl as he protectively circled around the horse and rider.* Whatever it was she was suddenly alert and reaching for her knife if she needed to defend herself.

Uttering a sigh of relief, Margaret relaxed as she looked down at a sea of curious native villagers' faces. Most kept a safe distance, as Sebastian was a fierce deterrent. One man, though, came close enough to be easily heard.

'I am Chief Kojo, your horse and striped leopard have wandered into out village.' There was wariness to his words. *My experience interacting with white people has been fraught with danger.*

'My name is Margaret Munroe. I apologize if we've alarmed you. We mean no harm to you or your village. I must beg you for sanctuary as my life is in danger. My father is... was...' Margaret found the words choking her and unable to finish her sentence.

'Of course!' Kojo nodded, 'Your father is the great Doctor. He has performed many miracles amongst our people. You're more than welcome Miss.'

Sliding down from Sophie's back, Margaret said with heartfelt gratitude. 'Thank you! You're most generous. Oh!' This last cry was uttered as her legs buckled beneath her and she began to collapse. The Chief reached out to stop Margaret from falling, and a gasp arose from the villagers as Sebastian lowered into a crouch ready to attack Kojo.

'No Sebastian! It's all right!' Margaret threw out her hand to command the zealous tiger. 'We're amongst friends.'

There was a moment of hesitation as Sebastian appeared to be considering the situation, but at last he stretched his taunt muscles and placidly lay down. Only when he had relaxed did Margaret finally look away from Sebastian to glance up at Chief Kojo.

'I'm sorry. We've had rather a nightmare of a night. Sebastian is just a little over protective.' She allowed the young woman, who came forward, to assist her remove her canvas bag.

'Come Miss Munroe, and tell me how we may assist you, while breakfast is prepared for you.' Kojo led Margaret and Sebastian, who rose as they moved towards the pavilion where the smell of delicious food was wafting towards them. Margaret was prepared to be led, but would not forget her duties.

'Sophie! My horse! I must see her fed and watered.'

The Chief smiled and indicated to the villager who was already leading Sophie away to be cared for. 'All will be taken care of Miss. Come.' Lightly laying her hand on Sebastian's neck, Margaret gratefully obeyed.

I'll Put You In Danger

The meal was excellent but Margaret ate very little. *I am exhausted but I'm very worried that my presence in the village will put more innocent lives at risk.* Chief Kojo listened attentively and sympathetically as Margaret explained what had been occurring the past week. He was extremely distressed to learn of the murder Margaret's parents and lamented that their loss would severely affect the entire region.

Kojo dismissed her fears that his people stood in any sort of danger, and stated that a messenger would immediately set out to find Richard Evans. Watching everyone and everything that went on around them, Sebastian refused to leave Margaret's side for even a second.

Kojo was extremely wary of this large, silent animal, but wasn't surprised that Sebastian followed them into a hut where the Chief said Margaret could sleep. She penned a brief note for Richard before sinking, thankfully onto the comfortable straw mattress bed. Sebastian stretched out alongside her and it wasn't too long before they were both sound asleep.

No Escape In Sleep

Although sleep was easily obtained, it was not so easily kept. Dark and disturbing dreams haunted Margaret's sleep. Scenes from her encounter with the Major replayed over and over again. Every possible alternative to Lieutenant Gibbs' death played endlessly as blood flooded every image until Margaret woke up screaming. Elliott wouldn't die from the wound if his colleagues looked after him, but that didn't stop Margaret dreaming his death.

Sebastian sat up alert beside Margaret; her cry had startled him out of his slumber. *There is no one around so I can't tell what is wrong.* He sat staring at her whilst her breathing, which had been quite fast and ragged, slowed. Margaret wrapped her arms around Sebastian's neck and pressed her face into his fur.

'It's all right Seb. It was only a dream. Sorry if I startled you.'

Sebastian relaxed at the sound of her reassuring tone, and comforted her by licking Margaret's cheek.

Can You Help Us?

A concerned native young woman looked into the hut. 'Are you in trouble Miss?'

Margaret managed a wan smile. 'No, just bad dreams, I hope I haven't disturbed anyone?' She reassured the teenager.

'Only worry for your safety.' The girl came a little closer although she kept a wary eye on Sebastian. 'I am Efia, Chief Kojo's daughter. You are Doctor Munroe's daughter, yes?' The girl looked around nervously as Margaret agreed. 'Chief said we were not to worry you, but I desperately need your help. My Mother has been brought to bed for birth of latest child, but all is not well. She is in so much pain, so unlike any other time.'

Margaret immediately jumped to her feet. 'Of course I'll assist if I'm able. How many children does your mother have?' She followed Efia across the village and was surprised when the girl held up both her hands, fingers spread.

'Ten children! My goodness! Sebastian, you'd best stay out here.' Margaret left the tiger outside of the hut they entered, as the sight of such a large and strange animal might upset the Chief's wife.

Efia ran across to kneel beside her mother's bed and taking the hand that reached out to her, she quickly explained Margaret's presence.

Serwa, Efia's mother, nodded frantically and held her free hand out to Margaret. 'Miss Munroe… Please grant us your wisdom.' Tears streamed down her face as her features contorted in extreme pain.

The devotion between mother and daughter is like a knife thrust into my breast. I'll never be able to touch my own mother's hand again, or hear her voice but I must force down my own feelings of loss if I am to help Serwa.

'I… I need to wash my hands, and then I have to see what is happening with your baby.' The words came automatically as if Margaret had no control over them. Efia showed her a hand basin where there was also soap and a towel.

With her hands as clean as she could get them, Margaret knelt at the end of Serwa's bed and gently folded back the sheet so that her legs were exposed. Mother and daughter waited anxiously as Margaret made her preliminary examination. Her worried expression did not reassure them.

'You're fully dilated Serwa. I should see the head ready to come out. I fear your baby may not have turned and is trying to come feet first.'

'Is that dangerous?' Efia looked worried at her mother.

Margaret nodded, 'To mother and baby.'

'Oh Miss Munroe,' Serwa cried. 'Is there nothing you can do?'

Margaret inhaled slowly. 'Yes, with Efia's help, we can deliver this baby.'

'What do we need to do?' Efia's face shone with hope.

'Normally, because baby's head and shoulders are the largest part, the rest of the body simply slips out after they are through. In this instance, while I help baby's bottom to come out, Efia, you will need to push on Serwa's abdomen to assist the head through.'

Serwa gritted her teeth as she experienced another contraction. 'What about the cord?'

'I'll keep an eye on that as the baby comes out,' reassured Margaret. 'Next contraction, I want you to push with all you've got.'

All three women were extremely nervous as Efia laid her hands on her mother's stomach to add additional leverage, and Margaret reached inside Serwa to grasp hold of the baby's hips.

As Serwa and Efia pushed with the next contraction, Margaret pulled the baby's bottom out into the open. The child's legs were pressed against his body and Margaret couldn't straighten them until the feet were clear of the womb. Waiting for the next contraction, with the little boy baby half out; Serwa was able to catch her breath. Margaret smiled supportively as she made certain that the umbilical cord wasn't tangled with the baby's head.

'This time I really need you to push hard, Efia, to help your mama,' instructed Margaret, working frantically to get the baby's arms through the right way to prevent damaging his limbs. One shoulder had to be eased out at a time, and then finally a huge push for the head. As Efia comforted Serwa, Margaret quickly wiped the newborn's face, clearing his mouth and nose. The sound of his cry rang throughout the hut and seemed to echo in the tears of all three women.

Wiping him down, Margaret gladly handed the baby to Serwa, wrapped in a sheet.

'Congratulations! You have a beautiful son!'

Efia raced out to tell her father and Margaret covered Serwa up for visitors.

'Oh the sack is still inside!' Serwa tried to pull on the umbilical cord, but Margaret stopped her.

'The placenta will come out on its own in a couple of minutes. To force it out can cause unnecessary bleeding.'

Serwa wasn't prepared to argue with her, lying back as she looked adoringly at her new son.

Announcing A Son

Chief Kojo burst into the hut and sat down on the bed beside his wife, who proudly showed him their son.

'He is beautiful! You are beautiful!' He affectionately kissed his wife.

'I beg your permission to name our son, Munroe. In honour of Miss Munroe, who surely saved both our lives,' Serwa was a little nervous, as it was Kojo's place to name their children. He wasn't angry, though, and in fact felt it only fitting.

'Your wish is granted. Munroe you shall be little man.' This time Kojo kissed Serwa and the baby before rising to his feet, he left the hut to announce to the village the birth of his new son.

A cheer rose outside, and Serwa sighed contently, *I have pleased my husband with another healthy son.* Margaret was seriously troubled, and as Efia and her female relatives returned, she left them so that she could clean up.

Frowning deep in thought, Margate scrubbed her hands free from blood at the local well and didn't hear Chief Kojo approach her. She jumped, startled when he spoke her name. Sebastian had joined her as soon as she had left the hut, and now lay on the ground beside her.

'Efia told me that the difficulties could have been life threatening. I am in your debt, Miss Munroe.'

Margaret's frown quickly came back. 'There is no debt Chief, you offered me sanctuary. There is something I must speak to you about...'

Seeing her frown, Kojo was worried that there might still a danger to his wife and new son. Margaret quickly reassured him that they weren't in any immediate danger.

I Have A Request

Taking a deep breath, she decided to plunge straight in. 'I don't think that Serwa will survive another pregnancy. She obviously loves you very much, and would never… deny herself to you, but another pregnancy must be avoided. I've seen it in other villages where the Chief's wife can no longer bear any more children and he turns to younger women, breaking his wife's heart.'

Concern crept into Margaret's features, as she feared she might have annoyed Kojo. To her amazement, he nodded his head in agreement.

'Are there means of prevention other than abstinence?'

Breathing a sigh of relief, Margaret nodded.

'Good! I am very fond of my wife. I do not particularly wish for another.'

Margaret couldn't help but laugh. 'They take so long to train just the way you want them too!'

'That is what Serwa would say about me!' The Chief smiled.

'Oh and just think another set of in-laws!'

Kojo threw up his hands in defeat. 'No, no! Not that! An argument that has no answer. You have more than convinced me.'

'You've greatly relieved my mind, Chief.' Margaret's smile vanished and Sebastian rose to his feet, growling as the sound of many horse hooves could be heard approaching the village.

'Quickly hide, Miss!' Kojo ordered, but it was too late to seek cover as a very angry Major Marconi and his men rode into sight.

Marconi's Revenge

Instinctively Margaret reached down to grasp Sebastian by the nape of his neck as her eyes scanned frantically for sight of the Lieutenant. His horse was attached to Sophie's cart, but it was Private Fraser who held the reins. Margaret felt her heart skip a beat and her throat close up making it momentarily impossible to breathe. It didn't take long for her anger to surface and she went for Major Marconi.

'What have you done? Where is Lieutenant Gibbs? Have you killed one of your own men?'

Calmly the Major dismounted from his horse and drew his gloves off. 'Gibbs is still alive for the moment. You should be more concerned about what I'm going to do to you.'

'I don't think so!' Kojo moved protectively towards Margaret, but she had no thoughts about her own safety at that moment. She ran to the cart and leapt into the back.

'Elliott! What has he done to you?' The Lieutenant lay in the cart so still that Margaret was afraid that it was too late. 'Oh my…!' She reached out a trembling hand to touch Elliott's wrist to check his pulse.

'Broken but not yet defeated.' His words were little more than a whisper, and brought a sob to Margaret's throat.

'What has he done?'

Private Fraser leant on the side of the cart. 'Lieutenant Gibbs refused to tell the Major where you would disappear to. When he lost your tracks, he broke the Lieutenant's leg as well as several ribs. I've not been able to re-bandage the bullet wound yet.'

Margaret became totally professional, 'I need your assistance Private. We need to strip him down to his undergarments so that I can set his leg and tend to the other wounds.' She jumped down from the cart and ignoring the Major, Margaret walked across to Chief Kojo.

'Could I please use the hut I slept in to work on the Lieutenant's injuries?'

'Of course Miss Munroe! Our village is yours. Anything you need, just ask.'

'Thank you.'

'Ahem!' The polite clearing of the Major's throat distracted Margaret from the soldiers who assisted the Private to carry Elliott from the cart. 'Aren't you forgetting something?' Marconi asked. His eyes full of anger belied his calm tone.

Margaret looked at him in surprise. 'Not now Major! I must repair the damage you've inflicted. You'll have to wait.' She turned away to direct the soldiers to the hut, but the Major's pretence at patience snapped.

'I couldn't care less if Elliott's leg falls off! You're not going to go another minute without knowing my revenge.' He grabbed hold of her arm and dragged her into his painful embrace.

Margaret stood frozen, looking up into his face with shock and horror. He leered in satisfaction but he was wrong if he thought that her reaction was fear for her own safety.

'I cannot believe you have no compassion for one of your own men. I thought you were a heartless idiot, but I was wrong. You're nothing but a monster! Not everyone gets what he or she wants and most children eventually grow out of throwing tantrums. You obviously have not! Your revenge will be no less sweet if you have to wait half an hour. Perhaps you could spend that time contemplating if the path you're treading isn't leading you straight to Hell and damnation.' Margaret tried to pull away, but the Major's hold was like steel.

'You've a sharp tongue, but you'll soon learn that you're not so brave. I will break your spirit before this day is through.'

Chief Kojo clapped his hands forcefully together. 'Enough! Remove your hands from the lady. She is under my protection.'

Although the Major snarled at the interruption, he took proper stock of his surroundings for the first time. Every villager was present, the men armed with spears and knives and although primitive weapons, they outnumbered the soldiers twenty to one. Sebastian too was growing restless, pacing up and down. *I am looking for the first sign of an opening where I can attack Marconi without harming my mistress.* Twisting Margaret round, the Major used her as a shield as he drew out a pistol to hold against her temple.

'Kill me and she dies too!'

Timely Arrival

'I always thought you were something of a drama queen!' The droll tone so familiar to Margaret caused Marconi to release her as he spun round to face Richard Evans as he dismounted from his horse. Margaret gave a cry of delight as she flew into his arms and raised her face to be kissed. Well that was what Richard later claimed as his defence. He now kissed her passionately. No one present could have any doubts as to their feelings for each other.

'Oh Richard, I'm so relieved to see you!' She buried her face into his shoulder as she fought against the tears that were building up inside.

'You're not even safe with an armed military escort, my poor kitten! I think I'll just have to keep you under my constant observation from now on.' While he soothed Margaret's fears, Richard was taking in the situation before them.

'Oh, the Lieutenant!' Margaret reluctantly drew away from him, 'He's badly injured! I must help him,' she explained.

'Go, I'll take care of things here.'

Margaret hesitated, but Richard smiled reassuringly. She ran off to the hut and although her thoughts were mostly on the medical task ahead, a part of her brain wondered, *how will Richard sort this all out?*

Just privately, the Professor was also wondering how to deal with this mess, but none of his concerns reflected on his features as he approached Chief Kojo.

'Thank you for your message Chief. I'm glad that I could arrive before the situation got completely out of hand.' The two men shook hands.

'You're indeed a welcome sight Professor Evans. In the short time Miss Munroe has been with us, she has become a true friend beyond measure.'

'Yes, she does have this ability to make herself indispensable.' Richard removed his glasses to polish them.

'When you've quite finished with your meaningless conversation!' Marconi was getting more annoyed every second that Richard ignored him. The Professor now turned to him as if perceiving the Major for the first time.

'Patience is definitely not your forte is it? Nor are manners. Then again, there appears to be quite a few social graces that you seem to be missing!' As Richard's tone hardened, Sebastian came up beside him, ready to support any attack that he instigated.

'That's rich coming from you! Do you deny that you're a married man and that you're carrying on with that girl?'

Richard sighed. 'Yes I am married, but I'm not having an affair with Margaret.' *I don't see this as being the time or place for this conversation, but there is little I can do about it while Marconi still holds onto his gun.*

The Major snorted in disbelief. 'Ridiculous! We all saw the way you kissed that whore.'

Instead of getting angry, Richard smiled. 'Jealous? I'm not surprised! You always did think yourself irresistible to women, and now you've met your match in Margaret. How that must wound your pride, your fragile ego!'

Marconi raised his pistol to aim at Richard, but his arm had barely left his side before Sebastian had sprung forward and added fresh teeth marks into the Major's arm forcing him to drop the gun to the ground. Marconi swore colourfully as he clutched his once again bleeding arm.

'Very stupid Major.' The Professor shook his head, 'You leave me no alternative in the action I must now take.'

Take Your Clothes Off

Entering the hut, Margaret found Private Fraser arguing with Lieutenant Gibbs as the soldiers tried to remove his clothes. Margaret, fresh from being mauled by Marconi, was not prepared to put up with Elliott's embarrassment.

'Get your clothes off now or I'll do it for you!' She pulled out her knife and ruthlessly ripped up the seam of his trouser leg. The soldiers stared at her amazed, but she was not finished surprising them.

'I want everyone out of here except Fraser. I need a large bowl, some clean water and lots of linen that I can use for bandages.' Margaret pulled out of her backpack her medical kit and when the soldiers didn't move, there was a snap in her voice.

'Have you all gone deaf? I need these supplies now!'

Kneeling down, Margaret tore off Elliott's shirt so that she could get to the bullet wound. Her expression was so forbidding that Elliott Gibbs thought better of pointing out that Margaret was quickly leaving him with nothing to wear at all. The soldiers scurried off to follow orders and only Mathew Fraser, who had remained obediently behind, dared to ask a question.

'What do you need me to do?' He unwrapped the blood soaked bandage around the Lieutenant's arm, while Margaret laid out the contents of her medical kit. She didn't immediately answer as she inspected Elliott's wound and was satisfied that it was as clean as possible.

'I'm sorry, is it Matthew Fraser or Fraser Matthew?'

'Matthew Fraser, Miss. Matt to my friends.'

'First I want to wash, dry and rewrap the Lieutenant's arm. There is very little we can do about the ribs, we could bandage his chest, but we will need all the bandages for his leg. Can you get Elliott's boots off? If that ankle has become too swollen, we will have to cut the boot off.'

Elliott was moved to protest. 'Steady on Margaret! The rate you're cutting up my clothes I'll have nothing to keep me respectable!' The look she gave him made the Lieutenant feel like a naughty two year old.

'If the swelling isn't reduced, you could lose your foot. Now stop being a hindrance!'

'Yes ma'am!' Elliott replied meekly, and glancing up at Matthew and pulled a face. The Private bit down on his bottom lip to stop laughing. Margaret cast them both a speaking glance, but said nothing as she tended to the bullet hole in the Lieutenant's shoulder.

The soldiers returned, with not only the items Margaret had sent them for, but also two straight sticks. One soldier, having once seen a cast set on a broken limb before, thought the sticks would help keep the leg straight while it healed. Margaret readily agreed and thanked them for their efforts.

They jumped, startled as the Lieutenant cried out in pain as his boots were removed. Cutting them hadn't been necessary, but they had still been extremely difficult to pull off. The soldiers gratefully accepted Margaret's orders to leave the hut. They felt helpless to assist Lieutenant Gibbs and just quietly one or two of them were thinking that they should have killed the Major when they had the opportunity.

Margaret finished off the bandage around Elliott's shoulder and laid a tender hand against his forehead. *He is sweating, but not to the point where I think that he has a fever, yet.* From the medical kit she removed a small sealed phial and a hypodermic needle and carefully transferred the clear liquid into the syringe.

Elliott opened one eye to look up at her. 'Are you going to put me out my misery?'

Margaret made certain that there were no air bubbles in the syringe before she answered, 'No, only out of pain.' She leant over him to inject into his undamaged arm and was surprised when his fingers suddenly grasped hold of her wrist.

'I never betrayed you!'

Margaret smiled. 'I know. If he had forced it out of you, you would've been here sooner. Don't worry, everything will be all right.' She pressed her lips against his brow and his eyes closed as he released her hand.

'Right then Matthew we need water in the big bowl, add this powder and stir well for a minute or two. Into this mixture we place the bandages, unwrapped, to soak up the moisture. Then we wrap them wet around the broken leg. Any questions?'

Matthew Fraser nodded. 'What is the powder?'

'Plaster of Paris. Probably not as much as we really need, but it should keep Elliott from damaging his leg while it heals.'

Satisfied, Matthew started unrolling the strips of linen and bandages and added them to the bowl when the liquid plaster was ready. Margaret positioned the two sticks on either side of the Lieutenant's broken leg and wrapped a dry bandage from knee to ankle. When the Private looked questioningly at her, she explained.

'It should prevent us ripping all the hair off his leg when the cast eventually comes off.' Matthew pulled a pained expression and agreed that it was a wise and humane precaution.

They had to work reasonably fast, wrapping the wet bandages around and around the broken limb, as the plaster of Paris would set rapidly. It was a messy job, with both Margaret and Matthew being covered from fingers to elbows in the plaster as they worked. This worried Matthew, but Margaret assured him that if they washed immediately after they had finished, they wouldn't have casts of their own.

Lieutenant Gibbs was quiet, docile, but still conscious. He meekly obeyed any order given if his position needed to change to allow his Doctors better access to his leg. The painkiller worked quickly, and although he could feel everything that was being done to him, he didn't feel any pain. Only when Margaret stuck a pin into his toes did Elliott finally make a protest. She only smiled and stated that it meant that they hadn't cut off the circulation to his foot.

Elliott didn't know if that was good or bad, and was relieved when they finally tidied up and left him in peace, as they went to wash off any plaster from themselves. *I no longer care that I'm nearly naked, or that the Major is likely to kill us all. I'm just glad to be free from pain for the moment, and to be able to give into the darkness that is beckoning me to join it.* The future was someone else's worry, as Elliott finally gave into sleep.

Sebastian's Justice

Sardonic laughter rang throughout the village. 'You have no power over me!' gloated Marconi.

Richard smiled coolly. 'There you're very much mistaken. In this District I'm not only a Justice of the Peace, but I am also a Marshall. That means that I not only have the power to arrest and detain a person for questioning, but also the ability to command all and any British Officers or troops that enter this region.' He paused for effect. 'That Major Marconi includes you!'

Marconi's laughter died. 'I'll see you in Hell first!'

'And I can have you arrested for insubordination, apart from the rest of your crimes. Don't make this any harder on yourself.'

'I will never submit to your orders!'

'You have no choice.' Nonchalantly Richard shrugged his shoulders.

'I have a multitude of choices!' The Major raised his fists, but before he could even strike Richard, he found himself flat on his back with a huge tiger standing on his chest. Sebastian glanced back at Richard waiting for his orders, but growled in warning when Marconi tried to move beneath him.

Richard didn't immediately relieve the Major of the large cat that pinned him down. 'I'm very impressed Sebastian. I hadn't expected such patience from you.' Richard affectionately scratched the tiger behind the ears.

'How is that Professor?' asked the Chief. *I had never seen any animal move so quickly before.*

'Well I had half expected Seb to have ripped the Major's throat out by now. He has offered him enough reason to!'

Marconi roared in anger. 'Get this fucking walking rug off me before I bash its fucking ugly head in!'

Richard tut-tutted. 'Did you know that Sebastian dislikes bad language as much as Margaret does? I'm half tempted to do the world a favour and allow Sebastian to tear you to pieces. Margaret wouldn't like him to get a taste for human flesh, so perhaps it is best that you don't eat him Sebastian.'

The tiger yawned, as if bored with the game anyway and languidly stepped off Marconi. He decided on his own form of revenge and as he wandered back to stand beside Richard, Sebastian lifted his tail and sprayed the Major.

Kojo raised his hand to cover his broad smile of amusement as Richard choked on a laugh. Shaking in fury, Marconi rose to his feet, absolutely soaked in urine, and reached for the pistol he had earlier been forced to drop.

'When I have finished with that beast, I'll mount its fucking head on a stick! By God I will not be humiliated like this.'

The Professor wore an innocent expression as he spread his hands wide in front of him. 'How would you like to be humiliated then? We're very accommodating if you have a preferred style.'

Kojo could not stop laughing.

'Damn you Evans! Damn you all to Hell!' Marconi raised his gun once more to aim at Richard. 'Now we'll see who'll be laughing last!'

'Not with that gun you won't,' stated Chief Kojo, opening out his hand to reveal the bullets from the Major's pistol. He had removed them whilst the Major's attention had been focused on Richard.

Mutiny!

Major Marconi's shoulders slumped in defeat until he saw the return of the rest of his men from assisting Margaret.

'Come men! You won't let me be insulted like this! Kill them! Kill them all!' His eyes held a wild crazy look as he ran up to join the other soldiers. When they reached for their weapons, it was not at the villagers they aimed, but at their Commanding Officer.

'It's over, Major. You've gone too far,' stated the Sergeant.

'We should've stopped you when you attacked Lieutenant Gibbs. He was right to stand up against you,' added another soldier.

'Mutiny!' roared the Major. 'Weak minded fools! You've let that bleeding heart Gibbs brainwash you. What price is loyalty?'

The Sergeant shook his head. 'Loyalty stopped us killing you last night. You'll accompany us back to Accra to face Court Martial.'

Marconi went into manic laughter. 'You'll have to catch me first!' He made a mad dash for his horse, springing up onto its back and riding off before anyone could react. The soldiers glanced to Richard for orders.

'Do we go after him, Professor Evans?'

Richard shook his head. 'Sooner or later, he'll have to be hunted down but with or without him, Marconi will be Court Martialled, and become a wanted fugitive. You'll have to return to Accra to report. I'll be sending in a detailed account.'

'What about the Lieutenant?'

Richard did not immediately answer. *A lot depends upon when Margaret feels Elliott is up to any sort of travelling.* 'He won't be able to go with you, but I mean to take him back to my farm until he is fit enough to travel back to town.'

How Is The Patient?

Appearing like a couple of ghosts, with their white plaster covered arms, Margaret and Private Fraser ignored the assembled group as they hurried to the well to wash off the plaster before it set. Everybody watched them, waiting for not only some sort of comment about Major Marconi's whereabouts, but also a report on the Lieutenant's condition.

Margaret, though, was more interested in Matthew scrubbing harder on his arms. Not until their arms were completely clean, and the odd spot of plaster removed from Margaret's face, did they even notice that they were the centre of attention. Matthew Fraser turned bright red under so many watchful eyes, but Margaret merely raised her eyebrows in surprise.

'Has something ultra-exciting happened? What have you done with the Major?' Margaret calmly asked; wiping her dripping wet arms on a towel that Efia supplied.

Smiling, Richard brushed a wisp of hair away from her face. 'Unable to defend himself against overwhelming odds, Marconi has decided to flee rather than face his punishment like a man.'

'Oh, he scarpered! What about this lot?' Margaret pointed to the other soldiers. 'Did they finally revolt against his madness?'

The Sergeant stiffened in indignation. 'He wanted us to kill everyone here Miss! That is going too far!'

Absently pulling on Sebastian's ears, Margaret mused thoughtfully. 'Yes, I suppose it is difficult to cover up something like a massacre!'

This caused an outcry of protest from the soldiers, all determined to defend their position of having to follow orders. Margaret smiled at how easily they had risen to the bait, but Richard openly laughed at her ability to touch a raw nerve.

'How is Lieutenant Gibbs?' Although he was in fact interested, Richard used the question as a distraction ploy.

'The Lieutenant will live. His leg has been set in plaster; it just needs to dry before he can be moved. The bullet wound is clean, but due to the blood he lost, I'm worried about Elliott becoming feverish. It isn't a big concern, but he's not in any fit state to travel a long distance.' There was a general sigh of relief at the good news.

'Gibbs won't be going back to Accra with his comrades,' explained Richard. 'He'll return to my farm until he is fit.'

'Good! That is excellent, then I'll be able to keep a close eye on his progress. Thank you!' *I'm very pleased with Richard for volunteering to look after Elliott without having to be asked. It isn't that he's a selfish man, but when he is in serious work mode, his focus is normally fixed quite firmly on that. To take on someone who will need a fair amount of nursing, which will take up quite a lot of his time, impresses me,* thought Margaret.

Richard didn't see it this way at all. *Lieutenant Gibbs did everything he could to protect Margaret, and has been injured doing this. To me, one good turn deserves another, and no inconvenience enters my thoughts when it comes to Margaret.* Chief Kojo offered them all an evening meal and the hospitality of his village for the night. Elliott Gibbs couldn't be moved before the morning, so Margaret and Richard gratefully accepted.

The other soldiers were more embarrassed about their presence in the village. Richard pointed out that their horses could do with a full night's rest before they started the arduous trek back to the capital city. This was hard to argue with, so they also accepted the Chief's offer. Peace settled in the village, but just to be sure that it stayed that way, Kojo posted guards around the perimeter. *It is unlikely that Major Marconi would return, but if he does, I want to be prepared,* decided the Chief.

A Restless Night

A rough night was spent in the hut that Margaret shared with Richard and Elliott. As she predicted the Lieutenant did become feverish and didn't always comprehend where he was or what had happened. Margaret patiently explained again and again as she bathed his face and forced him to drink lots of water.

He complained a little peevishly about being water logged and when the obvious result occurred Elliott refused to allow Margaret to help him relieve himself. Richard came to the rescue with an empty bottle and evicted Margaret from the room for the procedure. She muttered something under her breath about men being big babies, but didn't return until Richard had settled Elliott back onto his pillow.

It wasn't until the wee (no pun intended) hours of the morning that the Lieutenant finally fell into a deep sleep which meant that his nurses could get a couple of hours rest before dawn. Even so, Margaret still woke at regular intervals to check on Elliott and cool his fevered brow. The only one to spend a restful night was Sebastian. *I was spoilt at dinner and with a very full belly I am happy to leave Richard in charge of our protection.*

WEDNESDAY

Elliott's Concerns

It wasn't surprising then that the morning was quite advanced by the time Margaret and Richard finally emerged from the hut. Although Lieutenant Gibbs was still feverish, he was more lucid. The other soldiers were hesitant to leave one of their own, but they couldn't offer the medical care that Margaret could give him. Nor was he up to the journey to Accra. It would be tiring just to get Gibbs to Richard's farm.

As the sound of the horses' hooves faded as the soldiers left the village, Elliott Gibbs finally relaxed. *I'm more worried about their journey than my own. If they come across Major Marconi, they might be forced to either take him prisoner or kill him if they can't bring him in safely. They're loyal men who have been forced to revolt against their Commanding Officer.*

There's no way to prevent news reaching the appropriate authorities, as the Professor will be sending a full report as soon as we reach his farm. There'll be serious consequences to face and unless we can capture the Major, we'll have a difficult time proving his insane behaviour. Lapsing once more into sleep, Elliott hadn't time to dwell on this or any other problem.

Let's Go Home

The morning had almost gone before Margaret felt that it was safe to finally move Elliott. It took two men to assist the Lieutenant into the back of the cart. Sebastian jumped in beside him and settled down for the trip as

Richard harnessed Sophie up to the shafts. Margaret secured Richard's and the Lieutenant's horses to the back of the cart.

Whilst they had waited for Elliott's condition to improve, Margaret had visited Serwa and baby Munroe. Both were doing well, and Margaret was surprised when the older woman hugged her tightly. Kojo now handed Margaret up to the box seat beside Richard, but retained a grip on her hand.

'Know that you will always find refuge here, Miss Munroe.'

'Thank you.' Margaret was deeply touched. 'I hope that my next visit won't be so eventful.' The whole village turned out to wave good-bye and Margaret knew some regret to be leaving them.

I Like Uneventful

The journey home was peaceful and un-eventful, but even so Richard did not relax his alert attention for trouble until they finally drew up outside his own stables. *Although I hope that we've seen the last of Major Marconi, I seriously doubted it will actually be the case.* Margaret couldn't think of anything but getting Elliott into a bed and checking his injuries after a bumpy ride.

Word had travelled to the farm from the southern village that Richard had rushed off to rescue Margaret, so Kobbi and Manu were eager for news upon their return. Margaret hugged them both, and said she would explain everything once she had seen to the Lieutenant's needs. The boys made themselves useful by helping out and it wasn't long before Elliott had been given a sponge bath, his wound redressed, clothed in one of Richard's nightshirts, and settled into Richard's bed.

Dalila made them an early dinner and as night settled around them, Margaret told her story. The boys plied her with hundreds of questions until Dalila said enough was enough and sent them home.

Richard brewed a sleeping draught for Margaret and Elliott while the Housekeeper made up one of the couches as a bed for him. Dalila would not hear of any bed sharing, and promised to stay if Richard needed a hand during the night. *I hope that the sleeping potion will knock them out for at least most of the night, and foresee few problems until morning.*

Having assisted Elliott to the bathroom they all settled down, happy that this latest adventure was finally behind them

THURSDAY
An Improvement

As sunshine streamed through the windows the next morning, Elliott awoke feeling a lot more optimistic about his situation. *My fever has passed, the feeling that my head is stuffed full of cotton wool has gone, and although my injuries pain me, I am alive and incredibly hungry.* With a little bit of difficulty, he swung his legs over the side of the bed and attempted to sit up. His head swam and his vision blurred causing Elliott to cling to the bedside table for support.

Having heard him groan, Richard strolled into the bedroom, a piece of toast in one hand. He was about to raise the toast to his lips when Elliott seized it and immediately devoured it.

'Well, that's a good sign,' Richard said as his eyebrows rose. 'But I don't think the Doctor wants you to leave your bed today.'

The Lieutenant grimaced. 'Some things are more important!'

Richard supported Elliott to his feet and helped him to hop to the bathroom. He let him have some personal space, but quickly returned when Elliott called out to him several minutes later. Struggling back to bed, Elliott sighed wistfully.

'What I wouldn't give to see something other than these four walls!'

Richard grinned, 'Stir crazy already?' He asked sympathetically.

Elliott shrugged. 'I wouldn't mind some fresh air.'

Deep in thought Richard scratched his chin. 'I think Doctor Margaret wanted you to stay in bed today but I'll ask if you can have time out for good behaviour.'

Wincing, Elliott repositioned his shoulder to ease the pain. 'Right now I'd accept anything I can get.'

'I'll see what the boss says.' Richard strolled out of the room.

I'm Angry All The Time!

After an undisturbed and deep sleep, Margaret had risen early, and finished breakfast before Richard even reached the table. She left him to enjoy his breakfast in peace and went to his study where she carefully wrote down, as accurate as she could, an account of Major Marconi's conduct since his arrival at the farm.

She had just signed her name at the bottom of the last sheet of paper, when Richard came in to relay Elliott's request. Frowning, Margaret stared down at the quill in her hand as she thought it through, but eventually she shook her head.

'No, we can open the windows to let some breeze through but Elliott stays in bed until tomorrow.'

'I think you should tell him.' Richard shrugged his shoulders fatalistically.

'Thanks for nothing!' Rising to her feet, Margaret poked her tongue out at him.

He laughed. 'I've a few letters to write before I send a courier off to town. Ask Dalila if it is possible to have some cake. I expect Father Gerard will come to see you today.'

Margaret dropped a kiss on the top of his head as Richard sat down in the chair she had just vacated. He looked up at her, pleased but also puzzled.

'What was that for?'

'I don't think I ever thanked you properly for coming to rescue me.' Her voice sounded very young and insecure. Richard placed his arms around her waist.

'Sebastian did most the work. I just wish Marconi wasn't still on the loose.'

Margaret slipped onto his lap and wrapping her arms around his neck, pressed her face into Richard's shoulder.

'Oh Richard; that night the Major tried to… When he shot Elliott and threatened to kill Seb and me… I was so angry that I think I really could've killed him. I know it's wrong, but at that moment, I felt that even God wouldn't blame me for ridding the world of such a loathsome creature.'

Richard forced Margaret's face up to look at him. 'If you had been alone, then perhaps it may have been necessary to kill Marconi. Once you had knocked him unconscious, the best thing you could do was leave it to the other soldiers to deal with him. It's a pity they couldn't immediately stand up to him, but they got there in the end.'

Shaking her head, Margaret rubbed a hand against her eyes. 'I don't understand what is happening to me, Richard. I just get so angry all the time! It is like there is a volcano bubbling inside me waiting to explode. I wasn't always this… aggressive was I?' She caught him raising his eyes to the ceiling and choking on a laugh Margaret thumped his arm. 'Richard! Answer me honestly!'

Exhaling slowly, the Professor chose his words carefully, 'You've always been very passionate and ready to speak out about certain subjects; the treatment of natives, of animals, and injustice. You've lived a fairly sheltered life at the Haven. Edward and Isabella taught you strong morals and ethics, but there has been very little to grate against these ideals.'

'You've had little opportunity to deal with hired killers, insanely vain Majors or a family most people would want to disown. Most importantly though, you're grieving for the only parents you've ever known. A great deal of your anger stems from that point. This faceless person, more than likely family, is the root of all your problems.'

'There is also guilt, your own. You blame yourself for your parents' deaths, and that they were killed to get to you. Just like the senseless slaughter of Jack Phillips and his hunting party. That guilt is fuelling the anger, the volcano, if you like, and it makes you more reactive to little annoyances.'

Margaret laid her head against Richard's shoulder and closed her eyes. 'Am I being very difficult to live with?'

Richard chuckled, 'Of course not! Apart from my messy work habits, I don't seem to be annoying you and you don't seem inclined to want to kill me. You're just a little more sensitive and that is perfectly normal. Now don't you have a patient to see?' He briefly kissed her forehead. Margaret reluctantly rose from his lap, and left Richard to the solitude of the cosy study.

What A Fuss

Elliott was sitting up in bed, eating his way through a substantial breakfast when Margaret entered the bedroom. He grinned up at her.

'The condemned man's last hearty meal!' He explained.

Margaret laughed. 'I hardly think so! I'm glad to see you have your appetite back. Apart from that, how are you feeling?' She sat down on the edge of the bed and briefly rested her hand on his forehead.

Elliott took a gulp of coffee before answering, 'My head is clear, my shoulder aches, my leg itches and my ribs hurt when I breathe. Aside from that, I feel hot and restless.'

Margaret shook her head. 'We'll get you up tomorrow.'

He shrugged, using only his good shoulder. 'Oh well, I thought I'd at least ask.'

She rose from the bed and as Elliott had finished eating, took his tray out to the kitchen. Elliott lay back on his pillows.

Mail Arrives

The Lieutenant was overwhelmed when Danso presented to him a pair of crutches that he had made. The kindness he had received from everyone left him only able to stammer his thanks as he tried inadequately to express his gratitude.

Elliott was shakily trying out his new means of getting around, (in total disregard to Margaret's orders) when Father Gerard arrived, and with him the mail. Gerard wanted to hear all about Margaret's adventure, and she, in return, how the rescue of the kidnapped girls had gone. They had tea on the verandah; Elliott was allowed to join them so long as he kept his damaged leg raised. He tired quickly though, and wasn't sorry to settle down once more in bed.

During the swapping of stories, the mail had been ignored, but the hunger for news soon had Richard sorting the correspondence into two piles. The bundle he handed to Margaret was as large as his own. Using the small knife she carried at all times, Margaret nervously ripped open her letters. She barely glanced at the contents of each letter before opening the next.

'Condolences from John Foster, which must be Mama's older brother, condolences from Hester Barnsby and family, and a list of demands from Grandfather Foster. Oh!' Margaret opened a more official looking envelope and finding it to be from her parents' lawyers; she read this letter more carefully. Richard had sorted through his own mail, but finding nothing of urgency, he put it aside and continued to talk to Father Gerard.

In an excited state, Margaret grabbed hold of Richard's arm. 'Oh, you have got to read this! Oh I beg your pardon.' Margaret caught herself up as she had interrupted their conversation.

Gerard smiled indulgently. 'Never mind, my dear, you obviously have interesting news.'

Flattening out the letter, Margaret said, 'Apparently my Grandmama, Elizabeth Foster, didn't trust her husband's lawyers to deal ethically with the Barnsby inheritance and hired someone else, Sinclair and Associates. They wrote to tell me that they'll continue to manage the inheritance until it is ready to be discharged. They'll even arrange for someone to explain in detail what it entails and answer any questions I might have. If I'm not happy with their handling of the matter, they'll recommend several other law firms. What they warn me against is being coerced into using Grandfather's lawyers. I say, they are frank aren't they?' She handed the letter to Richard.

Gerard sighed deeply. 'Law is a tricky thing. I haven't met many lawyers, but I had always thought it a rather ruthless profession. This firm obviously doesn't wish you to fall to any unscrupulous practices your relatives may use to relieve you of your birthright.'

Folding the letter, Richard grunted. 'If only we had known the extent of the threat before they could kill Edward and Isabella!'

Insufferable Man!

A gasp escaped from Margaret and Richard realized that his words may have been a little insensitive. She hadn't heard him though, as she was reading through her Grandfather's letter.

'I don't believe the nerve of that man!' The sudden burst of anger startled both men, even Sebastian, who had come out to stretch along the verandah, looked up at Margaret in concern.

'My own Grandfather expects me to… Actually demands that I… Oh what an insufferable man! I cannot even bring myself to speak his words!' Throwing down the remainder of her correspondence, Margaret jumped up and strode away without explanation. She felt too furious to speak. Richard picked up the offending letter and quickly read it. Reaching the end, he glanced up and across to Sebastian.

'Follow Margaret and see that she comes to no harm,' he ordered. The tiger immediately rose and trotted off in the direction his mistress had taken.

'What on earth is it, my son?' Gerard was starting to feel frightened.

'Warren Foster is sending his grandson, Cedric Barnsby to determine if the Haven is worthwhile continuing as a family property, or selling it.'

'Heaven help us! Has the man no sensitivities at all?' Gerard was deeply shocked.

'It doesn't end there, Father, Warren demands that Margaret show Cedric the ropes and go over the books with him. Not only that, but he suggests that Margaret should make herself pleasant to her cousin so that if he takes a fancy to her, her cousin might take care of her. She shouldn't expect marriage, but that would depend upon how well she pleases her cousin.' Although Richard spoke calmly, his lips were thin in anger.

'That is absolutely inhuman! Does he at least express any sorrow at the death of his daughter and her husband?'

Richard shook his head. 'No! Only suggestions on how Margaret may please her cousin, Cedric.' He handed Gerard the letter.

'Curse that man! He is truly a monster!' The Priest read the demands for himself before throwing it onto the table with disgust.

Coming out onto the verandah, Dalila bent down to take away the tea tray when she caught sight of both their faces. Filled with alarm, she straightened immediately and demanded to know what had happened to annoy them so. Gerard explained as Richard felt his throat close up on the words. They had expected the Housekeeper to be justifiable angry, but were taken aback when she exploded.

'That barbarian! That vile loathsome creature! He would force his own granddaughter to prostitute herself just to have a roof over her head? Let him show his face around here and I'll teach him what we do with evil abominations like him!' She stomped back into the kitchen, and could be heard slamming pots around as she worked. Stunned, Richard and Gerard could only stare at each other.

'I hope I never have cause to anger Dalila.' Father Gerard rose to his feet, preparing to leave.

Sighing, Richard scratched his head. 'I just hope this cousin doesn't do anything to incur Dalila's wrath.'

Gerard shrugged. 'If he is anything like his grandfather, then it will be more than likely.'

Richard buried his head in his hands, 'As if they haven't had excitement around here!'

Leave Her Alone

Throughout the day Richard had Manu and Kobbi check up on Margaret at hourly intervals. She had headed down to the river and sat in the shade of a tree, staring across the water. Sebastian spent most of his time sitting beside her, but when he got too hot, he encouraged Margaret to go for a swim with him.

The boys didn't attempt to talk to Margaret or intrude upon her dark musings. They supplied her with lunch and a bottle of fresh water, and although the food was gone the next time they checked on her, they weren't sure that Margaret had actually eaten it.

Kobbi regularly reported to Richard, who spent most of the day between working and keeping an eye on Elliott. The Lieutenant, learning of Warren Foster's letter was just as horrified as everyone else. *I don't understand why Richard doesn't go after Margaret, but I assume that the Professor knows what is best for her.* Elliott wasn't reluctant to remain in bed, as he seemed to tire so quickly. He didn't argue when Richard supplied him with several fiction books, and told him to stay put. That wasn't hard to obey as he slept on and off during the day.

Margaret Returns

As the day wore on and the light began to fade, Richard became more worried about Margaret's absence. He would have headed out to bring her home, but there was a small explosion in the experiment room and it was essential that it was cleaned up immediately, so that it didn't start a fire or contaminate his other experiments.

A search for Margaret wasn't needed anyway as she made her way back to the house across the field. Sebastian trotted along behind to make sure that she didn't walk off on another trek. Reaching the verandah they met Nbulungi and Adwoa and Margaret smiled for the first time in many hours.

As Adwoa gurgled and held her hands out to Margaret for a cuddle, Sebastian continued inside the house to find Richard and let him know that they were safely returned. Margaret took the baby girl into her arms and swung her around causing Adwoa to laugh in delight. Nbulungi smiled at the complete faith the baby had in Margaret as she flew through the air.

For that brief moment the lines of worry had disappeared from Margaret's features; but that moment wasn't to last very long. As Ricard came out to greet her return, she handed Adwoa back to Nbulungi.

'I'm sorry. I'm so sorry.' Margaret whispered, raising her eyes to look up into Richard's concerned face. His features relaxed in fondness.

'We're so going to have to work on some anger management for you, or you'll self-destruct.'

Margaret sighed deeply. 'I just don't understand who I am anymore.'

'You've had so much to deal with lately that I'm not surprised you're over loaded.' He kept his tone soft and supportive. 'Come on, you need to eat something.'

'I've not been hungry, but I have kept up my water so I'm not dehydrated but…' Margaret stumbled slightly and Richard placed his arm around her to steady her footsteps.

He sighed, 'I know you're upset but you can't stop eating. It can be just as harmful as if you went too long without water.'

The What Ifs

A lengthy silence followed as Richard led her inside to prepare for dinner. When Margaret spoke again, her voice was so soft that Richard had to lower his head to hear her. 'What really annoys me is the 'what ifs' that I cannot stop thinking about. What if there was no inheritance? What if the only way I could survive was to degrade myself with a stranger just so that I had somewhere to live? If I was in that position, would my grandfather still be as uncaring about my welfare and my feelings?'

'You're torturing yourself about things that you have no control over. From what your Grandmother told me of her husband, he always was a hard hearted bastard. That is why it isn't surprising that she came north with you and your parents. To help Isabella raise you was one of the only great joys in her life.'

Margaret sighed. 'I still miss Nanna, even though it is over five years since she died.'

Tenderly Richard kissed the top of her head. 'Elizabeth was a major part of your life while growing up. She taught you while Isabella ran the farm and Edward operated his clinic.'

Tears began to roll uncontrollably down Margaret's cheeks. 'I miss them so much it hurts. I feel so empty and alone.'

Richard brushed her tears away before forcing Margaret to drink some water. 'I will always be here for you.'

You Need To Eat

'I'm not very hungry. If you don't mind I'll just go to bed.' Margaret brushed her hand against Richard's cheek as she rose to her feet.

'All right, but take a jug of water with you and a couple of biscuits in case you feel hungry later.' He ordered and was surprised when she meekly obeyed him.

Dalila placed a plate on the table and looked significantly at Richard. 'You need to eat something, Professor.' This was not a suggestion, but an order. As he hesitated, and glanced back at the curtain that led to Margaret's bedroom, Dalila understood his thoughts.

'Sit and eat Sir. I'll check up on Miss Margaret.' The Housekeeper didn't wait for a reply, and as she headed for the door, Richard was forced to obey.

With the first mouthful of food, he realized that he was in fact quite hungry. *I had thought that with all that had occurred lately that I would have no appetite, but it isn't too long before my plate is empty and I am able to relax my body as well as my mind.*

Dalila reported that Margaret had fallen asleep and with Richard's assistance she got Elliott fed and settled into bed. She finally headed home to her family.

With his stomach full, Richard felt less tired. He spent a couple of hours working before he was ready to turn in. Having checked that both patients were fast asleep, Richard finally sought his couch. *I hope that we can possibly have a few drama free days in which to recover.*

FRIDAY

First Class Idiot

Margaret was a little sheepish as she emerged from her room the next morning and joined Richard and Elliott at the table for breakfast.

'How are you feeling kitten?' There was such tenderness in Richard's voice as he gently kissed her forehead, but he didn't touch her in any other way. *I need to keep her at arm's length until I sort out my own affairs.*

'Like a first class idiot!' Margaret admitted ruefully.

Richard smiled sympathetically 'Oh no, not first class, third maybe, but not first!' He was rewarded by a hint of a smile from Margaret.

'I no longer appear to have any control over what is happening to my life.'

Elliott sat at the table with his bad leg propped up on another chair. He had found a pack of cards and had been playing Patience.

'Considering all that has happened,' he said, 'that's not at all surprising. You've suffered an enormous shock. Your life will never be the same again, and that'll take time to adjust.'

Pausing as he filled his pipe, Richard studied Elliott for several minutes before he finally spoke. 'True, but unfortunately until the enemy is vanquished, there is no time for the luxury of grief. This person will be looking for any sign of weakness to attack.' Lighting his pipe, Richard called to Sebastian as he headed for the back door. The tiger got up from where he had settled on the floor beside Margaret's chair, and followed the Professor outside.

'I'm just going to check on some of my outdoor experiments,' Richard explained. 'I thought Sebastian could do with the exercise.' As he disappeared with the tiger happily following, Elliott sat frowning deep in thought. It wasn't until Dalila walked passed that he finally spoke.

'Dalila, do you know what happened to my rifle and pistols? If there is trouble coming, I'd like to check and clean my weapons so that they are ready to use.'

Startled, Dalila glanced from Elliott to Margaret. 'I'm not entirely sure Mr. Elliott. Any weapons on the property are Danso's responsibility. I'll find out for you.'

Nodding, Elliott's expression didn't immediately relax. 'Thank you! I just want to be able to do my part in any melee.'

Looking silently from Elliott's wounded shoulder to his broken leg; Dalila refrained from comment and momentarily left her patients to find out about the Lieutenant's guns.

Two Reluctant Patients

That morning was a very quiet one in the house. Once Elliott had cleaned, oiled and reloaded his guns, he set up a coffee table beside Margaret on the lounge and tried to teach her several card games. As Margaret knew only non-gambling games, it took a while for her to grasp the concept of bidding, even if it was only for fictional amounts.

Although Richard joined them for lunch, he withdrew to his experiment room to work. Dalila continuously plied Margaret with jugs of fresh cool water all day and plenty of small meals to satisfy her lack of appetite.

It appeared as if Richard's desire for an uneventful, peaceful day was about to be fulfilled. Kobbi and Manu sat quietly on the verandah playing cards. While Sebastian was warming his belly in the rays of the late afternoon sun and Margaret sat beside them still staring out into space.

Visitors From Accra

Manu was moved to protest when Sebastian suddenly jumped to his feet, and sent all the cards flying as he dashed to the steps. He stood there growling with his tail swishing angrily. Moments later the two boys heard what had upset Sebastian and they were also on their feet as two horseback riders and a wagon approached the house.

Kobbi sent Manu inside to get Richard and Elliott as he withdrew his hunting knife, positioning himself in front of Margaret. As if the possibility of danger had penetrated her trance, Margaret suddenly sat up straight and alert. She reached out to lace her fingers through the fur at the tiger's neck.

Hobbling out as fast as he could on his crutches, Elliott was followed by Manu who was carefully carrying the Lieutenant's rifle. Sitting down on the top step, Elliott swapped his crutches for the rifle. Dalia stood in the doorway as Danso and Fynn came running from the stables.

The two riders came out of their saddles and the driver of the wagon took the reins of their horses as they stepped towards the waiting group. They halted in their tracks as Elliott raised his rifle at them. One gentleman raised his eyebrows as he calmly surveyed the scene before him.

'My God, the reports said things were unsettled up here, but I never expected such a reception!'

The Lieutenant refused to lower his gun. 'Identify yourselves!'

'Charles Cedric Barnsby, but please call me Cedric. My business partner Phillip Danbar and my servant Albert.'

'If you're carrying any weapons please hand them over.'

Fynn obeyed Elliott's signal and approached to take any guns the new arrivals might possess. Margaret rose to her feet and came down the steps to greet the men.

'My apologies if we seem inhospitable but we have learnt that it is better to be cautious than dead.'

Having relinquished his arms to Fynn, Cedric Barnsby bowed. 'You must be my cousin Margaret Barnsby.'

Margaret stiffened, her eyes flashed in momentary anger, 'Munroe! I was legally adopted.'

In silent support Dalila came to stand beside Margaret, the women were careful to make sure that they didn't block the Lieutenant's line of fire.

'I'm sorry. Grandfather always refers to you as the Barnsby curse, so I only think of you as a Barnsby.' Margaret took a step back in horror.

'That is outrageous!' Dalila's maternal instincts were roused as she put her arm around Margaret's shoulder. 'Miss Margaret, you'd best leave this to the Professor to handle.' She turned her around and led her into the house.

Elliott wasn't satisfied yet about their identity. 'Do you have proof of who you are?'

Cedric's eyebrows rose again in mockery. 'Who are you to be asking?'

'Forgive me for being out of uniform, I am Lieutenant Elliott Gibbs. Have you any papers?'

'What if I refuse to hand them over?' Cedric crossed his arms.

Elliott smiled. 'I'll shoot your right knee cap off for starters.'

Phillip Danbar was moved to protest. 'For God's sake Rick give him what he wants! You know they went through hell up here, why make matters worse?' He grabbed hold of his friend's arm as he tried to reason with him.

'A sensible suggestion!' Richard's dry voice from the doorway behind Elliott caused him to jump startled. The Professor came to stand on the steps with his hands buried in his trouser pockets.

'I am Richard Evans. I couldn't get my Housekeeper to tell me what you said to distress Margaret, but we'll deal with that later. Right now I suggest you stand very, very still and don't make a sound!'

Cedric opened his mouth but Richard held up a warning finger. 'Believe me Mr. Barnsby, your life depends upon it.'

He bent down and said something to Sebastian that Elliott couldn't hear. The tiger looked up at Richard and then across at the two newcomers. He leapt up and ran full speed straight at the men. Phillip swallowed hard as he tried to contain a whimper. Cedric fought the instinct to run and closed his eyes waiting for the attack.

Sebastian brushed passed them and pounced upon a large venomous snake that had been slithering towards the men. His huge paw crushed the snake's head so that he was safe from its deadly fangs as he ripped the body apart.

Glancing around, Cedric swore colourfully as Phillip, who had turned a shade of green, threw up. Ignoring them, Sebastian trotted back to Richard with the snake's body in his mouth.

'Well done Seb!' He stroked the tiger's head. 'Why don't you go and enjoy that snack while I deal with this?'

Sebastian glanced back once at the new men before taking his prize off to the shade of a tree.

'Why the bloody hell didn't you warn us?' demanded Cedric.

Richard shook his head. 'You might've panicked and run. It would have been impossible to prevent one of you from being bitten then.'

He took off his glasses and cleaned them before putting them back on. 'I believe the Lieutenant asked for identification.

My people will look after your horses if you would care to step inside.'

Cedric Barnsby

Cedric grabbed a saddle bag off his horse and moved cautiously up the steps passed Elliott as he and Phillip followed Richard into the house. Manu and Kobbi helped Elliott to his feet and took his rifle so that he could use his crutches to get inside.

Margaret was nowhere to be seen, but Dalila came out of Margaret's bedroom, rather tight lipped. She met the questioning look Richard cast at her and shook her head. Richard calmly glanced over the documents that Cedric withdrew from the saddlebag. Satisfied, the Professor handed them back.

'What did you say to upset Margaret?' He quietly asked.

Cedric shrugged. 'Look I'm sorry about that. You'd have to understand my Grandfather's lousy sense of humour. For as long as I can remember Warren Foster has called her a curse because of the chaos that occurred due to her birth.'

Elliott's mouth dropped open in surprise. Dalila choked in disgust, but Richard calmly said, 'I see! It is advisable that you do not quote Warren Foster around here, he's not exactly our favourite person at the moment.'

'He's not anyone's favourite person! Period!'

Richard continued as if Cedric hadn't spoken. 'And if you speak derogatorily again about Margaret, I'll cut out your tongue and feed it to you.'

'You must be bloody joking!' Cedric went extremely pale.

Richard looked at him over the top of his glasses. 'I'm as serious as the Lieutenant was about blowing your kneecaps off!'

'Why you cocky little bastard!' Cedric grabbed hold of Richard by the lapel of his shirt but was interrupted by a voice from outside.

'All right Bert, that will do!' said the quiet, weary voice from the doorway. The driver of the wagon stepped into the room, discarding his hat, gloves and overcoat to reveal a very well dressed young man.

'I told you Phil that a macho Cedric wouldn't go down well. Better that they take me just as I am.' He said, smoothing back beautifully wavy hair from his eyes.

From where he sat on a couch, Elliott watched him warily. 'You're Cedric Barnsby then?'

An exquisite bow answered him. 'I do apologize for our ruse, but Phillip tried to convince me that rough and tough men of the bush would relate better to Bert than to me.'

Richard could see what he meant. *Cedric is extremely slender with a face like Adonis, a soft voice and mannerisms that are, well, quite effeminate. There is one thing bothering me, and that is the similarities in features but not mannerisms between Albert and Cedric.*

'All right Albert, perhaps you should head back to Accra tomorrow now that I'm me again.' Cedric waited until the servant had departed before sitting delicately down at the table and smiled up at Richard.

'Uncanny isn't it? The similarities? Bert, along with many others in Accra, is the son from the wrong side of the blanket. What women saw in such a rude, obnoxious and often violent man as my father, I will never understand.' Cedric sighed as he shook his head. Phillip sat down beside him and laid a hand on his arm.

'Rick, you're going to have to explain and apologize to your cousin. Bert has really made a mess of this.'

Sighing again, Cedric rose to his feet and brushed a fleck of dust from his trousers. 'As always, Phil, you are correct. Perhaps Professor Evans you could accompany me to Margaret's room?'

'That won't be necessary.' Margaret had joined them without being seen or heard. Cedric immediately stepped towards her and taking her hand into his own, he raised it to his lips. 'My dear cousin, I'm so sorry. Our switch wasn't made for the purpose to distress you.'

Margaret gently disengaged her hand. 'I still don't understand why you felt it necessary. I think if I had met you first I would've liked you.'

He placed his hand against his chest as he admitted. 'My father was always disappointed in me. He wanted me to be more like... Well anyone else so long as it wasn't who I was. I'm just grateful that he died before he could completely destroy me.' He smiled sympathetically at Margaret's look of horror. *I could never be relieved at the death of one of my parents.*

'You must think me heartless, but you are fortunate to never have known the Barnsby brothers. They were an explosion just waiting to happen. I'm sorry to say my brother; Clay has our father's temper and bad habits.' He escorted Margaret to the table, seated her before sitting down again.

Grandfather's Orders

'I was extremely sorry to hear about your parents' murder, cousin. Your mother's letters about everyday life at the farm were one of the only things that kept my mother sane. She wasn't strong like her sisters, and my father's rages made her a nervous wreck. If it wasn't for the fear of leaving us children with him, I'm sure she would have fled up here to join you.'

'No one should live in fear like that!' Margaret jumped to her feet and disappeared into her bedroom to reappear with her grandfather's letter. 'You may or may not already know what he wrote to me.' She handed the letter to Cedric as she sat down again.

'My dear cousin, this is disgraceful! I had no idea he was this cruel! Was his intention to punish you or me?' Cedric had become quite flushed in embarrassment as he passed the letter to Phillip.

Richard studied Cedric thoughtfully. 'Why would Foster want to punish you?'

Cedric sighed. 'He, too, disapproves of me. I'm not what a grandson should be and no matter how much he bullies me, am never likely to be.'

'How horrible!' Margaret placed her hand sympathetically over her cousin's. 'No wonder my parents wanted to get as far away as they could from the family!'

Phillip laid the letter down onto the dining table. 'That is so typical of the old man! Do you think he knows?' He asked Cedric, who cast a cautious glance at Margaret.

'No, no, just his usual attempt at being nasty!'

Richard and Elliott exchanged puzzled looks, but neither of them understood the meaning of the other men's conversation.

Cedric wasn't prepared to enlighten them either. 'Is it possible to put us up for a day, or if inconvenient, a change of horses and a guide?'

Richard inclined his head. 'You're more than welcome to stay with us and a guide is available whenever you need one. I assume, though, that Margaret would be going with you to show you the farm's operations?'

'My cousin's assistance would be greatly appreciated, but I, unlike my grandfather, had no intention of causing her any additional pain.'

Sighing, Margaret shook her head. 'I must return to the Haven. I want to see my parents' graves as well as collect any belongings grandfather has graciously allowed me to have.'

Cedric didn't miss the touch of sarcasm in Margaret's voice and smiled sympathetically. 'Welcome to the family my dear! Believe me you were much better off being well out of it all.'

As Margaret knew not how to answer this, it was a welcome respite when Dalila appeared with the offer of cold drinks.

I Must Do This

It was decided that the journey to the Haven would begin first thing the next morning. That way they wouldn't have to camp overnight. Elliott wanted to accompany Margaret, but both she and Richard firmly vetoed him going anywhere. *It's essential for him to rest if he is to heal,* decided Margaret. *I don't see why Richard or Father Gerard need to go as well, as it could be at least a week before I return to Richard's farm.*

Although Richard has denied that I am distracting him from his work I'm all too aware of the important nature of his research and experiments. I can't see Cedric as being a danger to me, and I wonder what he would say about our assassin fears being family related?

The rest of the day, thankfully was a quiet one. Albert approached Margaret and apologized for what he had said. He admitted that having always been referred to as Bert the Bastard; he was insensitive to being called names. Margaret was again horrified and was again left feeling that she did not want to have anything to do with this cruel and inhumane family.

Sebastian's History

Later, Phillip came across Margaret sitting on the verandah brushing Sebastian. The tiger obviously didn't mind this grooming, because he readily rolled on to his back so that Margaret could brush his belly. Phillip looked on in awe.

'That is amazing!'

Sebastian was immediately on his feet and standing in front of Margaret to protect her. She pulled loose fur out of the brush and added it to the pile beside her.

'It is necessary to bath and brush Sebastian occasionally to keep him free from fleas, ticks and such like.' Margaret explained, patting the tiger's back reassuringly.

'Even so; to see such a wild creature acting like a domestic pet,' Phillip offered his hand to Sebastian to show that it was weaponless. The tiger lay down again beside Margaret and Phillip lowered himself into a chair.

'How does a tiger come to be in Africa?' Phillip asked.

'When I was 14, a big game hunter living up north had been stocking his property with exotic game from all over the world. Sheena, Sebastian's mother, was captured in India and shipped over here. What the hunters didn't know was that Sheena was pregnant at the time. It was a stressful journey and Sebastian was the only cub to survive.'

'While the bearers were carting the tigers north, they were set upon by Ashanti warriors and wounded they ended up at our hospital. Papa did all he could to save Sheena but she had suffered too much damage and died. Sebastian was too young for the bearers to deliver to their boss as he needed to be hand reared. So he's been with me ever since.'

Father Gerard's Decision

The sound of a horse approaching the house at a sedate pace caused Sebastian to rise to his feet once more. The lone rider was no stranger, though, and the tiger sat down again as he recognised Father Gerard. The Priest flung his reins over a railing before stepping up onto the verandah. Phillip rose nervously to his feet as the large German made an impressive figure.

'Father Gerard, this is Phillip Danbar,' introduced Margaret. The two men shook hands, but Gerard wore a frown as he addressed Margaret.

'Danbar? I thought your cousin's name was Barnsby?'

'I'm a friend of Cedric Barnsby,' Phillip explained as they both sat down.

'Come for a bit of adventure huh? Danbar? I knew a fellow of that name out in these parts. Old enough to be your father, but he never had any children, well legitimate ones any way! Gold mining was his obsession. Don't suppose he was any relation?'

Phillip laughed. 'That sound like Uncle Ernest.'

'Ernie! That's it! Well now how about a drink for an old man?' Gerard said, even though Margaret was already rising to her feet and she disappeared inside with Sebastian close on her heels.

Stepping out of the house, Cedric was startled to find Phillip in conversation with a stranger. 'Good evening, I'm Cedric Barnsby. There is no need to introduce yourself, Father. Aunt Isabella's letters described you perfectly.' The two men shook hands.

'I hope you've not brought your grandfather with you Mr. Barnsby. He won't be welcome here after his callous words to Margaret.'

Cedric sighed. 'Ah yes! That infernal letter! I'm not surprised it has upset everyone. I have no intention to force my cousin to degrade herself so that she has a roof over her head.'

'I am glad to hear that!' There was a note of steel in the Priest's voice that belied his good humoured features.

'We've just been discussing Uncle Ernest, apparently Father Gerard knew him.'

Cedric's face broke into a broad smile, 'Old Ernie? The mad uncle you were never allowed to ask about? Was he really such a wild card?'

Gerard's smile was reminiscent. 'Always ready for a bit of fun. Full of energy and mischief, no one had a bad word to say about Ernie. Generous too, if his neighbours were having lean times, he would share what he had. He may have had a few odd habits but who doesn't?'

Cedric laughed. 'Now that is the sort of relative I'd like to have. Mine are rather boring and dull.'

Phillip shook his head, 'Hardly that Rick! A husband and wife who murder each other. Their child adopted by her aunt and uncle and they flee to the jungle. Your grandmother leaves her husband and goes with them. Let alone what your brother Clay and cousin Stephen have got up to in the past!'

Cedric threw his hands up in defeat. 'I must learn not to make rash statements in front of a friend who has known me from the cradle!'

When Margaret brought out drinks for everyone, Cedric took the tray from her and assisted in serving the refreshment. It gave him the opportunity to draw her to one side for a more private conversation.

'Are you absolutely certain that you need to come with us tomorrow? I just wish to spare you as much heartache as possible.'

Grateful for his concern, Margaret managed a smile. 'I'm afraid it is essential; for my own sake and for yours. I don't feel that I can truly accept that my parents are dead until I see their graves.'

Cedric lay a sympathetically a hand on her shoulder. 'I understand, but why for my sake?'

'The people at the Haven will be waiting for me to return. If you show up alone, you could be considered as a hostile takeover. You would be dead before you're even able to explain your legal right to be there. The workers are very loyal to my parents and their future now hangs in the balance.'

Cedric stroked his chin as he considered this. 'So really we need your protection.' There was a lurking smile in his eyes that Margaret did not fail to see.

'Indeed yes! The stories that Grandmama told about her husband made us all believe that he was some kind of demon. The villagers will be afraid of their fate in his hands.'

Cedric sighed. 'If they actually met him, they'd know that their fears are justified!'

'Margaret,' Father Gerard's deep voice brought them back to the group. 'Danbar has been telling me that you're returning to the Haven tomorrow. What time are we leaving in the morning?'

'We?' Cedric's eyebrows rose in surprise.

'Of course, the Lieutenant must recover from his wounds and Richard is busy with his work. Besides which, I want to make certain that those who died have been properly buried,' explained Gerard.

Margaret laid her hand over his. 'Thank you Father. I didn't wish to impose upon you, but I would be grateful for your support. There is no need to set off at first light; after breakfast would be a suitable time.'

Gerard patted her hand, 'Good! Ja! I'll be here then.'

Phillip's brow creased into a frown. 'How dangerous is it the closer we get to Ashanti land?'

Margaret's thoughts flew back to Manu's butchered village. 'Nothing can be taken for granted. Not the land, the animals or the people. My father's reputation with the surrounding villages means we shall be welcomed and left alone.'

'We'll be sufficiently armed,' Gerard added. 'You'll take Kobbi with you, but what of the boy and the baby?'

Margaret rested one side of the cold glass against her forehead. 'They'll remain here. Adwoa is bonding with Nbulungi and I don't wish to break that connection.'

'Good!' Father Gerard rose to his feet. 'I'll just have a word with Richard,' he said as he strode into the house.

Father Gerard didn't remain long at the farm. He regretfully declined joining them for dinner as he had a great deal to do if he was to be ready for an early start the next day. Richard made no mention of what he discussed with the Priest, and no one tried to force him to reveal the conversation.

Wouldn't You Rather Go?

Whether or not the Professor was disappointed that Gerard and not he would escort Margaret home wasn't evident by his mood or manner. He was a genial host during dinner and even sat through a couple of hands of cards before suggesting an early night.

As he assisted Elliott to bed, the Lieutenant finally asked the question that was burning on his lips.

'Wouldn't you rather be going with Margaret tomorrow?'

Richard shook his head. 'It's more logical this way.' At Elliott's stunned expression, Richard smiled. 'I may be a fair shot but Gerard is a crack marksman. Surprising for a priest but he has been out here a long time. Believe me Margaret will be well protected.'

'But the horror she is going back to!'

His smile disappearing, Richard nodded. 'I know. Even if I was there, I couldn't take the pain away. Margaret must deal with the loss before she can move on.'

Elliott made room for Richard to join him in the bed. They would share so that the couches were free for Cedric and Phillip.

'That will be so hard,' Elliott added.

Richard nodded, putting out the candle. 'Unfortunately that's life!'

SATURDAY

A Not So Restful Night

Even though they didn't plan an early start, Margaret was still up and dressed in male attire as usual at dawn. Dalila found her seated on the verandah; her knees brought up under her chin as she stared unseeing ahead. The Housekeeper heart ached at the look of forlorn and knew that no one could take this journey for her.

'Have you had anything to eat yet Miss Margaret?'

Shaking her head, Margaret came back to the present. 'No, I didn't want to wake any one.' She uncoiled herself and rose to her feet. 'Shall I start the toast?'

The two women entered the house together. 'You could set the table for me, and then we'll see what else needs doing.' They worked quietly away at the routine activity, for the moment it distracted Margaret from her worries.

When Richard emerged from his bedroom, he didn't look like he had slept very well. He was moving slightly awkwardly and seemed to be in some pain. Immediately solicitous, Margaret wanted to know if there was anything that she could do to help him.

He managed a rueful grin. 'I don't recommend sharing a bed with a man with a cast who tosses and turns.'

'So you barely slept? But why are you so sore?'

Richard looked away as colour flooded across his tanned cheeks. 'I copped the cast in a rather sensitive area.'

Frowning, Margaret had to think about what he said for a minute before realization struck her, 'Oh dear! I'm not sure what to recommend for that.'

'I'll be all right.' He headed to the bathroom as their guests on the couches began to stir.

Breakfast was rather a subdued meal as Margaret ate what Dalila put in front of her because she knew she needed to prepare for the arduous journey ahead and not because she was hungry. Having finished his own breakfast outside, Sebastian reappeared and cleaned up any leftovers. There was nothing wrong with his appetite.

Why Aren't I Going?

Margaret slipped two pebbles into her pocket for luck like her father had always done when travelling to the city but would leave the bags of pebble people behind with Richard. *They'd always brought Papa back safely to us. That memory makes me realize that returning to the Haven; I will be inundated by reminders of my parents.*

A rather upset Manu dragged Margaret out to sit on the steps of the verandah. 'Don't you like me any more, Miss Margaret?'

She placed an arm around Manu's shoulders. 'Of course I do!'

'Then why is Kobbi going with you and not me?' The tears he had manfully been trying to contain began to fall.

'It's not because I don't want you with me, but you and Adwoa will be much safer here. Out there is someone who wants to kill me. Also there is someone who wanted to destroy your whole village. Taking you with me might expose you to double the danger. Kobbi wants to see if his family and friends survived.'

Manu sniffed. 'I see.'

'Besides which,' Margaret wiped his tears away. 'I have an important job for you here. You're Adwoa's only link to her family. She is only a baby; she wouldn't understand that you meant to come back. It would be very disturbing for her if you weren't here to protect her.'

'Protect her? Me?' The 10-year-old boy looked incredulous.

Margaret nodded. 'Who kept her safe through the attack on the village? Who brought her safely here? You did! You're the big brother she needs to look out for her.'

'We're not siblings.' Manu shook his head.

Margaret sighed. 'You may be the closest thing you have to each other as kin. Blood counts! Adwoa's mother knew that she could trust you to look after her baby. Until we discover who would want to destroy your family, it's best to remain out of sight. I won't be away long, and Richard has a couple of his people investigating the destruction of your village and several others which have suffered the same fate. They should report back soon.'

'Wouldn't it be safer for you to stay here too?'

Sadly she nodded. 'Yes, but I have business that must be taken care of at the Haven.'

Manu hugged her tightly. 'Hurry back to us Miss Margaret.'

Tears shone in Margaret's eyes as she returned his embrace. 'I will.'

Setting Off

Father Gerard arrived as Fynn and Albert were finishing harnessing up the horses and wagons. Albert would return to Accra once he had seen his half-brother set off in the opposite direction. Phillip and Cedric shook hands with Richard before mounting their horses. Kobbi hugged Manu before he jumped up onto the box seat of Richard's wagon and took the reins from Fynn. Sebastian leapt easily into the back of the wagon, and settled down. Margaret was trying to reassure a teary eyed Dalila that the journey was going to be all right this time.

Managing to disentangle herself from the Housekeeper, Margaret was submitted to a bear like hug from Elliott. *I won't be there to protect her this time and I feel the inadequacy of my condition.*

'I'll be all right! Don't fuss or I'll start to cry!' Although Margaret joked, it was close to the truth. Richard extracted Margaret from the Lieutenant's hold and escorted her to the waiting wagon.

'You'll be back before you know it.' Richard reassured in his calm, no nonsense manner. He took her hand and held it for a moment. 'Just promise me that you'll be careful.'

Knowing that if she spoke, she would start crying, Margaret nodded her head before throwing her arms around Richard's neck to embrace him. A little surprised at her open display of affection, he returned her hug and pressed a gentle kiss on the top of her hair.

'Come on kitten, it's time to go.' Richard unlocked her arms and assisted her up on to the box seat beside Kobbi. There was no stopping her tears now, and Margaret uttered a sob as Richard pressed the palm of her hand against his lips before releasing her.

Being Left Behind

The convoy headed off with Father Gerard leading the way. Richard remained standing where they had left him until they were out of sight. He walked slowly back up the steps to join a solemn Dalila, Elliott and Manu.

'Don't start imagining horrific scenarios,' ordered Richard. 'It'll be all right! We must believe that or we'll all be basket cases by the time Margaret returns!'

Nodding, Elliott exhaled slowly. 'Yeah, it's just… She makes you care a whole damn lot about what happens to her.'

Dalila looked at him startled. 'You're not falling in love with Miss Margaret are you?'

Elliott blushed. 'Aren't we all? Oh I don't mean in the husband and wife kind of way... It's just... Margaret is special, that's all!'

'Amen to that!' Dalila placed her arm around Manu's shoulder. 'Come along young man. I believe Fynn could use some help in the stables today.' She led him away, everyone knowing that what the Housekeeper had said wasn't true but it was important to keep busy.

The Necessary Journey

The morning's travelling was marked without incident, and they stopped in the heat of the day to have lunch and rest the horses. A strange subdued atmosphere hung over the group. Their conversation was light and meaningless as the real possibility of danger made them ultra-aware of every little thing around them.

Kobbi was wary of the three strangers. *I know that it's possibly someone in Miss Margaret's own family wants her dead, but somehow this cousin doesn't seem to be the murdering type. Mr Cedric is a puzzle to me, I've never met anyone like him before.* Even so, when Cedric noticed the youth watching him, he smiled and Kobbi couldn't help but smile back.

Father Gerard snoozed as Phillip and Margaret debated Darwinism. It wasn't long, though, before they were heading off once more. As every hour brought them closer and closer to the Haven, more than one stomach was tied up in knots. As the sun began to set, they all wondered what would be waiting for them.

As the surroundings became more familiar, Margaret became quieter and paler. Her whole body began to shake as they entered the Haven's perimeter, and although Father Gerard knew that it wasn't cold, that made her tremble, he placed a blanket around her.

Guards were still positioned around the farm and there were looks of surprise and relief to see Margaret return. They bowed and raised their hats as the convoy rode past. Margaret's face had frozen so that she could neither speak nor smile, but she managed to raise her hand to acknowledge the guards' salutes.

The workers will have gone home for the day, which I'm grateful for, as I'm not able to deal with a lot of people. As the horses slowed down outside the main house, tears were streaming down Margaret's cheeks. The memories were so raw and painful. *I half expect to see my mother glide down the front stairs to greet us as she always did at our return from the jungle.*

I Need To See Them!

As Busara, the Housekeeper, ran down to meet them; Margaret realized, *I'll never see my mother again! Never to hear her soft no nonsense voice, her gentle laugh or the beautiful singing voice that rang out every Sunday.*

'I can't deal with this,' Margaret whispered, rigid with fear.

Father Gerard lifted her down out of the wagon. 'You've come this far, dear child! You must go on!'

Busara watched cautiously, not knowing what to do. Wanting so much to comfort Margaret, but realised that she was about to explode.

'I… I must see them.' Margaret's words were barely audible.

'Tomorrow. You don't have to deal with everything straight away.' Gerard tried to guide her into the house, but Margaret remained like a stone statue.

She raised pleading eyes to his face. 'Please! I need to see them! I have to know…' Her voice broke off as she found it impossible to complete the sentence.

Unable to bear her pain Cedric turned away to focus on organizing the stabling of the horses and the removal of their luggage.

Busara placed her arm around Margaret's waist but addressed Gerard, 'It's all right Father. I'll take her to where they lie. If you could look after the gentlemen till I return.'

Gerard could do nothing but nod in agreement. *This is more painful for me than I thought it would be. Until this moment, I hadn't recognized my own loss of two good friends.* Both Cedric and Phillip felt like intruders and desperately out of place. Father Gerard pulled himself together and urged the young men to follow him into the house. *I'll have to try and make them feel welcome, but the feelings of intrusion and awkwardness is not going to go away very easily.*

How Am I supposed To Go On?

Margaret's feet felt like they were made of concrete as the Housekeeper led her to the place where the graves of Isabella and Edward Munroe now lay beside that of her grandmother, Elizabeth Foster.

Beautiful headstones had been erected with the names etched into them. Both the new mounds of earth were completely covered with a colourful array of flowers. Tears flowing uncontrollably, Margaret fell to her knees and sobbed.

'Miss Margaret?' *I'm not sure whether I should stay or leave.*

Margaret raised her face and managed a weak smile. 'I'll be all right Busara. I'll come back to the house before it gets dark,' she promised. As Busara left she thought, *I don't like the idea of leaving Miss Margaret, but she obviously needs time alone to say goodbye to her parents.*

Margaret laid a hand on top of each mound. 'Please forgive me!' She begged as her tears splashed down on to her hands. 'I should never have left you! We were a family. I should've shared the same fate. How could you leave me behind? How am I supposed to go on without you?' She collapsed beside the graves, sobbing uncontrollable, as she asked over and over again, 'Why?'

For a long time Margaret lay like this, her crying the only other sound to be heard apart from the breeze blowing in the trees. The light was rapidly fading but Margaret didn't leave her vigil. She jumped slightly when she felt Sebastian beside her and tried to lick away her tears. Slowly Margaret struggled to sit upright and placed her arms around the tiger's neck.

'I just don't understand Seb! Why did they have to be taken away?'

Sebastian, naturally, had no answers for her, but sat very still while Margaret clung to him for comfort. The sun had completely disappeared by the time Margaret finally managed to rise to her feet. *I'm not afraid of the dark, but I am vaguely aware that darkness is an ally to someone trying to kill me, so I must reluctantly leave my parents' graves and head back to the house.*

Overpowering Grief

Here, the knife in the breast is thrust deeper as memories flood in on me; the delicate scent of my mother's perfume, the book still lying open where my father had left it. A thousand and one little things that serve as a reminder of the parents so cruelly snatched from me, the life I'll never have again. Every sight, every sound, every smell is an overpowering memory, and it is too much for me to accept. She started crying hysterically. Gerard tried to restrain her in the fear that she could try and hurt herself, but Margaret broke away, screaming.

Sebastian was as supportive as the next man, but a high pitched wail he could not deal with. He backed away and waited outside for the storm to quieten down. The men looked helplessly at each other, but Busara just tut-tutted. She took Margaret by the shoulders and led her off to her bedroom. She had been prepared for this collapse and had ready a sleeping draught to knock Margaret out for a few hours.

Busara prepared them a cold supper, and although none of them felt like eating, they went through the motions. Cedric sighed, *we hadn't known what to expect when we finally arrived and the result is rather disturbing. Our welcome hasn't been hostile, but Margaret's grief is overpowering.*

There was no protest when Father Gerard suggested an early night after such a long ride. Busara made up a couple of couches for the visitors and Gerard was reluctant to use the master bedroom. *I may be more in command of my grief, but I cannot sleep in their bed.* Sebastian crept into Margaret's room when she was asleep, intent upon watching over her.

SUNDAY

Nightmares

Cedric had not slept well. He had been tired enough after another full day of riding, but Margaret's grief had touched him deeply. He had dreamt that, having been accused of killing Isabella and Edward, he was being strung up on a huge cross. As he screamed his innocence, the locals had built a fire at his feet and set it alight. He could almost feel the rough sandpapery sensation of the flames licking his face.

Cedric jerked awake. *Flames are not rough and sandpapery!* Sebastian was sitting beside his couch, licking his face to get him to wake up. A drowsy Phillip still lay on the opposite couch, but was propped up on one elbow.

'You were moaning,' Phillip explained as Sebastian raised his paw to pat Cedric's shoulder to make sure he was awake.

Cedric looked dubiously at the large cat that was nose to nose with him. 'He wasn't trying to eat me was he?'

A laugh came from the dining table where Father Gerard was leisurely eating his breakfast, 'Nein! He's very gentle if you're not a threat.'

Satisfied that Cedric was all right, Sebastian rose to his feet and silently padded out of the house. Sitting up, Cedric ran a hand a couple of times over his face.

'I'm not used to dealing with nightmares.'

Father Gerard's eyebrows rose. 'A cold shower will set you right.'

Cedric shivered in horror. 'No thank you! Are you going to allow Margaret to sleep in?' He rose and stretched. Gerard paused in raising his coffee cup to his lips.

'Margaret is not only already up and dressed, but has been out of the house for at least an hour.'

Cedric looked startle. 'I hope she isn't alone.'

Gerard continued to drink his coffee, 'Nein! She is with Yao, the Haven Property Manager. I believe she intends to address the locals.'

'I'd better get cleaned up if I'm to attend that.' Cedric headed for the bathroom.

'Is that wise?' Phillip was frowning.

Cedric paused to look back at him. 'Better to be open with these people than thought to be hiding in the house too frightened to meet them.'

Gerard nodded, 'Ja! Good point. I'll let Busara know that you're ready for breakfast.'

'Thank you.' Cedric went to wash and change. *I'm not certain that the knot in my stomach will actually allow me to eat anything.*

Margaret's Assurances

A large pavilion had been erected many years ago as a shady place to spend the lunch break. During the hottest time of the day, a couple of hours' rest made the hard slog of farming more endurable. Now, at the beginning of a new day, not only the workers, but also nearly all of the villagers gathered in the pavilion.

Word had spread like wildfire that Margaret had returned, and they were agog to not only hear of her adventures, but also learn of their own future. To a silent audience, Margaret had just got to the part where she learnt that the Haven reverts back to her Grandfather, when Cedric joined her.

An outcry rose, not at his presence, but at Margaret's words. Not only were they all loyal to Margaret, but the villagers had heard many stories from Elizabeth Foster about her husband. The thought of him taking over frightened them and Margaret waited until they had settled down a little before she continued to address them.

'It's not at all likely that Grandfather would ever come here personally. What he plans to do with the Haven will depend upon how viable he thinks it is. It doesn't matter if he intends to keep the property or sell it. Either way, whoever runs the Haven they'll need a work force and what better than one that is already familiar with the farm and locality? Don't fear for your livelihood. You will be taken care of.' At Margaret's calm but insistent words, the villagers' alarm eased a little.

Margaret turned to Cedric and surprised him by taking his hand. 'It would be wise to make it seem like we are best of friends. Being Grandfather's agent won't be easy for you,' she whispered before turning back to address the group.

'This is my cousin Cedric Barnsby, and although he is here to assess the worth of the farm, he's not our enemy. With his help, I may be able to buy the Haven back from my Grandfather when I come into my inheritance.'

The glares that had been cast at Cedric now altered to looks of approval.

'Any questions he may have I want you to answer as honestly and courteously as possible. To ensure your place here I must convince my grandfather that you're reliable and trustworthy. I know that you all are, but we must send back a good report.'

Looking across at Yao, Margaret asked, 'Has payment continued even though Mama…' she broke off, her throat closing up and she fought to contain a sob. For a moment she closed her eyes as she attempted to overcome the desire to burst into tears. As she swayed unsteadily, Cedric placed his arm around her waist to steady her. Yao hastened to answer so that Margaret didn't need to complete the question.

'Yes Miss Margaret. Busara showed me how Mrs. did pay day. All is in order.'

Margaret exhaled slowly and opening her eyes, they were gleaming with unshed tears. 'Good!' She included the villagers in her next words. 'Work will continue as normal, and payments will be as normal. Nothing changes until we find out what Grandfather Foster decides. Don't worry about the future. I'll take care of everything.'

Cedric could feel Margaret begin to collapse and he tightened his hold on her.

'Work as normal then,' said Yao. 'Tonight, Busara asked me to inform you that there will be a wake-feast to say goodbye to our beloved brothers and sisters. Anyone able to assist in the preparation, see Busara.'

Margaret Collapses

A cry went out through the crowd as Margaret's legs finally crumbled and Cedric scooped her up into his arms. She had passed out.

'If I can leave you in charge, Yao, I'll take her back up to the house?' asked Cedric, not happy by the lack of colour in Margaret's cheeks.

'Of course Mr. Cedric, Be careful with her.'

'I intend to!'

When Cedric burst into the house carrying Margaret, Father Gerard knocked over his chair in his haste to get to his feet.

'What happened?' He demanded as Cedric laid his fair armful on a lounge.

'She fainted. Too emotional.' Hearing commotion, Busara had rushed in.

'We need water Busara!' Gerard ordered checking Margaret's pulse. The Housekeeper returned with not only a glass and a jug but also a cloth and a bowl of water. Soaking the cloth, she laid it on Margaret's forehead and removed her boots before raising her legs.

Margaret slowly opened her eyes. 'What happened?' She accepted the glass of water that Gerard pressed into her hand and drank it all down.

'You fainted,' explained Cedric, straightening up from where he had been kneeling beside her.

'Did I make a fool of myself?'

Cedric couldn't help smiling, 'Not at all! You spoke very well until you tried to mention your mother. I think they'll understand that is a raw subject for a while.'

'Ja! Ja!' Nodding, Gerard patted her hand. 'Now, you must rest.'

Margaret shook her head. 'There is too much to do. I have to see how much damage they did to the hospital, and then there are the farm accounts. Cedric will want to see them.' She tried to get up, but the Priest held her down.

'Nein! All that must wait. Now you rest. I will have no arguments!' Margaret had never heard him so forceful.

'It's just…'

Sighing, Gerard took her hand, 'Ja! You wish it all to be over and done with, I know! To run around like a chook with its head cut off is not going to help you. You're emotionally unstable. Trust me to advise you.'

Margaret nodded. 'I'll go and lie down on my own bed then.' Cedric assisted her to her feet, but Busara escorted her to her bedroom.

What We Came Here To Do

Cedric and Phillip glanced at each other and then back to Father Gerard.

'What happens now?' asked Cedric

Father Gerard stroked his beard as he thought about it. 'You should talk to Yao about an overview of the running of the farm, Herr Barnsby. If you want to help, Herr Danbar, see Busara about what you can do. Tonight's feast is very important, and there is a great deal of work to be done.'

Cedric frowned. 'Is this wake really suitable for Margaret? She is on very shaky ground as it is.'

'Margaret has grown up with this tradition. It would be alien to her if a wake wasn't held for her parents. There will be good food, lots of reminiscent stories, laughter, and ja, lots of tears. It'll be painful to watch Margaret cry her heart out, but tonight she might just sleep a little easier.'

Cedric meekly accepted the rebuke. 'I'll go and find the Manager.'

'Wear a hat,' called out Phillip as Cedric headed for the door, and he paused to pull his hat off the coat rack. Having carefully donned his headwear, Cedric sighed as he flicked dust off his jacket sleeve.

'It must really tickle the old man's warped humour to have sent me on such a disagreeable mission. I wonder if he'll be disappointed if we make it back alive?'

Father Gerard looked startled, but Phillip only laughed.

'No man could be as bad as that can he?' asked the Priest.

Phillip shrugged his shoulders elegantly. 'You've never actually met Warren Foster have you?' He left it at that as he went in search of the Housekeeper.

Gerard pulled himself together and went to inspect the damage to the hospital. *I want to see it for myself before letting Margaret anywhere near it!*

Not Right Now

Father Gerard came back to the house from his visit to the hospital, rather pale. The assassins had set the hospital alight, and not all the patients had managed to escape the burning building. The villagers had removed the remains and given them a proper burial along with those killed defending the farm.

A smell of death still hangs over the hospital and the only sane thing to do will be to completely demolish the building. Not that I can see Warren Foster continuing to supply medical assistance to the local people, or anyone else for that matter.

Quietly opening Margaret's bedroom door to check if she was still sleeping, Father Gerard was momentarily horrified when he saw that her room was completely empty. His heart began to race as panic started to set in. *Has Margaret left the house? Where would she go? In what state of mind is she in? What is she capable of doing? Where to start my search?* In despair, Gerard called out, 'Margaret?' He had no real expectation of receiving a reply and nearly fainted when he heard her voice.

'I'm here.'

As his heartbeat slowed to a more normal speed, Father Gerard actually noticed that the door to the main bedroom was open and a long white tail was sticking out.

Unconscious of what he was doing, Gerard crossed himself in relief. 'Thank you God!' He stepped carefully over Sebastian who lay sprawled out on the floor of the bedroom and received another shock. Margaret, although she was crying, was actually neatly packing her parents clothing into a trunk.

'Dear child! There's no need for you to do this straight away.'

Margaret managed a weak smile. 'It has got to be done some time, and I can't just lie on my bed and feel sorry for myself.'

'What if you get to keep the Haven?'

She shook her head. 'Let's be honest, Father that isn't likely is it? I can't see my Grandfather suddenly changing his character. I'm not certain that I could continue to live here day after day with constant reminders of my parents. I would never, for a single second, be able to stop thinking how monstrous it is that their innocent lives were cut short.'

Gerard sat down on the edge of the bed. 'Do you think you won't think about it every day, no matter where you lived?'

Inclining her head, Margaret accepted that. 'More than likely, but there wouldn't be everywhere a visual reminder of the travesty.'

Gerard couldn't argue with that. 'What about these people? What will happen to them if you just give up the fight?'

Anger sparked in her eyes. 'I'm not giving up! Whatever Grandfather decides to do with the Haven I will ensure that he takes care of the villagers! I will not allow him to cast them aside like a pair of old shoes!' This show of spirit soothed some of Father's concern about Margaret. He bent over to stroke Sebastian's head.

'Keep an eye on her please.' Rising to his feet, Gerard decided he needed some fresh air, and some time alone to regain his composure.

Together We Grieve

The midday meal was a cold compilation thrown together by Margaret, as Busara was very busy cooking for the feast. That afternoon, Cedric sat down with the farm's accounts while Phillip and Sebastian went with Margaret to inspect the hospital. Gerard had tried to dissuade Margaret from going, but she had to see the damage for herself. *Gone are the days when my innocence can be protected. There is no hiding any more from reality; it is there in my face and issuing a challenge. I'm not about to run; I have to face the enemy and not flinch!*

The men finished up work for the day and after a quick wash they soon joined their women. The aroma of the cooking meat was mouth watering and enticing with everyone eager to get the feast started. No one, though, would touch so much as a mouthful until Margaret appeared.

An absolute silence fell over those assembled as the back door to the house opened. Phillip dragged in a sharp breath and Cedric's eyebrows rose into his hairline. Neither had seen Margaret in a dress before and the one she was wearing now was absolutely stunning. It was startling in its severity of black and was amazing in its contrast to her white hair, which was elegantly styled into a topknot.

'She is absolutely beautiful!' Phillip's whispered exclamation caused Father Gerard to smile.

'She is no matter what she wears.'

Phillip blushed. 'Yes, but… That is a majestic picture!'

The Priest chuckled. 'Tonight Margaret is a Queen! When she leaves this place she will be dethroned.'

Phillip shook his head. 'No! It won't matter who ends up owning the Haven, Margaret will always be the rightful ruler in their hearts.'

'Which does not bode well for the new owners, ja?' Gerard nodded.

Yao and Busara approached Margaret and bowed low. In return she hugged them both before addressing all gathered in the pavilion.

'My friends! I thank each and every one of you for your efforts and support, not just today, but since our first arrival at the Haven. We've shared so much together during the years that it is only fitting that we now share our grief for the loved ones we have all lost. As we share this meal, we'll remember good times and hard times, but most importantly we will remember that we've never given up on each other, and with God's help, we never will!'

A thunderous applause rang out from the villagers. 'Three cheers for Miss Margaret!' Someone called out. Tears entered Margaret's eyes as they cheered her.

'Thank you my friends! Now let's eat!' Another cheer followed and the feast officially began.

Rather limply Margaret sat down beside Father Gerard as the crowds filed out of the pavilion to be served. Phillip and Cedric had risen to join the queue, but paused as Margaret closed her eyes and sighed.

'Won't you get something to eat cousin?' asked Cedric, rather worried at how pale she looked.

'Later; when everyone else is fed, go on, you don't want to miss out. You might never attend a feast like this again.'

The two young men glanced across at Father Gerard, but he nodded. 'It's all right. I'll stay with her.'

As they departed, Margaret said to Gerard, 'I'm all right. Go and get some dinner, Father. I have Sebastian here.' Margaret reached out to run her fingers through the tiger's fur as he sat quietly beside her.

'Do not move please.' Gerard went to join Phillip and Cedric and didn't see the single tear that fell down Margaret's cheek.

The evening was exactly as Father Gerard had predicted. There was a lot of laughter, a lot of tears, tremendous food and continuous story telling. Margaret was awfully silent, contributing little to the conversations and managed to eat very little of the meal that Cedric brought her.

'Do you remember when we…' stories continued well after sundown. Phillip felt more than at any other time, that he and Cedric were intruders. *We aren't a part of this world, a part of these memories and yet the villagers do not shun us for this. We had been made welcome because Margaret had vouched for us,* mused Cedric. *So as we listen to the reminiscing, we learn about a type of family alien to the metropolis. This family is not about blood, money or possessions; it is about loyalty, fairness, sharing the good and the bad and returning to the community more than you take from it.* Cedric wasn't surprised that his cousin spent most of the evening in tears, he was deeply moved himself. *Margaret has lost not just her parents but a whole village full of family. The lifestyle the Munroes had created was probably the nearest thing to heaven. Who is prepared to kill to get it though, and what is their next move?*

MONDAY

Packing Up

After such a long night, it wasn't surprising that Cedric and Phillip slept in. Margaret finished emptying her parents' bedroom and started on the next room. She was surprised that even though they had lived a simple life, they had accumulated quite a lot of personal possessions.

Even though Grandfather Foster had been very limiting in what I'm allowed to have, I'm going to take what I want. Although I'll leave enough Manchester for whoever takes over the farm, but there are certain things, that either Grandmama or Mama had embroidered, like bed quilts, that I will not let go.

Cedric agreed, promising to help move everything out of the house if she wanted it. Margaret was touched, but she could not take the furniture. It wouldn't be fair to the person taking over, and Richard didn't really have room for another house-full of furniture. Cedric insisted that Margaret take the good silver cutlery, which was only used for special occasions. It had been a wedding present to Isabella and Edward from Felicia.

Halfies!

A scream from outside had Father Gerard grabbing his rifle and following the others out towards the shouting. It was some time before they could make out what was being screamed.

'Halfies! Halfies! We're under attack by Halfies!'

A gang of horsemen could be seen approaching, but Phillip glanced across to Margaret and asked, 'What is a Harpy?'

'Not Harpy, but Halfies,' explained Margaret as she shook her head. 'They're a band of illegitimate children of white farmers and native women. These particular half-bloods are rarely acknowledged by their fathers and have joined forces to become a band of outlaws. What they cannot steal, they destroy.'

'So what do they want here?' Phillip asked as men came running from all over the farm, armed with anything they could lay their hands on.

Father Gerard checked the sights of his gun. 'They must have heard about the Munroes' deaths and hope to lay claim to the Haven.'

'Over my dead body!' Yao growled and was seconded by the other workers.

Cedric heaved a deep sigh. 'It shouldn't come to that!' He promised. 'Kobbi, could you fetch my pistols from my bag?' The youth ran back into the house as the horsemen came to a thundering halt in front of the waiting group.

Calmly, Cedric lit a cigarette as the Halfies dismounted from their horses.

Yao swallowed hard and stepped forward. 'This is private property! What do you want here?' Yao tried to put confidence into his voice even though he didn't feel it.

The leader's lip twisted into a sneer. 'The Munroes are dead, so we're here to stake our claim. Lay down your arms and the takeover can be a peaceful one.'

'Never!' Yao snarled into the leader's face. The Haven workers moved forward a little to back up their Manager. Tension crackled in the air as both sides waited impatiently for the other to make a move.

'What is your name?' Cedric's calm question broke the tension, and those gathered looked at him in surprise.

'What?'

Cedric carefully flicked cigarette ash off his sleeve. 'I asked, "What is your name?"'

'What's it to you?' The leader sized up Cedric. *This fine gentleman is no threat!*

Cedric blew a smoke ring. 'You see, I like to at least know the name of the man I am going to kill.'

The leader and his gang burst into laughter. 'You? This ain't England Governor! We're not some fox y'r hunting! You have to look a man in the eyes as you pull the trigger.'

'Vermin is still vermin! No matter how it is packaged! At the moment this land belongs to Warren Foster and as his grandson and his representative, I'm currently in charge. If you don't leave, I'll have to demonstrate my authority.'

'Hey! Is that prissy bastard calling us vermin?' called out one of the Halfies.

'Enough talk, let's kill them all now!' screamed another.

The leader held up is hand. 'Settle down lads. You'll have your bloodletting.'

Stubbing out his cigarette, Cedric shook his head. 'I don't think so, unless you're of course referring to your own blood. This community out numbers you about one hundred to one; fire a shot and you won't leave this place alive.'

The leader laughed. 'We don't have to kill them all, Governor! Just enough for the rest to get the message.'

Yao's hands were tightly clenched into fists of rage. 'While Miss Margaret still breathes, we are her people! We would rather die than work for you!'

'Well then, that's easily fixed.' The leader leapt forward and grabbing hold of Margaret and held her tightly against him with a knife at her throat.

'Once I've torn the breath from her pretty throat, I'll do the same to you Mr. Prissy.'

Cedric shook his head, raising his hand to stop Yao from rushing forward. He had seen a movement out of the corner of his eye.

'I don't think so! Tell me, have you met Sebastian?'

As the white tiger pounced from where he'd been creeping up on the group, the leader swung round, momentarily releasing Margaret. Phillip grabbed hold of Margaret and drew her to safety as Sebastian landed on the leader bringing him to the ground.

Snarling, the leader tried to stab Sebastian, causing Margaret to cry out in fear, but the tiger was far too quick and agile for the human. His great fangs sank into the leader's arm and refused to release him until the knife fell out of his hand. The Halfies reached for their weapons to assist their boss, but Cedric shook a finger at them.

'No, no! Spill one drop of the tiger's blood and you'll wish that I had killed you speedily!' He glanced across at Margaret. 'Call him to you.'

Margaret obeyed and Sebastian reluctantly left his captive victim. Kobbi came running up with Cedric's guns. A couple of the gang came forward to assist their leader to his feet and stop the blood gushing from his wounded arm.

'You don't know who you're messing with!' snarled the leader.

Uttering a deep sigh, Cedric said, 'Well, you wouldn't tell me your name would you?' He checked his weapons before slipping it into the band of his trousers.

The leader spluttered in anger, but eventually spat out, 'Damien!'

'Thank you. At least we have something to put on your headstone.'

One of the other Halfies snorted in disgust. 'You don't stand a chance against us! You're a soft bastard from city living!'

'You know nothing about the city if you think life is easy there!'

'Enough of all this chatter,' yelled the leader, 'surrender to us and no one will get hurt!'

Cedric shook his head. 'No; I think not. Leave now and do not return.' His next words were addressed to Yao. 'How long does it take to reach the property boundary?'

Although surprised, Yao immediately answered, 'Half an hour, riding hard, about an hour or so if you don't push the horses, Sir.'

'Right then, you have 30 minutes Damien to get off this property. After that my people have permission to shoot a warning shot if you come close to the boundary and to shoot to kill if you cross the boundary. Any questions?'

'Who's going to make us leave? You?' The leader was now looking rather wan with the amount of blood he had lost. *But I'm determined to stand my ground, and not lose face in front of my men.*

'I dislike violence, and would prefer to settle this peacefully, but I won't permit vermin to overrun property under my command!'

Roaring in outrage, the leader drew his gun, but before he could pull the trigger, he was toppling backwards. A bullet was firmly planted between his eyes. Cedric had been too quick for him. After a few seconds of shock, guns were out and ready, but no one started shooting.

Tension escalated as everyone waited for something to happen. Margaret reached down to lay a hand on Sebastian's neck to keep him still. Any sudden movement could start a gun battle.

'You'll pay for that mister!'

'I think not! Half an hour is decreasing with every minute you waste. Look carefully around you. You're outnumbered and don't stand a chance of surviving a battle.' Cedric removed his fob watch from his pocket and checked the time.

The Halfies looked at each other and then at the large number of villagers gathered to defend the farm. They lowered their weapons as they realized the truth in what Cedric said. The gang, rather subdued, mounted their horses but Cedric hadn't quite finished.

'What do you know of the massacre of a village just south of here?'

'We had nothing to do with that!' A Halfy was quick to reply.

'I haven't accused you of involvement. I just want any information you may have as to who the attackers actually were.' Cedric's calm tone soothed their hackles slightly.

'Word is that the Ashanti King Peponi thinks someone is trying to kill him and replace him with someone in his family. So anyone remotely connected to the King is being executed.'

Cedric checked his watch again, 'Half an hour gentlemen. Step foot on this land again and you will die!'

The Halfies didn't need to be told twice, they turned their horses and sped away. A sigh of relief spread through the villagers. Cedric's handling of the situation had meant no loss of lives; to the villagers anyway. He went up in their esteem and respect.

'Someone should make sure that they do leave,' suggested Phillip.

Cedric nodded. 'I intend to ride out after them.'

'I'll get the horses saddled,' said Kobbi as he ran back to the stables.

'Sir, I want a team to go with you,' Yao suggested.

Cedric nodded. 'They'll need to be armed. We have to be prepared if they try to double back on us. Phillip, I want you to stay here.'

His face showed his disappointment. 'Don't you trust me Rick?'

Cedric reached out to lay his hand on Phillip's shoulder, 'More than anyone in this world! That is why I want you here to protect my cousin.'

Margaret tugged playfully upon Sebastian's ears. 'What am I? A fragile china doll?' She spoke only loud enough for Father Gerard to hear as she realized something quite significant was passing between the two old friends.

Margaret didn't protest as she was urged back into the house. Yao organized riders to accompany Cedric, and a team of men to dig another grave.

The Pebble People

In her packing, Margaret had left her own bedroom for last. This was the hardest room to do. With all the memories it contained. For the most part, Margaret wanted to be alone while she worked, but eventually as the afternoon had worn on, she finally emerged, tear-stained, back into the real world. In her arms was a beautiful china doll that she was redressing. Sitting down on one of the lounges, Margaret began to brush the doll's hair and restyle it. Cedric had already returned from seeing off the Halfies, and raised his eyebrows in surprise.

'My dear cousin, where have you been hiding such an attractive young lady? I insist that you introduce us.'

'This is Bethwyn.' Margaret smiled a little. 'Papa brought her back from Accra when I was about five. At that time Mama had suffered yet another miscarriage, and I had asked Papa to see if he could bring back from town a baby brother or sister so that Mama wouldn't have to suffer any more.'

'Bethwyn became my little sister. We did everything together. I suppose a doll like this should not be played with, but put on a shelf to be admired. We both ended up with scratches and bruises, but Mama patched us up and sent us back out to play.' She wiped away a tear as she recalled her happy childhood. Cedric placed his arm around her shoulder as he sat on the couch beside her.

'I'm sorry! I didn't mean to upset you further.'

Margaret shook her head. 'I've so many wonderful memories of my life with my parents. Reminiscing about those good times helps me to stop thinking about their senseless deaths.' Cedric squeezed her shoulders in understanding.

Leaning forward where he sat on the couch opposite, Phillip asked, 'Did your father regularly travel to the metropolis? I thought as a Doctor, he was kept fairly busy up here.'

Margaret nodded. 'Oh yes, there was always plenty to do on the farm apart from the surgery and the hospital. Once a year, though, Papa went to the city. We have regular drivers who take the produce to town, and collecting any normal supplies, but equipment and supplies for the hospital, Papa would take care of himself.'

Phillip looked amazed. 'It must have been a worry while he was gone. It's a long way to go.'

Sitting Bethwyn down beside her, Margaret smiled. 'I never worried about Papa as I sent a couple of my pebble people with him each time to protect him.'

Phillip and Cedric stared at each other in confusion. Sitting at the table reading a book, Father Gerard suddenly moved uncomfortably. *I know what is coming next and these questions are going to lead to some awkward revelations. There is no way I can prevent it happening; I just hope that I can minimize the pain.*

'So who are the pebble people?' asked Phillip, 'Are they a tribe in these parts?'

Margaret laughed. 'They're not real people but clear pebbles I found on the farm. I sometimes felt lonely so I made characters out of the pebbles.' As she explained,

Margaret slipped her hand into her pocket and drew out the couple of pebble people she had been carrying since leaving Richard's farm. She handed them to Cedric whose smile vanished as he looked carefully at the pebbles.

'My dear cousin, these aren't pebbles!' Cedric rose to pass the stones to Phillip to examine. Father Gerard laid down his book and came across joining them.

Phillip studied the pebbles before glancing up at Margaret. 'Didn't anyone ever tell you what these really are?'

Looking bewildered by their excited manner, Margaret shook her head. 'I don't see what the fuss is about! They're only pebbles. Papa said that friends were priceless and that you should always look after them even if they're only stones, plants or animals.'

'Margaret,' Cedric sat down again beside her and took one of the hands. 'Your pebbles are actually diamonds!'

Margaret laughed. 'But they don't look anything like the diamond in Mama's ring!'

'That is how they look once cut, shaped and polished. This is their natural form.' Phillip explained. Margaret looked at Father Gerard and his face told her that he already knew about this.

'You knew? Why didn't anyone tell me?'

Gerard shrugged. 'Would it have made any difference to you or your life at the Haven?'

Margaret conceded that the Priest had a point. 'Not really I suppose.' She paused in thought. 'Does this have anything to do with why someone wants to kill my parents? How many people would actually know the pebble people were really valuable?'

Father Gerard shook his head. 'Very few knew the truth; your parents and myself. I doubt Richard realized.'

'Then how would anyone outside know about them?'

'Your mother would have mentioned it, Rick, if she knew surely?' asked Phillip.

Cedric agreed. 'This isn't known in the family. If one of us does know, he or she is keeping it quiet.'

'But how would they find out about it?' asked Phillip.

Cedric looked at his cousin. 'You mentioned that your father took a couple of pebbles to town. Did they ever return with him?'

Margaret shook her head. 'No, he said to ensure a safe journey back to us, he had to set the pebble people free in town. It never worried me as there were plenty of them.'

'Plenty of them?' Phillip groaned in disbelief, 'You must be sitting on top of a lucrative diamond mine!'

Rising to his feet, Cedric began to pace. 'He probably used them to help purchase medical supplies.'

'Doctor Munroe would most likely have gone to a jewellery dealer,' Phillip nodded. 'I can think of a few who would rather cut out their tongues than reveal their client's secrets.'

Margaret frowned as she tried to follow what they were saying. 'Then how did someone in the family find out about the pebbles? Sorry diamonds?'

Cedric spread his arms out in front of him. 'At the moment we can only speculate. A customer may have inadvertently overheard the transaction. One of the employees may have been hard up for money and sold the information to a family member. Someone may have seen Uncle Edward going into the store and realized he wasn't buying but selling.'

Likely Suspects

'The real question is, children, who benefits?' enquired Gerard.

Cedric didn't even need time to think about this as he answered immediately, 'Warren Foster!'

'For the farm, but does he gain for the inheritance?' Gerard added.

Cedric tugged on his ear. 'Not directly. Here, do you have some blank paper, so that I can draw a family tree?'

Margaret jumped to her feet and disappeared into the office before returning with several blank sheets. Accepting the paper, and a pencil Margaret had also brought, Cedric sat down at the dining table and worked diligently for nearly ten minutes. During this time it was useless to question or speak to him, as he would only wave an impatient hand at them.

When he was finished drawing up the family tree, Cedric looked up and smiled wearily. 'Until it's put on paper, I hadn't realized how big the Foster clan is! Come and have a look. We can use this as a guide to narrow our lists of suspects.'

As the others drew the dining chairs around him, Cedric created three columns on a separate piece of paper, heading the columns Farm, Inheritance, and Farm Inheritance. Under each heading he then added Warren Foster as first suspect.

'I still don't see how your grandfather benefits through Margaret's inheritance,' said Phillip.

Cedric's smile turned cunning. 'He doesn't! Not for himself, but my brother Clay is one of his favourite grandsons.'

'Even so…'

'Let me start at the beginning and I'll try to make it all clearer. Firstly we can eliminate the great grandchildren from any plot, the eldest is only eleven.' Cedric slashed a line through Warren Foster's great grandchildren.

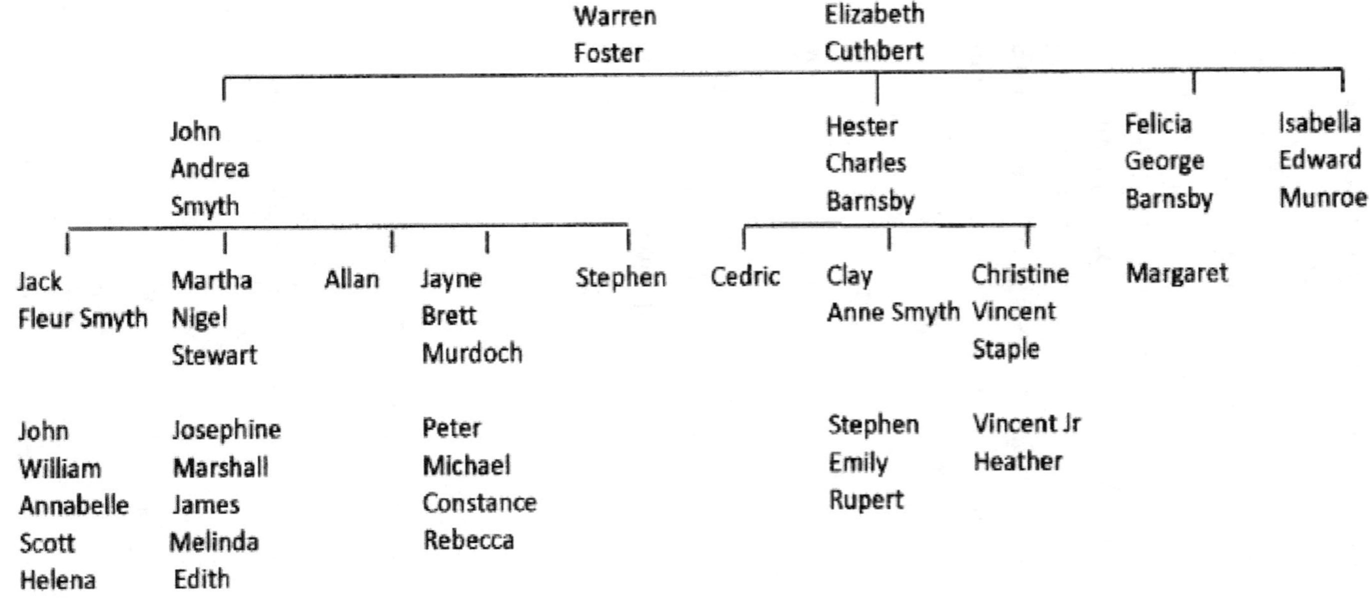

Tiger's Eyes

Warren
Foster

Elizabeth
Cuthbert

John
Andrea
Smyth

Hester
Charles
Barnsby

Felicia
George
Barnsby

Isabella
Edward
Munroe

Jack
Fleur Smyth

Martha
Nigel
Stewart

Allan

Jayne
Brett
Murdoch

Stephen

Cedric

Clay
Anne Smyth

Christine
Vincent
Staple

Margaret

John
William
Annabelle
Scott
Helena

Josephine
Marshall
James
Melinda
Edith
Graham

Peter
Michael
Constance
Rebecca

Stephen
Emily
Rupert

Vincent Jr
Heather

Father Gerard looked displeased at all the work Cedric had just ruined. 'If you weren't going to include the little ones Herr Barnsby, why draw them in the first place?'

'That's a good point,' Phillip added.

Cedric sighed deeply. 'They may not be relevant as themselves, but do indicate perhaps their parents need for money to support them.' Both Gerard and Phillip acknowledged that made sense. 'If I may continue? Next we can rule out family already dead.'

Cedric crossed through Isabella and Edward Munroe, Felicia and George Barnsby, Charles Barnsby, Elizabeth Foster and Andrea Foster.

'Now, if we start with suspects for the family only. Firstly Warren Foster, for himself or for someone else. So who is desperate for money, and who could convince grandfather to give them the farm? John, Warren's only son is in charge of the family business. No serious vices, more like Isabella than Hester or Felicia. Sensible, no nonsense and practical! He has his hands full with the business, and no money worries.' Cedric paused to gratefully accept Busara's offer of refreshments.

'John has five children. Jack, the eldest, is very pious. A bit of a prude actually, but looking to take on the family business. Martha married a really nice bloke. Nigel Stewart has been running one of his father-in-law's farms, but he has spoken to me to keep my eyes open for a farm of his own. Nigel wants to be his own boss.'

Father Gerard interrupted. 'Forgive me, but why ask you?'

Cedric's eyebrows rose. 'Because that is what I do! I'm in Real Estate.'

'Is that one of Barnsby's Holdings interests?' Margaret asked.

'Hell no!' Cedric burst out laughing, 'I wouldn't work for Barnsby Holdings even if it promised to make me a King!'

'Isn't it usual for sons, especially eldest sons, to follow in their father's footsteps?' Margaret frowned in confusion.

'Perhaps my dear cousin, but there was nothing there for me, Clay still works for them even though I told him it would only make him bitter.' Cedric crossed off John, Jack and Martha before continuing to dissect the family.

'Allan and I get on quite well. He's in London and in charge of Foster interests there. Allan is having the time of his life in the great metropolis and has no interest in coming back to Africa.' Cedric crossed him off the list and thoughtfully tapped his pencil beside the next name.

'Our first Foster possibility. Jayne made a disastrous marriage. Everyone thought Brett Murdoch was a wealthy businessman, but it was only after they were married that it was discovered he was a con-artist and a trickster. They live off John's benevolence and are always desperate for money. The problem is that Grandfather despises Brett and wouldn't give him such a windfall. Also a farm would be too much work for a lazy lizard like Brett. We'll have to leave them as a question mark.'

'The last Foster is Stephen. He and my brother Clay were pretty chummy at one time. They got into all sorts of mischief and trouble. It was pretty harmless at first, but then it turned rather nasty. Grandfather hauled them over the coals. Clay settled down a bit, but Stephen continued on a destructive course; Drugs, drink, gambling and women. To get Stephen away from easy reach of temptation, an out of the way farm would be ideal. Is that good enough reason though to kill your own daughter and granddaughter?'

Circling Jayne's name and her husband's as well as Stephen, Cedric then wrote them under the first column. His brow puckered in thought, he sat back to study the family tree.

'A little far-fetched, but not impossible. Warren Foster could be doing this for Clay. He has always been bitter about losing control of Barnsby Holding,' Cedric added his brother's name to the first column.

'I don't understand,' Margaret said. 'I thought the company was split evenly between George and Charles Barnsby.'

Cedric nodded. 'That is correct and when George died, his 50% was placed into a trust for when you turn 25.'

'What happened to your father's shares? Were they split between you and your brother and sister?'

'You don't know?' Cedric looked surprised. 'Of course not, sorry! My father and Stephen were like two peas in a pod; gambling, women, drink and mountains of debt. To keep gambling, my father tried to get a loan from the bank, but they knew he'd never pay it back. So he approached your lawyers. The only deal they would make was to buy part of his shares. He could purchase them back if he was ever able to but that never happened.'

'By the time he died, most of his shares were gone. Your lawyers offered to buy the remaining shares at really good market value as Mama had been left with massive debts. Therefore Barnsby Holdings is or will be yours 100%.'

Father Gerard whistled in disbelief. 'No wonder your brother is bitter, his father gambled away his inheritance.'

'So what happens to my inheritance if I die before I marry or turn 25?' Margaret wanted to keep them on track.

Scratching his head, Cedric pulled a face. 'Not exactly certain about that. It reverts back to the other stockholder, my father, but with his death, I'm not sure if it then goes to me solely or more likely split between the three of us. Knowing father he would've tried to cut me out as much as possible. If he could arrange it, he would've left it all to Clay.'

'Is a third of the company worth killing for?' Gerard asked.

'Most definitely! Clay would, if he could get away with it. Christine is happily married with no real money problems. Mama managed to arrange a decent dowry for her before Father bankrupted us. Besides which, her husband, Vincent may be only a younger son of an Earl, but he is doing well at his own business.'

'I don't need the money, Phillip and I are doing quite well and our needs are simple. I worry about Mama sometimes, but having got rid of that impossibly large house and moved into something more comfortable with a friend she seems much happier.'

Clay's name was added to the second column and after a pause for deliberation; Cedric added it also to the third column.

Why Do They Despise You?

'Unfortunately,' Cedric added, 'you have only my word that I didn't have your parents killed and have no intention of killing you. Barnsby Holdings means nothing to me, and there is no way in this lifetime, or even the next, would Grandfather do anything for me. That was the only thing he and my father agreed upon, how much of a disappointment I was!'

'I don't understand why.' Margaret shook her head in confusion. 'I certainly like you better than the first Cedric I met. Not that that was actually Albert either; he just got carried away. So what did you do wrong? I mean, you're handsome, polite, and intelligent, if what you say is true, then successful in your own business. Is it because you're not yet married and have produced a pack of children?'

Phillip and Cedric exchanged a speaking glance, but there was no way they could escape Margaret's questions.

'I was never manly enough for them. I... I will probably never marry because although I may like women,

I cannot ever love one.' Cedric tried to choose his words very carefully.

Still confused, Margaret asked, 'Is love always necessary for marriage?'

'Not always.' Cedric smiled. 'The problem is that I love someone already.'

'And you cannot marry them?'

'No.'

Father Gerard started to move uncomfortable in his seat, but there was nothing he could say to satisfy Margaret's enquiring mind beyond the truth.

'Are they already married?' She asked.

'No,' Cedric sighed. 'You see Margaret; I'm in love with Phillip.' He finally admitted.

Margaret looked at him blankly, and then across to Phillip who was bright red in embarrassment. 'Forgive my ignorance, but that isn't exactly normal is it?'

Father Gerard interjected. 'Nein, my child, but it does happen. More often than you realise. It's not always possible to control how we feel about others. I'm sure Herr Sigmund Freud would have a great deal to say about it, but it will be many, many years before people can be more open about same gender relationships.'

Margaret slowly shook her head. 'I still don't understand, but it's not my business. It doesn't change my liking you, and it has led us away from finding a killer.'

Cedric took her hand into his. 'It really hasn't changed your opinion of me?'

'No, just a little puzzled but I'm learning that there is so much about the world I do not know.' Margaret smiled.

Phillip reached over to embrace Margaret before they turned their focus back to the columns of suspects.

How Does This Help Us?

'So,' Cedric brought them back on track. 'We have three most likely candidates. Forget Jayne and Brett, they may need money, but are really unlikely to get anything out of Grandfather. Knowing that it could be Warren Foster, Stephen or Clay, gets us where?'

Knowing who it is, is that going to help us prevent them killing me? A shiver ran through Margaret as it hit home. *Someone in my family does actually want me dead.*

Phillip looked puzzled. 'Do we gain anything by narrowing down the possibilities?'

Surprising them all, Cedric suddenly smiled. '"Know thine enemy!" I don't know where I heard that but it's true. I may not be able to bring back Margaret's parents, but we should be able to prevent her death. We must head back to Accra as soon as possible. I need to confront Grandfather face to face. It's necessary to expose these plots.'

'What if further attempts on Margaret's life have already been set into motion?' asked Gerard.

Cedric looked surprised. 'Don't you feel that you and Professor Evans are capable of continuing to protect Margaret?'

'Of course we are!' Gerard grunted in disgust. 'I'm just getting tired of the mounting death toll! I am after all a man of God!'

'Once I've sorted things out back in Accra, there shouldn't be any further attempts. It would make things easier if Margaret could be married before she's 25. There are still several months to go before she can accept her inheritance.'

'We're working on it,' Gerard admitted, ignoring Margaret's blushing protests.

'Father Gerard!'

Despite the seriousness of the situation, Cedric was momentarily distracted by the hint of romance. 'So which delectable young man is it then? The handsome but wounded Lieutenant? The only delay would be acquiring a marriage license. You could've organized that by now Padre. That leaves us with the stoic and studious Professor. Apart from the common decency of Margaret's bereavement what could be the problem?' Margaret exchanged glances with Gerard.

Cedric's eyebrows rose. 'I see! I couldn't recall if he was wearing a wedding ring or not. Is this a solvable problem?'

'Ja! Ja!' Gerard sighed. 'But we need more time.'

'That is something we're running out of Father.'

Phillip tapped Cedric's list of suspects. 'If Warren Foster is behind all this, then he won't stop until he succeeds!'

A rueful smile flittered across Margaret's features. 'You're such a comfort Phillip. I just know that I'm going to sleep peacefully tonight!'

Cedric grinned at her sarcasm. 'Phillip can be a little over dramatic at times, but unfortunately the danger is very real. I'll try to bring an end to all of this when I return to Accra. In the meantime, I suggest you sleep with a knife or a pistol under your pillow.'

Sighing, Margaret picked up the diamonds off the table and studied them carefully. 'Who would have thought that so much trouble could be caused by such little things?'

Cedric placed his arm around Margaret's shoulders. 'They won't get away with this, I promise you.'

A tear fell down her cheek. 'Thank you. Tell him; tell Grandfather, I would've willingly given it all to him if it could have meant that my parents would be alive today.' Rising swiftly to her feet, Margaret ran out of the house. No one immediately followed as they realized that she needed time alone.

I Will Never Be Here Again

Cedric spent the rest of the day going over the farm accounts as he wrote up his appraisal report. He discussed with Yao and Busara about leaving them in charge until Warren Foster made a decision about the Haven. Father Gerard and Phillip, assisted by many young hands, loaded up the cart with the boxes and trunks, which Margaret had packed.

It had been decided that they would leave first thing the next morning. Phillip and Cedric would escort Margaret and Gerard back to Richard before heading down to the city.

Margaret double-checked every room to make certain that she did not leave anything important behind. *Deep in my heart, I know I'll never be back and before we leave I need to seek some alone time, kneeling beside my parents' graves. They had been the centre of my world, and I am never going to see them again.*

Father Gerard packed up all the medical implements and supplies that he could salvage, and they were also loaded onto the cart. Sebastian kept a close vigilance upon Margaret, as a depressed atmosphere descended upon the farm.

The villagers had been told of their departure, and no matter how much they wanted Margaret to stay, they knew that she could not do so. Cedric repeated his promise that he would ensure that the village was taken care of. *Despite my dislike for violence, I'm preparing for a war that I am determined not to lose. One way or another, I am going to make the guilty pay! Even if it is my own Grandfather!*

Marrying For The Right Reasons

Before turning in for the night, Cedric took a walk around the outside of the house to ensure that security was strong and impregnable. While he strolled, Cedric smoked a cigar. Phillip tolerated him smoking cigarettes, but didn't like cigars. So he never smoked near the house. As he stepped up onto the verandah, he didn't toss his cigar butt, concerned about starting a fire, so he made certain it was out before burying it.

About to enter the house, Cedric jumped startled, as he realized that someone was sitting on the verandah. His gun was drawn before recognizing his cousin. Raising his free hand to wipe away the sweat that beaded his brow, Cedric's voice wasn't quite steady.

'My dear Margaret! I could've killed you! I thought you had gone to bed!' He holstered his weapon as he sank onto the seat beside her.

'Sorry I startled you. I couldn't sleep.' Margaret had her legs pulled up against her chest and her cheek lay on her knees.

I can tell, despite the limitations of light that she has been crying. He gently drew Margaret into his arms to comfort her.

Margaret took the handkerchief that Cedric offered to her, and wiped away her tears. 'I have known no other home but this one. Now it may never be possible to return. We didn't need the pebble people, or the farm or even this inheritance, so long as we had each other.'

Cedric stroked his hand down her hair. 'Some people are just too greedy. They want it all and it doesn't matter who gets hurt.'

Margaret buried her face into her cousin's shoulder, and they sat silently together for some time. Cedric felt Sebastian brush passed them and down the steps into the garden. *I don't know why I'm surprised at the tiger's presence; I should've expected him to be on guard over Margaret.* The tiger obviously felt that Margaret was safe with her cousin, so he went out to stretch his legs.

'Can I ask you a question that is rather personal?' Cedric had a ticklish query that needed to be carefully worded. Margaret sat up as she dried her tears.

'Of course, I need not answer if I'm not comfortable.'

He didn't immediately rush into speech as he debated his right to interfere in his cousin's life.

'What is it Cedric?' His hesitation alarmed Margaret.

Cedric exhaled slowly. 'What is your reason for wanting to marry Professor Evans? Is it necessity because you've lost your home? Is it because of this inheritance? Or do you actually love him?' He waited for Margaret to explode at the impertinence of his questions. *I am relieved that reaction didn't eventuate.*

'For a long time I have cared very deeply for Richard. I tried to suppress the development of anything more substantial as I always knew he was married. I didn't know until recently that he cares for me, and that his marriage was one of convenience only.'

'Richard would offer me a home even if we could only ever be friends. The money means very little to either of us, but if being wed means that I'm no longer in danger, then that is why the inevitable is being pushed forward as fast as is possible.'

Cedric leant forward, his hands tightly clasped together. 'It's just that I don't want you rushing into something that you may regret later. Are you certain that it is love you feel and not just the need to cling to someone in this time of need?'

Rising to her feet, Margaret paced the verandah. 'I don't know how well I'll explain this, so please bear with me. It wasn't love at first sight; I was only 14, after all. We spar, but we don't fight. I don't swoon just because Richard looks at me. Oh, I'm making a mess of this!' Margaret pressed her hands against her heated cheeks.

When Is A Kiss Just A Kiss?

Cedric chuckled. 'Keep going, you're getting there.'

Margaret sighed. 'Well, I like him more than any other man I've met. I enjoy being in his company, and when he touches me…' She broke off in embarrassment.

'Yes? Has he made love to you already?'

Margaret uttered a startled sound. 'No, no! Richard kissed me and… and caressed my… my breasts.'

Cedric was on his feet, standing right behind her. 'And how did it make you feel?'

I can't believe that I am revealing all of this to my cousin. 'I felt light headed, weak in the knees and wanted it to never end!'

'Have you been kissed like that by anyone else?'

Screwing up her nose, Margaret thought about the question for a moment before she answered, 'Major Marconi tried to kiss me and put his paws all over me!' A shiver of horror ran through her. Smiling, Cedric placed his hands upon his cousin's shoulders.

'I take it from that tone of disgust that you did not like his advances?'

'Well, I did knee him in the groin!'

'Ouch!' He laughed. 'What I'm trying to say is if the Professor is the only one to have ever kissed you, are you certain your feelings wouldn't be the same if you were kissed by someone else? Not the Major obviously.'

Leaning back against him, Margaret took a moment to consider the question. 'I don't know. The only example of something similar is when Elliott Gibbs puts his arm around my shoulder, compared to when Richard does. From Elliott, I get the feeling of protection. From Richard, I get that but something more. There is a funny sensation in my stomach, like butterflies are running loose inside me.'

Cedric's hand caressed lightly up and down Margaret's arm. 'How do you feel when either Phillip or I embrace you?'

A shiver ran through Margaret. *I'm not sure that I like where this conversation is heading.* 'I... I don't know! But what you're doing now has me a little nervous,' she admitted.

'Nervous excited or nervous scared?' Cedric turned her round to face him; his hands still lay lightly on her shoulders.

'Just ... Just nervous.'

Chuckling, Cedric suddenly lowered his head and kissed Margaret on the lips. Not just a momentarily peck, but a proper kiss. She froze in confusion but when one of his hands trailed down to caress her breast, Margaret shoved him away. Hard.

'No! You mustn't do that!'

Cedric watched her calmly, 'Why; because I'm your cousin?'

Margaret blurted out, 'No, because you're not Richard!' Startled by the sudden revelation, her hand flew to cover her mouth. 'Oh!'

Cedric, though, was smiling. 'That came straight from the heart, you didn't have time to stop and think about it. Good girl!'

Frowning, Margaret took a couple of steps back to place some space between them. 'I don't understand!'

'I do though!' They both jumped at the sound of Phillip's voice from the doorway.

Cedric's eyebrows rose. 'Been there long?' His tone was light but not anxious.

Phillip inclined his head a little, 'Long enough. Are you satisfied about your cousin's feelings for Professor Evans?'

Cedric ran his eyes over Phillip from head to toe. 'Not quite yet. One more experiment I think.' He grasped hold of Margaret's arm and propelled her across the verandah so that she collided with Phillip. Instinctively Phillip reached out to steady her.

'I don't think this is a good idea Rick.'

Cedric grinned. 'I do! I don't want my cousin to settle for anything but what is best for her.'

Margaret slipped out of Phillip's hold and put up a hand to her dishevelled hair. 'I think you're being very silly, Cedric, and not at all fair to your friend. Making him uncomfortable by trying to force him to do something obviously distasteful to him!'

Phillip looked startled. 'I never said it would be distasteful. Just that it wasn't a good idea!'

As his eyes narrowed, Cedric gaze never left his friend's face. 'You want to, don't you? You want to know if I was right. You'll always wonder if I was right or not!'

Shaking her head, Margaret moved towards the door. 'I'll leave you to play your mind games. I'm going to bed!'

'No!' Phillip grasped hold of her hand and drew her into his arms.

'Oh really! I…' Margaret never got to finish her protest as Phillip's mouth descended upon hers. She pushed against him, but his hold on her wasn't easily broken.

'Well?' Cedric asked when Phillip finally released Margaret, but she wasn't sure whom he was actually addressing.

'I never expected such despicable behaviour from either of you! Why you want to humiliate me I don't know. I had thought I'd found at least one decent relative!' Tearfully, Margaret managed to get as far as the door before Phillip grasped her around the waist to prevent her leaving.

Margaret struggled for a minute but went absolutely still when she realized it was useless to resist. 'Please let me go!' Her tone was cool and a little hurt.

'Not until you let me explain my dear cousin.' Cedric tried to take her hand, but she refused to let him have it.

'I think you've said and done enough already! Please release me!'

Cedric's eyes narrowed momentarily. 'Petulant child aren't you? I had to discover how deep your loyalty for Richard Evans ran. Was it just the excitement of your first real kiss, or was it something more personal. If you had reacted in the same way to being kissed by someone else, I would have strongly urged you to reconsider marriage to the Professor at this highly emotional time. The fact that you rejected both of us showed how true your feelings are for Richard. A harsh lesson but you must be certain about taking a large step after such a horrendous couple of weeks.'

Phillip finally released Margaret, but she didn't move.

'There is so much I do not know or understand about the world.'

This time when Cedric took her hand, Margaret did not pull away. 'Don't limit yourself! There are immense possibilities out there. Don't settle for something just because it is familiar.'

Margaret shook her head. 'This is where I belong. I would feel lost in a big city. Besides which I have responsibilities here. Sebastian couldn't survive in a city or probably even in another country. Manu and Adwoa are my responsibility until we take care of the Ashanti King. Besides which, I do love Richard.'

Cedric surprised her by smiling. 'And you would be happy in that life?'

'Oh very much so!'

He squeezed her hand. 'That's all that I want.'

TUESDAY
Parting Is Such Sweet Sorrow

A sombre mood hung over the farm the following morning as the workers and the villagers gathered to farewell Margaret; perhaps forever. While the horses were being prepared, Margaret knelt for the last time beside her parents' graves. She removed the dead flowers and replaced them with fresh ones she had just picked. Tears fell, making speech impossible as the knot grew in her throat. *There is nothing more I can say that I hadn't already said, but even so I find it impossible to just get up and walk away.*

When it was time to depart, Father Gerard came to take her hand and lead a reluctant Margaret to the waiting crowd. She tried to dry her tears and put on a brave face but many of the villagers were also crying. Margaret had to be handed up on to the box seat of the wagon now laden with possessions from the Haven.

Kobbi had the reins, which was just as well as Margaret would not have been able to see clearly. Yao had arranged armed riders to travel with them to the property boundary. It was a sad journey and one that saw little conversation, as they each dwelt upon their own private thoughts.

A Restless Tiger

After they stopped for lunch and rested the horses, Sebastian became restless. *It's as if I don't know what to do with myself as I change regularly from the box seat to the wagon tray and then walking beside the horses.* Margaret suggested that he went for run to work out his agitation.

Sebastian hesitated about leaving Margaret, but there were four men as well as Kobbi, and he was soon disappearing up the trail ahead of them. Margaret wished, *that my own discord could be overcome so easily, but I know it is going to take a great deal of time for me to come to terms with everything that has happened.*

Another Ambush

They were only a mile or so from Richard's farm when they heard the sound of fast approaching horses. *At first I thought that it might be Richard riding out to meet us, but the fact that the horses sound like they are being pushed hard, worries me.* Glancing around at her companions, she realized that they had already considered this, and weapons were appearing.

A shiver of fear ran through Margaret in dread of a possible gun battle. *Who will protect the interests of the Haven workers, or tell the world what really happened to my parents, if we're all killed now? Do I need to spend the next few months constantly having to worry about someone attempting to kill me?* As the riders came into view, these questions were momentarily pushed aside. They were in serious trouble as the newcomers outnumbered them two to one.

Father Gerard drew his group to one side of the track in the hope, minute perhaps, that these riders were just going to pass them. This hope was dashed as the approaching horses were pulled up in front of them in a spray of dust. The heavily sweating horses snorted and tossed their heads in disapproval of this treatment. The riders ignored their protests as they watched the group cautiously, and their leader urged his horse forward.

'Miss Munroe?' He asked politely.

Margaret saw little point in denying it, so she nodded. 'Yes, can I help you?'

The leader smiled. 'No Miss Munroe, we're here to help you. Your family in Accra was deeply distressed to hear of the murder of your parents and we were hired by your cousin to ensure your safety.'

Her eyebrows raised, Margaret glanced briefly at Cedric, 'How considerate! Which cousin exactly would that be?'

'Cedric Barnsby.'

'Isn't that nice of my cousin?' Margaret saw Cedric slightly shake his head and felt a knot of fear tighten in her stomach.

The leader didn't catch the irony in her voice and continued to smile. 'Indeed he was very particular about how we were to take care of you and your companions.'

'I'm sure he was!' Cedric drawled, his finger tightening around his gun.

Margaret sighed deeply. 'At what point are you going to kill all of us, or were your orders to just get rid of me?'

The leader's smile suddenly vanished. 'What on earth are you talking about? Our orders were to protect you.'

Father Gerard tut-tutted. 'Don't play games please! The man who hired you used someone else's name.'

Out of curiosity, Phillip asked, 'What does a human life cost now a days?'

'Are you people insane?' The leader demanded. 'Why can you not see that we're here to assist you?'

'Because I am Cedric Barnsby!' answered Cedric.

There was a prolonged silence, which was eventually broken by the leader. 'Damn! Well I suppose we can get down to business then!' The riders had all drawn their weapons and were waiting for orders to begin shooting.

'So what were your orders?' Margaret asked calmly. 'Were you to kill just me or all of us?'

'Clean sweep of the lot, love!' The leader glanced over at Cedric. 'Whoever stole your monarch doesn't think much of you! He said to give special attention to two prissy gents.'

Rolling his eyes, Cedric sighed. 'That sounds like something Clay would say. Did he happen to warn you that one of the dandy's could shoot both your eyes out before you could even raise your gun?'

The other riders glanced at each other a little concerned but the leader only laughed.

'No one is fast enough to do that!'

Cedric's eyes twinkled mischievously. 'Try me!'

The two men locked eyes and their bodies tensed as they waited for the other to make a significant move. The other riders held their collective breath, but Margaret's patience snapped.

'Stop being so childish, both of you!'

As their tense muscles eased, neither man could stop himself from grinning like naughty schoolboys.

'Sorry cousin,' apologized Cedric, 'but my prowess with a gun is one thing that I will not tolerate criticism.'

'Well I don't doubt your skill, Cedric! I saw you outdraw that Halfy!'

The leader laughed a little nervously. 'If you're trying to psyche me out…'

'I don't have to.' Margaret shook her head. 'No one is killing anyone. Whatever you were being paid, it isn't enough to die for.'

'Sweetheart, we're not the ones who are going to be dying.' The leader raised his weapon to point at Margaret, but before he could pull the trigger, something small and sharp pierced his neck. He had only enough time to determine that it wasn't a wasp or a bee, but a dart, before he fell off his horse. The leader was dead before he even hit the ground.

To The Rescue

Out of the trees appeared nearly the entire workforce from Richard's farm as they surrounded the two groups. The would-be assassins raised their guns, but the sheer weight of numbers was against them and they allowed their weapons to be taken without a fight. The villagers and their weapons may have been more primitive, but they were still deadly and numerous.

Sebastian bounded onto the scene closely followed by Richard on horseback. Margaret had never been happier to see anyone in her life. Father Gerard urged his horse forward to meet Richard as Sebastian leant his massive front paws on the box seat of the wagon to see if Margaret was all right. She wrapped her arms around his neck and laughed in relief at their well-timed arrival.

'My dear boy, you cannot know how glad we are to see you!' Father Gerard warmly grasped Richard's hand. 'But how on earth did you know we were in trouble and get here so quickly?'

The Professor's eyebrows rose in surprise. 'When Sebastian arrived alone and in an agitated state, I assumed that he'd been sent to get help. Is that not the case?' He glanced across to Margaret who shook her head.

'Sebastian was restless so I told him to run off his frustration. I wonder if he did know we were in trouble.' She kissed Sebastian on the nose before sliding off the box seat.

Margaret checked on the leader to ensure that he actually was deceased and beyond her aid before approaching Richard's horse. With very little effort, Richard lifted her up onto the horse to sit in his arms. He looked at her closely, noticing the stress lines on her face.

'You've had a hard time of it, kitten. I should've come with you when you went home.' Tenderly Richard kissed her forehead as she laid her cheek against his shoulder.

'It was always going to be heartbreaking,' answered Gerard.

Richard nodded, stroking his hand against Margaret's hair. 'I know, but I should've been there for support.'

All this time Cedric had not removed his hand from the butt of his gun. 'Perhaps we should decide what we're going to do with these fellows,' he suggested. Gerard agreed, but stressed that their elimination was not an option. *Too many people have died already.*

'I wasn't going to suggest that!' Cedric drawled. 'We can either let them go or escort them to the closest town and hand them over to the authorities.'

Richard continued to stroke Margaret's hair and the assassins looked hopefully towards him. None of them liked the idea of being executed or handed to the police.

'They won't get more than a slap on the wrist, all they can be charged with is being guns for hire. Conditions for release will have to apply. They must never come near Margaret or the farm, and they must sign a statement in regards to who hired them.'

The men breathed a sigh of relief. They were prepared to sign anything if it meant their freedom. The calm way the Professor spoke reassured them. When he next spoke there was a cold, hard, steel edge to his voice that sent a chill down their spines.

'Understand this; come anywhere near my intended wife without a valid reason, and I'll blow your brains out. You should pray for a swift merciful death. If anything happens to Margaret, I will make your death slow and painful. Do you understand me?'

Unable to speak, the men merely nodded their heads.

'Acceptable?' Richard glanced across at Cedric, who also nodded in agreement.

Sliding off Richard's horse, Margaret hunted through her belongings on the wagon and produced a sheet of paper, an ink pot and a pen. One man wrote down how they were hired and the others all signed it. Cedric read it through before folding the paper and putting it into his pocket. They all looked at Richard for orders.

'Get out of here then!'

The men looked at him stunned. A twinkle entered Richard's eyes, 'Or perhaps you prefer the option of a bullet?'

'No! No!' The assassins turned their horses and rode off, leaving their guns and the villagers behind them.

When Will This End?

Richard no longer sat as upright in the saddle and exhaled slowly in relief.

'What about him?' asked Phillip, nodding his head towards where the dead man laid.

'We'll take him with us; he can be buried on the farm with the other dead hired guns.' Richard paused, *another family will have to be informed of the death of a love one.* 'I'll organize his personal effects and hopefully some identity to go with you when you leave for Accra,' he added.

Father Gerard asked a couple of the natives to lift the corpse onto his horse and secure him in place. Margaret ascended once more to the box seat of the wagon beside Kobbi.

'How many more attempts will be made before this is over?' She couldn't hide the slight tremor in her voice.

'None!' The certainty in Cedric's words surprised them all.

'Once I'm back in the Metropolis I'll sort this out once and for all.' He urged his horse closer to Margaret and held out his hand to her and she took it as she smiled gratefully.

'Thank you.'

'We'd best get moving,' suggested Father Gerard, 'if we're to get home before sunset.'

The convoy moved on and although everyone was thankful that a massacre had been avoided, they remained alert for any other trouble. After all, this was the jungle, and not all the predators were human.

Safely Home Again

The remainder of the village turned out to welcome their return. Margaret was touched by their response and by their concern for her well-being. She tried to smile, but she was extremely tired, and her throat tightened upon any words she may have wanted to utter. A protest was forced from her, though, when Elliott Gibbs lifted Margaret down from the wagon and swung her around in delight and relief.

'For goodness sake Elliott! Put me down immediately. Think of your poor leg, and if you've reopened that shoulder wound, I'll be very angry.'

Elliott allowed Margaret's feet to touch the ground, but he didn't release her from his bear hug. 'When Sebastian turned up alone, a hundred horrific possibilities ran through my head. Then Richard refused to let me come with him. I honestly thought that this time…'

Margaret ran a soothing hand over Elliott's back, reassuring him that they had managed to avert another attempt on her life.

Most of the villagers and workers headed home. A couple remained to deal with the horses, unloading the wagon, and the unpleasant task of burying the dead assassin leader. Dismounting from his horse, Cedric felt more than a little stiff. He was surprised glancing across at Richard that he was faintly smiling at Margaret and Elliott. *I had expected some sort of jealousy, but there is none.* Meeting Cedric's gaze, Richard's smile broadened.

'You can't but help care about Margaret. You've felt it too, haven't you?' Realizing that it pointless to deny it, Cedric nodded.

'Come on,' Richard urged them all inside. 'Something delicious from Dalila and a hot bath I think.'

Cedric stretched his aching muscles. 'I won't say no to that!'

Father Gerard remained outside to oversee the burial of the leader. *I must say a prayer for the man's soul, and another of thanks that this time it hadn't been necessary for more people to die.* When another mound had been created, the Priest took the personal effects that Fynn had removed from the body, and joined the others inside.

Manu was just as excited and relieved to have Margaret and Kobbi safely home again. He wanted to know all that had happened while they were away, but didn't press for answers as Margaret looked extremely worn out.

Grateful not to be bombarded with questions; she encouraged Manu to tell her all about what he had been doing the past few days. Watching her as she lay back on the couch, Phillip wondered, *is she in fact taking in the boy's chatter?* When Margaret asked a question pertinent to what Manu was saying, Phillip was left in no doubt that Margaret was truly focused on the boy. He wondered, *how she can stay so focused? I suppose the normality of Manu's news about every day, normal things actually has a remarkable soothing effect. It makes the terror we'd experienced seem less real.* Calm had descended over them by the time Kobbi took Manu to Dalila's home to have their own dinner.

They bathed, had a simple meal, and dressed for bed. They could discuss innocent topics; talk about the Haven would wait until the morning. Elliott produced a pack of cards and he, Cedric and Phillip played a few light hearted games. After the meal, Father Gerard headed home. Richard did offer a bed for the night, but the Priest thanked him, saying he wanted his own bed and familiar surroundings.

Dalila rewarded Sebastian with a large plate of raw meat which he consumed at an incredible rate before stretching himself out on the floor to nap. Margaret wrote down an account of not only the attempt against them on the way home, but also the attempt of the Halfies to take over the Haven.

Richard sorted through the dead man's possessions so that they could put a name on the wooden cross that would be erected over his grave. These possessions were then wrapped up in brown paper for Cedric to take to the authorities. Richard added a brief note to Margaret's letter and sealed it without reading it. This surprised her as she had offered it to him to read. *I want to wait until Margaret is ready to tell me about the whole trip.*

Lying with her head resting in Richard's lap, Margaret was listening to him describe his latest research findings. *Tuning into their conversation for a moment,* Cedric was astounded, *I am completely at a loss and fail to see how Margaret, without a University education, cannot only understand but also contribute to such a highly technical discussion.* He wondered, *was this due to the unofficial training Margaret had received from her Doctor father, or is it just because she takes an interest in the Professor's work?*

Comfort

'I'm sorry.' Sitting up, Margaret placed her hand over her mouth as she yawned. 'I'm off to bed.'

Richard withdrew his fob watch to glance at the time. 'I don't suppose any of us will be up late tonight, Kitten.' As Margaret made her way to the bathroom, Sebastian raised his head to see what was going on.

Cedric waited until Margaret was out of hearing before addressing Richard, 'You need to be with her tonight.'

Richard stiffened in indignation. 'It's not possible! Even if I was single it wouldn't be appropriate!'

'For goodness sake, man! I'm not telling you to make love to Margaret. She'll need you! Your mere presence, your strength, the realness of you to make her nightmares seem less overwhelming,'

The rigidity left Richard's body. 'All right, but I must make sure that I finish off my paperwork tonight.' He disappeared into his study.

Shuffling the cards, Elliott looked a little dubious. 'He's procrastinating.'

Cedric nodded. 'Yes, but he will go to her. He knows that he's the only one who can comfort her.'

Richard remained up to see Elliott off to bed before he finally bowed to pressure and stepped silently into Margaret's room to join her. She was asleep, but stirred when Richard slid into bed beside her.

'Richard? Is everything all right?'

'Shh! It's fine. Your cousin thought you might need a big stuffed toy to cuddle through the night.' As she turned towards him, he wrapped his arms securely around her. Margaret chuckled as she pressed her cheek against Richard's chest. 'If I wanted that, I would have Sebastian up here! Are you all right with this?'

'Don't you trust me?' Richard sighed deeply.

'Of course I do! Don't change the subject. I don't want you to spend a night of torture just to comfort me.'

He traced a finger lightly over her cheek. 'I think I can contain myself! Now go to sleep again. I'll be here if you need me.'

Margaret snuggled into him and sighed. 'Just maybe, the nightmares won't come tonight.'

We both know that isn't likely to happen, but I'm not about to dampen her enthusiasm. Removing his glasses to place on the bedside table, Richard closed his eyes and tried very hard not to think about the supple and very close body beside him. *This isn't a time for romance,* he reminded himself before eventually he fell asleep.

WEDNESDAY

An Armed Escort

It rained during the night but had stopped before the sun had even begun to peek over the horizon. The earth smelt fresh and clean, and the trees sparkled with water droplets that either dropped to the ground or quickly dried in the morning sunshine. The air was crisp with a slight breeze that foretold of the fine weather to follow, making it a good day for travelling.

After a hearty breakfast, the horses were saddled up so that Cedric and his friend could get through as many miles as possible before nightfall. Dalila provided them with a bounty of food for the journey and ensured that they had a fresh supply of water.

Standing on the verandah, watching the preparations for departure, Margaret placed a small drawstring bag into her cousin's hand.

'What's this?' He looked at her surprised.

'A couple of pebble people, I mean diamonds, if that is what they actually are,' explained Margaret.

'I don't understand. Do you want me to sell them for you? Do you need money? If so…'

Margaret waved her hand to stop him. 'No, no. You'll need to take proof to an expert and get their opinion before you accuse your brother or grandfather. I mean you'll look foolish if you accuse them of killing for a diamond mine when they may only be pebbles.'

Cedric grinned, slipping the sachet into his shirt pocket. 'You're so right little cousin.' He took both of her hands between his. 'Once this is sorted out I'll come back to see you. There'll be a great deal of paperwork for you, I'm afraid, especially once you're married.'

Margaret blushed and he affectionately pinched her chin. 'Will I have to come to Accra?' She asked.

Cedric wasn't certain, but Richard nodded. 'Unless your lawyers are prepared to send a representative out here, you'll have to go to them.'

The horses were ready, and both Cedric and Phillip embraced Margaret before they mounted their horses. They were taken aback when a couple of loaded wagons with two drivers each joined the convoy.

Cedric's eyebrows rose in surprise as he looked down at Richard. 'Is this your subtle way of supplying us with an escort, Professor?'

Richard smiled, 'No, well sort of. Those killers may be waiting to ambush you. I've a shipment due to send at the end of the week, but we've managed to push it forward a couple of days to coincide with your trip.'

Cedric chuckled. 'A ready answer for everything, I like that! Take care of my little cousin, Professor. I hope to be back in time to give the bride away, but if the opportunity presents itself early, take it firmly with both hands.' He glanced across at Phillip and nodded. They led the convoy through the farm gates and on their way to Accra.

What Happens Now?

Work resumed as normal, but Elliott and Richard sat down on the verandah with Margaret so that she could divulge all the events of the past few days. Richard, though, was more interested in Cedric's exposure of the pebble people as diamonds and the candidates of possibilities to Margaret's attackers.

'Diamonds? Are you sure about that?' Richard asked, incredulous.

Margaret shrugged her shoulders. 'That's why I gave a couple of pebble people to Cedric to verify his theory.'

Elliott was shocked for a different reason, 'But Margaret your own grandfather! How could he ruthlessly decide to murder not only his own daughter, but also his granddaughter? He must either truly love this brother of Cedric's, or be completely insane.'

Margaret's smile was a little grim. 'In my childhood, we would scare ourselves silly listening to horror and ghost stories. Sometimes these stories were made up, but the true stories Grandmama told about Warren Foster were the ones that gave me nightmares. He is a very evil man.'

Frowning, Elliott shook his head. 'Why did she marry him?'

Margaret sighed. 'No choice really, it was an arranged marriage, like a merger between two companies. Grandmama remained until her children were married, and then moved in with my parents. My real parents, not biological parents.'

'Didn't that create a scandal?' Richard asked *I'm surprised she waited that long to leave Warren but it was probably necessary to protect the children from their father.*

'Not at all. At that time Papa's mother and two younger sisters were living with them. Grandmama Munroe apparently was very ill and Grandmama Foster came to help not only care for her but also to help chaperone the sisters. Apparently there was quite a to do when Grandmama Foster decided to come to the Haven with us.'

Richard stretched his legs out in front of him and crossed them at the ankles. 'That was the best move your parents could have made. To get as far away as possible from the rest of your family,' He sighed deeply, removing his glasses to give them a polish before replacing them back on his nose.

'So what happens now?' Elliott reached out to run his hand down Sebastian's back as he walked passed going towards Margaret.

'Hmm! A rough assumption is that Cedric will hopefully get back to the Metropolis alive and verify what exactly the pebble people are. He'll discover who told his grandfather or brother what Edward Munroe was selling and finally confront his grandfather and/or brother. The problem is that there is probably very little actual evidence against either man for a court to convict them.'

Margaret scratched Sebastian behind the ears as she frowned in concentration. 'Even if it can't be proved, revealing the truth to the public would create a scandal wouldn't it?'

Richard nodded. 'Yes, it could also destroy Warren's business empire as well. Proven or not, no one wants to do business with a suspected cold-blooded murderer!'

'What about us?' Elliott seemed to be more anxious about the future than was his nature.

Slowly Richard exhaled as he considered this question. 'Well, firstly you have to get well again and back on your feet before you're able to travel. At some point you'll have to report to Headquarters in Accra and account for the incident with Marconi. I've sent word out to as many surrounding villages as possible about the assault on Manu's village. If any other survivors turn up they'll be looked after and sent to us.'

Richard reached over to take Margaret's hand. 'I don't want to get your hopes up kitten, but the possibilities are slender at best.'

Margaret nodded, not immediately trusting herself to speak. She cleared her throat. 'You've tried, that is all anyone can do.'

'As for our little family here, basically we wait. For another possible attempt on Margaret, for news from England about

Alice, and maybe even the opportunity to deal with the Ashanti King Peponi. Otherwise it's business as usual.'

Our Future

Elliott's features relaxed into a cheeky grin. 'There is also a wedding to prepare for!' Margaret blushed and glanced up shyly at Richard, but he was looking grave.

'A dream come true, but until there is a shred of hope of that happening, I'm not letting myself get carried away in case of disappointment.'

Elliott's mouth fell open in surprise. 'But hang it all, that's not fair! Something good must come out of this nightmare! You two belong together! I want a happy ending!'

Stunned by his outburst, Richard's eyes opened wide as Margaret gasped in surprise.

'Richard, I hope our babies don't get this stroppy when they don't get what they want.' Margaret's tone was mild but held a suspicion of a quiver of laughter.

'I'm not a baby!' Elliott protested.

Richard smiled down into her eyes as he slid his arm through hers and she leant her cheek against his shoulder. 'Have you thought of any names you would like?' Margaret laughed, her eyes twinkling.

'Actually I have. Our eldest son should be Rick.'

'Does that mean that the eldest girl will be Margaret?' Elliott demanded.

Margaret screwed up her nose. 'Not quite. There are some pretty derivatives of it though, Megan or Margot.'

'Anything else?' Richard pressed a tender kiss against her forehead. *These sorts of thoughts are a lot more pleasant than dwelling on relatives who want to kill you.*

'Yes, I would like Bella for Mama, and Eddie for Papa. Perhaps Lizzie or Bethany for Grandmama. Oh, how many is that?'

Elliott did a quick count, 'Three girls and two boys.'

'Well then, our third son could be either Gerard or Elliott,' Margaret added.

Visibly touched by this, Elliott was at a loss for words. The twinkle in Margaret's eyes became more pronounced. 'Or we could be light years ahead of ourselves and call them Brooke, River, Glacier, Ridge, Lion and Fern.'

The men exchanged glances before Richard said, 'No, I think perhaps not!' There was a second of silence before all three burst into laughter. *We need that light hearted release,* mused Richard. *We've been through so much already, and it is far from over yet.*

Adding A Personal Touch

While Richard worked, Margaret and Elliott sorted through the trunks and boxes she had brought back from the Haven. A more personal touch was added to Margaret's bedroom and her favourite novels were placed on the shelves in the living room beside Richard's novels.

Elliott was a little hesitant about accepting Doctor Munroe's clothes, but he was taller and leaner than Richard, which made his attire less suitable for Elliott to wear. Elliott didn't want to be a constant reminder of Margaret's loss, but he couldn't deny that it would probably be many days yet before he could return to Accra and he needed to feel comfortable.

Dalila oohed over the intricate and detailed embroidery that Margaret's mother and grandmother had executed upon some of the Manchester. The Housekeeper immediately replaced the quilt on Margaret's bed with an embroidered one and suggested that they pack the remainder away for future use and prosperity. Manu, admiring the bedding, asked what that meant and Dalila told him that these items would become heirlooms to be handed down to and treasured by Margaret's children and grandchildren.

Several boxes were placed into storage and Margaret also put away the trunk of her mother's clothing. *I'm not yet ready to deal with the disposal of my mother's attire and I don't want to do anything hasty that I may later regret. One thing I will remove from my mother's trunk is her wedding dress. If it is going to be possible for me to marry Richard, I wish to do so in my mother's dress.* Dalila promised to help with any alterations, but until they heard about Alice, Dalila would keep the gown in her home. *Miss Margaret doesn't need the continuous reminder that time is conspiring against us.*

News From Chief Kojo

Margaret was sitting in the hammock with baby Adwoa and Manu in the afternoon, so that Nbulungi could rest. Sebastian lay stretched out beneath them, his tail flicking up occasionally to tease Adwoa who tried to catch it. The baby gurgled with delight every time she managed to capture the tiger's tail. Margaret was reading a story to them, when a rider came racing towards the house.

Sebastian sprang to his feet and took up a defensive posture in front of Margaret and the children. Before the native on the horse could stop and dismount; Kobbi, Fynn and Danso were there to meet him. Danso had a rifle in his hands just in case of trouble. The stranger jumped down and after a brief discussion with Danso, they took him into the house. Manu turned his concerned gaze towards Margaret.

'Should you go and see what it is all about?'

'No,' she shook her head. 'Richard will tell us if it's important. Protecting both of you is my priority at the moment.'

They didn't have long to wait, as Richard was soon seen coming out of the house towards them. He looked a little grim, and Margaret's heart began to beat faster as she feared more bad news.

'What's happened?' Margaret's voice came out little more than a whisper. 'Another village hasn't been destroyed, has it?' She took Manu's hand into her own, prepared for the worst.

Richard shook his head, as he squatted down in front of them. 'It's good news, Margaret. Your friend Chief Kojo sent the messenger. Apparently a group of youngsters staggered into their village begging sanctuary. It was at least a day before the Chief could get anything sensible out of any of them, but it seems that they're also survivors of the massacre on Manu's village.'

A cry escaped from Margaret, but it was a sound of joy. 'God be praised! Do they know of any other survivors? We must bring them here.' For a moment Richard didn't answer as he scratched Sebastian's back. This silence worried Margaret.

'Is there a problem? Don't you want them here? I can arrange to take them to the Haven if necessary.'

The Professor shook his head. 'If they are who they claim to be they will come here, there's no question about that.'

Frowning, Margaret reached out to grasp his arm. 'You doubt their identity? Why?'

He exhaled slowly. 'It could be a trick to get to Manu and Adwoa. I'm hoping that Manu may be able to recognize perhaps a name or two in the group. I don't suppose you know everyone from your village; no one will be upset if you can't identify these people.'

Manu glanced at Margaret who smiled reassuringly, then back to Richard; 'I'll try my best.'

Richard smiled. 'Good boy!' He withdrew from his trouser pocket a piece of paper the messenger had given him.

'The leader of the group is a girl, 16, and her name is Juba. There is also an older boy, about 18, called Pra, but Kojo writes that he seems mentally deficient. There is a five year old boy called Ohini, a ten year old boy called Sentwali and two girls about eight years old, Hola and Afia. There are also two toddlers, a girl, Mardea and a boy Chinua.'

Looking up from the letter, Richard actually held his breath as Manu stared at him intently. A single tear rolled down Manu's cheek and a look of horror crept into Margaret's face. The boy's next words were barely audible.

'I know them all!'

Uttering a cry of elation, Margaret hugged Manu, who began to cry. His tears were of joy that he and Adwoa were not all alone in the world. Richard breathed a sigh of relief.

'Juba is my cousin; Ohini lived next to us. Sentwali and I used to go fishing with our fathers. Hola is my sister, and I know the others.'

Richard took Adwoa into his arms so that Margaret could comfort Manu. Soon though, the tears were all gone.

'When can I see them?' Manu sniffed as he wiped the back of his hand across his face to remove his tears.

Richard checked the Chief's letter, 'In a day or two. They're in need of rest and care. They have a few minor wounds and burns, but Kojo will send them here as soon as he feels they're up to the journey.'

Still sniffing, Manu slipped off the hammock. 'May I go and tell Nbulungi the good news, Miss Margaret?'

She smiled at him. 'Of course you may. Don't disturb her though if she's asleep.' Manu promised before running off to the cottage.

Are Their Injuries Serious?

Margaret waited until the boy was out of earshot before she turned her gaze back to Richard. He was playing peek-a-boo with Adwoa, but looked up when Margaret slid out of the hammock.

'How badly are they injured?' She asked.

Richard straightened his position. 'The dagger and spear wounds are serious, but not life threatening now that they can be cared for.' He swallowed hard before continuing, 'Kojo fears for the older boy's sanity. One of the attackers had thrown the 16 year old Juba to the ground and instead of instantly killing her, he tried to rape her. The 18 year old, Pra was battling another attacker and couldn't immediately go to help her. According to the younger ones, Pra went psychotic.'

'He smashed his attacker's head with a rock before taking his dagger and slitting the throat of Juba's attacker. The blow was so vicious that it clean took the man's head off. Although he was dead, Pra kept stabbing him over and over again, until Juba managed to make him drop the knife. He's been in a catatonic state ever since.'

Closing her eyes Margaret managed to hold back the tears, but could not contain a sob, 'We must bring him out of that dark place to which he has descended, before it's too late.'

Placing his free arm around her shoulder, Richard led the way inside. 'We'll write back to Kojo immediately. We can go and get them if you like.'

'No,' Margaret shook her head. 'Kojo will know when they're fit to travel, I don't want to force them to move before they're ready.'

A confused Sebastian followed them up the steps. *There had been tears, shouts of joy, a lot of talk but I don't know if the news was good or bad. Anything that upsets Margaret isn't good in my book, but perhaps this one might not turn out to be so bad.*

Not Good News From Accra

After dinner a courier arrived with a letter for Elliott. He read it through silently before handing it to Richard.

'Damnation!' Margaret was startled to see Richard so angry as he waved a piece of paper in his hand.

'What's happened?' *Horrible possibilities flood into my brain as I try to imagine what could make my amiable Professor so agitated.*

Elliott Gibbs smiled reassuringly at her. 'It's nothing to panic over. My discharge papers have arrived from Accra.'

'Oh!' Margaret stared blankly at Richard's flushed features.

'Dishonourable discharge papers!' Richard snarled.

'Oh no!' Margaret shook her head in disbelief. 'How can they do that?' She took the letter Richard held out to her as proof the authorities in Accra had done just that.

'It's nothing to get worked up about,' soothed Elliott leaning back casually in his chair at the table. 'We should've expected this.'

'No we shouldn't!' Richard paced in his agitation. 'Didn't those idiots even read my reports? Well I am not going to let this happen!'

Elliott shook his head. 'It has already happened.'

Margaret looked up from the letter. 'What is this other nonsense? You have to report to Head Quarters immediately or they'll send guards to arrest you for desertion.' Her gaze rested on the cast upon the Lieutenant's leg. 'How were you supposed to travel to Accra with a broken leg, a hole in your shoulder and the amount of blood you had lost?'

Elliott chuckled, 'Calm down, both of you. There's nothing we can do for the moment to change the situation and sky rocketing your blood pressure is not going to help anyone.'

'How can you take this so calmly?' Richard sat down opposite him.

'Because I don't care! The time I've spent with you and Margaret... oh and Sebastian, of course, has made me realize that there are certain things that matter more than others. This is not one of them. I don't particularly want to end up in prison but I'll sort it all out, I hope, when I can finally travel to Accra.'

Margaret put her arms around Elliott from behind him. 'Well we're not going to let them haul you off to prison! We'll be with you in Accra.'

Elliott squeezed her hand. 'Thanks but you've enough problems to worry about. There's a mad King and an even madder grandfather to take care of.'

Richard shook his head. 'Don't forget that Marconi is still on the loose.' His eyes were twinkling in mischief.

Elliott nodded, 'Yeah! Wow! My problems really seem inconsequential in comparison to all that!'

'Even so,' Richard was finding it difficult to keep the tremor of laughter out of his voice, 'We will be going to the Capital with you as soon as we have settled the other survivors here.'

Margaret straightened, her face etched in worry lines. 'Yes, now we're back to the mad King.'

Richard took her hand between his. 'We'll deal with him, don't worry Margaret. No one will let Peponi harm any of the survivors.'

She smiled in gratitude at his support but a chill swept through her. *If protecting these children means a fight to the death, then I'm prepared to take it to that level. It's what my parents had done to protect me, and now what I must do to protect my own.*

THURSDAY

The other survivors

A squeal of delight from Manu heralded the arrival of one of Richard's men, driving the mare Sally and the covered wagon. As soon as they had heard about the other survivors, Richard had sent the vehicle to Chief Kojo's village so that when the children were ready to travel, they could be comfortable.

Only the women who will assist me, thought Dalila, *are on hand to welcome them. I feel that it will be better for the children not to be overwhelmed by too many people at once, or too many men either. Miss Margaret has sent Sebastian into the house so as to introduce him when the arrivals are a little less nervous of their surroundings.*

Manu tried to stand patiently beside Margaret as the driver assisted the survivors out of the cart, but when his younger sister, Hola, screamed out his name in delight, Manu ran forward to embrace her.

The 16 year old girl, Juba, glanced swiftly at Pra and lay a comforting hand on his arm but the older boy only had a simple smile on his face.

'J? M?' Pra forced out and Juba relaxed, smiling.

'Yes Pra, you remember Manu.'

Pra swept Manu up into a hug that was as gratifying as it was uncomfortable. Juba gently suggested that he put the younger boy down again.

'J?' Pra looked confused but Juba patted his hand reassuringly.

'It's all right, but we must introduce ourselves to Miss Munroe. She has offered us protection.'

Pra relaxed and obediently followed Juba and the other children to where Margaret was patiently waiting for them, smiling in welcome.

'Before you tell me all your names, we shall go sit down under the shade of a tree and Manu will organize some drinks for us.' Manu eagerly disappeared inside as Juba took the hands of the two toddlers and they followed Margaret out of the hot sun.

As they sat down on the grass, they looked at Margaret, expectantly.

'It doesn't matter if you don't remember everything that you see or hear today, but there is one thing that I want you to never forget,' Margaret paused until she was certain that she held their attention. *Well not the two toddlers, they're trying to catch butterflies.* 'While you're here, you are under my protection. We'll do everything within our power to keep you safe. Until this problem is resolved, you mustn't leave this property without an adult escort. I cannot protect you if I don't know where you are. Do you understand?'

The children nodded, even Pra, but as Margaret thought he was only copying the others, she raised a questioning eyebrow to Juba.

'It's all right Miss Margaret; I'll make sure he understands.' Juba promised.

Manu appeared carrying a jug of drink while Dalila brought out glasses on a tray. As Manu poured out drinks, Juba instructed the eight year old girls to watch the toddlers with their drinks so that she could draw Margaret aside. They didn't move far away and kept Pra in line of sight, but Juba did not want them to hear her question.

Juba Seeks Answers

'How much danger are we still in?'

'The Ashanti King is apparently trying to kill off all with his bloodline. If he learns that there are any survivors he will continue the slaughters until none remain.'

'That's insane!' Juba looked horrified. 'What have we ever done to Peponi?'

'I don't quite know.' Margaret shook her head. 'What I've been told is that Peponi is scared that his next of kin might attempt to remove him to take the throne. So he has decided to kill them before they kill him.'

'But we must be so remotely related to the King that I didn't even know anyone in the village was of his blood line.'

Margaret stroked the girl's hair. 'Insanity doesn't have to make sense. We'll deal with him when the time arises.'

Pra's Condition

'Right now I need to assess the state of all your injuries and how to best help Pra.'

Juba sighed as her eyes rested upon the older boy, placidly and gently holding a squirming toddler as Hola encouraged the little one to drink from the cup she held.

'He's already vastly improved Miss Margaret. After the… once he had…' A lump forming in Juba's throat made it impossible for her to continue. Margaret pressed her hand.

'I understand. He completely withdrew into himself didn't he?'

Juba nodded. 'It was like he was an empty shell. He couldn't think or act for himself. He wouldn't or couldn't utter a sound. Somehow he understood what I was saying and as long as I directed him, Pra would do anything.'

'With such young ones and everyone tired, scared and sore, it wasn't an easy journey. Pra would not sleep. There was nothing I could say that would allow him to close his eyes even for a couple of hours. Yet he continued on, tirelessly, protecting us, carrying the babies until we came to Chief Kojo's village.'

'Every day I'd tell Pra that we were going to find someone who could help us. So by the time we entered the village I think Pra understood that we were in no danger from these villagers. I feared that seeing grown men would cause Pra to… for it to trigger off another frenzied attack. Chief Kojo was so kind, and all his people were supportive.'

'Their medicine woman gave Pra an herbal remedy which made him sleep all night and nearly half the day. There was an improvement in Pra once he woke up. It was as if his brain had been switched on again. He wasn't back to his normal self but it was obvious he understood a lot more what was going on around him.'

'And the attempt to communicate verbally?' asked Margaret.

'You saw the effort it takes for him to make a sound. It's almost as if he's fighting against himself to be able to speak.'

Margaret pressed her hand against her own forehead. 'He's doing just that Juba. A part of his brain is trying to block out all memories to prevent having to relive and remember the horror you've just been through. It's trying to protect him but it also disables his ability to function as a normal person.'

'Will it be permanent?'

The older woman shook her head. 'No, from what you have described he's not beyond help. It will take time.'

Juba's brow puckered into a frown. 'How much time do we have before the Ashanti King comes to kill us?'

Margaret placed her arm around Juba's shoulders. 'Don't worry about that. I need you to concentrate upon ensuring that these children feel safe and comfortable here. I will deal with Peponi.'

Juba looked up at her, a little doubtfully. *This man has already had hundreds, possibly thousands of innocent people killed. What can one white woman do against such a man?* The quiet assurance and confidence in Margaret's voice had a soothing effect upon Juba's fears and knew a sense of relief to let someone else worry about their protection.

Big Kitty!

A squeal of delight and a cry of 'Kitty!' from one of the toddlers caused Margaret to turn swiftly as Richard approached with Sebastian beside him. The Professor's hand lay lightly on the tiger's neck but there would be nothing he could do if Sebastian bolted. They paused several feet away and Sebastian lay down to wait for the command for him to come closer.

Margaret knelt down beside Pra, who although he hadn't moved at the sight of Sebastian, he had stiffened.

'Pra, look at me.' Margaret ordered gently.

'M… M?' He raised his concerned eyes to Margaret's face.

'This is Richard Evans and beside him is Sebastian. Neither will harm you, in fact they'll help me to protect you. Please don't scream or run, it'll only upset him. Do you understand Pra? They are your friends.'

Pra's gaze returned to rest upon Sebastian but the tension left his body.

Responding to a signal from Margaret, Manu rose to his feet and walked calmly forward to sit down beside Sebastian. He began to pat the tiger to show his kin that they were safe. It was enough for one toddler, with another cry of 'Big Kitty!' Chinua tottered towards Sebastian, his hands stretched out in front of him. Pra stiffened again, but

Manu took the toddler into his lap and showed him how to stroke the tiger without pulling out handfuls of fur.

'Make sure the little one doesn't pull on Seb's whiskers, he wouldn't like that.' Richard quietly instructed Manu, who quickly moved Chinua's exploring hands away from Sebastian's face. The other children, spurred on by Chinua's success also wanted to pat the "Big Kitty".

When Sebastian had had enough he rose, stretched and slowly moved to stand beside Margaret. Smiling, she kissed him on the nose and scratched his ear.

'Good boy.' She praised before he turned and strolled away and out of view.

Juba's Emotional Crash

Manu showed his family around the house where mats lay on the floor of the living room, with the backs of the lounge suites positioned to protect them. Blankets and pillows sat in a neat pile as well as some spare clothing to tide the survivors over until Dalila had the opportunity to get their actual sizes.

Juba was so touched by the little things done for their comfort that she burst into tears. Pra became extremely agitated at her crying as he couldn't see the danger that could make her so upset. She couldn't stop crying to be able to explain to reassure Pra and Manu, not knowing what to tell the older boy, looked around helplessly for support.

Leaving Manu and his sister Hola to look after the others, Margaret drew Pra and Juba aside. She explained in simple words to Pra that Juba wasn't in danger that she had been so brave and strong for the children for so long that she was now exhausted. *I won't attempt to explain adrenalin to Pra; it would only be too confusing.*

Luckily it wasn't necessary as Pra appeared to understand that Juba needed emotional support and not a physical protector. He took Juba into his arms, so that she cried into his shoulder and he gently stroked her hair. Margaret left them alone to take Manu and the other children onto the verandah for something to eat.

Nbulungi brought Adwoa out to join the other survivors and she stayed with them. She encouraged Juba to eat something and Margaret was happy enough to leave them alone with Nbulungi.

A Romantic Interlude

Wandering around to the other side of the verandah, Margaret joined Richard and the Lieutenant as they savoured some of Richard's homemade wine. Smiling up at her with such a warm look in his eyes, which brought an instant flush to Margaret's cheeks, Richard held out his hand to her. Taking his hand, she found herself drawn down onto his lap and into a gentle kiss.

'Ooh! You taste like honey!' exclaimed Margaret.

Both Richard and Elliott laughed.

'We were just discussing whether or not this latest wine was too sweet.' The Professor explained, holding his own glass up to Margaret's lips. She took a small sip and smiled.

'Oh no, I like it.'

'It is too sweet then!' Richard sighed.

Margaret thumped his arm, 'Beast!' Elliott laughed as Richard placed his glass down out of harm's way before licking off the droplets of wine that had spilt onto his hand.

With a touch of devilry in his eyes, Richard kissed her again, this time with no restraint. Margaret melted against him, giving into the intoxicating pleasure until the sound of a chair creaking brought back her ethical dilemma.

She pushed gently against Richard's shoulder and drawing away from him, she cast a guilty glance at Elliott who was attempting to rise out of his chair quietly.

Margaret slipped off Richard's lap and sat down in her own chair.

'Don't go Elliott, I apologise for embarrassing you. My common sense seems to fly out the window whenever Richard kisses me. How can something that feels so right be apparently so wrong?' There was a delicate blush to Margaret's cheeks that caused Richard to smile a little guiltily. Elliott settling back into his chair only laughed but neither men had an answer to give her.

Richard chuckled, coming to her rescue. 'How are the survivors settling in?' Margaret grasped the life line gratefully and they led away from more embarrassing conversations of a personal nature.

A Sigh Of Relief

Margaret gave the children as much time as they wanted with her. She also gave them space to be alone when they needed it. Just so long as they were visible or accompanied. There was more than one sigh of relief when the day ended peacefully and as the guards silently patrolled the farm, there was still a nervous edge to the air. *Until it is finally over, none of us will sleep completely easy*, sighed Margaret.

FRIDAY

A Restless Night

The whole night was not to be completely restful. Manu and Adwoa wanted to sleep alongside the other children. This wouldn't have been a problem except Adwoa became grizzly and unsettled as her gums became enflamed and tender again as she was teething. Manu tried to keep her quiet but eventually Margaret heard her and took the baby outside. Pra, who still wasn't sleeping much, went out to sit beside Margaret as she nursed Adwoa.

Once the baby had settled down, Richard's gel cooling her gums and she chewed on a hard biscuit; Margaret offered Adwoa to Pra to hold. He adamantly shook his head. Nervously he patted Adwoa gently on the head but didn't want to hold her. Margaret chatted quietly to Pra, not really expecting him to answer but knew that he was listening while on the look out for danger.

Sebastian had come out of the house with them and lay stretched on the verandah floor at Margaret's feet. He was just as watchful as Pra for danger but didn't consider the young man to be part of that threat to his mistress.

Eventually Adwoa slept but Margaret didn't take her back inside as she knew that the respite would be short lived. She laid her head back on the cushion and closed her eyes but she didn't sleep. *Too many thoughts and fears are running through my brain to allow sleep to come. Not that I think that I would get much sleep anyway as Adwoa's gums are very enflamed and sore.* During the early hours of the morning, Pra and Margaret took the baby across to the hammock so that her crying didn't disturb the rest of the household.

Sebastian was restless. *There is not only the feeling in the air that trouble is coming, but also Adwoa's cries hurt my ears.* The big cat patrolled the immediate area, always returning to Margaret's side and even staying a while whenever Adwoa was quiet again.

More Trouble Arrives

So there was quite a sense of relief when the sun began to rise to dispel the dark enemy that surrounded them. Richard, taking Adwoa and giving her a bottle, nursed the baby while he ate his own breakfast. As Dalila fussed about feeding the other children, and Lieutenant Gibbs, Richard suggested that Margaret try to get a couple of hours sleep.

Shaking her head, she pressed a tender kiss against his forehead and said, 'I only need a cold shower and a cup of tea as there is too much work to be done.'

The Professor was about to order her to rest, but was frowned at by Dalila. Obediently he closed his mouth again but Pra was not as easily satisfied as he tried to follow Margaret into the bathroom.

'Ma… Ma?'

Smiling, she pressed his hand. 'It's all right Pra. Have something to eat and watch over the children, I won't be long.'

The troubled young man looked around the table at his family and obediently sat down to also eat.

Two shots were heard close in succession and caused Elliott to swear. Not because he was startled by the gunshots like Margaret who had jumped; but as he had leapt up from the dining table, he had smashed his damaged leg against it.

'Damn! Where's my rifle?' The Lieutenant reached for his crutches which were leaning against the wall behind him. 'Two shots,' he explained, 'Is the signal that one of the sentry guards has been found either dead or wounded. We may only have minutes to hide these children!'

Pra wrapped his fingers tightly around the knife beside his plate and looked towards Margaret for guidance.

'Ma... Ma?'

Margaret nodded. 'You and Juba take the little ones into the kitchen and stand guard over them. I'll deal with this.' The quiet confidence in her voice reassured all the children as Juba scooped up both the toddlers and Manu took Adwoa from Richard to also protect his kin.

King Peponi

Sebastian pressed himself close to Margaret's side as Richard strode towards the rifle that hung on the wall beside the front door. A piercing scream from outside broke through Dalila's calm. Her eyes widened in horror and she stiffened as she had recognized the voice. Before Richard could take down the rifle, three men entered the house; one had an arm around Nbulungi's waist, a knife pressed against her throat.

Outside, outraged Fynn and Danso as well as the rest of the villagers were being held back by more Ashanti strangers. Dalila moved instinctively towards her pregnant daughter but Margaret laid her hand on her arm to stop her. Margaret stepped forward, scrutinizing the three Ashanti men in turn.

'King Peponi?' her enquiry was polite, yet un-necessary as she recognized the insane gleam in the eyes of the man who held Nbulungi. He acknowledged her with a nod of his head. Margaret locked her eyes squarely upon him.

'Now that you've forced your way inside, let the girl go. You no longer need a hostage; or are you using her to shield yourself?'

The King's laugh sent a chill down Margaret's spine but she maintained an impassive face. 'Tell your men folk to drop their weapons and I'll release the whore.'

Margaret placed her hand on Sebastian's neck as he had not liked the King's tone and was ready to attack. Without having to be asked Elliott lowered his rifle to the ground as he thought, *We need to get Nbulungi out of harm's way before we can deal with this mad man.* Peponi pushed his hostage away in disgust and Nbulungi ran to the protection of her mother's arms sobbing in relief. Richard glanced briefly at Pra but the youth stood like a rock in front of his family.

'Take Nbulungi away, Dalila, this doesn't concern either of you.' Richard's quiet order caused the Ashanti King to turn blazing eyes towards him.

'They do not have my permission to leave!'

Richard's eyebrows rose and a supercilious expression appeared as he looked over the rim of his glasses at the King. 'Are they of your blood?' His quiet but stern question surprised the Ashanti leader.

'No.'

'Then this does not involve them.' Richard transferred his gaze to Dalila. 'Take Nbulungi away and calm her down.'

Dalila looked once at the Ashanti King but didn't disobey, leading her daughter into Margaret's bedroom to lie down.

'This can be very simple,' stated King Peponi, 'Hand over any survivors and your people needn't get hurt.'

Margaret shook her head. 'No!' Her calm refusal was not a surprise but caused Peponi to sigh.

'I wanna avoid bloodshed.'

Margaret was startled into laughing. 'Too late for that, don't you think? I won't permit you to harm these children or anyone else for that matter. I have claimed guardianship over the survivors. They're my kin now.'

'If you or your villagers try to stop me claiming my blood then you too will die.'

'I don't think so,' Margaret's calm assurance surprised even Richard.

I realize that any sign of fear, alarm or anger from Margaret could snap clean through the minute hold Pra has upon sanity. 'You shall not sully this place with the blood of the innocent!' Richard added, 'Leave now or you won't leave here alive!' It seemed like such a ridiculous statement coming from peaceful Richard, but no one felt like laughing.

King Peponi threw his hands up in a magnificent gesture. 'I'm not so easy to get rid of, white man. It was foreseen that once I consumed all of my blood that I shall be immortal!'

'Poppycock!' Margaret's exclamation seemed to quite succinctly sum up how they were all feeling. 'I have never heard such utter nonsense in all my life! Do you really believe that slaughtering every single person who carries your bloodline will make you live forever?' The edge of scorn in Margaret's voice made both Sebastian and Pra move restlessly but neither sprang into action.

'It has been foretold!' The King made another grand gesture with his hands. 'Now stand aside woman.' As he moved towards the children Margaret placed herself in the way.

'No! You'll have to kill me first.'

Peponi shrugged. 'So be it!' With lightning speed he drew his knife and lunged at her. She had been expecting the attack and easily moved out of his reach, but Peponi was quicker than she had anticipated and the blade slashed against her arm. Blood spurted, Sebastian growled but it was Richard who reacted by punching Peponi in the face so hard that he fell to the floor, dropping the knife.

One of the King's guards took a step towards Richard but never touched him as Sebastian leapt across the fallen King and brought the other man down flat onto his back and stood on his chest. The second guard raised his knife to attack Sebastian but Margaret's calm voice stopped him.

'I wouldn't do that if you valve your life,' she pressed a handkerchief against her arm to slow the blood loss. 'He'll kill you and your friend before you can even touch him.'

The tiger bared his teeth and the man lowered his weapon. Sebastian lifted his tail but Margaret knowing what he was about to do, commanded him to stop.

'Not in the house Sebastian! Just sit on the one you've got!'

Disappointed Sebastian planted his bottom down on the prisoner and angrily flicked his tail. *One wrong move, and I'll have you!*

A Stand Off

At the sight of blood dripping down Margaret's arm, Pra had tightened his grip on the table knife in his hand and took a step forward.

'Ma… Ma?'

Margaret turned to face him. 'Pra, stay with your children.'

Pra's eyes widened in horror, 'Ma… Ma!' He raised his free hand in warning but it was too late. King Peponi had sprung to his feet and snatching up his fallen blade, he seized Margaret from behind and pressed the already bloodied knife against her throat. Pra raised his own weapon as Sebastian stood up on his prisoner and Richard's hands clenched into fists but the King shook his head.

'None of you are fast enough to reach me before I could slit her pretty throat!'

All the men stood perfectly still except Richard who held up his hand to command the tiger not to move.

'Seb, if you jump him, Margaret could get hurt!'

Margaret kept her eyes on Pra but she spoke to Peponi. 'Killing me will not make these honourable people just give the innocent to you for slaughter.' She kept her voice calm but there was no hiding her scorn.

The King laughed and caressed the edge of his blade against her jaw. 'I think your man would do anything to prevent your death.'

Margaret transferred her gaze from Pra to Manu and locked her eyes with the younger boy's. 'These children are my children! They are my kin and that makes them his responsibility as well. Harm any of us and you won't leave this farm alive.'

Margaret held Manu's gaze before lowering her eyes to the young man's free hand which sat upon the hunting knife at his waist. She shook her head slightly as Manu was about to follow her gaze. Margaret directed his eyes towards her own hand. It was all done in seconds but Margaret knew, *I have to do whatever is necessary to prevent a bloodbath; even if it cost me, my own life.* Richard didn't take his eyes off Margaret's face but it was to the Ashanti King he spoke.

'Peponi!'

The King turned his head to look at Richard, an arrogant sneer on his face as he expected Richard to agree to anything to save her. The King's grip loosened slightly on the knife at Margaret's throat. Richard exhaled slowly; *I hope that whatever Margaret has planned is going to work.*

'No deal!' Richard declared.

Peponi's jaw wasn't the only one that dropped in surprise but that moment of shock was enough time for Margaret to act. Before Peponi could bring the blade back against her throat, she sank her teeth into his hand causing her captor to swear. As his hold loosened around her waist, Margaret caught the knife that Manu threw at her and twisting to face Peponi, plunged the weapon straight into his chest.

There was a look of astonishment on the King's face as he clung to Margaret, trying to hold himself up but her aim had been true and had pierced his heart. As Peponi collapsed, in a last ditch effort to inflict a fatal wound upon Margaret, he tried to run his own blade into her but Sebastian was not having any of that. The tiger leapt from on top of his prisoner and brought the King crashing down, his great fangs sinking purposefully into the arm that held the weapon. It was lifeless fingers, though, that the blade fell from as the King Peponi gasped his last breath before he hit the floor.

I Am Their Champion!

Recovering from their stupor, the Ashanti guards, one leaping to his feet, were ready to avenge their King's death but both Richard and Sebastian were faster to react. The tiger knocked down again his previous prisoner as Richard grabbed the rifle off the wall and pointed it at the other Ashanti warrior at the same time as Elliott picked up his own rifle.

'Don't move!' Richard's voice was almost inaudible as he was overwhelmed by anger.

Margaret raised her hand to where the King's knife had nicked her throat and blood was streaming down the front of her shirt. 'Enough blood has been spilt. I need you alive to carry out my orders when you go back to Ashanti,' she said.

Manu gave baby Adwoa to his sister Hola and rushed forward with the medical kit, always kept in the kitchen, to assist Margaret stop the bleeding.

The guard still standing curled his lip in a sneer. 'The death of our King must be avenged!'

Margaret shook her head, allowing Manu to press a cloth against her throat and didn't argue as he led her to sit down on the nearest lounge.

'I think not. My life and that of the children I protect were in danger. I defended myself. Peponi was warned what would result if he did not disarm.'

'The children must return to Ashanti with us.'

'No, not yet, until they're of age, as their guardian and champion you will have to follow my orders!'

'Never! A woman, and a white one at that, as our ruler? Never!'

Margaret tore the sleeve of her shirt to allow Manu to bandage her arm where the King had first wounded her.

'Calm yourself,' she advised. 'That is the last thing I want also. I have a solution but first I want your people outside to lay down their arms. There will be no more killing.'

The guard stared hard at her for a minute passing his tongue over suddenly dry lips. 'What would stop you then killing us all?'

'My word!' Margaret sighed wearily. 'So long as none of our people have been harmed, your people will all leave here alive.'

Elliott pointed with his gun towards the front door. 'Come on! Let's get on with it! This business is starting to bore me!'

Sebastian stepped off his captive and allowed him to leave with Elliott, who limped painfully out. Richard picked up the Ashanti's discarded weapons, throwing them onto the table before kneeling down beside Margaret to check on the state of her injuries. Satisfied with the repair job done by Manu, Richard moved across to stand in front of Pra.

'You did very well Pra. You protected your family from harm. You've all been very brave.' Gently Richard laid his hand on Pra's shoulder who raised questioning eyes to the Professor's face.

"Pro… Prof…'

Richard shook his head. 'It's not over yet, Pra, but you're safe now.'

A Council Of Elders

It wasn't too long before Elliott escorted the two guards back into the house. 'No one has been injured and they've given up their weapons. None of them seemed interested in a fight once they heard that Peponi was dead,' he explained, pushing the Ashanti men onto a couple of kitchen chairs. 'It's safe now Margaret if you want the children to go over to Dalila's home while you deal with this lot.'

She shook her head. 'Not yet. I want to be certain that they're happy with what I decide is appropriate.' Margaret gestured for Pra to bring his family to sit down around her. Not until they were settled, did she turn her attention to the guards.

'I do not want to be your Queen or ruler but for the moment I speak for these children. There is a great deal of work to be done. A near impossible task but you must discover who exactly is next in line for the throne. The body of the King must be taken back to Ashanti despite the evil he has committed he should be with his ancestors.'

'In the meantime a council of the wisest elders shall be called to take over the rule of your people. When the survivors reach their majority, if none wish to rule, which I wouldn't blame them, then the elders must decide if they will continue to govern or find a means of appointing a successor.'

There was a moment of silence to digest the information. Juba glanced across at Manu and nodded. He agreed, 'Sounds fair, Miss Margaret, but…' Manu hesitated putting into words the hurt, torment and anger he felt.

Margaret tenderly laid her hand against his cheek. 'I know, justice, though, Manu, and not revenge. I feel that the men following Peponi's orders were doing so unwillingly,' she transferred her gaze to the guards. 'What did he threaten you with?'

They exchanged a speaking glance between them before one answered, 'The King would have our own families slaughtered. If we tried to tell or warn anyone, he would have killed every one of our blood.'

Margaret nodded in understanding of their fears. 'Even so, you will have to face some punishment. You did not have to let him terrorize you like that.'

The guards shifted uncomfortably in their seats and glanced at each other in horror. Margaret managed a tired smile. 'Don't look so worried, you get to live and it won't hurt one bit.' Her reassurance lightened their fears.

'You must serve the council elders to restore order and control. So long as the acts are lawful, you shall be a servant to your people. Any more bloodshed and you will all face white man's laws.'

The relief was evident in the eyes of the Ashanti men. 'Yes Ma'am.' They rose to their feet but then hesitated as they looked down at the body of their former King before raising their eyes to their new leader.

'Take him with you. Perform your funeral rites as you see fit. I am tempted to cut off his head and mount it onto a pole so that your people can see the result of this madness but there has been enough horror.' Margaret glanced down at Juba and Manu, her eyebrows raised. 'Do you wish to add anything my children?'

They shook their heads but Pra was frowning as his tormented brain tried to assimilate all the information that he had heard.

'Ma… Ma?'

'Yes Pra?'

'Bad… men… go?'

'Yes Pra.'

'Fam… lee… safe?'

'Yes Pra.'

Great big tears of relief ran down the troubled boy's cheeks as his body was wracked with sobs. Pra could finally let go of all the emotions he had locked away deep inside to keep his family alive. He buried his head in Margaret's lap and she ran a soothing hand over his head as he cried.

Still So Much To Do

Richard, satisfied that Pra's mood wouldn't lead to a violent outburst, turned his attention towards the two Ashanti men, 'Time to leave gentlemen. Any attempt to harm Margaret or any of the survivors will be harshly dealt with. Is that understood?'

The guards bent down to pick up Peponi's body. 'Yes Sir.' Elliott followed them outside with Sebastian to see the interlopers on their way off the property. A sigh of relief went through the children as they began to realize what had just taken place.

Dalila and Nbulungi emerged from the bedroom and scooped up the children to share their joy. Dalila tut-tutted over the blood stained floor but Margaret thought it was more important that the youngsters were settled and comforted. Dalila decided to take them and Nbulungi back to her home. *I'll have to rid the main house of King Peponi's presence before I allow the children to return.*

Margaret wasn't sorry to hand over the care of the children to someone else for a while. *What with a sleepless night, a violent confrontation and the loss of blood, I need time to come to terms with the fact that I have just killed another human being.*

Keeping his alert gaze upon Margaret's face, Richard sat down on the lounge beside her. She was so deep in thought that she didn't react even when he took her hand between his own. He spoke her name twice before she finally brought her eyes up to his concerned face. A slow smile appeared as she raised her free hand to caress against his cheek.

'I must do something about that rug. That blood will stain it if left to dry.' Margaret got to her feet but Richard retained his grasp on her hand.

'Margaret…'

She wouldn't allow him to finish. 'It's all right. Really! You were right, though, I'm feeling very tired. I might have that cat nap you suggested, but this rug needs soaking first.'

'Do you want to talk about what has just happened?' He still wouldn't let her go.

'Of course! But… It just doesn't feel that important any more. I know I'll have to come to terms with having killed someone but there is still so much we have to deal with before we can relax and analysis what we should or should not have done.'

'Someone in my family still wants me dead, there might be serious repercussions from Peponi's death and Pra and the other survivors will need our help to cope with the massacre of their loved ones.' On these last words her voice wavered. Richard's fingers tightened around hers but she managed to smile, reassuringly.

'Go to bed then, I'll clean up here,' Richard laughed as she looked startled. 'What? I'm not completely useless you know.'

'Of course I know that.' Margaret shook her head. 'It's just that I don't expect you to clean up after me.' She gently drew her hand out of his and bent down to roll up the rug. The loss of blood, though, had impaired her equilibrium and she wavered uncertainly as she quickly straightened up again.

'Oh!'

Richard was on his feet at once, his hands surrounding her waist to support Margaret as her knees buckled slightly. Her exclamation of surprise changed to one of annoyance.

'Oh! How ridiculous!'

Richard urged her back down onto the lounge before rolling up the strip of carpet. Dalila bustled back into the room, a sprig of herbs in her hand.

'I'll take that Sir. I suggest you take Miss Margaret outside for a while as I intend to cleanse the house of that man's evil spirit.' As the Housekeeper was shooing them towards the door, Richard offered Margaret his arm for support as she stood up once more. Dalila picked up the rug and took it to the laundry to soak before she set alight her sprig of herbs and used the smoke it produced to sweep the air clean of the dead King's presence.

Sebastian, Kobbi and Elliott joined Margaret and Richard on the verandah.

'I wouldn't go in if I were you,' Richard stated, 'Dalila is fumigating. We're going to head down to the river for a while; you're more than welcome to join us.'

Elliott shook his head. 'Thanks but my leg is killing me. I'll sit here on the verandah and wait for the escort I sent out with the Ashanti warriors to return.'

Kobbi patted Sebastian on the back. 'Come on Seb, I'll race you to the river!' He broke into a run and after casting a questioning look at Margaret, the tiger was soon on Kobbi's heels and overtaking. As Richard and Margaret followed more sedately he thought, *It has been one hell of a way to start the day and I only hope that there are no more surprises in the immediate future.*

We Can't All Go To Accra

While Margaret slept in the shade of the trees beside the river, Father Gerard arrived and Richard calmly explained all that had taken place. The Priest was not calm at all in response as he thanked God that a massacre had been prevented. Once Gerard had composed himself, they were able to discuss what preparations they needed to make for the journey down to the Capital city.

Father Gerard and Kobbi would remain at the farm to protect the children with the aid of the villagers. Elliott Gibbs needed to return to Accra to deal with his dishonourable discharge. *Not that I really care too deeply about that as the whole experience with Marconi has disillusioned me to the army,* thought Elliott.

As far as we're aware, mused Richard, *the mad Major is still on the loose and that is one of the main dangers that we might have to face. The other hazard is if Cedric has failed to stop their grandfather from his attempts to kill Margaret. Although I know it's illogical, I am worried more about the appearance of Marconi than any number of hired assassins because Margaret is more likely to lose control over the Major and possible kill him. I know it would probably be justifiable but I don't want her to get into the habit of killing people.*

The hardest decision they had to make was whether or not Sebastian would go to Accra with them. *Tiger and Mistress have never been apart since the day he had arrived at the Haven with his injured mother,* debated Richard. *To separate them would be inhumane but whereas the local villagers know Sebastian and respect his presence, in the city he might cause chaos and a panic. Also there will be far more people and vehicles and noise than either Sebastian or Margaret are accustomed to and it could be very disconcerting for them. On the other hand, there is no one I trust more to protect Margaret to the death.*

That fact overruled any doubts for Richard and perhaps any problems could be prevented by having Sebastian on a leash.

You Should Stay Here

It rained that afternoon forcing them back inside, or at least to the verandah as Dalila had all the windows and doors flung open to allow the herbs to cleanse the house. Father Gerard spent some time with the children and was surprised at how far Pra had come since he had first arrived at the farm. Although words were still a struggle to emerge, he did manage to make himself understood.

The two toddlers took an instant liking to the Priest as the feel of his bushy beard made them gurgle with laughter. *I'm worried,* sighed Father Gerard, *by how quiet and withdrawn Margaret appears but I know that Richard is keeping a close watch over her.*

Richard, though, wouldn't force Margaret to talk but wait until she was ready to confine her worries to him. Elliott was frustrated by the silence but a warning look from Richard caused him to bite his tongue. So when Margaret finally spoke, the Lieutenant jumped startled.

'I think you should remain here Richard.'

'No.'

'Elliott and I will be able to manage.'

'No.'

'Richard your work needs you to be here.'

'No.'

'I would feel more confident about leaving the children if you were here to protect them.'

'No. Gerard is more than capable of looking after the children.'

'Richard…'

'No Margaret! It doesn't matter what you conjure up, I'm not letting you out of my sight again. No offence to Elliott but I am not having a repeat performance. My work can wait and Gerard is a much better marksman and councillor than I could ever be to the survivors.' The Professor knocked out the dottle from his pipe before slipping it into his pocket. He strode off, putting an end to the argument to consult with Father Gerard.

I Can't Lose Him Too

Only waiting until Richard was out of ear shot, Elliott finally spoke, 'Not wishing to get my head snapped off but I don't think there is anything you can do or say to stop him from coming with us.'

'I had to try.' Margaret sighed.

'Why?'

'I'm afraid of putting him in danger. I don't think that I could cope if I lost him as well.'

Elliott shook his head. 'He has the right to do all in his power to protect you.'

'That doesn't stop me worrying.'

He laughed. 'Didn't think it would but that's what happens when you love someone.' Margaret blushed but didn't reply. He reached over and placed his hand over hers. 'This will all be over soon, Margaret. You have got to keep the faith.'

She managed a small smile. 'Right now I'm having a hard enough time just keeping alive!'

'Let Richard and I worry about that. Do you think it is safe to go back into the house yet?'

Margaret nodded. 'Oh yes. I'd better go and help Dalila with dinner.' Rising to her feet, she stretched carefully so as to not aggravate her injuries.

Elliott grimaced. 'You'll be sorer tomorrow.'

Margaret laughed, 'But alive, Elliott!' There was no arguing with that logic.

SATURDAY

Heading South

They started out at first light the next morning, Elliott was assisted into the cart beside Sebastian and the provisions for the journey. Margaret sat on the box of the cart beside Richard who was holding the reins. They would be accompanied by four armed guards, two riding a little way ahead of them.

As they set off Margaret glanced over her shoulder at the children who were enthusiastically waving to them and she wondered, *am I doing the right thing? What if I come back and the children have been murdered? What if I don't return at all? How many more people are going to die before this adventure is over?* She tried to shake off her doubts and concentrate upon what she needed to achieve in Accra. As this wasn't a pleasant task, it was not surprising that she was extremely quiet as the day moved on.

By the time they stopped to eat and rest in the midday heat, all their nerves were shredded to pieces with not knowing if or when they should expect another attack from Warren Foster, or even the mad, bad Major Marconi.

Sebastian was so restless that he was getting snappy. As the four guards were going to rest, Margaret sent the tiger out to patrol and work off his excess spleen, only wishing that she could remove her own frustrations so easily.

Focus On The Here And Now

Richard was acutely aware of Margaret's frustration and suggested that, while the guards rested, they took a walk to stretch their legs. Elliott protested that they shouldn't split up but Richard patted the gun holster on his hip.

'We're not going far,' he reassured, leading Margaret away from the group.

'Are you sure we should go out of sight?' Margaret glanced back to where Elliott sat on the ground looking worried.

'I want you to forget all your worries for half an hour.'

Margaret laughed as they entered the trees. 'How on earth do you plan to make that happen?' She was surprised to see a flush travel across Richard's tanned features.

'By being only in the here and now,' He stopped walking and drew her backwards into his arms so that her back was pressed against his chest. His hands shook slightly around her waist. 'Concentrate upon the present, forget the past and don't worry about the future, now is all that matters.'

I'm a little nervous about how close Richard is standing and I wonder how this is supposed to relax me? 'Do you mean right now?' She asked.

'Yes,' he murmured against her hair.

'How is this going to relax me? I'm standing here alone in the arms of a married man whom I would dearly love to kiss me but it is morally and ethically wrong.'

Richard sighed, 'I just want to give you half an hour where you didn't have to think but just feel; to be lost in a moment of enjoyment. To forget the trauma that you've been made to endure.'

He released her but as she turned around, Margaret took his hands between her own. 'It was a kind thought Richard. I do appreciate it but the guilt afterwards would make the stress even worse.'

'In the eyes of the law...'

Margaret shook her head. 'No Richard, in the eyes of God, you're still lawfully married to Alice. Until we're both free...'

It was Richards turn to interrupt, 'What do you mean "both free"? You're not secretly married to someone that I don't know about?'

This caused Margaret to laugh. 'No, if I was already married it would be pointless for my grandfather to try and kill me for my inheritance.' Although this had been said lightly, the gravity of it wiped the smile from her face.

'What I meant was that until this business with my family is settled it isn't safe for me to marry anyone. To put someone else I love in danger frightens me more than facing Grandfather Foster. That is why I didn't want you to come to Accra.'

Richard placed his hands on either side of Margaret's face as he gently kissed her. 'Oh Margaret, I would've gone crazy not knowing what was happening to you.'

I Have A Message For You

Despite her misgivings, Margaret allowed the kiss to deepen as she put her arms around his neck, but it was Richard who broke away and pulled her behind him. It wasn't to assist Margaret to keep her moral objections, but because Richard had heard someone approaching. His gun was in his hand and ready to kill any intruder.

'Whoa! Easy there cowboy!' A white man was being led by one of their native guards and Sebastian. The sight of the white man who spoke did not make Richard lower his weapon. In fact it made him aim more determinedly at the intruder. *This is one of the men who had ambushed Margaret on the way back from the Haven.* The man saw that recognition in Richard's face and held up his hands in fear.

'No, no. I know what you're thinking. I'm not crazy to come anywhere near you but I was sent with a message from Phillip Danbar.'

The native nodded. 'Sebastian seemed to agree Professor, something about a letter he has.'

Richard's eyebrows rose to assume his supercilious expression. 'When exactly did Sebastian learn to read?' He didn't take his eyes off the intruder.

'No sir,' said the guard. 'It was something about how it smelt.' He handed over the letter being careful not to get between Richard's gun and the intruder.

Margaret raised the paper to her nose; she looked up startled at Richard.

'They're right. I recognise that scent. That's Cedric.'

'It could still be a trap,' Richard wasn't prepared to risk Margaret's life without proper investigation.

'Mr Danbar knew that you wouldn't be easy to convince so he gave me a sort of password. He said to say that, "The Pebble people are real." He said you'd understand.'

The guard looked suspicious. 'There is no tribe called the Pebbles.'

Richard slowly lowered his weapon. 'That's all right Santos, I know what he's talking about. What does it say, Margaret?'

'*Dear Margaret and Richard,*

I know you'll be suspicious that I've used this man as a courier but he has been a great assistance to me. Cedric has gone missing and I'm afraid that Warren Foster has killed him after he went to see him about the pebbles and so forth. I beg you to get here as soon as possible. I can't put everything in writing. I'll tell you when you get here.

Please hurry, Phillip.'

Kenneth's Story

Richard looked at the intruder. 'So how did you come to be involved and what has happened?' He holstered his gun which made the other man relax a little.

'My name is Kenneth Knox, and I want to say up front that I deeply regret being a part of the attempt to kill Miss Munro.'

Richard waved this aside. 'All right, get on with your story. Unless it convinces me, I might still kill you.'

'Don't get trigger happy! Some of this I only know second hand but I'll start at the beginning before I even came into it all.' Kenneth took a deep breath before continuing, 'When Phillip and Cedric got back to Accra they took the Pebbles to be professionally assessed and once they knew they were real, they went and saw an old friend in the police force. They gave him the pebbles and all the information they had. The copper also got hold of the Professor's reports.'

'He told Cedric to leave it to him to investigate but Cedric insisted on going to see his grandfather. He wouldn't let Phillip go with him but when Cedric never came home, Phillip went looking for him. I won't go into the hissy fit Phillip threw at the grandfather's but his trail finally led him to finding Cedric's horse outside a brothel. That's when I came into the picture.'

Margaret's face was blank as she looked to Richard for enlightenment. 'What's a brothel?'

'It houses prostitutes,' explained Kenneth, but received only that bewildered look again.

'I'm sorry to be so dense, but I don't understand. What is a brothel or a prostitute?'

Kenneth looked stunned at Richard. 'She really is such an innocent?'

Richard nodded. 'Oh yes! Perhaps I had better explain,' He suggested and addressing Margaret, he continued, 'a prostitute is a person who has sexual intercourse for money.'

'Oh!' Margaret frowned in disbelief. 'That doesn't sound like Cedric. He didn't seem the unfaithful type.'

Richard shrugged. 'He kissed you didn't he?' Kenneth's eyes nearly boggled out of his head at how casually Richard sounded.

Margaret only laughed. 'Well so did Phillip, but how did he come to trust you?' She asked Kenneth but he was too stunned to speak for a moment.

'Uh, well I'd been transacting some business there and happened to see that the person who left the horse wasn't Cedric.'

'That doesn't mean Phillip would trust you?' Margaret still looked puzzled.

'Well I sort of smoothed things over as Phillip created a scene in the brothel. I also took him home as he was a little hysterical.'

Richard was sceptical but Margaret could believe that Phillip would lose control. *I would probably be hysterical if it was Richard who was missing in such a disturbing situation.*

'How long before we can continue to Accra, Richard?' *I'm determined to get going to Accra as soon as possible but I know that the horses need to rest.*

Richard pulled out his pocket watch and slowly nodded, 'Half an hour more should be fine; we haven't been pushing the pace up to this point.' He led them back to the main group. 'We'll have to watch that the horses don't suffer in this heat as we forge on.'

Richard relayed his orders to the others before suddenly turning back upon Kenneth Knox. 'You're on probation Mr. Knox, any attempt against Miss Munroe and I will kill you instantly, understood?' The fierceness of his gaze was enough to rob Kenneth of speech and all he could do was nod his head.

It Was Never Going To Be Easy

I'd always known that I wasn't going to be easily accepted but I hadn't thought that it would be such a stressful journey back to Accra, debated Kenneth Knox. *Not only am I aware that Richard Evan's eyes are upon me, but also those of Sebastian, Elliott Gibbs and the native guards.* By the time they set up camp for the night his nerves were almost as raw as Margaret's about facing her grandfather.

Kenneth meekly took the food he was offered and sat at a short distance from the main group. Margaret took pity on him and went to sit beside Kenneth despite the disapproving gaze of the other men.

'You knew that it would be hard to return to us. You don't know the hell that we've been through,' explained Margaret.

He exhaled slowly, 'I hadn't thought beyond getting here and convincing Professor Evans not to kill me on sight.'

Margaret smiled as she glanced across to where Richard's eye never left them. 'What on earth made you agree to come?'

Kenneth scratched his head. 'I don't know. Phillip Danbar was just so desperate and had already told me the whole story. He felt you'd have to believe me otherwise I must be a suicidal idiot!'

Sebastian came to sit between them, curling his body around Margaret's back, his tail laying possessively across her lap. She caressed the tiger's head.

'I'm fine, Seb. We'll face enough trouble when we reach Accra without us creating more waves.' She playfully pulled Sebastian's ear before rising and crossing to lay her hand on Richard's shoulder. 'I'm going to sleep.'

He gently pressed her fingers allowing her to draw her hand away after she had returned the pressure. 'We'll leave just before dawn breaks. Even with a decent rest during the hottest time of the day, we should reach Accra before nightfall tomorrow.'

Margaret nodded. 'I'll want to see Grandfather as soon as we arrive!'

Elliott's head rose in surprise. 'That's not a good idea. You'll be exhausted and we must see Phillip and the police first. One wrong move and it could cost Cedric his life.'

There was a pause of silence before Margaret finally nodded. 'All right, but I must warn you, I don't know how much more I can take before I crack completely.

The Female Of The Species

As Margaret headed for the cart, the eyes of Elliott and Richard met in the flickering light of the camp fire.

The Professor's eyebrows rose expressively. 'That actually frightens me more than anything else we've been through so far.' Richard removed his glasses and polished them absently.

'It should frighten you,' Kenneth Knox picked up his plate and joined the group around the fire, 'the only thing worse than a hysterical woman is a hysterical man.' He shuddered in memory. 'When Miss Munroe does crack, and I do mean when and not if, just make sure that anything that could be used as a weapon is kept out of her reach. I know something of Old Man Foster and he could enrage a saint. He'll easily be able to push his granddaughter over the edge.'

Richard rose to his feet and stretched his arms above his head. 'If that is indeed the case, Mr. Knox, then we won't have to worry about weapons... Margaret will be capable of killing him with her bare hands.' He called Sebastian to his side. 'I'll take first watch. Get some sleep, tomorrow will be a long hard ride.' The Professor and Sebastian left the group to patrol the immediate area.

The Unknown Entity

Kenneth Knox glanced across to Elliott Gibbs to find the Lieutenant looking even more worried. 'What additional problems have you thought of, Soldier?'

Elliott met his gaze. 'I've seen Margaret lose her temper but I don't think she is the one we need to worry about losing control.'

Kenneth's eyebrows rose. 'Are you a bigger threat, Soldier?'

Elliott smiled and glanced down at his plastered leg. 'Not in my condition, no, throughout all this Professor Evans has remained fairly cool, calm and collected.'

'And that worries you more?'

The Lieutenant nodded. 'Oh yes! I can guess how Margaret will react but Richard is an unknown entity. We could all be in serious danger if Richard Evans ever lost control.'

'Surely you're over reacting?'

Elliott struggled to his feet. 'Pray that I am. Goodnight Knox.' He left him to prepare for an uneasy night.

SUNDAY

A Pre-Dawn Attack

The night passed quietly and uneventful as the guard was changed at regular intervals. Before the dawn light had begun to disperse the darkness, Margaret stirred. She passed the native guard on duty and assured him that she was all right as she went to visit a bush. The pre-dawn sounds of birds, animals and nature had just begun when Margaret had woken.

Now, though, as she made her way back to the camp, those sounds had suddenly ceased. Margaret reached for the knife on the band of her trousers before she even found the native guard laid out cold. Bending down to check if the guard was still alive, she felt the movement behind her before she heard it and turned suddenly, the knife steady in her hand to defend herself. She wasn't quick enough as the blade was knocked out of her hand and she was grabbed around the waist while a hand covered her mouth.

Margaret finally cracked and Richard was correct, she did not require any weapon to be dangerous. She bit hard upon the hand over her mouth as she stamped the heel of her boot down on her attacker's foot. Her elbow slammed backwards into his ribs but although she fought like a tiger, and he swore as he pulled his hand away from her mouth; he was too strong for her to break away.

'Did you really think that I was that easy to get rid of?' The familiar and loathsome voice caused Margaret to stiffen in disgust.

'Marconi!'

He laughed into her ear. 'So you do remember! Good! I want you to know who your master is!'

As one of his hands travelled up her body to cup Margaret's breasts she screamed, 'When Hell freezes over!' Margaret thrust her foot backwards, hopefully aiming for his groin. There was a brief moment of satisfaction when the severity of his swearing told her that she had succeeded. Major Marconi had loosed his hold on her so that Margaret could pull away.

While he clutched his groin in agony, Margaret scrabbled around trying to find her knife in the grey light. With her weapon back in her hand, Margaret sprang upon Marconi, knocking him to the ground and driving the knife violently down towards his chest. The Major managed to catch his breath, having been temporarily winded, and rolled enough to avoid being stabbed but was unable to dislodge Margaret from on top of him.

He tried to wrestle the knife from her but only managed to get his arm slashed. As Margaret plunged the knife down again she screamed, 'Never!' She was seized from behind and dragged off the Major.

'Margaret, no!' Richard had to exert all his strength to stop Margaret from continuing to attack the Major. Kenneth Knox took the blade out of her hand as Richard pulled her into his arms to calm her down. Marconi attempted to rise but found a pistol lined up with his nose.

'I don't know what your deal is mister,' warned Kenneth, cocking the gun, 'But move a muscle and I'll blow your fucking head off!'

The rage was still so deep and so explosive that it took some time for the Professor to get Margaret to stop thumping her fists against his chest and resume some sanity. Elliott checked the unconscious native before he assisted one of the other guards to drag Major Marconi to his feet and bind his hands securely.

Killing Could Become A Habit

Margaret gave a sudden gasp and collapsed against Richard's shoulder and began to cry. 'I'm sorry! I'm so sorry Richard.'

He soothingly stroked her hair. 'It's all right; I look good black and blue. We had to stop you killing him; you can't afford to make killing a habit.' Richard looked across at Marconi who was exchanging heated words with Elliott, 'Even if the Major does deserve it!'

Margaret managed a watery laugh. 'This has got to end Richard! I'm going crazy, I don't know if I'm going to be able to control myself ever again. I just seem to explode at everything.'

Richard's eyebrows rose. 'This is hardly an insignificant incident. Anyone would get upset if they were grabbed in the dark and about to be dragged away to be raped and maybe murdered.'

'It sounds logical when you describe it like that.' Margaret gave another watery laugh.

Santos, the guard, dragged Elliott away from his urge to pound Major Marconi into a bloody pulp. 'So do we dismember him here or take him with us to Accra?' asked Kenneth, who was reluctantly bandaging Marconi's arm where Margaret's blade had slashed him.

'I vote for dismemberment now!' Elliott added but was shushed by Richard.

'So long as he doesn't give us any trouble, he'll arrive alive at Accra.' Richard was interrupted by a string of expletives from the Major. 'For goodness sake, Knox, gag the prisoner or I'll be tempted to personally wire his jaw shut!' In the pre-dawn light they all stared at the Professor in stunned surprise. A boyish grin passed over his features. 'What? If Sebastian was here, I would be urging him to urinate on him! Again!' They all laughed, except Marconi, who was having a handkerchief stuffed into his mouth and Margaret who was looking around for the tiger.

'Where is Seb?' A note of panic had entered her voice.

Richard pressed her shoulder reassuringly. 'I sent Sebastian hunting as he was too agitated to sit still.'

Setting Off Once Again

Elliott glanced up at the increasing light in the sky. 'Should we get started before it gets too hot, or do you want something to eat?' Richard glanced around at the faces of the assembled group and as they all shook their heads, he decided that they would push on towards Accra. Margaret attended to the guard's head, which was more bruised than battered as Elliott and Kenneth struggled to get Major Marconi into the back of the cart.

As the Major would have to share the cart with Elliott, Margaret suggested that they knock him out cold for a while so that the Lieutenant wouldn't be tempted to kill him. There was a tussle between the two young men as to who would actually knock out Marconi. Without saying a word, Richard picked up Elliott's rifle and using it like a cricket bat cracked the Major over the head.

As he fell to the ground, Richard turned to Elliott and Kenneth. 'Am I going to have any trouble with either of you?'

They exchanged a hurried glance at each other before replying, 'No, no trouble here!' They quickly moved out of the Professor's reach and finished saddling the horses.

A Very Tense Journey

If the ride to Accra had been tense before, now that they were accompanied by Major Marconi, the tension level was off the chart. When Sebastian joined their group, they had stopped for the midday meal and rest, the tiger took deep exception to the presence of Marconi. It took a great deal of persuading and coaxing from Margaret to prevent Sebastian from tearing the Major apart. It took a great deal of begging from Elliott so that Sebastian didn't then vent his anger by urinating on him. *I'm especially concerned about this as I have to share the cart with the Major and he will stink, really stink, if Sebastian has his way. There is no way I can escape either as I can hardly ride with my leg in plaster.*

Reaching Accra

Humans and horses alike were about to drop with exhaustion when they finally pulled up outside of the Inn, the Cameriere Canto, that Doctor Munroe usually patronised when he came to Accra. Even though it was after midnight, Franco Gio came out to greet them as Richard lifted Margaret down from the box before assisting Elliott out of the cart.

'Professor Evans! So long it has been since we see you! Signorina Margaret! The last time I saw you were only as high as my heart! Oh, how I wept when we heard the news of the murder of your saintly parents and this must be Sebastian!' Franco dragged Margaret into his welcoming arms despite the fact that she was sadly travel stained. Margaret burst into tears as the Innkeeper held her against his ample frame, stroking her hair.

'Now, now, Bambina, you're tired and hungry. My Maria will whip up a tasty plate of food, then bed.'

Margaret wiped away her tears, 'Oh no Signor Gio, don't get your wife up just to feed us, and we'll make do with whatever is left over from dinner.'

Franco started to lead Margaret inside but Richard didn't follow and he gestured for Kenneth Knox to join him. 'Take care of them Franco, I need to get Major Marconi down to the police station.' Richard briefly took the hand a worried Margaret held out to him. 'I'll be back as soon as I can. Elliott, you're in charge.' Richard and Kenneth dragged the Major out of the cart and down the road. Margaret waited until the Professor was out of sight before she finally allowed Franco to lead them inside.

MONDAY
I Feel As Bad As I Look!

Maria Gio had insisted on cooking a fresh meal while rooms upstairs were made up for them. A bath had been offered, but all they wanted was to collapse into the soft pillowing mattress of their beds. Margaret didn't see Richard until she was soaking in a bath the next morning. Sebastian lay stretched out on the bathroom floor as he was guarding Margaret but he didn't react at Richard's entrance.

At first she was a little embarrassed by his unannounced arrival but Margaret studied the Professor closely before she finally said, 'Do you mind if I say something?'

A weary smile flitted across Richard's face. 'I know I feel as rotten as I must look.'

Margaret sat up in the bath and squeezed the excess water out of her long blonde hair. 'Did you get any sleep at all?'

'Only a couple of hours, I intended to send Knox to get Phillip later this morning but the Police Inspector insisted on us seeing him immediately. Hop out and I'll change the dressing on your wounds. Oh, I am so looking forward to that bath!' Richard held up a towel to wrap around Margaret.

'So where are we with our plan, or did Phillip talk you silly?' She asked as Richard stripped off his clothes and lowered himself into the bath with a groan.

'I had no trouble getting the Inspector to take Marconi off our hands. Apparently mine hasn't been the only report about the Major that has reached Accra.'

Margaret soaped up a sponge and started to clean Richard's arms and chest.

'What about our little problem?'

Richard took the sponge and scrubbed himself clean. 'Complications have arisen. One of the workers from the jewellers your father sold the diamonds to has disappeared. The Inspector thinks Warren Foster is cleaning up anyone who could implicate him with your parents' murders.' He doused his head with soapy water.

'So my grandfather will try to eliminate us next?'

'If he can.' Richard sighed, 'Scared kitten?'

The laugh that escaped from Margaret was rather hard. 'What is death compared to what he has already done? Soak awhile, I'm going down to have breakfast with Elliott.' She kissed him on his newly cleaned forehead before Sebastian led the way out of the bathroom.

You Need To Eat

It was nearly two hours later before a sheepish but clean Richard joined them downstairs. 'Sorry, I fell asleep,' admitted the Professor, shaking his head at Maria as she tried to interest him in breakfast. 'No thank you, I'm not really hungry.' Margaret ignored this and said something fluently in Italian.

'Ignorarlo, Maria, un piatto di cibo per favore.'

Maria chuckled and hurried back to the kitchen. Richard wearily raised an eyebrow as he studied Margaret who was in an attractive midnight blue dress.

'Have I been put in my place?' He asked.

Margaret smiled, 'no, but you do need to eat something. Phillip and his nice Inspector have been to see us already.'

Richard pulled out his fob watch and grinned. 'I wonder if they had any sleep at all. Had the Inspector managed to do what I asked?'

Elliott chuckled as he cleared space for Maria to place Richard's breakfast on the table. 'Inspector Fletcher is very efficient. My hearing is scheduled for three pm today. The lawyers are drowning in paperwork. The only word from the Foster camp was Uncle John.'

Richard paused in raising a piece of toast to his lips, 'Nothing from Grandfather at all?'

Margaret shook her head. 'Still I don't feel that he is a man who would come to us. We'll have to confront the lion in his own den.'

Richard continued with his breakfast and when he felt a wet nose against his knee, passed down a rasher of bacon to Sebastian under the table. *Although I'm used to being around people, the noises of the city are unsettling, and I'm sticking close to Margaret.* Sebastian had already had a huge bowl of raw meat but wasn't objecting to sharing Richard's breakfast until Margaret caught them.

'Eat your breakfast Richard, I can't face a lion alone!'

He placed his hand over hers. 'Even an old and toothless lion?'

Margaret couldn't manage to raise a smile at his attempt to tease her, 'They're the most dangerous and unpredictable as they have nothing to lose!'

Elliott glanced swiftly from one to the other. 'We're talking about a human being not an animal!'

Margaret's eyebrows rose, 'Are you sure?' She left the room, Sebastian at her heels, before her pent up emotions got the better of her.

The Lion's Den

A much calmer Margaret, (*I'm concerned that she is too calm,* mused Richard) stood with the Professor on the doorstep of her grandfather's house. Despite the heat of the day and the uncomfortable dress Margaret wore, she displayed the only sign of agitation through the hand she gently laid upon Sebastian's neck. It was shaking. *One doesn't normally go calling upon one's relations with a fully grown tiger but when Richard had suggested leaving Seb behind at the Inn with Elliott, I had said, 'no.' We've never been apart and I want to demonstrate to my grandfather that I am not a helpless female!*

As Richard wondered, *should I be armed?* He chuckled as he dismissed this idea as a true visiting faux pas. This was reinforced as a Butler answered the door and bowed as he let them inside. A very proper Butler, Samson, whose only indication that anything was out of the ordinary was a faint rise of an eyebrow.

'Mr Foster has Mr John with him at the moment Miss Margaret. If you would like to wait in the drawing room?' Samson indicated to follow him down a lavishly decorated corridor. *The opulence and just over the top wealth seems vulgar to me for although the Haven was comfortable it wasn't ostentatious,* puzzled Margaret.

'Eh, your beast?' Samson paused, opening the door for them to pass through.

'Stays by my side!' Margaret insisted, a tightness to her voice caused Richard to cast a concerned glance in her direction and once she was seated, he laid a hand on her shoulder. Sebastian prowled around the overly decorated room before lying down at Margaret's feet.

Small talk seemed pointless so Richard studied the paintings in the room. *Too many of them are of Warren Foster. I'm not certain that I am ready to deal with that level of egotism and perhaps ruthlessness.*

Heathen Child!

They were kept waiting for nearly twenty minutes. *As each minute passes, I wish that I had brought my gun with me! I would like nothing better to place a bullet between the old man's eyes and put us all out of their misery.* An elderly man strode proudly, even arrogantly, into the drawing room. Richard rose to his feet, expecting a battle to ensue.

Margaret drew in a deep breath and raised her eyes to finally meet her grandfather. The old man had a cold greeting freeze upon his lips as he stared dumbfounded at the granddaughter he hadn't seen since the day she was born.

'Felicia!' Warren Foster reached out for his deceased daughter but was stopped by his son standing behind him.

'No Father, this is Margaret, Felicia's daughter,' John Foster said and then lay his hand on his father's arm but Warren couldn't stop staring at Margaret. She dragged her eyes away from her grandfather to rest upon her uncle.

'May I present Professor Richard Evans, my mentor and protector?' Margaret then laid her hand on Sebastian's head. 'Also Sebastian, who protects us all.'

Warren Foster finally saw something other than his granddaughter. 'Get that disgusting beast out of my house! How dare you bring a wild animal into my presence?' He yelled, his colour rising alarmingly across is jowls.

Margaret rose regally to her feet. 'Then perhaps you shouldn't have so many pictures of yourself! There is only one disgusting beast in this room and it is not my Sebastian! Do you even care that your daughter and husband were murdered three weeks ago? Do you care that I'm now homeless? Do you care that one of your grandsons is missing? Do you care about anything but yourself?' With each accusation Margaret fought to keep her voice under control, as Sebastian, who had also risen, would most likely attack the instant he perceived a threat to Margaret.

'How dare you? Get out of my sight, heathen child! You are the cause for the entire devilry that had befallen my beautiful Felicia. You're the devil's spawn, born to dead parents; you bring death and despair to all who dare to love you! Beware of mating with this creature Professor or you too will die a horrible death!' His voice rose ever increasingly in volume causing Richard to lay a commanding hand on Sebastian's neck as the tiger growled threateningly.

'For the love of God man will you shut up? Attacking Margaret will only see your throat ripped out!'

'Don't threaten me!' Warren stepped towards them but Sebastian's flash of sharp teeth kept him from touching either visitor.

Worthless Little Stones!

Margaret held up a hand to calm the situation. 'I came not to bandy words with you sir, but to discover what was so important that it cost my parents their lives. I certainly hope that it had nothing to do with these pebbles.' Margaret emptied a small bag of pebbles into her hand, spilling them all over the floor.

'Stupid worthless little stones!' She moved her hand so that the pebbles remaining in her hand caught the sunlight and gleamed. Warren Foster all but salivated at the sight of the uncut diamonds.

Frowning, John bent down to pick up a handful of the stones off the floor. 'I was led to believe that Isabella's and Edward's death was the result of a random Halfies attack.'

Richard shook his head. 'No, it was a planned assassination. Like the several attempts after that upon Margaret's life.'

John rolled the stones around in his hand. 'Do you have any proof of murder?'

'Inspector Fletcher has taken over the investigation. He seems a very competent officer and is following several leads.' There was a moment's pause as Richard allowed these words to sink in.

Warren Foster exploded. 'If you're suggesting that anything will lead to my door then you can all go to Hell!'

'Deliver your own messages!' retorted Margaret, 'Foolishly I thought you would want to know the details of your daughter's murder from a family member rather than a cold police report. Obviously I was wrong and I'll not waste any more of your time, or more importantly, mine. Goodbye!' Margaret sailed majestically out of the drawing room, her entourage followed meekly in her wake.

A Majestic Exit

John was hot on her heels. 'Margaret, please, don't leave in anger. We're all upset about your parents' murders. Give it a couple of days and perhaps we can all talk a little more rationally.'

'It was nice to finally meet you Uncle John but I'm not sure I have anything else to say to that monster. I promise that if anything has happened to Cedric I will bring your house down around your heads. You'll be left with nothing but disgrace, dishonour, chaos and a shattered family!'

Margaret's exit was interrupted at the front door by the sight of Samson the Butler, collapsing to one knee as he clutched his chest. The frozen maiden thawed immediately as Margaret reached out to assist him into a nearby chair.

'Are you alright? Richard call someone to bring a glass of water please.'

The Butler grasped hold of Margaret's hand between both of his, 'No, no, it was just a momentary dizziness, please do not trouble yourself.'

'Nonsense, it is obvious that you need to rest.'

'So now you're an expert on my servants too!' sneered Warren.

Margaret's hands momentarily tightened into fists, 'Oh for goodness sake! Have you no humanity what so ever? You really are the demon Grandmama described.' On that superb exit line, Margaret stormed out the front door.

Richard paused momentarily to suggest a strong cup of tea to the embarrassed Butler before following her and Sebastian out into the sunshine and fresh air.

Insider Information

Richard expected Margaret to explode so he was surprised when she started to laugh. Signalling for a carriage to take them back to the Cameriere Canto Inn, Margaret waited until they were inside the vehicle before confiding in Richard. She placed a short note into his hands.

'Mr Cedric is being held in the cellar, Samson.'

The Professor looked up in surprise. 'How on earth...?'

'When the Butler collapsed he pressed that note into my hand as I helped him up,' Margaret explained.

'But why?'

Margaret shook her head, 'I don't know, oh, I can't wait to hand this over to Inspector Fletcher! Surely it is enough to allow him to search that mausoleum?'

'Yes...' The hesitance of Richard's answer caused Margaret to look at him worried.

'What is it Richard? You have doubts?'

He shook his head, 'It just seems a coincidence that the Butler comes forward with this information now.'

'Do you think it's some sort of trap?'

'I don't know, kitten, but it'll be up to the Inspector to decide.'

Margaret caressed her hand down Richard's cheek, 'Doubting Thomas! We will get through all of this.'

Richard's stern expression relaxed as he laughed. 'Yes we've come this far. Still it would be foolish to relax our defences just yet.'

Margaret sighed. 'Oh yes, the last thing we could possibly do is relax!' *That was said so seriously that I'm worried that it is an omen of impending disaster,* worried Richard.

Disaster was the last thing on their minds as they handed the Butler's note to Inspector Fletcher. He was pleased with this turn of events and raced off to get a Judge to sign a search warrant. Richard checked the time before he slipped his fob watch back into his pocket. 'We need to consider some lunch before Elliott's hearing this afternoon.' As if these were the magic words that summons a genie, Maria Gio bustled into the room offering a menu of choice dishes.

Clever Minx!

After the sumptuous feast that Maria lay before them, it was just as well that they had time for a quick siesta otherwise they might commit the sin of falling asleep during Elliott's hearing. Elliott had already limped upstairs but Margaret remained at the table keeping Richard company as he finished his coffee. The Professor sat back in his chair, his eyes half closed as he watched Margaret's restless hands.

She picked up a sugar cube from the bowl in front of Richard and wetting her thumb and index finger she gently rolled the sugar cube between them. As Margaret re-wet her fingers the sharp edges had softened and started to take on a familiar shape. Richard's eye widened and he burst into laughter.

'Oh you cheeky kitten! I've been wondering about your actions ever since you recklessly spilled those "diamonds" in front of your grandfather.'

Margaret chuckled. 'They may not hold any value to me, but I'm not so careless with evidence.' She threw the sugar cube into the air and it was neatly caught in his mouth by Sebastian. 'I came up with the idea at breakfast that I could disconcert grandfather by appearing to throw the diamonds away. When we saw Phillip this morning I asked him to procure for me some cheap quartz stones.'

Richard rose to his feet and held out his hand to Margaret. 'You could have warned me, kitten, I thought my jaw would drop to the floor when you pulled that trick. Come on, we could do with an hour or two of sleep. The hearing could be very emotional as you'll have to relive all the events leading up to today.'

Margaret laid her hand upon his arm and permitted Richard to lead her and Sebastian up the stairs. 'Do you think Elliott will want to stay in the Gold Coast once everything has been settled?'

Richard's eyebrows rose, 'I don't know. He might be so disenchanted that he could leave Africa and return to England.'

'I hope not.' Margaret sighed.

'Do I have a rival for your heart?' His tone was light and teasing but he knew a moment of doubt as an icy cold hand tightened around his heart..

'No, but I do like Elliott and I would be sorry if he was to also disappear from my life.'

Richard reassuringly patted her hand. 'Yes, so will I. Perhaps we can convince him to stick around.'

'I've got an idea.'

'Well hang on to it. If we get through this we could use some ideas.'

'If?' Margaret paused outside her bedroom.

Richard smiled. 'Sorry, when we get through this. Margaret... we're not safe yet!'

She caressed her hand down his cheek. 'I know, but I do feel safe with you. I don't think there is anything else that they can throw at us.'

'Of course kitten,' Richard waited for Margaret to pass through the open doorway before addressing Sebastian, 'Keep watch Seb, this isn't over yet.' He waited until the tiger had entered the room before propping a chair against the closed door and checked his gun before sitting down. *I might lose out on some sleep but I am not going to let Margaret die on my watch!*

Court Martial

Elliott Gibbs' throat was sore and constricting upon him as he found he could no longer talk. With Margaret and Richard on either side of him, Elliott sat in front of a panel of senior officers as they presided over Elliott's dishonourable discharge.

There had been a protest when Margaret had walked into the hearing with Sebastian. She offered to wait outside until her evidence was needed but as most of the evidence was related to her, it was necessary for them both to remain.

Sebastian lay down behind their chairs but the tiger took exception when Major Marconi was brought into the room. Richard placed a calming hand on his neck as the Major was seated at the table beside theirs. During the emotive hearing there wasn't only the addition of the other members of Marconi's unit but also one civilian.

At the back of the room sat John Foster. He didn't interfere in the proceedings at any point but simply sat there with his head bowed as he listened while Margaret recounted all that had happened since the moment Isabella Munroe had ordered her daughter to flee the only home she had ever known.

Agonising Wait

Now while they waited as the panel of officers deliberated Elliott ran through the evidence they had just delivered. *I wonder if I've said enough? Could I have stressed more Marconi's mania that led me to commit mutiny?* He opened his mouth to speak, to say again how Marconi had betrayed everything it meant to be an officer and a gentleman, but the words wouldn't come out, as Elliott's throat refused to let him make a sound. He swallowed hard on the lump in his throat as he struggled to breathe normally.

A cool hand was placed upon his arm and all the anxiety and doubt drained immediately out of him. Closing his mouth Elliott glanced down at Richard's hand on his arm and took in a deep breath. Releasing it slowly Elliott felt the doubt and panic leave him and raising his eye to meet Richard's, he managed to smile.

'Thank you,' Elliott whispered.

Major Raoul Marconi leant forward to look passed Richard to sneer at Elliott. 'Are you wetting yourself over there Lieutenant?'

One of Richard's eyebrows rose slowly as Sebastian's head came up and he growled at Marconi. 'Don't mention urine in front of Seb, he might get ideas that you're just not going to like!' Richard drawled.

The Major cast a nervous glance down at the tiger and decided to keep his mouth shut. Margaret leant forward and laid her hand upon the Lieutenant's other arm.

'Boys behave; the Generals seem to have reached a decision.'

All heads turned back to the panel of senior officers as they finished their discussions.

'Lieutenant Gibbs, we apologise for not waiting to hear your side of the story and we rescind your dishonourable discharge. It's not acceptable to defy your Commanding Officer but we see now that to protect Miss Munroe you were left with no other choice.' The General in the middle turned his attention now to Major Marconi, who didn't look at all worried as he wore a smug expression.

'Major, you'll be stripped of your Commission and remain in custody until we determine your sentence. Is there anything else you would like to say in your defence Major?'

Totally Inappropriate!

As Major Marconi calmly rose to his feet, he straightened his uniform jacket and looked not at the panel of officers but at Margaret. The slow leering glance he cast down her body caused Margaret to tightly clench her hands so that her fingernails dug deeply into her palms. Smiling, the Major finally looked up at the panel.

'If you had the chance to fuck such a beautiful woman wouldn't you pursue every conceivable opportunity?'

Margaret gasped as she flushed in embarrassment. The central General banged his gavel in anger and Sebastian rose to his feet and began to growl.

'Major Marconi! It is not appropriate to use that language in this forum!'

The Major's smile widened as he leered at Margaret. 'Oh but it is appropriate! That is exactly what I want to do to her! I want to fuck her brains out!'

Richard immediately reached down to place his hand upon Sebastian's neck to stop the tiger from launching himself upon Marconi. 'Seb, go sit by Margaret, the Major isn't worth it!' He spoke quietly and calmly as he rhythmically stroked his hand along the tiger's fur.

Marconi threw his head back as he laughed. 'I'm just honest about what I feel. Can Professor Evans tell me that he doesn't want to fuck Margaret? Or perhaps he has already had her naked and beneath him. Maybe I should ask him for a performance report? It might be the closest I ever get to fucking her myself!'

Elliott rose to his feet as the General continued to bang his gavel. Margaret grasped Elliott by the arm and drew him back down into his chair.

'Ignore the Major, he's all mouth,' suggested Margaret.

Sinking back down, Elliott glanced across to see how Richard was reacting to Marconi's tirade. The Professor's face was a mask of indifference as he urged Sebastian to sit on the other side of the desk beside Margaret where the tiger wouldn't be able to see Marconi.

Richard raised his eyes calmly to the panel of soldiers. 'If these proceedings are concluded, gentlemen, I would like to remove Miss Munroe from having to hear any further offensive remarks from Marconi.'

A sneer curled the Major's lip. 'You haven't had her have you? Noble Professor or are you impotent?'

Richard sighed as he rose to his feet and reluctantly held up his left hand. 'No, Marconi, I am married.' *Regardless of how I feel about my marriage, I have always worn my wedding ring.*

The Major nearly fell over his chair as he looked quickly from Richard to Margaret. 'The two of you are married?'

Richard shook his head as he took off his glasses and calmly cleaned them. 'Not that it's any of your business but until I can finalise a divorce, I'm not free to ask Margaret to marry me.' Placing his glasses back on Richard took a step towards Marconi. 'You're a disgusting excuse for an officer and a human being!' Just as calmly as Richard tackled anything else he clenched his fist and hit the Major so hard that he flew backwards, landing on his backside.

Elliott's jaw dropped in amazement as Richard just as calmly held out his hand to Margaret and looped her hand through his arm.

'I've got to know,' Elliott said, 'Was that because Marconi called you impotent, what he said about Margaret, or because he's just a colossal ass?'

There was a hint of a smile on the Professor's stoic features, 'Mainly what he said about Margaret but all three reasons are justifiable! Are you ready to go?' Richard's free hand was under Elliott's elbow to assist him to his feet.

'More than ready!' Supporting himself on his crutches Elliott hauled himself up.

Man Versus Beast

After a brief moment of amazement, Marconi scrambled up onto his feet and had to be held back by two guards from launching himself at Richard.

'Son of a fucking bitch! I'll kill you if I can ever lay my hands on you!' The venom of the Major's words wasn't lost on Sebastian who immediately placed himself in front of Margaret and Richard.

The room went perfectly still as man and cat locked eyes. Margaret stretched out her hand towards Sebastian's neck to restrain him, but Richard arrested her hand before it made contact and gently drew it away. As she looked up, questioningly at him, Richard smiled slightly as he shook his head. *I don't want anything to distract the tiger.* Everyone in the room collectively held their breath as they waited to see what would occur. Sebastian was unleashed and even if he had been no one person could have restrained him if he attacked.

As if suddenly realising the danger he was in, the Major paled and unconsciously his hand brushed against his wounded arm where Sebastian had bitten him the night he had first tried to rape Margaret. Sweat beaded on the Major's brow and the smell of fear wafted through the room.

Eyes still locked between the Major and the tiger, neither moved but Sebastian lifted his top lip and bared his enormous fangs as he gave a low deep growl. A different smell filled the air as Major Marconi lost complete control of his bowels and fainted in fright.

Uttering a soft chuckle Richard finally laid his hand upon Sebastian's back. 'Let's go home little man; the Major is no longer a threat to anyone!' He led his friends out of the hearing, not looking back at the destroyed mess that the guards were left to clean up.

John Foster was nowhere to be seen as they left the building but Margaret wasn't interested in his whereabouts as she only wanted to celebrate Elliott's vindication. Richard sighed, *I only want to make sure that we get safely back to the Inn. Until Warren Foster has been brought to justice, Margaret's life is still very much in danger.*

They attracted considerable attention as they travelled back to the Cameriere Canto Inn, mainly because they travelled with a fully grown tiger. If there were any agents of Warren Foster's amongst the people watching them then there was no way they were even going to contemplate attacking Margaret, mainly because they travelled with a fully grown tiger.

A Little Stress Release

Both Maria and Franco Gio were expressive in their joy at the result of Elliott's hearing and promised an impressive feast that evening. Elliott was left in charge of protecting Margaret while Richard finally admitted that he was exhausted and Margaret convinced him to go upstairs and sleep.

Sebastian was restless. *I dislike all the strange noises, the mass of buildings, and I am still anxious that my Mistress is in danger.* To relieve this tension Elliott borrowed a fresh horse, tethered it up to the cart and took Margaret and Sebastian just outside of the city so that the tiger could run free for a little while.

Margaret willingly changed back into male attire and took the opportunity to run just as free. Elliott was armed, remaining on high alert and also took two of the native guards with them. It was a relaxing time for them all, except Elliott, who didn't let his guard down until they returned to the Inn as night began to fall.

Inappropriate Behaviour

Feeling so much lighter in heart and spirit, Margaret bounded into the private room in the Cameriere Canto Inn and settled upon Richard's lap unaware that anyone else was in the room. she wrapped her arms around his neck and kissed him. Although the Professor placed his hands about Margaret's waist it was more to support than embrace her.

'You do realise that you're kissing a married man don't you?' The unfamiliar voice caused Margaret to leap to her feet, her hand instinctively reaching for the dagger on her belt, not from embarrassment, but to defend herself and Richard. Her stance relaxed slightly when she recognised John Foster.

'A technicality Uncle John, for all we know Richard may well be a widower.'

One eyebrow of the older man rose. 'Is that how Isabella and Mother raised you? Would they be proud of you right now?'

Fire and anger leapt into Margaret's eyes as her hands tightened into fists. 'Don't speak of my mother and grandmother! For all we know you were a part of the murder of my parents, over two dozen villagers, a hunting party and the several attempts upon my own life!'

Richard reached out to take one of Margaret's hands to calm her down. 'Your uncle went to Elliott's hearing to find out what really happened. He wouldn't need to do that if he was in league with your grandfather.'

Margaret took a deep breath but didn't lower her weapon. 'It could be a front to find out how much we've managed to discover, or how deeply he too is implicated!'

John rose swiftly to his feet in anger but Richard defused the tension by chuckling, 'Claws kitten! I need you both to calm down.'

Taking deep breathes, Margaret's hands dropped as her body began to relax. After a moment John Foster resumed his seat as Margaret sank into the chair beside Richard.

'There is one thing I really want to know Uncle John,' Margaret started and took another deep breath before she continued, 'with such a vast fortune at his fingertips within the Foster Empire, why didn't Grandfather use those resources to assist Clay rather than commit murder and other atrocities for the Haven and my supposed inheritance?'

A weary smile adorned the older man's features, 'Mainly because he doesn't...'

Inspector Fletcher Has News

They were interrupted by the entrance of Elliott, Sebastian and Inspector Fletcher.

'My apologies for intruding,' stated the policeman, his eyebrows rising slightly at the sight of John Foster. 'I thought you'd want to know the problem immediately.' All eyes were upon the Inspector, except those of John who moved uncomfortably in his chair as Sebastian paused to sniff him. As John started to rise out of his seat, Richard glanced across to warn him.

'Sit still Mr. Foster! If Seb associates you with the visit this morning to your father any sudden movement could be seen as a sign of aggression.'

'Sebastian come here baby!' Margaret gently coaxed and held out her hand to caress the tiger's head as he crossed the room to sit beside her.

A nervous laugh escaped from John as he struggled to regain his composure, 'Baby?' His disbelief was understandable as Sebastian was a fully grown tiger in his prime. His pure white fur with chocolate stripes covered 700 pounds of muscle and he was nearly nine feet long excluding his tail.

Sebastian curled his tail around his body as he elevated his head so Margaret scratched him under his chin. A low rumbling sound came from deep in the tiger's chest as he closed his eyes, but the very tip of his tail twitched to show that he was not completely happy about the presence of this stranger.

'I suppose it is silly,' admitted Margaret, 'that I still think of Seb as the baby I hand raised. At the moment, though, with so much chaos in my life I tend to cling to what little I have left.' She indicated for Elliott and the Inspector to be seated. The policeman cast a significant glance at John Foster before his raised eyebrow asked Richard the question he didn't wish to articulate.

'It's all right Inspector, we...' the Professor broke off as Margaret cast him a look, 'sorry, I believe that John Foster isn't involved in Warren Foster's activities.'

'Well,' the Inspector started hesitantly, 'there's not a single Judge in Accra that will sign the warrant to search Warren Foster's home.'

John nodded, 'Father was always very good at getting dirt on people of influence but as I was about to tell Margaret and the Professor you won't need the warrant.'

Inspector Fletcher looked more than a little sceptical. 'Without a warrant I need the owner's permission to search the house and I don't see Warren Foster agreeing to that!'

John agreed, 'That would indeed be the case if Father owned the house.'

This Is All My Fault

Seeing that he had stunned them all into silence, John Foster continued, 'A couple of years ago Father had a serious health scare. Thinking it was the end and being the miser that he is, Father was adamant that there wouldn't be extensive death duties; so all aspects of the company, all assets, and all properties were signed over to me. Any un-entailed fortune Father gave to Clay.'

Reaching out to take Margaret's hand Richard asked, 'I don't want to know exact amounts but was that a lot of money?'

A grimace appeared on John's face. 'It should have lasted through several generations, but Clay has his father's diseases; he's a gambler and an alcoholic.' He passed a shaking hand across his eyes.

'Oh Margaret, it's my fault your parents are dead,' continued John. 'Father came to me for money for Clay and I said, "no". Not unless certain conditions were met. That he stopped his drinking and gambling. You see the houses that Clay and his mother Hester live in are Foster property, rent free. Also the allowance that Hester receives because her husband left her with nothing also comes from me!'

Margaret's entire body stiffened, 'So the only way Grandfather could raise money for his favourite grandson was for the Haven to return to his hands and the Barnsby inheritance.'

Sadly John shook his head, 'If Father had read the legal documents, when he transferred the business over to me, properly then he would have known that the Haven would not return to him as it was also signed over to me along with all the other Foster properties. If the goal was the Barnsby fortune then you would be the sole target. Isabella and Edward's deaths would be merely collateral damage!'

A strangled cry emanated from Margaret and her hand lying on Sebastian's neck tightened to the point where he uttered a sharp protest. Margaret released her grip and apologised to the tiger.

'Collateral damage? They could still be alive if it wasn't for Grandfather wanting me dead? That is going to haunt me for the rest of my life!' Tears welled in her eyes and began to roll down her cheeks as Margaret fought to keep calm.

'I'm sorry, but until we can question Father, we won't know if he knew the truth about the Haven or not,' John added.

John's Permission

Elliott had remained a silent observer throughout this exchange but now voiced a query that was causing him to frown. 'Hang on a minute, if Warren is basically your pensioner how did he raise the money necessary to hire not one but two teams of assassins?'

Sighing deeply John Foster didn't immediately answer, 'I think Father has had someone copy the paintings in the house and sold the originals. When I was five I'd drawn on one of those masterpieces. Although the Housekeeper cleaned it so that Father never found out, in a certain light you can still see where I had drawn. I happened to look at that painting today and that mark is no longer visible. That is why I came to the Lieutenant's hearing, to discover if Father could possibly have been involved!'

'What conclusions have you come to?' quietly asked Richard.

John dragged in a deep shuddering breath 'I knew he was an utter bastard, forgive my language Margaret, but capable of murder... You have my permission to search my Father's house, Inspector, and any other properties that belong to Foster Industries.'

As Margaret buried her face into Richard's shoulder, he tenderly stroked her hair and looked up at Inspector Fletcher. 'I recommend you have a Doctor with you when you search!' He cast the policeman a significant look.

The policeman nodded as he rose to his feet. 'Phillip will also want to be present.'

'Is that a good idea?' John asked, 'He can be a little volatile.'

Margaret raised her head and took the handkerchief that Richard offered. 'He should be there; Cedric will need him.'

'I'll organise that immediately,' stated the Inspector, 'shall I meet you there Mr. Foster?'

'Yes, but I think Margaret should be there as well. It's time Father answered all of Margaret's questions.' John paused as he cast a critical glance down at Margaret's attire, 'Perhaps you should change first; Father would probably have a heart attack if he saw you dressed like a boy.'

It's Time To End This

He was a little surprised when Margaret obediently rose to her feet without protest. She followed Inspector Fletcher out of the room and Sebastian went with her up to her room. A relieved sigh was uttered by her uncle and he looked apologetically from Richard to Elliott.

'Sorry but I've never been in the presence of such a large wild animal.'

Taking off his glasses to clean them, Richard said, 'You do realise that wanting Margaret there at the denouncement means also that Sebastian will be there?'

John straightened his jacket, 'Yes of course, a little bit of fear could work in our favour.'

Elliott leant upon his crutches, 'or kill you all!'

Putting his glasses back on Richard sighed, 'Being so cheerful keeps me going,' he drawled as he rose to his feet, 'It's time to finish this... once and for all!'

I Insist That He Comes Too!

Margaret didn't keep them waiting long as she only slipped into her midnight blue dress. She didn't wear the petticoats and bustle that were the current fashion. As Richard turned Margaret around to do up her cuffs of her long sleeves, John opened his mouth to say something, but glancing up and seeing Richard's raised eyebrow, he closed his mouth again.

This is going to be hard enough to get through without alienating the girl and her very protective, very large, tiger, said Richard's look. Clearing his throat, John rose to his feet.

'Shall we head off now or do you think Inspector Fletcher needs more time?'

Richard pulled out his fob watch, 'So long as he doesn't have too much trouble with Phillip, we should be on time if we're walking.'

Margaret glanced across at Elliott as she straightened her jacket. 'So I take it Elliott won't be accompanying us then? Am I supposed to leave Sebastian behind as well?'

Not hesitating for even a second, John said, 'Oh I insist on his coming with us!'

Richard smiled as Margaret looked surprised and she attached a leash to the tiger's collar. 'Does that mean you're getting used to him?' She asked.

John rose to his feet, 'not in the least, but he does make an excellent bodyguard.'

Chuckling Richard took one of Margaret's trembling hands and threaded it through the crook of his arm. 'We should be back in plenty of time for dinner, Elliott.' His calm assurance was a soothing tonic to Margaret's on edge nerves. Richard's tone suggested that they were merely going for a stroll rather than the denouncement of a murderer.

A Show Of Force

A carriage containing Inspector Fletcher, Doctor O'Brien and Phillip had just pulled up outside of Warren Foster's home when the walking party approached from the opposite direction. Four or five police officers were patiently waiting for the Inspector to issue his orders. Inspector Fletcher introduced the Doctor as John knocked on the door. Samson, upon seeing the enclave, silently stepped back to allow them to enter.

'Mr Foster is in his study,' was all the Butler said, bowing his head as Margaret entered.

'Good!' Inspector Fletcher was in complete charge now. 'I want all the servants brought together in the kitchen. Nothing is to be moved or destroyed. No one is to leave without my permission. Leggett help Jones round up the servants. Samson I'll want the keys to the cellar.'

The Butler nodded, 'Only Mr. Foster or his valet Bedford have keys Sir.'

'Jones get the keys off Bedford and keep a close eye on him. He's probably the only servant Mr. Foster has taken into his confidence.' Inspector Fletcher gestured towards the study door, 'Shall we get this over with Mr. Foster?' he asked John.

Confrontation

Taking a deep breath, John was a little annoyed that the hand he extended to open the study door was not exactly steady. He preceded the Inspector and another Constable inside. Everyone else waited outside as son confronted father.

'I know the truth Father. How did you think you were going to get away with so many murders?'

From where he sat behind his desk, Warren Foster looked up annoyed at this intrusion. 'What on earth are you talking about John? What is that man doing in my house? Get out!' an arthritic finger pointed at Inspector Fletcher. Moving around the desk, John opened the top drawer and removed a bunch of keys.

'My house Father, you signed all property over to me, remember? Would you like to accompany us to the cellar?' John handed the keys across to the Inspector.

'Not really!' This was said so flippantly that the Inspector wondered, *Had the Butler been lying or has Cedric been moved already?*

The Constable was left in the study to ensure that nothing was destroyed by Warren Foster as the Inspector followed Samson along the corridor to the door that led down to the cellar. Phillip fell in beside the policeman determined to go with them but the Inspector gently laid his hand upon Phillip's shoulder.

'We don't know what state Cedric could be in.'

Phillip stood steadfast as Margaret came forward to lay her hand upon Phillip's arm and she offered, 'Do you want me to go first?'

Richard was moved to protest, 'Margaret no!'

She turned to the Professor and smiled 'I'm in no danger Richard, the Inspector will be there to protect me and if you're still worried, Sebastian will go with us.'

As the Inspector reassuringly tapped his sidearm, Richard reluctantly nodded.

The Wine Cellar

Entering the cellar, Sebastian stuck close to Margaret's skirt as they followed Inspector Fletcher down a set of stairs and through row upon row of bottles of wine. The lights were dim but there was enough illumination that additional lanterns were not needed. There were racks of wine bottles lining all the walls, as well as two independent rows in the middle of the room; but there was no sign of any human occupant.

'Uncle John is there a secret door in the cellar?' Margaret called up the stairs.

John appeared at the top of the staircase, 'Not to my knowledge but it wouldn't surprise me.' He was firmly but gently put to one side as Richard glanced down at the cellar's structure. 'The left wall is load bearing, so are the front and back walls.'

The Inspector strode across to the right hand wall as it was the only one not mentioned. He carefully wriggled several wine racks until one section in the middle came towards him. Pulling the section of racks all the way from the wall he revealed a locked door. Inspector Fletcher sorted through the keys that John had given him.

Sebastian and Margaret stood silently beside him as the Inspector tried two different keys. Neither opened the door and Margaret began to wonder how they could break down the door when the third key the Inspector tried fitted perfectly into the lock. The door swung towards them and the Inspector gestured for Margaret to remain where she was until he had investigated.

This hidden room was also dimly lit, the artificial light the only source of illumination and would be pitch black when extinguished. There was a bucket in the far corner, a crate with a glass, a jug of water and an empty plate. A metal cot took up most of the room with a lumpy mattress and a body laid curled up upon it facing the wall away from the door, his wrists were in a pair of handcuffs and chained to the front leg of the cot.

The body was so still, no movement had resulted from the door being opened. Its clothes were torn and covered all over with dirt and blood. Swallowing hard on the lump in his throat,

Inspector Fletcher reached out a not entirely steady hand and touched the body's shoulder.

'Cedric?' He uttered a sigh of relief as the body moved, turning slowly over in recognition of the policeman's voice.

'Donald?' The question came out of parched lips. Nodding Inspector Fletcher squeezed Cedric's shoulder before leaving the room.

'Give him some water,' he ordered Margaret before striding back to the stairs and up to the entrance way. 'Send the Doctor down Phillip; we'll bring Cedric up to you in a minute!' Not waiting for an answer or the Doctor to descend, Donald Fletcher sorted through the keys once more looking for a very small key for the handcuffs as he went back into the hidden room.

I Want To Kill Him!

It was such a touching scene that the Inspector stopped in the doorway and stared. Margaret knelt beside the cot, cradling her cousin's head against her breasts as he cried and Sebastian sympathetically licked Cedric's hand. Fletcher moved out of the Doctor's way and freed Cedric's hand from the cuffs before returning upstairs.

He didn't think he could watch as the Doctor examined the prisoner. Phillip took a hasty step towards the policeman before faltering as his eyes desperately swept Fletcher's face.

'He's alive!' The Inspector laid his hand on Phillip's to stop him from running down to his partner. 'Let the Doctor tend to him.' He cleared his throat before continuing, 'Phillip, they didn't just imprison him...'

Phillip's face collapsed in horror and Richard placed a supporting arm around him as his legs started to tremble, 'Oh God! How badly...' Phillip could not finish his question.

'Beaten black and blue, his clothes are soaked in blood. The Doctor will be able to tell us if it is anything more serious than that,' replied the Inspector.

Richard's soft voice in his ear caused Phillip to stiffen his spine and not fall apart, 'Pull yourself together Phillip! You must be his rock! Cedric's strength!'

Taking a deep breath Phillip used the back of his hand to thrust away his tears as he drew away from Richard's support.

'I'm going to kill him!'

Richard grabbed hold of Phillip by the shoulders and stopped him storming off towards the study. 'No! Do that and Inspector Fletcher will be forced to arrest you! How is you being in prison for the rest of your life going to help Cedric? For murder you could even face the death penalty!'

'I want Warren Foster to know pain!' Phillip said through clenched teeth.

'He will, believe me! Even with his wealth and connections Warren cannot escape prison! Innocent people are dead by his design, he may even face the noose for all of this,' promised Richard.

Doctor's Preliminary Report

As Phillip fought to regain control of his rampaging emotions, the Inspector took a blanket which Samson wordlessly handed to him and headed down the stairs to wait outside in the cellar with Margaret and Sebastian as Doctor O'Brien briefly examined Cedric for broken bones and other internal damage.

Packing up his medical bag the Doctor gestured for Margaret to go in and sit with Cedric and wrap the blanket around him to cover the tattered remains of his clothes.

'Well Doc?' Inspector Fletcher led the medical man out of hearing of either the patient or his partner above them.

'Nothing broken, except his spirit; I'll want to do a more thorough examination and keep him in hospital for a few days under strict observation. When I asked about removing what's left of his trousers to completely examine him Cedric began to panic so I didn't insist.'

Inspector Fletcher reeled backwards in shock, 'My God! Doctor, what did that monster do to his own grandson? Is he... still intact? Did he castrate Cedric? Sodomise him?'

The Doctor shook his head. 'I don't know, his clothes are covered with blood all over so until I can examine him properly, I won't know for certain.'

The policeman pulled himself together as Margaret appeared in the doorway with a supportive arm around Cedric as he staggered towards freedom. Taking his other side the Inspector took over keeping Cedric upright as Margaret, due to her own recent injuries, would not have had the strength needed to assist Cedric up the stairs. Although a sob escaped from Phillip, he remained steadfast as he accepted Cedric into his arms.

'I'm sorry to have to do this Cedric, but I want to ask you a couple of questions in the presence of your grandfather,' said Inspector Fletcher, 'We had hoped that the jewellery clerk would be with you. Now we have to move quickly to prevent his execution. If he isn't already dead.'

Phillip shook his head but taking a deep breath Cedric nodded and squeezed Phillip's hand. The policeman assisted Cedric with Phillip's help into Warren's study settling him comfortably into a chair before dismissing the Constable.

'Bring the witness in please Constable. Doctor have a seat in the hall with Margaret, I won't keep you long.'

Margaret exchanged a look with Richard at the sudden drop in temperature around the Inspector but the Professor shrugged and nodded towards the front door where the Constable was leading Kenneth Knox into the study. Margaret's lips parted to say hello but Kenneth refused to glance in hers or anyone's direction.

An Eye Witness

The Inspector tried to shut the door but Richard objected, 'Oh no Inspector, no closed door secret meetings!' The two men locked eyes and held their gaze for at least a minute before the Inspector finally submitted.

'Do not interrupt,' he ordered before turning to address Kenneth. 'I understand that you were present when your boss Abe Conan was hired to assassinate Margaret Munroe.'

'Yes Sir,' replied Kenneth, looking nervously around the room. 'Do you see that man present?' Kenneth took a good long look around as those waiting outside held their breath. 'He sort of looked like that bloke.' Kenneth pointed to Cedric.

'That's impossible!' Phillip cried out.

'Be quiet!' ordered Fletcher, 'You're not certain Knox?'

Kenneth screwed up his nose. 'The face is sort of right but it can't be this broken wreck of a man.'

Inspector Fletcher placed a piece of paper into Cedric's hand. 'Read this please.' Struggling to focus his eyes, Cedric silently read the note.

Fletcher cleared his throat. 'Aloud please Cedric,' he said gently.

Colour drained further from Cedric's face. 'I can't say this, I don't use that sort of language,' he managed to say.

Kenneth shook his head, 'I don't know what you're playing at Inspector but the face may be almost right, but this isn't the man that hired us.'

Richard said from the doorway, 'Does your brother Clay look anything like you?'

'Not really,' replied Cedric.

An image flashed across Margaret's memory as she was taken back to when she first met Cedric and Phillip. Her gasp of surprise drew everyone's attention to her.

'Albert!' she exclaimed.

Inspector Fletcher demanded, 'Albert who?'

'Albert Bedford, my half-brother,' explained Cedric.

Richard had been watching Warren Foster when Margaret had said Albert's name and although the old man's face didn't change expression, he could not control the tick in the corner of his eye.

'Bedford, as in the name of Mr. Foster's valet?' asked Richard.

Cedric nodded, 'Albert's mother Gina was a maid at our home when father was alive. She was the valet's sister.'

'If Albert hired the assassins then his apartment is where we might find the jewellery clerk.' The Inspector was about to stalk out but Margaret halted his progress by stepping into the room and laying a hand on her cousin's sagging shoulder.

'Can Cedric go to the hospital now?'

Fletcher stopped and glanced back at the shattered shell of a man, 'I'm sorry! Yes of course. Constable, I want men at Albert's home immediately. Bring Albert and the clerk to me here. Take Mr. Knox to the kitchen for now and then come back to assist Phillip to raise Cedric to his feet. Look after him please Doctor.'

So You Had No Knowledge?

The Inspector waited until they had left before he turned to address Warren. 'So why would Albert want to kill the Munroe's? What would he get out of all of that?

He's illegitimate, he can't inherit Barnsby Holdings. Albert's not your grandson so he'd hardly expect to get his hands on the Haven!'

Warren Foster looked bored as he shrugged. 'How do I know what Bedford and his nephew have been up to?'

Fletcher sat down in a chair opposite Warren and steepled his fingertips. 'So you're saying that you had no knowledge that Cedric was locked up in the cellar bashed and brutalised.'

'Not in the least.'

'You had no idea that Albert had learnt that Edward Munroe had sold uncut diamonds to purchase medical supplies from the jewellery clerk?'

'Not in the least.'

'No idea that Albert hired at least two different groups of assassins to kill the Munroe's?'

'Not in the least.'

There followed a silence that the Inspector allowed to continue for several minutes. Margaret, though, was not prepared to let the mind games to continue.

'How did they raise the money to pay the assassins?'

'No idea Satan's sporn!' spat out Warren.

Calmly Richard tapped his hand against Seb's head. He and the tiger had quietly entered the study during the Inspector's questioning. 'Moderate your tone Mr Foster or your next words may be your last,' he spoke evenly as his fingers caressed along the tiger's spine and Seb began to growl.

'So Mr Foster,' Inspector Fletcher reclaimed Warren's attention. 'You're telling me that you had no knowledge of Albert's actions and had nothing to do with them?'

'That is correct Inspector!' Arrogance exuded from the man.

The Inspector's Bluff

The Inspector uttered a heartfelt sigh. 'Well then the only other alternative then is that Albert is working for Clay Barnsby. I'm sure that Albert will be able to confirm that once he's been arrested. Thank you for all your help Mr. Foster. Sorry to have taken up so much of your valuable time.' He turned and was striding out of the study when Warren called out.

'Wait! Clay had nothing to do with any of this!'

Fletcher turned back, 'No one else benefits from the deaths of Edward and Isabella Munroe and their adopted daughter Margaret. Albert gets nothing. There is only Clay or you. Unless you believe that Christine, Clay and Cedric's sister, is responsible. Perhaps you think that Cedric is really behind this and had himself imprisoned and bashed?'

'Cedric can't have organised the second set of assassins as he would've been on the way to the Haven with me when that was happening,' said Margaret.

Warren suddenly leant forward on his desk. 'But Cedric sent Albert home after you met at the Professor's,' he gloated. A significant silence fell after Warren's words.

'How did you know about that?' Fletcher quietly asked. 'How did you know that Albert even went with Phillip and Cedric?'

Warren's smile widened. 'Two Nancy boys travelling alone into the wilderness, Albert's the toughest walking muscle that Cedric knows.'

Margaret shook her head, 'I saw how Cedric handles a gun, and he didn't need hired muscle.'

An ugly look crossed Warren's features as he glared at his granddaughter. 'Did he show you his other weapon? Did that impress you too? Not that it would do him any good.' He swore in anger causing Margaret to blush, 'A bloody faggot for a grandson! If he was half the man Clay is, Cedric could have seduced this devil's child into marriage and taken possession of all of Barnsby Holdings!'

His temper building, Warren turned on his son. 'I blame you for saddling Clay with a bride with no dowry. He could have tamed this siren and it wouldn't have been necessary to kill anyone!'

John Finally Snaps

Richard had been watching John and the way the muscles along his jaw would spasm as he clenched his teeth. As John's face became flushed, Richard placed his hand under Margaret's elbow and drew her and Sebastian back into the corner of the room. The Professor was prepared when John exploded but the Inspector was taken by surprise and jumped but could not move, from his chair, out of the firing line.

'Have you gone completely insane?' John leant upon the desk to stare directly into his father's eyes. 'Saddled Clay with a bride? Saddled? As if Charles Barnsby and I had any choice in the matter after what Clay and his cousin, Stephen did to that girl? What would you have done Father? Paid her off like some sort of back street whore? Perhaps they should have gone to prison for what they did! Maybe Clay would have learnt that there were consequences to his actions! For God's sake Father, she was under age!'

'Stephen was just as responsible, why didn't he have to marry Anne? Why did it have to be Clay?' demanded Warren.

'Although he participated, Stephen wasn't the one who got Anne pregnant!'

A sob of disgust escaped from Margaret. *I'm learning more and more about my family that I would rather not have known.* In sympathy Richard took her hand and squeezed it reassuringly. The father and son battle continued oblivious to the audience.

'You always come down hard on Clay! You even put conditions on helping him when he gets into trouble!' retorted Warren.

'Getting help for his drinking and gambling so that Clay stops getting into debt is hardly an unfair condition!' John suddenly turned to Inspector Fletcher, 'Clay can't be bank rolling Albert to hire assassins as he has nothing left to sell!'

The Inspector was a little startled at being brought back into the argument so abruptly. 'Well someone with money is behind this, the assassins were paid half up front and the other half was to be paid on completion.'

'Well that can't be me,' sneered Warren, 'As John is so fond of telling everyone, he owns everything now!'

An Expert's Opinion

From the doorway Samson uttered a small cough. 'Forgive me for interrupting but a gentleman is here to see you Mr. John, a Mr. Vincent.'

'We're busy!' snarled Warren but John turned as a smile flittered for a nanosecond across his face.

'Show him in please Samson.' John ordered before adding to the Inspector, 'Mr. Vincent is an art expert I consulted earlier this afternoon.' Richard's eyes were resting upon Warren and saw the colour drain away from his face at his son's words.

Mr Vincent was a dapper little elderly man who glanced around in interest and professional curiosity as he entered the study before he shook John's extended hand. 'Marvellous collection Mr. Foster, truly marvellous, you were right about the Monet in the entrance that is a very clever copy.'

He moved smoothly around the desk to study the painting behind a seething Warren. 'Oh yes indeed, this

Renoir is also a copy. The Constable I'd have to study a little more closely but that seems to still be an original.'

John nodded, 'Thank you Mr Vincent, Samson, if you could escort Mr Vincent through the house so that he may inspect all the paintings.' Samson bowed and led the little gentleman out of the room again.

Why Should She Get It All?

'How can you betray me like this John?' demanded Warren.

'They weren't yours to sell Father! Then to use that money to pay someone to murder your own daughter, her husband and your granddaughter! What is wrong with you?'

'Unlike you I was taking care of kin.'

'Isabella and Margaret are also your kin! Or don't they matter because they're female?'

Warren thrust an angry finger towards Margaret, 'Why should that demon child get what should be Clay's? He is a Barnsby! She doesn't even bear the name of her father!'

'You're wrong!' Margaret quietly interjected, 'I do bear my father's name, the name of Munroe!' She added with pride.

Warren snorted in derision 'If you're claiming that Edward slept with Felecia...'

'That isn't what Margaret is saying Father!' corrected John before Warren could develop into a rant.

'George and Felicia Barnsby may have been my biological parents, but Isabella and Edward Munroe were even more my parents. They raised, loved, fed, clothed and taught me as their own child. Until you had them murdered I didn't even know that they weren't my biological parents.'

'I didn't know the pebbles I played with as a child were actually diamonds and therefore worth killing for. I didn't know that I was to inherit some so called fortune from a father I didn't know I had.' Margaret released Richard's hand as she approached the desk. Her voice was low and calm but tears fell down her cheeks. 'Do you want to know the really pathetic part of what you have done?' She kept her eyes locked upon Warren's.

'That you're still alive?' He sneered.

'If I had known about the inheritance, if I had known about the diamonds, if you had asked for them, I would have probably given them to you.'

Warren laughed harshly in disbelief as he rose to his feet, 'Impossible girl! Just give away a fortune!'

Margaret nodded, 'You just don't understand Grandfather, I don't need it! Have never needed it! I had everything that I could ever want and you took away from me what actually was priceless to me. My parents, my friends, and my home! Little pebbles mean nothing compared to the people you ruthlessly had killed in cold blood! They were what mattered to me! No money could ever replace them. Now tell me Warren Foster was it worth it?'

'Devil's child! Why couldn't you have died in your mother's womb?' snarled Warren, 'I curse the day you were born! You took my beautiful Felicia and my Elizabeth away from me! Then to learn that the useless piece of land I had given Isabella was actually a diamond bonanza! That Charles Barnsby had gambled away his share of the Incorporation and you were going to get that too! It wasn't fair! It wasn't right! So I had to do something before you were 25! 'I recruited Bedford and Albert to frame Cedric so that Clay would get everything. Clay had nothing to do with any of this!'

I'll Do It Myself!

Warren ripped open the top drawer of his desk and pulled out a pistol. As he raised it to point directly at Margaret, Richard released his hold on Sebastian's leash. As

Warren pulled the trigger, Richard lunged forward to push Margaret out of the way as he drew out his own weapon. Sebastian fastened his powerful jaws upon Warren's arm, forcing him to drop the gun as he screamed.

BANG! BANG! BANG!

Three shots were fired almost at exactly the same time but not from the same gun. Sebastian released Warren and returned to where Richard was gently lowering Margaret to the floor, his hand pressed against her right shoulder as blood spread across and down the sleeve of her dress. Sebastian had spoiled Warren's aim so that he had only wounded Margaret.

Warren held his damaged arm against his chest but could not understand why there was so much blood under his hand. Not until he raised his eyes to see Inspector Fletcher now on his feet with his own pistol still in his hand. As Warren had pulled out his gun from the drawer, the policeman had instinctively risen and drawn his own weapon. They had fired almost simultaneously but the Inspector's aim had not been hampered by Sebastian's attack. *Even so I had thought to only wound and disarm Foster. As I had wanted to take him in alive. The true kill shot had been Richard's.*

In slow motion Warren raised his hand to the bullet wound in his chest and as his legs began to collapse beneath him, John raced around the desk to support him back into his chair. Like Richard, John applied pressure to the wound but Richard's bullet had pierced Warren Foster's heart.

'Tell me...' Warren croaked feebly grabbing hold of John's jacket lapel, 'Tell me the devil's child is dead!'

John glanced down at Margaret as Richard was pressing his handkerchief against her wound. He glanced back at his father dying in his arms.

'No Father, Margaret is only wounded.'

The scream of defeat seemed to echo around the room even after the breath had finally left Warren's body for the last time.

Albert's Arrest

Samson and two policemen had come running at the sound of the gun shots. Richard sent the Butler to retrieve a medical kit and one of the policemen to fetch a Doctor. As John closed his father's eyes, Inspector Fletcher slowly returned his gun to the holster on his hip.

No one spoke, not even when Samson returned with medical supplies and assisted Richard to remove Margaret's jacket so that they could bind her wound until the Doctor arrived.

The first words spoken came when a handcuffed Albert and a bewildered clerk, Elijah Bernstein, were escorted into the house by two policemen. Albert cast a dispassionate glance at the dead body and shrugged.

'He wouldn't have survived prison anyway.'

Inspector Fletcher stared hard at Albert. The physical similarities between Albert and Cedric were offset by the differences in their speech, mannerisms and personality. Finally Fletcher turned his attention to the clerk.

'Have you been mistreated Mr Bernstein?'

The Jewish boy, he was barely 19, shook his head. 'I don't understand, I thought he was Cedric Barnsby but the policeman said his name is actually Albert Bedford!'

'Go with the officer and he'll take your statement.' The Inspector transferred his gaze to Albert, 'Anything you'd like to tell me?'

Albert smiled, 'Not without my lawyer!'

The Inspector sighed, 'Take him and his uncle away, I'll join you at the police station once their lawyer has arrived.' He ordered one of the Constables.

The Doctor Returns

Doctor O'Brien didn't wait for Samson to announce him when he arrived at the house but sailed straight into the study. He bent down for a moment to check Margaret's wound before rising to his feet again. 'Strip her down to the waist,' the Doctor curtly ordered Richard before moving to examine Warren Foster. John uttered a protest about Margaret's modesty and the Doctor snapped at Richard, 'Keep up the pressure for a moment Professor Evans!'

Doctor O'Brien did a quick examination of Warren and nodded to the Inspector. 'He's dead. The wagon will be here shortly for the body. Now then the two of you get out!' He spoke to John and Fletcher as he knelt down again beside Margaret.

The Inspector immediately headed for the door but John was still not satisfied.

'He is a married man!' John pointed to Richard as he began to undo Margaret's dress. Snarling the Doctor picked up a scalpel and sliced it down the front of Margaret's dress to speed up the process. 'I'll need an assistant as I dig the bullet out. Now get the hell out!' Doctor O'Brien helped Richard ease the blood soaked sleeves of the dress down Margaret's arms.

Richard was puzzled by the Doctor's behaviour. *I don't understand the savagery that possesses the Doctor and with that sharp scrapple in his hand I am not prepared to ask.* The thin chemise under Margaret's dress had to be removed as it too was soaked in her blood.

The bullet had missed the collarbone but was lodged in the flesh just above Margaret's breast. The scrapple made short work of the chemise and the Doctor simply grunted a thanks as Samson deposited a bowl of hot water beside him before fleeing the room again.

The wound bled only sluggishly now as Doctor O'Brien filled a syringe to dull the pain as he removed the bullet. Placing the injection into her right arm the Doctor used the time to wait for it to start to work to clean away the blood from Margaret's breast and arm, and to sterilise the forceps he would be using.

Sweat beaded Margaret's brow as she gritted her teeth and held on tightly to Richard's hand as the Doctor probed into the wound. He sighed with relief as he withdrew a complete bullet. *If it had shattered it could have meant the need for an operation to remove the fragments.* Cleansing and dressing the wound the Doctor pressed a tender hand against Margaret's cheek before rising to his feet.

'Thank you Doctor,' Margaret's voice was little more than a whisper. 'Cedric? How is he?'

Laying her jacket over the top of Margaret, Richard looked up sharply at the Doctor who choked. Margaret raised concerned eyes to the stricken man's face. Not able to meet Margaret's imploring gaze Doctor O'Brien leant over to whisper something into Richard's ear.

The Professor swallowed hard on the bile that rose in his throat and didn't object as the Doctor fled from the room. Margaret looked up questioning into Richard's face.

'Richard? What did they do to Cedric?'

He cleared his throat as he attempted to find the gentlest way to describe what Warren had inflicted upon his own grandson.

'Kitten, it's better if you don't know.' *I know it's a cop out but I just can't inflict those images upon her fragile psyche.* He placed a gentle kiss against Margaret's forehead as two tears rolled down her cheeks.

Redressing Margaret

They heard the Inspector finally lose his cool demure as he swore colourfully. Assisting Margaret to sit up, Richard assumed that the Doctor must have told the

Inspector about Cedric's condition. As he was assisting Margaret off the floor and into a chair Samson quietly re-entered the study and he held a blouse and a long skirt in his hands.

'Mrs Samson thought this might keep Miss Margaret decent until you get back to the Inn.'

Richard held out his hand for the clothes, 'Thank you Samson and thank your wife that was very thoughtful.'

The Butler bowed his head and closed the door behind him as he left so Margaret could have some privacy as Richard helped her re-dress. When Margaret finally rose to leave she left the blood stained dress and chemise on the floor. *Even if it could be mended and cleaned I doubt that I could ever bring myself to wear it again.*

As expected the Inspector had already left, but one policeman stood guard outside the study while several others continued to search the house for evidence against Warren Foster. Even though he had confessed, Inspector Fletcher was not completely convinced that Warren had been the only one involved in the whole affair. John organised a carriage to take Margaret straight back to the Inn.

Richard Reports

As time had begun to run into evening, Elliott had begun to worry so when Richard led Margaret into the private parlour in different clothes from the ones she had left in, Elliott leapt to his feet in concern.

'What on earth happened? I was starting to get worried!' Elliott drew out a chair and assisted Richard to lower Margaret into it.

She raised pleading eye to Richard, 'I can't go through it again.' He laid his hand over hers.

'There is time before dinner, would you like to lie down in your room?'

When Margaret nodded Richard helped her up once more and escorted her and Sebastian upstairs.

On his way back to Elliott, the Professor promised to have a brief word with Franco Gio as well as procuring two large brandies. By the time Richard had finished explaining what had occurred at Warren Foster's house, Elliott was in need of the stiff drink.

'My God, Richard! There was no need for them to torture Cedric! How bad was it that you refused to tell Margaret the extent of Cedric's injuries?'

The hand that Richard ran over his face wasn't exactly steady. 'Bashed, whipped, fed only gruel and water,' he dragged in a shuddering breath and Elliott knew worse was to follow. 'They raped him repeatedly and... they cut him.' Richard found that he could not say the words and he gestured helplessly to his groin.

'Not cut off?' Elliott winced, at the thought.

Shaking his head Richard managed to continue, 'No, but although the cuts will heal, they'll leave scars. He'll always have a reminder of what his grandfather allowed him to suffer. The Doctor can't yet be certain that the cuts were deep enough to cause damage to function.'

'His own grandson, that man was a monster!' Elliott took another sip of his brandy. 'Do you intend to ever tell Margaret?'

Richard shook his head. 'Not unless Cedric wants her to know. She's learnt far too many family secrets today and I don't wish to overload her with any more.'

Is It Over Then?

Removing a handkerchief from his trousers' pocket Elliott wiped his forehead. 'So is it all over? Is Margaret safe?'

'That would depend...' Richard finished his brandy.

'On what?'

'Whether Warren Foster was telling the truth about Clay's involvement in this affair.'

'Do you think Clay is innocent?' Richard adjusted the gun that once again adorned his hip.

'Not in the least!'

An Unexpected Visitor

Maria Gio did not disappoint as she produced a magnificent feast for the party that evening. Margaret slid out of the conversation to concentrate on trying to eat with the limited use of her right arm. Her silence didn't go un-noticed, but her companions didn't force her to participate.

They were surprised when John Foster arrived. He apologised for interrupting their meal, he only wanted to drop something off to Margaret. She came out of her shell long enough to ask him to join them. Initially John refused but when she managed to smile he relented.

'When did you last have something to eat Uncle John?' Margaret's concern touched him.

'Breakfast...'

Having risen to his feet at John's entrance, Richard now brought another chair across to the table. As John sat down Elliott poured him a glass of wine using Margaret's glass as she wasn't using it.

Those assembled around the table allowed John to fill his plate and just eat as they returned to their previous conversation. Only when his plate had been emptied and Elliott was refilling his glass did they look to include him. He smiled gratefully as he raised a napkin to his lips.

'Thank you, I'd thought that I wasn't hungry but it was obviously what I needed.' John slipped his hand into the inside pocket of his jacket.

The resulting action was instantaneous. Both Richard and Elliott laid their hands on their right hips where they each had a gun holster. Correctly interpreting their response, John froze.

'I'm not reaching for a gun. This apple is nothing like its tree! Margaret, open my jacket and reach into the pocket please.' John slowly withdrew his empty hand out of his jacket and Margaret drew out an envelope. Her two protectors relaxed as she laid it on the table.

'That's for you Margaret.' John laid his hand over the top of one of hers. She shook her head.

'I don't want your money Uncle John.'

'It's not money. It's the deeds to the Haven. Even before your parents were murdered I intended that the Haven would pass to you. I never spoke to Father about it; I didn't know he was interested in it or your inheritance. I'm so sorry!'

Tears filled Margaret's eyes and she couldn't manage to say any more than, 'Thank you.' *But what had once been home to me could never be so ever again.*

'What about Clay?' asked Richard.

John shrugged as he uttered a sigh. 'The Inspector's people found absolutely no evidence at the house or in Albert's flat that Clay was actively involved in any of this business.'

What Lies Ahead?

The issue was allowed to be dropped as Maria cleared the table and brought out dessert. The sweet confectionary lightened their mood.

'So what happens now?' Margaret asked.

Elliott swirled the port around in his glass, 'Well, I have three months left to serve in my commission and after that I'll leave the army.'

Margaret felt her fingernails press deep into the palms of her hands as she asked him, 'Will you go back to England then?'

He smiled affectionately at her, 'No, I think I'll stick around the Gold Coast for a while and see what turns up.'

'Well...?' Margaret started slowly, choosing her words carefully, 'I'm going to need someone I trust to manage the Haven.'

Elliott glanced back at Margaret as his eyes widened in surprise. 'I think... I think I'd like that.'

Richard took off his glasses to clean them, 'And we're only a day's ride away so you need not feel too lonely.'

John said to Richard, 'I suppose you'll now have a second to do something about getting yourself a divorce before you can get married again.'

'Yes, but it seems now that Margaret is no longer in danger that she won't need me.' Placing his glasses on again, Richard sighed.

'I don't need you,' Margaret's quiet words caused those assembled to gasp in shock. Richard felt his chest constrict around his heart but he fought to keep from showing any emotion. Margaret laid her good hand over Richard's as she tried to smile.

'I don't need to be with you, I want to be with you! I want you to feel the same way and not just because you feel the need to protect me!'

Sighing in relief, Richard slid his hand from under hers to cup Margaret's face and kissed her passionately. She uttered a sob as her good arm slipped around Richard's neck and she willingly kissed him back.

'Well,' said a slightly embarrassed John, 'That seems pretty definite then!' As the couple drew away blushing, they joined with the others as they laughed. When John rose to his feet that it was time that he left. Margaret protested, but secretly she was not sorry to call it a night as she was incredibly tired and in pain.

Not If But When!

Margaret was safely tucked up in bed with Sebastian sprawled beside her when Richard came in to check on her. Despite Margaret's protest that she preferred fresh air, Richard shut and locked the French doors that led out to a small balcony before drawing the curtains closed.

The Professor methodically checked every square inch of the room as he doused all the candles except for one on the bedside table. Briefly he paused to caress his hand down Margaret's hair before giving Sebastian a solid pat and urged the tiger off the bed.

'I'll take Seb for a final walk before we all turn in for the night,' stated Richard as Sebastian slid onto the floor and stretched leisurely. The tiger cast her a searching glance but decided that it was safe enough to leave Margaret for a little while. *There just might be leftovers on offer in the kitchen.*

While Richard and Sebastian checked out the parameter of the Cameriere Canto Inn, Elliott hadn't changed into sleepwear yet as he prepared for a sleepless night. Seated in a comfortable arm chair, his rifle propped against his leg and his revolver in his lap, Elliott closed his eyes and tried to relax his body. *For Ricard and I it is not a case of if an attack is expected; but when.*

TUESDAY

A Painful Awakening

The bullet wound to Margaret's shoulder made sleep a little uncomfortable as it was the side she usually slept upon, so she was forced to sleep on her back. Thus Margaret managed to sleep for several hours until rolling over caused her to wake from the pain.

Struggling to sit up she glanced at the lit candle to see how far it had burned down. Then she reached across for a sachet that Doctor O'Brien had supplied her for pain and a glass of water.

The Cameriere Canto Inn had fallen silent as the last of the drinkers had been sent home an hour before and Margaret thought she heard the grandfather clock downstairs chime the hour. One o'clock. A shiver ran through her as she felt a light breeze blow aside the curtains at the French doors.

Frowning, but drowsy, Margaret thought, *hadn't Richard shut that curtain before taking Sebastian for a walk? Shouldn't Seb have come back by now?* Margaret felt around the bed to make sure the tiger wasn't there before she threw back the bedding and gave a quick glance at the floor to ensure that there was no large furry welcome mat.

Margaret was about to slip out of the bed to shut the window again when a solid shape moved swiftly towards her out of the limited range of the light of the lone candle.

Not Alone

A hand descended over her mouth as another pressed a sharp blade against her throat. 'Try to scream my pretty cousin and I'll slit your throat!' promised a menacing voice as the intruder sat down on the bed beside Margaret. Dressed entirely in black, the only part of him that was easily seen was his face.

'Cousin Clay I presume?' asked Margaret as the intruder removed his hand from her mouth, sliding his hand down her throat, Clay Barnsby raised Margaret's face so that he could study her by candle light.

'I can see how Grandfather could easily be misled; you do look just like Aunt Felicia.' Clay's hand continued to travel downwards and Margaret uttered a maidenly protest as he expertly undid the buttons of her nightgown. Clay pressed his knife just a little firmer against her throat as he peeled back her grown to reveal the bandages.

'I want to see where Grandfather wounded you. I've never known him to miss but I understand that your cat savaged him and spoiled his aim.'

Margaret chuckled at the description of Sebastian as if he was a domestic moggy. 'Sorry if it ruins your entire plans cousin.'

Sighing Clay ran his fingers down her cheek and along the jaw before caressing the line of her throat. 'Far too ambitious for the old man, but he's not the man he used to be in his prime.'

Margaret winced as his hand travelled over her shoulder and down her arm.

'So are you here to finish the job?' She asked lightly, not wishing to do or say anything that might provoke him. His hand came up to cup one firm, supple breast and Margaret's hands clenched into fists as she fought the desire to slap his face.

'I don't know... You are so very beautiful; I think I may be able to have even more fun by keeping you alive.' Not wishing to push her to lash out at him, Clay removed his hand from her breast.

You're Too Late!

'Just so you know killing me now you'll get nothing as I am already married!'

Clay sat very still as he scanned Margaret's face to determine if she was lying. 'I thought Professor Evans was already married?'

Margaret nodded, 'When we got back from Grandfather's this afternoon there was a letter from London from Richard's brother-in-law Peter Dickson.' Tears appeared in her eyes, 'Alice... Alice had succumbed to her illness so Richard was now a widower. A license and a quiet ceremony this evening and we both also made out our wills. Kill me and the money will go to Richard. Kill him too and it goes to his sister in England. You can never get your hands upon this accursed inheritance.'

Margaret remained silent as she allowed her cousin time to process all this information. Slowly Clay lowered his gaze from her face to rest upon her left hand. His body stiffened as he picked up her hand to look at the simple gold band that adorned her ring finger. Lowering her hand back into her lap, Clay suddenly burst into laughter.

'Nearly but not quite, cousin, I'm not so easily fooled by a glib story and a piece of jewellery. If this is your wedding night I would've found your husband in bed beside you claiming what is rightfully his.'

Sighing as a pained expression crossed Margaret's face, she pitied him. 'Richard is something you will never be... a true gentleman. With all the stress of the day as well as the pain from my recent but numerous injuries, he decided that we would wait until I was well enough to fully enjoy his attentions.' As a delicate hue swept across Margaret's features, Clay laughed again.

'Oh this is going to be even better than killing you! I can clearly see what I am destined to do; a Barnsby-Barnsby heir to rule the Barnsby Empire!'

A Change Of Plans

For the first time since Clay had sat down on the bed beside her, Margaret was now feeling nervous as Clay lowered his blade to shuck off his jacket. When he started to undo the buttons of his shirt, she protested, 'What do you think you're doing?'

Clay chuckled, 'What your husband should be doing, my sweet cousin, making you a woman! I wonder if you'll be able to stand to have your husband touch you once I make you scream in ecstasy?'

Margaret tried to edge back away from her cousin as he pulled his shirt free from his trousers but his hand latched painfully upon her wrist.

'Oh I'll scream all right! In terror! Do you really think that repeating history is going to work in your favour? Yes, I know that you and our cousin Stephen actually raped an innocent young lady!' Margaret gasped at the sudden anger that leapt into his eyes. Picking up his knife with his free hand, Clay slit down Margaret's nightgown and pulled it open to lay his hand against her stomach.

'My son inside of you? It will so be worth it. You never know you just might enjoy yourself!'

Margaret choked, 'Is that what you said to Anne Smythe when you raped her?'

His hand wrapped suddenly around her throat and Margaret realised that this time she had pushed him too far. For a moment the choking hold remained as Margaret desperately pulled at his fingers to release her. Laughing, Clay removed his hand before she blacked out.

'My God, Grandfather was right! I shall enjoy taming such a wild animal! A word of warning, wild cat, if you use your claws when I bed you, I might scratch back!'

Margaret was gasping for breath and was not capable of immediately answering him as Clay stripped off his shirt.

'Tell me...' her words came out as barely a whisper, 'Will Albert keep silent about your involvement with Grandfather to kill me and my parents for my inheritance?'

Kicking off his shoes, Clay immediately answered, 'Nothing to keep silent about as I wasn't involved. It should be fairly obvious that I had nothing to do with their plans.'

'Why?'

Clay unbuckled his trousers, and smiled wolfishly down at Margaret. 'If I had been involved you would definitely be dead by now and so would dear brother Cedric.'

While he drew off his trousers, Margaret valiantly tried to hold the sheet tightly around her. 'Please don't do this, do you want me to beg?'

Clay ripped the sheet out of her fingers as he chuckled. 'Oh yes, please beg.'

For a brief moment Margaret thought, *I might be able to avoid a physical confrontation.* 'Does that mean you won't rape me if I beg to your satisfaction?'

'Innocent child! No! The only thing more arousing than you begging me to stop would be if you put up a fight!' Clay, with almost tenderness, slipped Margaret's arms out of the remains of her nightgown.

'The violence actually turns you on?'

With one eyebrow raised, he gestured with this hand to his raging erection. As Clay knelt one knee on the bed, Margaret tensed up her body ready for action.

'How about not at all?'

Sweet cousin, do you still believe in fairy tales?'

Margaret actually smiled, 'Well if Prince Charming isn't going to save me at the last minute, then I'll just have to save myself!'

Turning The Tables

Margaret abruptly brought her knees up to her chest and then thrust both feet into Clay's groin. For the briefest moment she enjoyed the success as Clay swore colourfully as he clutched his privates and he bent over in agony. Margaret brought her knees back up to her chest and this time thrust her feet into Clay's face. As he toppled backwards, Margaret used her momentum to push Clay off balance and pin him to the floor beneath her.

On her way off the bed, Margaret grabbed the blade Clay had put down to strip off his clothes. He had been winded by the fall and was struggling to get his breath back as Margaret pressed the knife against his throat.

His attempt to throw Margaret off was thwarted as she reached beneath her and dug her fingernails into his penis. She was a little surprised when Clay started laughing.

'My God! Wild cat! I underestimated your power after so much loss of blood! You will truly be wasted on the Professor! Our son won't just rule an empire but could rule the world!'

'I will never let you rape me! I will never let you rape anyone again.' Her whole body was trembling in anger as she moved the knife away from Clay's throat intending to slam it into his black heart.

I Will Tame You!

He used her anger against her as he finally managed to throw Margaret off balance, knocking the knife out of her hand and tossing her onto her back as he rolled to land on top of her.

'You were saying sweet cousin?' Clay ran his hand down her throat to cup her breast, 'My God! I'm going to enjoy taming the wild cat. Before this night's over, I will have you screaming out my name.'

Margaret struggled to dislodge him but he was too heavy to shift. She reached up one hand and scratched her fingernails down his cheek.

'I'll scream it now, as I send you on your way to Hell!'

'I'm not going anywhere until I have made you mine!' As Margaret's blows went unheeded, Clay tore away the last shred of her clothes.

Springing The Trap

When Clay forced his knee between Margaret's bare thighs, he swore as a lantern was suddenly unshuttered from beside the armchair.

'Don't move Mr. Barnsby, believe me at this distance I'll easily put a bullet through your eyes!' Elliott's voice caused Margaret to jump startled.

Looking up at the pistol levelled calmly at him, Clay ceased his movements but did not get off Margaret. He glanced quickly to where he had thrown his knife, safely out of Margaret's reach, but now also out of his.

'Don't do it Clay,' stated a second voice as another lantern closer to the French windows was also unshuttered.

Clay's eyebrows raised, 'Inspector Fletcher? My goodness, cousin, this is getting kinkier by the minute! Does the Professor know how many different men you are servicing?'

'Watch your mouth!' snarled Elliott, losing some of his composure, 'The Inspector hoped that Margaret could get you to admit your involvement in the murder plots.'

Clay glanced up wickedly at the Inspector, 'That didn't exactly work out for you then?'

The internal door opened and the soft pad, pad, pad of large paws was heard entering the room. Glancing over his shoulder Clay watched as Richard, his sidearm drawn and Sebastian joined them. For the first time real fear descended upon Clay's features as softly the tiger came straight towards where he still lay on top of Margaret. Swallowing hard, Clay swore and was about to scramble to his feet but Richard's calm, quiet voice stopped him.

'Stay very still Mr. Barnsby. If he perceives that you've been hurting Margaret, Seb will tear your throat out before you can even get to your knees.'

Sebastian slowly walked around the pair on the floor, his deep blue eyes scanning the scene for context. Transferring his gaze to where the three other men stood or sat, all with firearms drawn, Sebastian gave a sharp 'humph' which nearly caused Clay to wet himself.

'Slowly Mr Barnsby, roll off Margaret and onto your back,' Richard instructed.

When Clay had obeyed, Richard assisted Margaret to her feet and into a dressing gown. Once she was safely seated upon the bed, Sebastian gave up his intense scrutiny of Clay and jumped up beside Margaret. As his companions let out a sigh of relief, Richard added, 'Now get up and put your clothes on. He's all yours Inspector.'

We Would Be Good Together

Rising and gathering up his discarded clothes and redressing, Clay gave a hard laugh, 'On what charges? I had nothing to do with Grandfather's murder plot.'

Inspector Fletcher shook his head, 'Tonight's actions will do for starters. Breaking and entering, menacing with a deadly weapon, threats to kill and attempted rape.'

'Misdemeanours,' Clay dismissed the charges with a wave of his hand, 'Especially if my cousin doesn't press any charges.' Margaret caressed her hand along the tiger's fur as Richard cast a serious eye over her bandages to ascertain if she was bleeding again from her tussle with Clay.

'Why shouldn't I press charges Clay? If you're concerned about the scandal to the family I'm afraid that that boat has well and truly sailed.'

Ignoring how intently Sebastian was watching him, Clay cupped Margaret's chin in his hand to raise her eyes to meet his. 'It's not too late, my goddess, annul your sham marriage to the Professor and I'll divorce Anne and together we can rule Barnsby Holdings and our children will rule the world! Barnsby-Foster joining with Barnsby-Foster stock! We'll be unstoppable!'

Elliott thumbed back the safety of his pistol but catching Richard's slight shake of his head, he lowered the pistol back into his lap.

'One major problem Clay,' stated Margaret, calmly pushing his hand away from her face.

'And what is that sweet cousin?'

Margaret smiled as she glanced up at Richard. 'I love Richard with every fibre of my being. You wouldn't even be a shadow of the man that he truly is!'

Anger surged through Clay, and ignoring the danger he stood in, his hand automatically came up to slap Margaret's face. He never made contact as Richard's hand intercepted Clay's. As their eyes met, Clay tried to pull his arm away but it was held in too tight a grasp.

'Attempt to strike Margaret again and I will break your arm!' calmly stated Richard as he released Clay.

Taking a step backwards, Clay massaged his ill-treated wrist, 'Well don't think for a minute that I'll stop trying to get back the birthright that should've been mine!'

I Was Bluffing!

Margaret watched with interest as Clay took another step backwards, this time towards his knife and the floor.

'What would you have done tonight if I hadn't told you that I was already married? If your intention was to kill me, how did you plan to get away with it?'

Clay waved an airy hand, 'I've a group of buddies who would've been prepared to swear that I was playing cards with them. I don't know if I could've gone through with murder though, even if you were single, I still think seducing you would've been much more enjoyable.'

Elliott chuckled, 'Do you think we should tell him?'

'Tell me what?' Clay now stood over the top of his blade.

Margaret smiled, 'I lied about getting married tonight.' Slipping off the wedding ring she held it up in front of her. 'That was Grandmama's, she told me to always have it with me and one day it could save my life.'

'Aren't you the cunning little Jade then?'

Out Of Patience

In one fluid movement Clay crouched down to pick up his knife before any of the other men could react. It was nothing to the speed and agility with which Sebastian reacted as he launched himself at Clay, knocking him onto his back. Sebastian stood over Clay, growling until he threw the knife away from him.

'I wasn't going to use the blade on Margaret,' Clay gasped under the heavy weight of Sebastian. *I can't believe I'm explaining my actions to a tiger,* 'I was simply going to use it to make my escape.'

The tiger's tail slashed the air from side to side as he refused to release his prisoner. Not even when Margaret called to him. With a deep sigh Richard moved forward and briefly patted Sebastian's head.

'Good boy!' Kneeling down on one knee, Richard placed his revolver against Clay's temple. 'Go back to Margaret; the Inspector will take your prisoner away,' he added to the tiger. Raising his eyes to meet Richard's, Sebastian looked at him for a brief moment before he turned away from his prey.

Clay breathed a sigh of relief as Richard hauled him to his feet and Inspector Fletcher secured his hands with handcuffs. Sebastian jumped back up onto the bed and lay down beside Margaret. His tail continued to flick to show how much he disliked the continuing presence of this man.

'Think about my proposal cousin, we could be incredible together,' Clay called out as the Inspector led him towards the internal door.

'Never going to happen, not in this life time, or even the next!' promised Margaret.

'This isn't over! I always get what I want!'

Margaret laughed, 'Good luck with that, and I hope you get everything you deserve!'

Can We Go Home Now?

Putting the safety catch back on his gun, Richard sank down onto the bed and gathered Margaret into his arms as she uttered a sob.

'Is it finally over?' she asked, 'Does anyone else want to try and kill me, or rape me?'

Elliott stretched his aching and stiff muscles, 'only Major Marconi and he's hopefully safely locked up in prison.'

Richard briefly pressed his lips against Margaret's forehead before rising to assist Elliott out of the arm chair. 'I'll just help Elliott to his room.' Richard waited until Elliott was fully supported on his crutches before picking up the Lieutenant's rifle and revolver.

'Richard!' Both men paused as they were about to leave the room.

'Yes kitten?'

'Can we go home now?'

'Right this minute?'

Elliott laughed as Richard received a look from both Margaret and Sebastian. A tired smile flittered across Richard's face.

'Soon.' He also carried Elliott's lantern so as they left the room the only light that remained was once again the solitary candle beside Margaret's bed. Shivering as she slipped under the covers, Margaret drew Sebastian down to lay close to her. *Protection against a room filled with dark shadows and even darker memories.*

Night Terrors

Margaret suddenly sat upright in bed, thrusting frantically at the bed covers that were encasing her. The screaming in her dreams transcended into the real world. Sebastian raised his head and licked her cheek to try and wake Margaret up and so stop the screaming.

In the armchair, Richard jerked awake; his revolver came up immediately to kill any intruder. The sight of the raised weapon broke through the last remnants of Margaret's dream.

'Richard, it's all right, it was just a dream about last night.' She called out reassuringly. The Professor dragged in a sharp breath as he ran a shaky hand across his face and slowly lowered his gun. Managing to untangle herself from her sheets, Margaret rose stiffly to her feet.

'Have you been there all night? Wouldn't it have been more comfortable on the bed with us?'

Rising to his feet, Richard stretched his cramped muscles. 'Master Sebastian takes up a lot of room. Besides...

I thought the armchair would help me to stay awake.' He checked Margaret's bandages for any bleeding. 'I'll change all your dressings this morning.'

She nodded absently, her thoughts were elsewhere. 'Why weren't you and Seb in the room when Clay broke in? Did the Inspector think you'd react before Clay could admit his involvement?'

'Yes, Fletcher thought I'd be tempted to shoot Clay the moment he entered or Seb would rip his throat out. The Inspector couldn't find any evidence of Clay's involvement at either your Grandfather's or Albert's homes.'

I Need To Know

Taking a step even closer to Richard, Margaret lowered his hand from her face to slip it into her dressing gown and up to cup her breast. Sighing in pleasure Margaret closed her eyes as Richard instinctively raised his other hand to cover both her breasts.

As his fingers gently stroked and teased, Richard momentarily forgot himself and he lowered his head to claim Margaret's mouth beneath his own. A blissful sigh escaped from her throat, her hands clutching Richard's shoulders to prevent him from drawing back.

For a moment he was caught up in the passion that they had both been suppressing for so long that it was some time before his conscious' nagging managed to get through the pleasure.

I am a gentleman, and still married to someone else, and Margaret is in a fragile state. Fighting the primal need to take possession of what he was being offered, Richard, managed to put some distance between them; which was not made easy as Margaret raised passion filled questioning eyes, trusting eyes, to meet his.

'I had to know,' she whispered in a sort of apology, 'if it would make my skin crawl like when Clay touched me.'

Richard tried to keep his face non-expressive, even though his chest was constricting painfully around his heart. 'Well what is the verdict?'

A delicate flush crept across Margaret's cheeks as she smiled shyly, 'How can we speed up your divorce? Do I have to wait until we're married before you can kiss me again?'

Laughing Richard felt the weight lift away from his chest as he wrapped his arms around Margaret's waist. Very willingly Richard kissed her again but kept a tight grasp upon his control before they were tempted to take it any further for the moment.

Next Time Shoot First!

A knock at the door caused Richard to release Margaret and reach for his gun but it was only Maria.

'I have drawn a bath for Senorita Margaret. Then I help her to dress, or do you prefer she stay in bed... to rest, Professor?' Maria didn't seem to be aware of the flushed features or their embarrassment at the thought of what they would prefer to be doing in that bed.

Richard cleared his throat, 'Dressed, Maria we have to see the lawyers.'

Margaret re-adjusted the dressing gown around her, 'And I want to visit Cedric in hospital,' she added.

Smiling Maria nodded. 'We take Sebastian down for breakfast or does he need to relieve himself?'

Placing his revolver back into the holster upon his hip, Richard said, 'I'll take him for a walk before I eat. Is Elliott up yet?' He gestured for Sebastian to come to his side.

Maria threw her hands up expressively, 'All Inn up now Professor! No one sleep through Senorita's screams.'

Pressing her hands against her heated cheeks, Margaret apologised but Maria waved this aside.

'Franco say next time there is an intruder, shoot first!' Maria led Margaret down the hall to the bathroom and assisted her to bathe and dress while Richard and Sebastian stretched their aching muscles.

Not Prepared To Relax Just Yet!

Before they took a short carriage ride to Margaret's lawyers, Elliott had been slightly surprised to see the gun once again positioned on Richard's hip after he had changed into fresh clothes and had his breakfast.

'With Major Marconi and Clay Barnsby now both in custody surely there is no longer any danger to Margaret?' When the two men were alone for a moment, Elliott queried this continuing level of security. 'What else could possibly be dangerous?'

Richard ran a hand over his forehead, 'I feel that we've missed something, a key element that links this mystery together.'

'What could we have missed? I thought this mystery had been solved?'

A tired smile appeared on Richard's face, 'If I knew what was missing then it would be less frustrating. Until it is identified I'm not scaling down security around Margaret.'

'Shall I re-arm and come with you?'

Richard patted him on the shoulder, 'No, I'll be able to think clearer once we all get a good night's sleep.'

Elliott shook his head, 'you seem so calm about all this danger.'

For the briefest moment Richard lowered his guard so that Elliott could see the torment in his eyes, 'I... I can still hear Margaret screaming. I wasn't happy about the Inspector's plan last night which is probably why he didn't want me in the room. It wasn't that I had any doubts about you being able to protect her when it became necessary.'

'Thank you very much!' Elliott drawled.

An attempt to smile failed to reach Richard's eyes, 'It's just that Margaret has been through so much already that to expose her needlessly to even more danger wasn't easy to swallow.'

'The Inspector had hoped that Clay would reveal his involvement to Margaret,' reasoned Elliott.

Richard sighed, 'I know! It's the only reason I allowed it to continue. But this time... any threat to Margaret... will be dealt with my way.'

Seeing the cold, ruthless, determination in Richard's face, Elliott swallowed hard upon the flicker of fear that rose within him. *It gives me no pleasure to know that I was right in predicting that Richard would be incredibly dangerous the moment he lost control. I just hope that I'm not in the way when Richard finally snaps.*

The Lawyer's Office

The clerk at the lawyer's office was apologetic as he showed Margaret, Richard and Sebastian into an empty office.

'I'm sorry Miss Munroe; Mr Greenberg is dealing with the fall out of your Grandfather's death and the art fraud. Mr Smythe will be with you in a moment. Can I get you anything while you're waiting, tea or coffee?'

Richard shook his head but Margaret turning away from the painting she was admiring, smiled. 'A glass of water, thank you.' As the clerk bowed and shut the door behind him, she looked back at the painting.

Richard sat down in the comfortable chair opposite the impressive desk, Sebastian lay down at his feet, but Margaret was restless and wandered around the office looking at all the artefacts, but mainly the pictures. Richard wondered, *Is she really studying the paintings or merely trying to keep from thinking about more disturbing thoughts?*

'Well kitten do you like what you see?' Even though Richard's voice was soft and gentle, Margaret still started at the break in the silence. She turned as she smiled.

'Oh yes, the artist is really talented and they seem all to be the same painter. They are signed only with 'A.S.' which is unusual.'

The door had opened as Margaret had replied and Richard looked quickly around, half expecting it to be the clerk returning with Margaret's water. His hand had strayed to his gun holster just in case it was trouble.

The Missing Link

It was actually the lawyer, Mr Smythe, and he smiled at Margaret. Behind the lawyer, the clerk slipped into the room and placed a glass of water on the desk before vanishing just as silently.

'The artist is my daughter Anne. Although she has her hands full with three young children she still paints when she is able.' Mr Smythe shook hands with both of them, but Richard's handshake was a little preoccupied.

His tired brain was trying to make sense and connections of everything he had heard since entering the lawyer's office and how it tied in with the missing inheritance had been eluding him.

'Anne... Anne Smythe... talented painter... as in Mrs Clay Barnsby?'

Margaret gasped as she realised where Richard was going. Mr Smythe stiffened in anger.

'Yes, but that is not a name I like to hear in my presence.'

Richard sympathised, 'I don't blame you! I'm sorry Sir, but I'm going to hurt you further. Would Anne do anything Clay told her to do?'

The muscle in Mr Smythe's cheek spasmed, 'Yes, she has always foolishly believed that Clay loves her and that he didn't...' the lawyer found the words stick like glue in his throat.

'Rape her?' whispered Margaret, 'like he tried to do to me last night.'

Mr Smythe's face collapsed in horror. 'My dear child, I'm so sorry! But what has Anne being a painter to do with Clay's crimes?'

Richard paused for a moment before he said quietly, 'To fund assassination attempts against Margaret and her parents, Warren Foster sold several of the masterpieces in his home but had them copied so that John Foster wasn't aware of his actions.'

'With all that happened yesterday, Margaret being wounded, Foster being killed, finding an imprisoned and brutalised Cedric and then Clay breaking into Margaret's room; it was easy to forget about the paintings. How did Foster find someone to copy the masterpieces? Who did Foster use to sell the originals so quietly that no one knew about it? Would Foster have enough power to force Anne to copy these paintings?'

The lawyer shook his head, 'No, Anne hated Warren Foster and how he encouraged Clay in his reckless pursuits.'

Richard smiled as Margaret sat down beside him. Her expressive face told him that she understood what that meant.

'Then Inspector Fletcher has his link between Clay and the murders. If Clay coerced or convinced his wife to copy the paintings then he had to know why his Grandfather was selling them.' Margaret scanned Richard's face and as he nodded she let out a sigh of relief.

'Is it enough?' She transferred her glance to the lawyer who had buried his head in his hands.

'Oh my poor Anne, the misery that man has caused over the years!' Mr Smythe lifted his head, horror etched on his face as he added, 'Does that make Anne an accessory? If she willingly and knowingly helped Clay and Warren, she could face the death penalty or life in prison!'

Reaching across the desk, Margaret laid her hand over Mr. Smythe's. 'You need to go to your daughter now and convince her to co-operate with Inspector Fletcher.'

The lawyer sadly shook his head, 'Anne will not turn on that cad.'

Dragging in a shuddering breath Margaret's voice shook a little as she admitted, 'Clay said last night that he could easily divorce Anne to marry me to produce... a Barnsby-Foster pure blood line to rule the Barnsby Empire.' *I hate having to repeat that loathsome creature's words but Mr Smythe needs something substantial to convince his daughter to hand her husband to the police.*

'Damnation!' exploded the lawyer, 'After everything that man has put my little girl through, he would throw her aside just to get his hands on your inheritance?'

'He wanted to get his hands on something else as well!' Richard decided not to voice that thought but said instead, 'Warren Foster said that Anne didn't have a considerable dowry.' Mr Smythe waved an exasperated hand.

'Compared to Miss Munroe's inheritance it would be a pittance but Foster was bitter as I pulled an old lawyer's trick.'

'You tied it up through the children?'

The lawyer nodded, 'Not that it slowed Clay down, and he forced Anne and his mother Hester to sell anything they could to bail him out again and again.'

'Margaret's right Mr Smythe, you need to go to your daughter, she'll need your support if the police search their home this morning,' urged Richard.

Mrs Anne Barnsby Nee Smythe

Rising to his feet Mr Smythe did up his jacket and was about to excuse himself to his clients when the clerk burst into the room ahead of a very irate young woman.

'I'm sorry Mr Smythe but I told her that you were occupied with clients.' The clerk tried to exonerate himself from this lapse in procedure.

'That's all right Durack, my daughter is exactly the person I need to see right now.'

The clerk accepted his superior's dismissal and fled the storm that was about to be unleashed.

'Anne, I'd like you to meet...'

Mrs Anne Barnsby nee Smythe didn't allow her father time to finish his introductions. 'Papa, Clay didn't come home last night and this morning a police person showed up at our home and said that Clay had been arrested! They're searching the house, heaven's knows what for!'

As Mr. Smythe eased his agitated daughter into a chair, Margaret silently handed her the glass of water and urged Anne to sip it and compose herself.

'Anne, where are the children?' There was an edge to the lawyer's voice that he was desperately trying to control.

'I took them to Mama. Please Papa; you have got to do something for Clay.'

Mr Smythe spoke carefully, 'Honey my hands are tied, Clay can't be represented by this firm as it is a conflict of interest. We represent Margaret Munroe.'

Rising abruptly to her feet again, Anne slammed the glass of water down on the desk before pacing the room. 'You've always hated Clay!' She accused her father.

'That has nothing to do with it Anne.'

Richard began to rise from his chair, 'Perhaps we should leave you to talk.'

Mr Smythe waved him back down, 'No, I want you as a witness as I ask Anne a few questions.' Putting aside his own feelings as a father, he grasped Anne firmly by the shoulders and looked her directly in the eyes.

'I want you to answer me honestly Anne, several paintings in Warren Foster's home have been discovered to be copies. Did you paint them?'

Taking a deep breath as she stared up at her father, Anne didn't immediately answer. 'Yes Papa,' she finally admitted.

'Did Warren or Clay ask you to copy them?'

'Clay.'

'Did he tell you why he wanted them copied?'

'Yes Papa.'

My Smythe bit back a groan and tried to remain professional. 'What was Clay's reason?'

She expressively shrugged her shoulders, reminding Richard of a naughty school child. 'Grandfather Foster had gone to Uncle John to help Clay with his debts but he had said, "No." Grandfather no longer had any assets but said if we copied the paintings and sold the original in London, Uncle John wouldn't know about it. I wasn't happy about the deceit but Clay promised me that it would pay his debts and he was going to give up gambling and cut down on his drinking.'

Margaret shook her head, 'Uncle John said he was prepared to pay Clay's debts if he stopped gambling and drinking.'

Casting a defiant look at her, Anne said, 'Clay said Uncle John wouldn't help, this was the only way to stop the debt collectors breaking Clay's legs.'

Mr Smythe tried to return them to the topic, 'Clay said the paintings were to pay his debts? Not that the money was for something else?'

'Clay said it would sort out his debts, what else could it mean but the money would be used to pay his debts?'

A weight lifted from the lawyer's heart but his next question would determine if his daughter was an accomplice or not with her husband and his grandfather.

'Some of the money from the paintings may have paid Clay's debts but the majority of it was given to Albert Bedford to arrange the assassinations of the Munroes for the farm and Miss Munroe's Barnsby inheritance.'

The horror on Anne's face was totally genuine and no one in the room was left in any doubt of Anne's innocence as she jumped to her feet. 'Oh Papa no! Clay can't have been involved! That is monstrous!'

Gently Mr Smythe eased his daughter back into her chair, 'Sweetheart, it gets worse. Clay was arrested last night for breaking and entering an Inn, menacing with a deadly weapon, threatening to kill and attempted rape.'

At the last word Anne went deathly pale. 'Was it this Munroe-Barnsby heiress?'

The lawyer nodded and he added, 'He... Clay told her that he wanted to produce a Barnsby-Foster heir and was prepared to marry Margaret to make that heir legitimate.'

Anne shook her head, 'That's impossible! Clay is already married!' Even as these words left her mouth the implications of what her father was trying to gently tell her hit home. 'After I stood by him through everything, he would toss me aside? I don't believe it!'

Taking a deep breath, Margaret finally said, 'It's true!'

Tears filled, angry eyes snapped to look properly at Margaret for the first time. Anne looked from Margaret to Richard, then down to Sebastian. Realisation finally hit Anne.

'You're Margaret Barnsby?'

Margaret stiffened slightly, 'Munroe,' she corrected quietly.

Swallowing hard Anne asked, 'It was going to be rape? It wasn't consensual? You didn't want to accept his offer of marriage?'

A shudder of revulsion ran through Margaret, 'I told him to go to Hell!'

Reassuringly Mr Smythe patted Anne's shoulder. 'Sit quietly for a moment while I complete my business with Miss Munroe and then I'll go with you to talk to the Inspector.'

Surprising News For Richard

Nodding Anne picked up her glass of water and sipped it as Mr Smythe returned to his chair behind the desk. 'I'm sorry Miss Munroe; you wanted to see us about something urgent?' he asked.

Richard drew out of the top inner pocket of his jacket the deeds to the Haven and pushed it across the desk towards the lawyer. On top of that he laid the bags of the pebble people.

'We felt,' said Margaret, 'that it would be safer for the lawyers to hang onto everything until all the paperwork has been sorted out and finalised.'

Mr Smythe opened up the deeds, but wasn't surprised by its contents, 'so John Foster is transferring the Haven to you. He mentioned it briefly several months ago. If we had done something about it sooner we might have prevented your parents' murders. I'm so sorry!' The lawyer whipped out a handkerchief and wiped his eyes.

Richard shook his head, 'They may have still died trying to protect Margaret when Foster went after her inheritance.'

Nodding his thanks, Mr Smythe drew out a document from Margaret's file as he stored the title deeds inside. 'A telegram was sent to London yesterday as you requested Professor Evans. The reply arrived only an hour ago. The official documents will of course be travelling by ship, so nothing can be done until they arrive in Accra.' He paused expecting a response from either Richard or Margaret, but they were both looking expectantly at him.

'Oh dear, didn't I say what the reply contained? Sorry Professor Evans your wife Alice died about two weeks ago. Your brother-in-law, Peter Dickson, has been tied up with legal red tape but boarded a ship to come to Accra as soon as he was able to clear everything up. He should be here any day now.'

Unable to speak, Richard just stared at the lawyer in disbelief. Margaret, though, had a very important question she needed answering.

'Why didn't Peter send us a telegram two weeks ago?'

Mr Smythe shrugged his shoulders. 'According to what is in the telegram Mr Dickson wanted to tell you himself, in person. There was no way he could be aware of the nightmare you were going through and the news would have come too late to save your parents. You would still have had to wait until the official documents arrived before you could be married.'

Both Margaret and Mr Smythe looked at Richard, expecting him to say something, anything, or show some sort of emotion. He just stared blankly ahead. Margaret reached out to lay her hand upon his arm.

'Richard? Are you all right? Did you hear what Mr Smythe said?'

Slowly Richard lowered his eyes to rest upon her hand for a moment before raising his gaze to Margret's face. He blinked twice and dragged in a deep breath.

'I think I must have lost my hearing.'

Margaret sank to her knees in front of Richard and cupped her hands around his face. 'Richard, Alice is gone, you're now a widower. Peter is on his way with the official documentation.' She spoke a little louder and clearer to try and penetrate his numbness.

'Is it finally over?' Richard stared disbelievingly into her face.

Smiling, Margaret stroked his cheek, 'Yes, Professor!'

'And you do still want to marry me?'

'Yes Professor.' Margaret shyly initiated the kiss that could have swept them on an erotic journey but a tolerant lawyer cleared his throat and Margaret reluctantly returned to her chair.

Richard was back with them. 'Can you organise a marriage license so that as soon as the papers arrive Margaret and I can be married immediately?'

Mr Smythe smiled, 'Yes of course, but don't you wish to enjoy some time as a single bachelor again before you re-marry?'

Taking Margaret's hand into his own, Richard pressed it to his lips. 'I've waited a long time for this young lady, I'm not going to wait a second more than is necessary to make her mine!'

As Margaret blushed, Mr Smythe added, 'Then all you have to decide is what you're going to do about the Barnsby inheritance.'

I Need Time To Think About It

Sighing Margaret brushed a weary hand across her brow, 'I'm going to need time to think about it. Right now this inheritance revolts me. I don't need it; I never wanted it; so it would be tempting to just get rid of it. But that would demean why my parents were murdered,' she paused as Anne gave a sob at her words. 'When you see Clay, tell him that! The people he and Grandfather murdered were more important than some birthright!' Taking a deep breath Margaret composed herself but she had been unable to keep the contempt out of her words.

Richard shook his head, 'I don't even know what the Foster or Barnsby Empires consist of.'

The lawyer was happy enough to move the conversation away from the emotions that threatened to consume Margaret.

'Foster is primarily imports and exports and Barnsby is a combination of real estate and commerce.'

'I understand your law firm has been running Barnsby Holdings since Charles Barnsby's death. The fact that Clay is prepared to commit murder then the company is doing well?' asked Richard.

Mr Smythe nodded, 'Very well, in fact better than when Charles and George Barnsby were running the business. We've not only updated, modernised and kept operating the assets but also ensured that the working conditions for the employees were improved.'

A Few Ideas

Breaking down, Anne covered her face with her hands as she cried. Margaret knelt down in front of her cousin's wife and wrapped her arms around her. She had half expected the grieving woman to reject her, but Anne accepted Margaret's comfort.

'How am I supposed to support my children?'

Margaret stroked her hand down Anne's hair and offered her a handkerchief to blow her nose. 'Even if I was the meanest bitch in the world and meant to cut the rest of the family out of the Barnsby inheritance, do you really think that Uncle John or your father would let you and Aunt Hester be reduced to begging or... or prostitution? Now take a drink of water and dry your eyes.' Margaret handed the glass to Anne and held it for her as Anne's fingers trembled. Once Anne had calmed down, Margaret returned to her chair.

'I won't know any details for certain until I've seen what sort of profits the business is making but I also want to talk to Uncle John about what is appropriate. I would like to see an annuity for Hester, and for Anne for their lifetime and regardless if they re-marry. I would like your ideas Mr Smythe of a trust fund for the children.' Margaret paused as Anne grasped her hand and sobbed out a thank you. Margaret patted her hand reassuringly.

'I'm thinking of a Board of Trustees to run everything, and if possible to have this legal firm as a major part of that Board?' As Margaret talked Mr Smythe had begun to take notes. Now he nodded.

'It would be an honour to continue to work for you Miss Munroe.'

'Thank you. A certain percentage of the annual profits should be set aside for, as you mentioned Mr Smyth, modernisation, development and training and improving conditions for employees.'

Again Mr Smythe nodded, 'What about the majority of the profit? Do you have any desire to expand the business or perhaps specialised in other realms?'

Richard watched as Margaret clenched her jaw and he saw the young girl becoming a woman.

'I have a couple of projects in mind. The return will be minimal if at all, hospitals and medical facilities where they're needed the most. Away from the cities.'

Richard added, 'Medical research?'

Sitting forward Margaret became animated, 'Yes, and animal sanctuaries; funding for schools to give women skills so that they have other choices than selling their bodies. Children need to be in schools and not factories or work houses. By giving them an education they can improve the fortunes of their families.'

Mr Smythe looked up from his notebook, 'You might consider a Foundation which reports to the Board and a separate committee for each charity or project which report to the Foundation.'

Margaret came back to reality with a laugh, 'A noble dream but it all depends upon what the company can withstand.'

Mr Smythe smiled, 'All this and more! There was a really good reason for Clay to want to get his hands upon Barnsby Holdings! We've not been slack in looking after your interests until you could claim your birthright.' Rising to his feet, Mr Smythe put away his notes into Margaret's file before placing the file and the bags of diamonds into his safe. 'If there isn't anything else Miss Munroe, I'll take Anne to see Inspector Fletcher.'

Visiting The Hospital

They all rose to their feet and Sebastian yawned as he stretched first his front and then his back legs. *I've been good all morning and think now would be a good time for a run or a snack, preferably both.* Following them out of the lawyer's office Sebastian glanced up at Margaret. Smiling down at the hungry tiger, Margaret patted his back.

'Sorry Seb, but we're going to see Cedric in hospital before we have lunch.'

Although Sebastian accepted the delay in any gratification as they took a carriage to the hospital; Richard, though, was a little concerned about taking a fully grown tiger into the hospital. *I'm not yet happy enough that Margaret is completely safe for her to go into the hospital alone.* Never without a small notepad and a pencil; the Professor jotted a brief note and sent an orderly with a message for Doctor O'Brien while they waited outside. However it was a highly stressed Phillip who came out to meet them.

'Thank goodness, you came Margaret!' Phillip embraced her. He looked like he hadn't slept, changed his clothes or even shaved since the previous morning.

'Doctor O'Brien sent me to bring you up through the service elevator; less chance of running into patients or visitors.' Phillip led all of them around to a back entrance of the hospital.

'Has something happened to Cedric? Has his conditioned worsened?' Margaret was becoming alarmed by Phillip's agitation.

'He won't eat!'

There was the occasional gasp as they walked passed an orderly or nurse but the collar and leash upon the tiger and Phillip's assurances meant that they weren't stopped. Entering the single room, Margaret dropped Sebastian's leash as a sob escaped from her.

Cedric lay in exactly the same position as when they had found him the previous day. Seb lay down in the corner of the room as Margaret sat on the bed beside her cousin. When he glanced up into her tear filled eyes, Cedric tried to shield his face.

'I don't want you to see me like this!'

Margaret gently drew his hands away and held them firmly between her own. 'Don't be silly cousin; you look better than you did yesterday.' She caressed her hand against his cheek and drew Cedric into her arms and let him cry.

Doctor O'Brien entered close behind them and having studied Cedric's charts, he permitted Richard to draw him to one side where no one around the bed could hear them.

'Phillip told us Cedric won't eat,' stated Richard, taking off his glasses to polish them before putting them back on again, 'Is he refusing to drink as well?'

The Doctor shook his head, 'He'll drink only water.'

Richard cast a brief glance back to the bed. 'Tell me the truth Doctor; with what they did to Cedric did they do any internal damage? Would the cuts on his penis cause pain when urinating? Are there any internal tears inside the… the anus? Part of it could be the fear of pain of doing further damage by expelling any waste.'

'Although tender, there is no serious damage to the anal passage.'

Deep in thought, Richard stroked his chin, 'They kept him on a minimalist diet of gruel and water; his stomach probably can't stand anything that isn't very bland or perhaps very liquid.'

'So what do you recommend Professor Evans?'

'Start Cedric off with milk, preferable pure clean milk, boiled if possible, for a couple of days, if his stomach appears to accept this, then move onto pureed food.'

Doctor O'Brien's eyebrows rose, 'Baby food?'

'Yes, but it'll have to be a careful balancing act between re-introducing food to Cedric's stomach and ensuing that he gets just enough fibre so that the waste expelled is soft enough to prevent causing any damage.'

The Doctor wiped a handkerchief across his brow as he exhaled slowly, 'Fruit will be a good start when we move to puree, the natural sugars will give him energy as well.'

The two men turned as a nurse came into the room and raised an objection over Margaret's actions. Margaret was sitting on the bed alongside Cedric with him leaning his head against her breast.

In one hand she held a small bowl in which she had crushed a couple of sugar cubes and added a few drops of water from his glass. Dipping her finger into the syrupy liquid, Margaret gently eased her finger between Cedric's lips. For a brief moment he refused but the sweetness broke down his resistance.

'Stop that at once! You have no right to do that! Get that dirty animal out of here!' screamed the nurse. Although Margaret looked up, she continued to wet her finger in the sugar and feed it into Cedric's mouth.

Doctor O'Brien strode forward, 'They're here with my permission. This is the first actual success since the patient was brought in! Now I want milk boiled, a couple of pints.' He propelled the nurse out of the room and closed the door on her protesting all the way. 'I'm going to cop it from the Matron, but this is progress, my dear boy!' The Doctor handed Cedric his glass of water to help wash down the sugar.

'Well done Margaret! What a natural mother you're going to make.'

Embarrassed Margaret managed a smile, 'I had to do something similar when Sebastian's mother had died and I had to bottle feed him.'

Tears welled in Phillip's eyes as a sigh of contentment was uttered by Cedric as he continued to accept Margaret's sugary offering. *It is so much like watching a mother nurse her child that I feel no jealousy at the intimacy between the cousins. I'm only filled with an overwhelming gratitude and relief that this must surely be the first step towards Cedric's recovery.*

Sitting in a chair on the opposite side of the bed from Margaret, Phillip was forced to bite back a sob of joy as Cedric's hand slid slowly across the top of his sheet to lie over Phillip's. They continued to sit like that until all the sugar was gone and Margaret used a little more water to dissolve the last remaining traces.

Holding Cedric's head up a little, Phillip assisted as Margaret slid the liquid down Cedric's throat. Gently they lowered Cedric back to lie down flat on the bed as Margaret slid off the bed onto the chair opposite Phillip.

Not until it seemed that Cedric had fallen asleep did Margaret finally rise to her feet. Doctor O'Brien's eyebrows nearly ascended into his hairline as he watched Margaret as she first gently kissed Cedric's lips and then leaning across the bed, kissed Phillip. Glancing swiftly at Richard, the Doctor was even more shocked that the Professor didn't show any sign of surprise, or even jealousy.

Catching the Doctor's look of bewilderment, Richard smiled, 'It's not a gesture of a sexual nature so there's nothing to be jealous about,' he explained.

The Doctor shook his head in disbelief, 'You really are the craziest people I have ever met! But honestly, I hope none of you ever change!' He led Margaret, Richard and Sebastian out of the hospital without incident before returning to his rounds.

A Sudden Arrival

Taking pity on the well behaved tiger, Richard procured a hamper from Maria and collecting Elliott, they headed out of the city so that Sebastian could run around while they had a picnic. Due to her injuries, Margaret wasn't able to run with Seb so she didn't change into male attire, but Elliott re-armed himself.

With Warren Foster dead, Clay Barnsby, Major Marconi, Albert and his uncle in custody I can't think of anyone else who could possibly be a threat to Margaret but as the old saying goes, "it's better to be safe than sorry." Elliott decided.

Sebastian had a great time stalking and chasing birds and when he finally grew tired of the sport he joined Margaret on the picnic blanket and happily cleaned up any leftovers. Then while the humans sat under the shade of a large tree, Seb took an after lunch siesta in the sun.

The tiger had just rolled over so that his belly was exposed to the warmth of the sun's rays when his ears suddenly perked upright and an instant later he was on his feet and fully alert as he stared off into the distance. His human companions had been dozing lightly but Seb's abrupt action snapped through the men's inertia. They all rose to their feet as the men both drew out their weapons.

'Well that's a fine welcome Ricky!' Recognising the voice as well as the face of the man who approached their group, Richard was already lowering his pistol. He was enveloped in a bear hug which crushed the wind out of him.

'Peter! You always sneak into a play when it is all but over!' Richard laughed as Peter Dickson released him so that he could breathe again.

'I was just about to post off your documents when news of the massacre of the Haven reached London. We didn't get more than sketchy details, but I knew trouble was brewing, so I hopped on the next ship leaving that day.' Peter placed his hand over Margaret's for a moment. 'I was indeed very sorry to hear of your parents' untimely death. They had been very good to Richard since he got here, and treated me like an old friend when I was last here.'

Richard interrupted only long enough to introduce Elliott as he holstered his gun before Peter continued,

'When my ship had docked in Accra, I was met by a gentleman representing your lawyers, Margaret,' said Peter, 'I was itching to see you, but you know these legal types, Ricky, everything has to follow the appropriate procedure. Meanwhile I got a peek at your official reports. Nasty time you've been having up here! Some nasty business going on down in the city too!'

'So it's finally over?' Tears welled in Margaret's eyes.

'Not quite!' Richard's eyes never wavered from Margaret's face. 'Margaret, I… '

She refused to let him continue. 'Before you say anything, give me your hand.' Startled, Richard held out his left hand to Margaret. Exhaling slowing, she removed his wedding ring and handed it to a bemused Peter.

'Now then, as a single man, you were about to say something?' Margaret asked.

Laughing, Richard wrapped his arms around her waist and swung her around before kissing her thoroughly. 'Impossible Imp! Do you want me to get down on one knee?'

Margaret's eyes twinkled. 'Would you?'

Peter hunted for something in his coat pocket as Richard dropped obligingly to one knee. 'You might need this.' Peter handed Richard a diamond ring. 'Believe me, the lawyers thought of everything!'

Elliott cleared his throat in embarrassment. 'Do you want us to leave?'

'Oh no!' Margaret cried out. 'I want witnesses that everything is above board!'

In absolute seriousness, Richard took Margaret's hand between his as he looked up into her eyes. 'Margaret Elizabeth Munroe, it is with great pleasure that I can finally and legally ask you for your hand in marriage. I will love, honour and cherish you for the rest of our lives, and possibly even beyond.'

Margaret sighed. 'I would be honoured to be your wife!'

Peter and Elliott cheered as Richard kissed Margaret's hand before slipping the diamond ring onto her finger. Rising to his feet. He took her into his arms and kissed her properly.

'I think,' Margaret said when she was allowed to speak again, 'It's time we went home!'

SATURDAY
Finally!

There were tears in Dalila's eyes as she brushed Margaret's hair before placing the veil and the ring of flowers that held it in place upon her head. Margaret looked a picture of radiance as Dalila applied the slightest hint of colour to her cheeks and lips. Margaret embraced the Housekeeper and said, 'Please don't cry, as it will start me off as well!'

Laughing Dalila mopped up her tears and smiled as she led Margaret, beautiful to behold in her mother's wedding dress, outside where Richard was waiting to marry her.

Standing facing Father Gerard, with Peter beside him and all of his workers and villagers seated behind, Richard felt his knees begin to shake as reality started to sink in. Exhaling slowly, Richard tried to overcome the shaking as Peter laid a comforting hand on his shoulder. They both turned to watch as Dalila's front door of her cottage opened and an equally nervous but absolutely stunning Margaret stepped out.

She took a deep breath and smiled as she took the arm of Kobbi and Manu. With the two young men on either side of her, Margaret walked up the aisle towards Richard, her eyes never wavering from his. As Margaret's smile grew, Richard felt all his nerves disappear and he smiled back. *This is perfect; this is a dream come true,* he thought.

Richard didn't even realize that he had been holding his breath since first laying eyes on Margaret until Peter pinched his arm forcing him to breathe again as he said, 'ouch'. Father Gerard cast a startled glance in his direction, but Richard had eyes for no one but Margaret.

Sitting in the front row, Elliott wasn't at all surprised by Richard's single mindedness, as Margaret did look absolutely breathtakingly beautiful. Silence fell over those gathered as Richard took both of Margaret's hands into his own, and raised one and then the other to his lips.

'I had to be sure that I wasn't just dreaming all of this.' Richard whispered against Margaret's ear. She laughed, her fingers momentarily tightening around his.

'Last chance to turn back.'

'Never!' Richard shook his head as he met the twinkle in her eyes.

They turned to face Father Gerard who was patiently waiting for them. 'Dearly beloved, we are gathered here today in the sight of God to marry this man Richard Evans to this woman Margaret Munroe.'

They spoke their vows clearly and confidently, but Richard's hand trembled slightly as he placed the ring upon Margaret's finger. An enormous cheer erupted as Richard took Father Gerard at his word and willingly kissed his bride. Dalila dabbed at her eyes as song and dancing erupted in celebration.

Our Future Assured

'So it's all finally over!' sighed Margaret in relief as they signed their marriage licence.

'Not quite!' drawled Richard, 'Phillip is going to keep us updated about Cedric's condition. Father Gerard will gather together all the survivors of King Peponi's massacres. You have to decide what you want to do with your inheritance as well as the Haven. Elliott has to serve out his time in the army and finally we need to discuss if you wish to go somewhere for our honeymoon.'

As he led his bride back into their house while Dalila and the other women set up a feast in their honour,

Margaret kissed Richard's cheek as Sebastian strolled alongside them.

'So long as I am with you, I don't need a special location.' She trailed one hand down along Sebastian's back. 'Do you think we could find a mate for Sebastian?'

Richard sighed, 'Oh great! So you want two fully grown tigers running loose! Don't you think I'm already going to have my hands full just keeping you out of trouble?'

'Hey! I don't go looking for trouble! I can't help it if I have greedy relatives. It won't change us will it? All that money?' At the doubt in her voice, Richard raised her hand to his lips as they entered the house.

'No! Isabella and Edward raised you to value something more important than wealth. Family, love, loyalty, honour, charity, community and honesty. I look forward to continuing their legacy with our own family.'

Laying her hand on his arm as she blushed, Margaret asked, 'can we start now?'

Richard's eyebrows rose. 'Start what?'

'Creating our family.' With a shy smile she led her husband into their bedroom and Sebastian tactfully waited outside.